MCCRA

We hope you enjoy this book. Please return or
renew it by the due date.

You can renew it at www.norfolk.gov.uk/libraries or
by using our free library app.

Otherwise you can phone 0344 800 8020 -
please have your library card and PIN ready.

You can sign up for email reminders too.

NORFOLK ITEM

D0785458

Also by Cat Schield

The Black Sheep's Secret Child
Little Secret, Red Hot Scandal
The Heir Affair
Upstairs Downstairs Baby
Substitute Seduction
Revenge with Benefits

Discover more at millsandboon.co.uk

TAKEN BY STORM

CAT SCHIELD

THE BILLIONAIRE'S BARGAIN

NAIMA SIMONE

MILLS & BOON

First Published in Great Britain 2019
by Mills & Boon, an imprint of HarperCollinsPublishers,
1 London Bridge Street, London, SE1 9GF

Taken by Storm © 2019 Harlequin Books S.A.
The Billionaire's Bargain © 2019 Naima Simone

Special thanks and acknowledgement are given to Cat Schield
for her contribution to the Dynasties: Secrets of the A-List series.

ISBN: 978-0-263-27183-6

0619

MIX
Paper from
responsible sources
FSC™ C007454

This book is produced from independently certified FSC™
paper to ensure responsible forest management.

For more information visit: www.harpercollins.co.uk/green

Printed and bound in Spain
by CPI, Barcelona

TAKEN BY
STORM

CAT SCHIELD

To my Desire sisters, Karen, Reese and Joss.
You put the fun in fungo!
It was a joy to work with each of you!

One

He's Just Not That Into You.

The title of Isabel Withers's favorite rom-com movie and, unfortunately, the theme of her love life. Or lack thereof. In fact, a better title might have been *He Doesn't Know You're Alive.*

The same couldn't be said for Isabel. She was dreamily, frustratingly, sexually, heart-palpitatingly aware every time Shane Adams stepped into The Opulence, a five-star luxury getaway resort an hour east of Seattle. The president in charge of Richmond Hotel Group wasn't just handsome, with his broad shoulders and piercing sable eyes. He wore aloofness like a magical cloak, enthralling Isabel at first sight.

Her movie title would go more like... *He Knows You're Alive, but Only as the Helpful Employee Who Drops Everything to Get Him What He Needs in the Hope That He'll Notice the Woman beneath the Uniform.*

"You just sighed." This statement came from Isabel's best friend, Aspen Wright.

Isabel shot her a look. "You've been sighing since Rich-

mond announced it was hosting its fifth anniversary retreat here."

With a sly smile that softened the lines of tension around
her eyes and mouth, Aspen replied, "I sigh to relieve tension." The creative genius behind the resort's lavish events,
Aspen was currently stressed to the nines after Matt Richmond hired A-lister event planner Teresa St. Claire to co-
ordinate Richmond's upcoming retreat. "You're sighing
because that chiseled hunk of you-can't-touch-this just
walked by."

Aspen was right and Isabel wasted no breath arguing.
"I can't help it. He's just so gorgeous."

"That he is. And all business."

Recognizing that Aspen was once again counseling her
to give up her crush, Isabel responded with the same stubborn determination that marked her rise from someone who
grew up wearing thrift-store clothes to The Opulence's head
concierge and self-appointed representative of all things
romantic at the resort.

"And that's exactly how I'm going to approach him this
time."

"Oh, honey—"

Isabel raised her hand like a determined traffic cop.
"Don't." She'd heard Aspen's lecture all too often and pre-
dicted what she was about to say. "I just know there's something between us. It's impossible for me to feel as strongly
about him as I do and have it be only one-sided."

"Says every stalker ever."

"I'm not a stalker."

"You find ways to run into the man at every turn."
Aspen ticked off each point on long, slender fingers. "You
know his schedule better than he does. You make sure he
has the best table whenever he dines at Overlook and that
his room is stocked with all his favorites whenever he stays
overnight."

"That's just part of the fine service we offer here at The Opulence," she said, waving away her over-the-top service to their executive. "And why wouldn't we want him to have the absolute best experience every time he comes here? It only improves his perception of the resort."

Aspen shrugged. "Some days I'm not sure he notices any of the positive features we have to offer. He's too busy trying to improve efficiency."

Rigidly organized and driven to improve the resort's already stellar efficiency, Shane was a formidable taskmaster and prone to terrifying the staff whenever he made an appearance. It wasn't that he was harsh with any of his employees, but the man was so focused on business that he simply forgot to smile when things went well.

"He needs someone to soften his edges," Isabel said. "Someone who can show him that the resort's success isn't just about providing consistent service, but that we pour our heart and soul into giving our customers a unique experience."

"Someone like you?"

Hearing the teasing lilt in Aspen's voice, Isabel released a wide grin. "Do you know of anyone better?"

"No," Aspen conceded. "Just don't be disappointed if you fail. I admire everything you've accomplished in the year since you arrived here, but that man's cold heart may be frozen too solid for even your warm touch to heat."

"I'm The Opulence's romance concierge." Isabel lifted her fist in a gesture of power and triumph. "I will not fail in my mission."

A champion of true love, Isabel believed that everyone had the perfect someone out there. Even Aspen, although the older woman scoffed every time Isabel brought the subject up. As for herself, Isabel daydreamed about Shane Adams, even as she recognized that they were opposite in almost every way.

Aspen regarded her with solemn eyes. "Maybe I'll stock up on ice cream and red wine just in case."

Automatically brushing off Aspen's cynicism, Isabel blew her friend a kiss and headed to the little office behind the front desk where she organized romantic events for the guests who came to The Opulence looking to celebrate or connect with their partner. Each experience was tailored to the couple's particular needs and wants thanks to a questionnaire that Isabel had developed over the last few months.

Although she had a degree in hotel management, Isabel's knack for customer service had evolved into a passion for delivering fantasy romance experiences after her first month at The Opulence when a dreamy weekend she'd planned had helped a long-married couple see that their marriage could be saved.

"Fighting for love one couple at a time," Isabel muttered as she settled into her desk chair and pulled up the presentation she'd been working on to convince Shane that they should actively promote The Opulence as a romantic destination.

Satisfied that the pitch had the right balance of facts and fancy to convince Shane this was a solid marketing strategy, Isabel dialed Shane's personal assistant. By the third ring, when Sheila picked up, Isabel's heart was hammering so hard she could barely hear herself ask the question she'd been rehearsing.

"Hi, Sheila, it's Isabel Withers from The Opulence."

"Hello, Isabel." Shane's assistant had a warm, inviting manner so unlike her brisk, all-business boss. "What can I do for you today?"

"I was hoping I could get a meeting with Shane while he's here. I have some ideas for the resort that I'd like to go over with him."

If Sheila found it odd that Isabel would skip over the resort's management and go straight to Shane, she gave no indication. In fact, Isabel had already mentioned her idea to Tom, but he hadn't grasped the value in it. Going over his head was a risk, but if she could convince Shane, the gamble would pay off.

"With the upcoming Richmond event, Shane's schedule is full," Sheila said.

"If you could squeeze me in," Isabel persisted, uncaring that she sounded desperate. "I'll take fifteen minutes. Whatever he can spare." Hell, she was so convinced her idea was a good one she was ready to chase him into an elevator and pitch him on the run.

"Well…" Sheila paused and Isabel could hear the keys clicking on her computer. "He's free for dinner tonight at eight."

Isabel didn't hesitate. "I'll take it." Dinner with Shane? A dream come true. "I'll get us a table at Overlook. Thanks, Sheila."

"I've added you to his schedule. And you're his last meeting of the day, so you won't have to rush."

Was it Isabel's imagination or did Shane's assistant sound as if she was smiling?

"Thanks for your help."

Hanging up with Sheila, Isabel exited the tiny office and made her way back to the concierge desk. The carpet seemed suspended over hundreds of springs because Isabel noticed an extra bounce in her stride. She noted several guests responding to her wide grin with smiles of their own. This only added to Isabel's bright mood.

The concierge currently assigned to the desk looked up from her computer as Isabel approached. "Shane Adams was looking for you a few minutes ago."

Isabel's nerves vibrated in a mixture of alarm and glee. "Did he say what about?"

"He wanted your report on the arrangements for extra activities during the Richmond retreat."

She'd already shared the information with Teresa St. Claire as well as The Opulence management team, but wasn't surprised that Shane Adams had requested the update, as well. He'd been quite hands-on these last few weeks leading up to corporate's massive event. And with good reason. This was a major opportunity to show off the best of the hotel's operation to A-listers and some of the wealthiest people in the country.

Although Isabel knew she could simply send Shane the report by email, she always grabbed any opportunity to speak to him in person. "Did he say where he'd be?"

"He's over there." Cindy pointed toward the front door, where Shane was currently deep in discussion with The Opulence's executive manager, Tom Busch.

As if suddenly aware he was being discussed, Shane glanced toward the concierge desk, and his keen brown gaze struck Isabel, knocking the breath from her lungs. That the man could land such a blow to her senses from clear across a room should've put Isabel's defenses on alert. Instead, she responded with a warm smile that hinted at the strength of her infatuation.

He blinked.

Isabel's heart leaped as his eyes narrowed and he seemed to truly take her in for the first time in a year. This was it. The moment she'd been waiting for. He would see her as a beautiful woman he desired and recognize that she was someone who strove to improve the hotel's reputation every chance she got.

And then it was over. Shane turned his attention back to the executive manager, dismissing Isabel from his thoughts.

She sagged like a leaky balloon.

Moments later, he ended his conversation and she headed his way. Clutched to her chest was the ten-page document detailing every guest's preferences, their requested spa services, rounds of golf, and the schedule of visits to area attractions including the local winery and those participating in unique interactive culinary experiences offered at Quintessential Chef.

"Here's the report you wanted," Isabel said, waiting in breathless silence for several heartbeats while Shane scanned the document.

With his attention focused elsewhere, she took several seconds to drink in the strong structure of his jaw and cheekbones. The ever-present dent between his eyebrows and surprisingly full, kissable lips. She shivered at the thought of how their softness would feel against her skin and wasn't prepared when he lifted his gaze and caught her staring at him.

His eyes narrowed as he silently studied her. Isabel bit her lip to stop herself from babbling out an apology for the infatuation he must've seen written all over her face, but his phone buzzed, interrupting his focus.

"If you have any questions, we can go over them tonight," Isabel said, rushing to make the offer before she lost his attention once more. "I've arranged for a table at Overlook at eight." Isabel barely paused for breath. Shane hadn't yet answered his phone—his gaze hadn't even drifted toward the demanding thing—and she was going to capitalize on every millisecond of his notice. "I'm really looking forward to our dinner."

Heart hammering with uncharacteristic vigor, Shane Adams regarded the plucky redhead standing before him while his phone's insistent buzz barely registered. Striving for detachment and finding it beyond his grasp, he surveyed Isabel's flawless pale skin, the thick dark lashes framing her lively hazel eyes, and her lush mouth painted a rosy pink while her words replayed in his head.

I've arranged a table at Overlook at eight.
I'm really looking forward to our dinner.

Had she just asked him out?

Since Isabel Withers had joined Richmond Hotel Group, he'd noticed a disturbing tendency to become distracted whenever he visited The Opulence. With her russet hair and lively personality a beacon for his attention, he'd pinpointed her as the source of his agitation. But it wasn't until midway through his first quarterly tour, when he caught himself trying to identify what about her perfume had caused him to lean forward and suck in a lungful of the lushly aromatic, sweet scent, that he realized what a danger she was to his disciplined professionalism.

"Ah—" Damn the woman. Her invitation left him gaping at her like an idiot. "I'm not sure my schedule—"

"Oh, don't worry. I already checked with Sheila. She said you were booked into meetings all day, but that you were free after eight. That's why I arranged for a table at Overlook then."

"You spoke to my assistant?"

Shane imagined the glee with which Sheila had fielded that particular phone call. She was constantly harping on him to take a little time out of his schedule to date. Although he never did anything to fix the situation, Shane recognized the need for balance in his life. Working eighty hours a week might not have been a problem for him, but he recognized his staff didn't have his endurance.

"Of course." Isabel's lips parted in a dazzling smile that made Shane's head spin. "I check with her every time you visit so I can make sure all your needs are met."

His needs?

Those two words sent sexual awareness rushing through him. He barely won the battle to keep his gaze from roaming down her slender frame, but that didn't stop him from speculating about the sort of curves hidden beneath the hotel's blue-and-gold uniform. Shane yanked his thoughts back under control. She was one of his employees. He couldn't go there. Ever.

Shane made a mental note to set up a date in the near future with one of the women he saw from time to time. He'd obviously neglected his *needs* as the Richmond retreat drew near.

He cleared his throat. "Well, I do need to eat," And it was a business dinner. Despite that momentary slip-up, he shouldn't have trouble keeping things strictly professional. "We should discuss the specific arrangements for each of the VIPs arriving next week."

Isabel nodded. "Actually, we have a meeting scheduled with Teresa tomorrow to go over those details. I have something else I'd like to discuss with you."

Something of a business nature? Her expression gave him no clue, but nothing in the last year indicated she was anything other than a professional. With a sinking feeling, he realized his earlier flare of personal interest was leading him to question her motives.

"Can you give me a hint what that might be?"

"I'd rather surprise you." She hit him with another bright smile, this time flavoring it with a dash of sly teasing. "I'd really appreciate if you'd come to dinner with an open mind."

Against his better judgment, Shane found himself utterly intrigued. "Why would you think I'd do otherwise?"

Her eyebrows rose at his question. "You have very strong opinions about everything done at the resort."

Although her measured tone and demeanor remained neutral, Shane recognized the point she was trying to make. He'd shown a heavy hand at The Opulence in the three years following Richmond Hotel Group's management of the resort. The place had been a chaotic mess when they'd won the contract. By instituting strict rules for how everything was done, from folding towels to welcoming the guests, he'd whipped the operations into shape in record time.

The turnaround had been instrumental in boosting him into the presidency of the Richmond Hotel Group division of Richmond Enterprises. He was proud of how the division had flourished with him at the helm. Of course, as more properties had been added to their management portfolio, he'd focused his attention on getting the newer ones up to RHG standards, leaving the earliest properties to function without as much oversight. For most this had worked out well.

Normally Shane didn't weigh in on staffing decisions at the hotel level, but he hadn't liked some of the reports that had been coming out of The Opulence. Tom Busch had been hired by the area manager ten months earlier to act as the hotel's executive manager, and the level of customer service had begun to drop.

The timing of this was not good with the fifth anniversary retreat for Richmond Enterprises taking place in less than two weeks. Everything needed to be running as smooth as glass. The smallest bump could have a catastrophic ripple effect.

"So, we're having dinner to talk about the resort?" he asked.

The shock on her face, quickly masked, sent a flurry of curses winging through his mind. Had he really just admitted to her that he'd assumed her invitation had been personal rather than business?

She gnawed on her lower lip and avoided his gaze. A betraying flush raced up her throat and turned her cheeks bright pink. Shane noticed his own skin becoming hotter with each breath. What was it about Isabel that consistently threw him off balance?

An awkward, breathy laugh escaped her. "Of course. You didn't think I was hitting on you, did you?"

"Well…no," Shane replied, but his response lacked conviction. He cleared his throat, discomfort rendering him less judicious than usual.

"And if I was?" The smile she threw at him had cheeky undertones.

Attraction flared anew, tightening his gut. The unwelcome sensation continued to disturb him. "I always keep my business relationships strictly professional."

"Of course," she repeated, nodding vigorously. "And it isn't as if I thought…" Hot color flushed her cheeks as she trailed off.

It occurred to Shane that this was the longest conversation he'd ever had with Isabel. He was starting to understand why all the management staff remarked on her winning personality as often as they praised her high level of customer service. She had a knack for drawing people in and making them like her.

"I imagine you have a lot of women hitting on you," she prompted when he declined to venture into the silence building between them. "After all, you're handsome, intelligent and successful."

"Not as many women as you think," he lied, easing her tension with a dry smile. "I work too much and play too little. Friends assure me I will end up a crusty old bachelor if I keep going like this."

Why was he discussing his personal life with a member of his staff? Because this slender redhead roused all sorts of unprofessional impulses.

"All it will take is the right woman."

He doubted that was true. "Spoken like a true romantic."

"You say 'romantic' like it's a dirty word."

He used his thumb to gesture at his chest. "Crusty old bachelor."

"You don't believe in romance?"

He was an emotionally shuttered workaholic. "Let's just say I don't have time for it."

"But do you believe in it?" she persisted, mesmerizing him with the specks of green shimmering in her hazel eyes.

"No."

The single, blunt syllable was meant to shut down the conversation. To his dismay, he underestimated the petite idealist. She grinned at him, her challenging smirk a too-late warning that he'd blundered into quicksand.

Before he could elaborate or explain, her smartphone buzzed. She shifted her attention to the screen and sighed.

"The Jamisons' wedding party has started to arrive early and we're not quite ready for them. I have to go. See you at eight." And then she was speeding off, her long strides taking her arresting presence beyond his reach.

In the back of his mind, a voice reminded Shane why he avoided engaging with this woman. All the information he gleaned about her from his management staff said she excelled at her job because she had a knack for reading people and providing them an experience they didn't even realize they wanted. Returning guests flocked to her concierge desk, knowing anything Isabel planned for them would be the perfect experience.

Alone with his thoughts, Shane found himself needing a bracing hit of brisk mountain air. He turned in the opposite direction and headed for a side door that led to the lower terrace. That the encounter had not gone his way didn't surprise Shane. Isabel's quick mind, passionate nature and eloquence were more than a match for his dogged determination and disciplined pragmatism.

He glanced at his watch as a cool fall breeze smacked his overheated face. He had four hours until their next meeting. Barely enough time for him to shore up his defenses. One thing was for certain, he needed his wits about him when dealing with Isabel Withers.

Two

"I can't believe you lied to me."

Teresa St. Claire shied away from the accusations blazing in Liam Christopher's eyes and shifted her attention toward the document clutched in his left hand. His father's will. The venom in his eyes lanced through her, cutting deep into her heart. It was as if every bit of rapport they'd developed these last few weeks had been erased in the time it took for her to use the bathroom.

Five minutes.

What could possibly have gone this wrong in such a short period of time?

When she'd slipped away from the yacht's lounge, he'd been relaxed and in a good mood, his obvious affection turning her bones to mush.

The last thing she expected on her return was to bear the brunt of his cold fury.

"I didn't. I haven't," she insisted, confused and off balance. "What's going on?"

The stack of papers fluttered as he gestured with them.

"My father left you twenty-five percent of his personal stock in Christopher Corporation."

He'd done what?

"That's crazy," Teresa murmured, barely able to breathe as she struggled to absorb that his father, her mentor, had left her a small fortune. "I don't understand."

Shock and dismay made her thoughts thick and gummy. Beneath her feet, the sixty-eight-meter yacht churned placidly through the calm waters of Puget Sound, but Teresa's equilibrium pitched and heaved. She tottered over to the closest chair and sat down.

Why would Linus leave me anything?

"…a year?" Liam had continued speaking, but she'd stopped listening. His voice had sounded muffled and indistinct as if she was hearing him while being submerged in water. "I need those shares back now."

The rage in Liam Christopher's voice sliced through the fog surrounding Teresa. Wincing at his fury, she blinked several times to clear her vision. When she glanced his way, she wished his features had remained indistinct.

She held out her hands in a conciliatory manner. "I missed what you said just now about the will's terms. Could you repeat the last part?" She forced a shaky laugh. "This is all overwhelming."

"My father put a clause in the will that states you can't divest yourself of the shares unless and until you spend a year on the board."

"What?" This additional complication on top of an already tricky situation threatened to overwhelm Teresa's ability to maintain some semblance of calm.

"Seems my father believed you'd be good for our company."

Obviously Liam disagreed.

Anger painted fiery blotches over his cheekbones. With

his eyes shooting steel and his jaw locked in stubborn lines, he vibrated with fury. The emotion highlighted his raw masculinity and set Teresa's heart to pounding for all the wrong reasons.

Stop it.

The man was poised to murder her and here she was, swooning over how gorgeous he looked.

"This whole thing is unacceptable," Liam snarled, bringing Teresa's attention back to the real problem. "You don't deserve those shares."

"Maybe not," she declared. *But why did your father want me to have them?*

Liam grabbed the arm of her chair and leaned toward her. "It seems pretty clear to me now that you've been underplaying your relationship with my father all along."

"That's not true," she insisted, sick of defending herself. "Look, I have no idea what Linus was thinking, giving me the shares."

"Don't you?" Liam declared, his voice low and savage.

Teresa ground her teeth together and fought to remain calm. "We did not have an affair." How many times would she have to make this same speech before he believed her?

He's never going to believe me. Just like he's never going to trust me.

The pair of declarations flashed through Teresa's mind like a lightning bolt, revealing the bleak landscape of her doomed relationship with Liam and leaving an afterimage of hopelessness imprinted on her brain.

"You're lying."

Teresa wanted to shriek in frustration and despair. How had they found their way back here again?

"What purpose does it serve me to lie to you at this point?" she asked, even as she recognized the futility of trying to reason with Liam. "Your father made a decision. I don't understand it any more than you do. Before your parents divorced, Linus and I were close, but he was my mentor. Nothing more."

She never would've slept with Liam if she thought he hadn't already accepted this. The disillusionment and melancholy unleashed by Liam's dagger thrust of accusations demonstrated just how right she'd been all those years to put her focus on her career and avoid romantic entanglements. Making her love life a low priority had been the right move all along.

"I'm going to make you give those shares back."

And for a moment she wished giving Liam back the shares would mean he might once again look at her the way he had when they'd made love. When that carefully constructed wall she'd raised around her heart to keep it safe and undamaged had shattered.

"You have a year to try," Teresa responded.

"It's not going to take a year."

Teresa met his eyes. "You can't intimidate me into selling you the stock."

"Selling?" Liam released a harsh laugh. "By the time I'm done with you, you're going to be begging me to take it off your hands."

Shane arrived ten minutes early for his dinner meeting with Isabel, expecting he'd be the first one to the table, only to find she'd beaten him. As the hostess led him to the table, the first thing he noticed was that Isabel had worn her hair down. The shimmering russet curtain spilled over her shoulders in a luxurious wave. Next, he realized she'd exchanged her hotel uniform for something white and lacy.

Bridal.

The impression popped into his head and he ruthlessly banished it before it took root.

"Good evening," he said, settling into the seat opposite her, relieved to see a presentation document placed to the left of his table setting. So, despite her attire, this was a business meeting after all.

"Good evening," she echoed. "Thank you again for meeting with me."

"Of course."

The waiter approached, and Shane glanced at Isabel's glass to see what she was having. The goblet held something clear and fizzy. Curious, but unwilling to ask, he ordered the same. When the drink arrived, he discovered it was plain club soda with a slice of lime.

After ordering dinner, he flipped through the bound document. Her presentation was well organized and brilliantly illustrated with catchy phrases and evocative photographs of beautiful couples enjoying each other at various settings in and around the resort.

"This looks quite thorough," he declared. "But I don't understand why you've come to me with this. Shouldn't you've taken it to Tom?"

"I did, but he wasn't…" Isabel trailed off. For the first time since he'd sat down, she displayed uncertainty. Her brows came together as she collected her thoughts. "That is, he's really good when it comes to the hotel's operations…"

Shane already knew that wasn't completely accurate, but stayed silent while she struggled to make her point without throwing her boss under the bus. As unusual as it was, Shane intended to hear the staff's opinions about the executive director and guessed Isabel would be more forthright than most.

"Anything you say here will remain between us," he assured her, before sitting back and letting her marshal her opinion without coaxing or interference.

"He just doesn't understand the heartbeat of the hotel. I thought maybe that would change as he grew more familiar with the staff and our clientele, but the direction he's gone with the promotions hasn't encouraged people to return."

She exhaled in a rush and then chuckled. "That didn't explain things very well, did it?"

She appeared unabashed by her stumble, and Shane found this intriguing. He'd never struggled to communicate his opinions. He simply stated his recommendations, confident that he'd thought the matter through and weighed all options.

Shane decided to table all talk of Tom for the moment. "How do you think we should promote the hotel?"

"As a romantic destination." She flashed a grin that struck him like a fist to the gut.

"What if I told you that Tom is focusing on corporate clients per my direction?"

"Then I'd say I'm here to change your mind."

"How do you intend to do that?"

The flickering candlelight revealed a sudden rush of color in her cheeks. "By showing you firsthand some of the most romantic places The Opulence has to offer."

Her suggestion filled him with mixed emotions. He was an executive of the company that employed her, and while he could justify tonight's dinner as a business meeting, she intrigued him both as a woman he was attracted to and as an individual who challenged his perspective on the hotel.

Retreating to the reason for tonight's dinner meeting, he picked up her presentation and began flipping through it again. "What's your vision for The Opulence?"

"The theme is…" Like a Broadway producer of old, she swept her hand in an arc above her head. *"Romance is the elixir of life."* She beamed at him, utterly convinced of her brilliance. "I think The Opulence is ideally suited as a romance destination, and the staff is ready to provide the perfect getaway experience. In fact, I'm gaining a reputation as a romance concierge."

"What does that mean?"

"You might say I have a knack for giving couples the

sort of memorable experiences that they rave about to their friends and family."

"What sort of experiences?"

"Mostly over-the-top romance. I want the hotel to be known as the best destination for a special evening or a first kiss. The covered bridge has been the site of several engagements and wedding ceremonies. And I've lost count of how many people have done photo shoots on the lower trail with the waterfall behind them. We have a first-class spa offering all sorts of luxury treatments geared toward couples. We score big points with honeymooners and people who are celebrating anniversaries."

Isabel's enthusiasm and pride washed over Shane, and he felt a stab of envy. When was the last time he'd felt that sort of passion for his work? He recoiled from the answer. Success was rewarding, but all too often he found himself in an ever-spinning circle of dissatisfaction. What did he have to show for all his hard work except more work and more responsibility? He certainly hadn't made his father proud of him. Nothing would do that. So why did he drive himself so hard?

"Romantic dinners in the Overlook." She gestured around them. "Or private, personalized feasts at Quintessential Chef. Who wouldn't want to come here for a small wedding or a lavish blowout affair?"

Her youthful enthusiasm made him feel ancient and too serious by contrast. It came as a surprise that her liveliness appealed to him. Like a bracing breath of fresh air in the morning. Or a caffeine jolt from a double espresso coffee. Her idealistic smiles and fun-loving ideas invited him to play and dream along with her. The part of him that he'd shut down in order to focus on his career awakened, and he found himself enjoying their exchange. A little too much.

Yet here he was, leaning in, ignoring common sense so he could focus on the woman across from him. Not the employee across from him, he noted as candlelight painted gold highlights in her lustrous red hair and added a mysterious bronze glint in her hazel eyes.

The freckles dusted across her nose gave her a girl-next-door look. Her earnest manner and playful smile buffed smooth the rough edges of his impatience and mellowed him. She moved her hands as she talked, prompting him to wonder: if he grasped them, could she speak?

The thought of touching her made his chest tighten. The sudden pain caused his cautious nature to flare. He shouldn't be thinking about her like someone he wanted to get to know personally. Just like he shouldn't have encouraged her to order the dessert she'd raved about. Even now her tongue flicked out to swipe a smear of chocolate off her lower lip, tempting him to pay the bill and hustle her up to his suite.

Of course he couldn't do that. This was a business dinner, a chance for her to pitch him her ideas. And they were all good ones. Her vision to promote the resort as Instagramable was exactly the sort of fresh idea he liked to see from his employees. He refused to jeopardize his professionalism or his career because she stirred his libido.

But it was more than just lust that she'd aroused. Isabel intrigued him. He admired her business sense even as her fanciful imaginings confounded him. Despite their opposite views, he wanted to hear her opinions even if he disagreed with them.

"I feel as if I've lost you," she said, noticing that his attention had wandered. "You don't believe that The Opulence is the perfect romantic destination."

"The hotel is successful because of its exceptional spa, first-class restaurants and outstanding reputation for events."

"But there's magic here, as well." She studied him for several seconds, her eyes narrowing in keen appraisal.

"There's a spot I highly recommend to our couples. I'll just have to prove to you that it's the perfect spot for a romantic first kiss."

Wait. Prove it to him? How?

"You're wasting your time."

Women had been trying to find his softer side—without success—since he was old enough to date. Most of the time he wasn't interested enough in them to want to explore past the surface. Sex was one thing. He believed in satisfying a woman in bed, leaving her breathless and sated before he slid back into his clothes and headed for the door. Lingering to snuggle and exchange confidences only led to attachments and took his focus away from work.

Romance meant tapping into his emotions and he had no intention of going there. He'd been raised by a father who valued hard work above all else and cynically avoided showing any emotion beyond annoyance and contempt for his troublesome son. Shane's mother had died when he was eight. He remembered crying at her funeral and how his father had shut him down, telling him to get over it. His mother wasn't coming back and she wouldn't be proud of him for being such a weakling.

"In terms of romance," he said, "you'll find me a hard sell."

From the expression on her face, he saw his mistake. By declaring he was immune, he'd just thrown down a gauntlet.

"What?" he demanded, anxiety and excitement blinking awake inside him.

Her delightful smile took up the challenge. "This is going to be interesting."

Following the bombshell of his father leaving Teresa shares of Christopher Corporation stock, Liam had traded several texts with Matt Richmond, but hadn't yet gotten his best friend on the phone to spill all that had happened regarding his father's will. Because of their similar fortunes and lifestyles, Matt had become someone Liam felt comfortable talking to about business as well as personal issues he might be having.

Which was why Liam wished he had his friend around to talk to about his chaotic emotions where Teresa was concerned. Instead, Matt was unreachable after deciding to extend his quick trip to the Big Apple into a romantic getaway to a destination unknown. Liam didn't want to envy Matt. The Richmond Enterprises CEO deserved to be happy. But Liam couldn't stop comparing his own failed love life to Matt's happy one and wishing he had better luck with women.

Why had Linus given Teresa shares when he could've bequeathed an equally generous amount in cash or property? Hell, if his father had given her the winery and villa in Tuscany, the yacht moored in the Cayman Islands and the vacation house in Bali, Liam might've been furious, but he could've let those things go and wiped Teresa St. Claire from his mind.

Instead, Linus had made it so that Teresa couldn't divest herself of the shares without giving a year of her time to the company's board. The ridiculous codicil put Liam in an untenable position of having to work side by side with a woman he didn't trust.

A woman he desired.

Someone who made him second-guess his perceptions about what he'd believed all his life. Someone who made him question his mother's stories about her failed marriage.

He'd opened himself up to the idea that the connection he felt toward Teresa might have potential. So he'd arranged to spend a perfect evening with her on the yacht. Expensive champagne, a gourmet dinner. A heartfelt apology over how he'd been so suspicious of her. All so he could set the stage for a romantic invitation to stay with him during the Richmond retreat. At the same time, he wanted Teresa there while he read the will, knowing it would be emotional.

He hadn't taken the step lightly. The move would reveal that she was important to him. That he trusted her. All that went up in smoke after the shocking discovery of his father's bequest. While Liam had been falling for her, she'd been lying to him. She'd played him for a fool, and it was long past time for Liam to accept that her innocent act was exactly that.

He'd believed her when she'd claimed that her relationship with his father had been strictly professional, but Linus's gift of twenty-five percent of his shares in Christopher Corporation told a different story.

And demanded further investigation.

His phone rang as he slid behind the wheel of his car. Liam sent his attention flickering toward the screen, where his mother's face had appeared. Ever since his father's death, Catherine Dupont—she'd returned to her maiden name after the divorce—had been avidly curious about her ex-husband's will. She'd received a significant settlement at the time of their divorce, but as Christopher Corporation continued to flourish and grow, she'd resented that her financial situation remained stagnant while Linus grew wealthier by the day.

"Why didn't you tell me you'd heard from your father's lawyer?" Catherine scolded him as soon as he'd greeted her.

Liam wondered how she'd found out. He'd been dodging her for nearly a week, still processing the document's shocking revelation, and wasn't prepared to deal with his mother's reaction when she heard what happened or to explain what his father had done.

"I've been busy." Liam wished he had a better excuse.

"And?" Catherine demanded, not waiting for her son to

respond before launching into her interrogation. "Did Linus leave you everything? Of course he did. I suppose he gave something to that secretary of his. She was too territorial for my taste, calling him at all hours with some excuse or another. I'm pretty sure she was in love with him. He was obviously flattered by all her attention. How much did he leave her?"

His mother's rapid-fire questions battered Liam, taking his irritation to new heights. He opened his mouth, determined to shut her down, only to realize that as weary as he'd grown of her suspicious and jaded view of the world, she'd been right to suspect something was going on between Linus and Teresa. This revelation took the edge off his temper toward his mother. Obviously she was right to assume the worst of people.

Yet even as he accepted this, a familiar darkness settled over his mood.

The time he'd spent with Teresa, making love to her, helping her when she freaked out about her brother. That had all been real. Hadn't it? Liam blew out a breath. In the span of a few short minutes, his entire world had gone topsy-turvy. Or maybe it was more the case that his ship had righted itself. Maybe his growing feelings for Teresa had been the anomaly. There was no question he'd felt less like himself over the last few weeks than ever before.

"Liam," his mother said impatiently. "Are you still there? Did you hear what I asked? Did your father leave money to his secretary?"

She never referred to Esther Smithers by her name.

"I'm not sure," he replied, barely remembering anything after the bombshell news that Teresa had received shares that should've been his.

"What do you mean you're not sure?" Her outrage came through loud and clear. "How can you not be sure? Didn't you read the will?"

"I didn't get a chance to read through the entire thing," he lied. He'd examined every word.

"Why not?"

"He left twenty-five percent of his shares in Christopher Corporation to Teresa St. Claire," Liam blurted out. He gave his mother a heartbeat to absorb the information before continuing, "Any idea why he might've done that?"

"To punish me, obviously."

Her answer was so ridiculous that Liam almost laughed. The only person damaged by Linus's last-minute decision to change his will was Liam. Not to mention his parents had been divorced for a decade. Yet he wasn't surprised that his mother continued to blame Teresa for some nonexistent affair. Catherine Dupont was incapable of letting go of any slight she'd ever received, real or imaginary.

Yet in this instance, his mother could be right about Teresa. Not that she'd had an affair with Linus. Weeks earlier Liam had accepted that she'd spoken the truth about that. But with his passion for her no longer muting his doubts about her, the voice at the back of his mind questioned if he'd missed something equally sinister about their connection.

Obviously more had gone on between them than just a simple mentor/mentee relationship. Had Linus given her the shares because she'd been blackmailing him? Maybe they hadn't slept together, but could he have stepped across the line in the early days of the relationship? Given the enormity of what she'd inherited from his father, it seemed realistic that she'd manipulated Linus somehow.

He made a note to call his private investigator and get the man to focus on his father and what skeletons might have been in his closet that Teresa could've exploited. But first, he needed to disengage himself from the woman railing in his ear.

"Mother," he interrupted when she paused for a rare

breath. Honestly, the woman had the lungs of an opera singer. "I need to make some calls. I will check in with you later."

And then, before she could launch into more of her vitriolic spin, he disconnected the call. He had plans to make regarding Teresa St. Claire. Once his strategies were set in motion, it wouldn't matter what she said or did in an effort to sway him. No amount of sexual chemistry or manipulation of his emotions to elicit his sympathy would stop him from recovering what was rightfully his.

Three

In the days following her dinner with Shane, Isabel manned the concierge desk with more than her usual good spirits. Unaffected by the gray skies and sporadic rains that plagued the area or the escalating tension felt by the staff as the Richmond anniversary retreat neared, Isabel hummed and grinned as she went about her day. How could she be anything other than gloriously happy? Not only had Shane been intrigued by her presentation, but also she had the distinct sense that she'd piqued his interest in a way that wasn't solely professional.

Something about the way he lingered after walking her to her car, as if he'd been reluctant for the evening to end, left her wondering if her flirting had gotten to him. What would he do if she leaned in and kissed him? Even as a delicious thrill chased up her spine, she recognized that he'd resist. He wasn't the type to make a pass at one of his employees. Too many scruples. But if she didn't work for him? Would he still rebuff her? The question preoccupied her as she awaited his return to the hotel that afternoon.

"Good afternoon," he intoned, his deep voice sending delicious shivers racing over her skin.

"Hi." She sounded breathless and silly, but he didn't seem to notice. "Are you ready to feel the romance?"

He didn't sigh, but his expression shifted into skeptical lines. "I'm ready to take your proof under advisement."

"Then let's go."

As with every time she drew within ten feet of the man, Isabel's pulse started behaving erratically. She glanced at Shane as they crossed the lobby. His distant expression made her sigh. He had no idea the sort of effect his height and powerful build coupled with his aloof manner had on the people around him. Or maybe he did and just didn't care.

"What's in the bag?" Shane eyed her tote as they emerged into the November afternoon.

"You'll see." Withholding information from him was a risk. The tactic either whetted his appetite or annoyed him. In fact, it was hard to tell how he was reacting. The man was always in control and she despaired of ever knocking him off balance.

In truth, she appreciated the repressed tension that vibrated in him. Like he was a powder keg set to explode any second. What would it take to ignite him? Would she survive the blast? Get to keep her job? Score the sex of a lifetime?

Isabel tried to match Shane's sedate stride, but her eagerness meant that most of her steps were on the balls of her feet. She moved like a small child eager to get to an ice cream truck, anticipating the joy of a treat on a hot day.

"There are several areas around the hotel that just scream 'kiss me,'" Isabel said, playing tour guide as she led the way toward the trail that wound beside the river above the falls. "The place I'm taking you is my favorite."

After several days of gloomy and damp weather, the sun

had poked out in the afternoon to highlight the fiery gold and orange of the autumn mountain foliage. The intermittent rains had soaked the earth and awakened the bracing scent of pine. Through the trees came the distant roar of Centennial Falls. Isabel listened to the steady crunch of their footsteps on the gravel path and noted the calm that settled over Shane as he sucked in a deep breath and let it out.

"There something about the air in the mountains, isn't there?" Isabel asked, unable to maintain her silence. "I'm glad the rain has finally stopped."

She winced at her inane conversational feint. Was she seriously discussing the weather with Shane?

"I've never spent this much time up here," he admitted.

No doubt he had larger, flashier properties that demanded his attention. Although known for its high-end luxury, The Opulence's rustic location made it more like a retreat or getaway destination.

"I really appreciate you driving up to meet with me today."

"Not a problem. I'll be making visits every day between now and the Richmond retreat next week."

"Of course." She tried not to let her disappointment show. Had she really thought he'd make a special trip up here just to meet with her? "Here we are."

The trail led to a covered bridge that spanned the river fifty feet before the top of the falls. It was a magical spot for couples, and Isabel had set the stage to prove it.

"This is your romantic spot?" he peered at the weathered wood structure doubtfully.

Isabel reached into her tote and pulled out two lighters, extending one to Shane. "You'll see what I mean when we're done."

Earlier she'd brought out dozens of hurricane lanterns and filled them with white candles. As the light faded, muting the shocking orange and brilliant yellow trees and deepening the cloudless sky to a rich cornflower blue, the setting would make a gorgeous shot.

Each took one side of the bridge and worked in companionable silence to light candle after candle. Some had been hung by chains from the rafters. Others sat on the railing or the ground. By the time they were finished, the glow of those flickering points of light filled Isabel with warm satisfaction.

"Okay, I'll admit this sets the stage," he said as he handed back the lighter.

Isabel tore her gaze from the covered bridge bathed in flickering candlelight and peered at Shane. He didn't sound like the stiff businessman she'd come to know. He shifted his attention away from her, but not before she saw grudging respect and understanding in his dark brown eyes.

Isabel wrapped her fingers around the tote bag's strap in order to keep from reaching out and touching him. If he was inspired by the romantic scene, then she'd done her job. Few could possibly be as dispassionate as this man beside her. Or maybe *dispassionate* wasn't the right word. Maybe *closed off* would be a better description. He claimed he didn't believe in romance. Perhaps his issue was that he didn't believe in love. Or was he merely afraid to give it a chance?

Had he been hurt by a woman? She found it hard to believe that anyone who'd penetrated Shane's shields could possibly want to hurt him. In a flash of insight, she perceived fragility beneath his take-charge attitude. Was that even possible? How could she imagine Shane being soft or breakable? The man was a slab of granite. Immovable. Unknowable.

"You feel the potential for romance, don't you?" Isabel probed. "The magic of this place that might prompt you to sweep a woman into your arms and kiss her."

"I'm not going to kiss you," he declared, his resistance clearly palpable.

"Of course you're not," she replied breezily. "You're my boss's boss's boss and that would be inappropriate." Her smile grew predatory. "But put that aside for a second and imagine there's something between us. Something that's worth exploring."

"I really can't."

"You want to make a huge impression on me and after hearing that the Overlook has fantastic cuisine and a stellar wine cellar, you decided to bring me up here for a delicious dinner. We share a decadent dessert and with the taste of chocolate on our tongues, we walk hand in hand to this spot."

Moving deliberately, she pressed forward, unsurprised when he retreated. She backed him up against the railing. Eyes narrowing, he made no protest even when her body stopped a few inches from his.

"My heart is racing. I'm tingling all over in anticipation of our first kiss." Her bold declaration caused him to raise his eyebrows.

He cleared his throat. "Okay, I get your point."

"We stop in the middle of the bridge and watch the first stars appear in the sky. You step in close." She seized the railing on either side of his waist, boxing him in.

"It's a very romantic spot." His voice had taken on a husky tenor. That was progress. "I concede that it's beautiful here and perfect for lovers."

Although Isabel had satisfied her purpose in coming here tonight, she was greedy for more. "You cup my cheek in your hand and whisper how you've been waiting all evening for this." She skimmed her fingers across his shoulder and slid her nails through his short hair. "I can't breathe. My knees are going all wobbly. We're alone in the flickering candlelight and you put your arms around me..."

She cleared her throat meaningfully and he exhaled as if in surrender. A second later his hands circled her waist. At first his grip was neutral, neither pulling her in nor pushing her away. Just indulging her bit of playacting. But as she leaned into him, his fingers tightened almost imperceptibly.

"And I give you a clear signal that I want you to kiss me."

She tugged his head down and lifted onto her toes to bring their lips in close proximity, stopping at the brink. This had to be his move. His choice. She could kiss him and no doubt he'd let her, but she needed him to want her. To be in this moment. To choose her. To step across that line.

"Isabel." Regret filled every syllable.

She tamped down her disappointment and reminded herself that she hadn't brought him here to seduce him. Not exactly. "Tell me you feel the romance," she murmured, letting none of her regret show.

His breath flowed across her lips as he sighed. "I feel it."

And in that moment, it was enough. Isabel eased away and tension flowed out of him.

"If I can get to you," she said, her confidence slowly refilling as she realized his hands continued to span her waist, "I can get to anyone."

She stepped back, conscious how fast the heat beneath her skin began to cool as soon as he stopped touching her.

"I'm not sure if it's the place or if it's you," he grumbled.

Her heart expanded in her chest, making it hard to breathe. "Come on," she told him, reining in her delight. "It's almost time. We have to go hide."

Hide? Hide where? And why?

Damn it! What had just happened?

Shane ground his teeth, recognizing that he'd let this ridiculous situation go on far too long. The dense woods on either side of the river lent a sense of privacy to their surroundings. He'd been lured into a mellow mood by the tranquil setting, the flickering glow of the candlelight and her inventive narration. Too late he realized that she'd ambushed him. And he'd almost kissed her. That would've been a mistake. A big one.

"Come on," Isabel said, taking his arm and tugging him in the opposite direction from which they'd come.

"Where are we going?" He demanded, pushing impatience into his voice. Silent curses filled Shane's mind. It was hard to resist her. "The hotel is the other way."

"There's something else you need to see."

Their footsteps thumped on the wood as they crossed the bridge and entered the forest on the other side. She tugged him into the shadow of a large pine tree.

"It's getting too dark to see anything."

This wasn't at all what he'd expected out of today's visit. Or was he just kidding himself? He'd studied her proposal and found it reasonable. He'd already decided to circumvent Tom Busch and let her work directly with the marketing department.

He could've just called her with the news. Instead, he was skulking around in the woods with the feisty redhead. To his amazement, despite the ridiculous situation he found himself in, he discovered he was intrigued.

"Can you please tell me what's going on?"

"Just be patient for a few more minutes and all will be revealed."

A slight breeze blew the aroma of pine and damp earth across his face. He filled his lungs with the cleansing air and found himself drawing in her perfume, as well. The intoxicating fragrance relaxed him.

"I really don't have time for this," he complained, but it was a feeble protest.

What was this woman doing to him? He was lurking in the woods, waiting for who knew what to happen. She'd taken his discipline and stubbornness and transformed it into curiosity and excitement until all he wanted was to be on this adventure with her.

"Can you at least give me a hint?"

"I set this up yesterday," she whispered, her entire body vibrating with excitement. "The candles. The perfect spot."

"What's going to happen?" Even as he asked the question, a couple came toward the bridge from the opposite side of the river.

"Here they come." Isabel reached into her seemingly bottomless tote bag and pulled out a camera with an enormous lens. It was the sort of thing sports and wildlife photographers might use.

"Are we spying on someone?" Despite his growing frustration, Shane pitched his voice low to match hers. "Is this something that could damage the hotel's reputation?"

"No, of course not."

"Why do you have the camera?"

"Don't be silly."

He was being silly?

"Then why…?"

"To capture it all, of course."

He didn't see how. The light was fading fast and the numerous candles barely pushed back the shadows beneath the covered bridge. "Capture what?"

"You'll see."

Biting back another demand for answers, Shane focused on the couple. It was obvious from the woman's body language as she caught sight of the candlelit bridge that she was delighted. Beside him Isabel peered through the camera's viewfinder. Caught up in the moment, Shane watched as the man took her hands and walked backward into the flickering light.

His heart gave a funny little jerk. They were both so obviously into each other. What would that be like, he wondered, to give himself completely over to another person?

His heart gave a hard yank when the man deposited a tender kiss on her lips before dropping to one knee before her. Her hands went to her mouth and she practically vibrated with excitement.

Although he and Isabel stood too far away to hear what the man had to say, it was pretty obvious what was going on and that the answer to the man's question was a definite yes.

Beside him Isabel grinned and snapped picture after picture, capturing the entire romantic event. With a sigh, Isabel lowered the camera and shot him a wry glance.

"Is this your first proposal?"

"Yes."

"What'd you think?"

"Okay, I get it," he muttered ungraciously. "This is a very romantic spot."

"Come on."

To Shane's dismay, as soon as it appeared as if the couple was done with their private moment, Isabel headed in their direction.

"Congratulations," she called as she approached. "That was the most romantic proposal I've ever seen."

Shane trailed after her, wondering if that was an exaggeration. As he closed the distance, he realized he recognized the newly engaged woman. He'd dated Kendall Chase for a year before she'd ended things, complaining that he was married to his career. And in typical Shane Adams fashion, he'd justified the breakup by throwing himself even harder into work.

Keeping busy distracted him from dwelling on how much he'd liked Kendall. Or from pondering if he'd been in a different place in his life whether he might've married her. She was perfect for him. A lawyer with a large, successful Seattle law firm, determined to make partner, she'd worked incredibly long hours. Well matched in their professional lives until her younger sister and best friend got engaged. After that Kendall started asking Shane hard questions about how he saw their future together and it became pretty obvious that they weren't going to make it.

That was two years ago. Obviously she moved on to someone who suited her better. Someone who could love her and wanted to spend the rest of his life with her. Seeing her happiness, Shane felt a hard lump form in his chest.

"This is all so amazing." Kendall wrapped her arms around her fiancé and gazed up at him adoringly. "I had no idea you could be so romantic."

"I had help." Her fiancé grinned at Isabel.

"Hi, Kendall. I'm Isabel Withers, the hotel's concierge. On behalf of The Opulence, I want to congratulate you on your engagement."

While the happy couple beamed, Shane wondered if Isabel had known about his past connection to Kendall. If she'd invited him to witness this event, intending to rub his nose in his romantic failure.

A quick glance at Isabel made him realize how ridiculous he was being. She was completely focused on the newly engaged couple. Her open and exhilarated expression demonstrated just how deeply committed she was to creating these romantic moments and then being there to watch the magic happen. Making people happy was her mission. And she was damned good at it.

Coming up to stand beside the concierge, Shane offered his own congratulations. As he shook the man's hand, he realized Kendall hadn't noticed him yet. Would she be as shocked to see him at her proposal as he was to be here?

"This is Shane Adams," Isabel said. "He's president of Richmond Hotel Group. They manage the hotel."

"Nice to meet you," Glenn said, but his greeting was drowned out as the woman beside him spoke up.

"Shane Adams?" Kendall blinked as if awakening from a wonderful dream, and her gaze shot in Shane's direction.

Her odd tone caused her fiancé to glance her way. "Do you know each other?"

From his question, Shane gathered Kendall hadn't mentioned him.

"We dated for a while," Kendall said, her tone indicating that period of time was a vague memory, inconsequential and forgettable. "That was over two years ago. I can't believe you're here. Now."

Shane cleared his throat. "Isabel brought me along today because she has this idea that we should promote The Opulence as a romance destination and wanted me to see firsthand what she was talking about."

Isabel's wide eyes as she watched the exchange demonstrated to Shane that the whole situation was one massive, awkward coincidence. "Let's get a few formal shots before you two head to the Overlook for dinner. Something that you could share with your family and friends on social media. I captured several of the actual proposal, but those were for you."

The couple agreed, and Isabel expertly maneuvered them into place and snapped pictures with the candlelight illuminating their happy faces and images of their hands together with her new diamond ring. Shane stepped back to watch it all, noting his appreciation of the way Isabel mixed professional customer service with romantic fantasy. The whole thing was accomplished in less than fifteen minutes and the couple was thrilled with the results. This convinced Shane that Glenn and Kendall—thanks to all Isabel's subtle salesmanship—would return in a year's time to tie the knot.

"Congratulations to both of you," Shane said. "I hope you'll be very happy."

While the couple walked away, Isabel spent several seconds going through the photos on her camera. When enough time had passed for them to be out of earshot, she glanced up at him.

"Was it weird watching your ex-girlfriend get engaged?"

"A bit," he admitted, feeling something unraveling inside him. "I'm glad she found somebody who suited her."

"Were you in love with her? I'm sorry. I shouldn't have asked that. It's too personal."

"I never gave the relationship a chance. She broke up with me because I worked too much."

"Was she in love with you?"

Shane blew out the candle nearest him. "We should probably be getting back to the hotel."

"Go ahead. I need to pack everything up."

Rather than leave her alone in the gathering dark, he spent the next twenty minutes helping her extinguish the candles and collect the hurricane lamps. Isabel fetched the wagon she'd hidden, and, working in silence, they loaded everything into boxes.

Although Isabel hadn't pursued an answer to her earlier question, Shane couldn't stop his churning thoughts. He'd never encouraged Kendall's emotional attachment to him. And even as she'd probed whether they had a future, he suspected if he'd proposed she wouldn't have agreed to marry him.

"Thanks for helping me pack up," Isabel said, her gratitude enveloping him like a soft blanket on a chilly night. "Sometimes romance is a lot of work."

While her jaunty tone gave the statement a lighthearted spin, Shane responded in a serious vein.

"Which explains why I'm single," he said. "What about you?"

"Me?" Isabel gusted out a laugh, obviously uncomfortable having the tables turned on her. "I guess I spend so much time focused on making other people's romantic dreams come true that I neglect my own."

"So you don't practice what you preach?"

"Maybe the right guy hasn't come along."

Shane snorted, thinking how she'd gotten into his head with all her talk of romance. "I think you could make any man the right guy."

"Even you?"

For several seconds he didn't know what to make of her question. They weren't in the least bit compatible. While he admired her for being hardworking, organized and professional, beneath her impeccable hotel uniform beat a fanciful, fun-loving heart he couldn't begin to relate to.

So why did he pause to considered how to answer? And why did his blood course hot and thick through his veins? Too late he realized she was flirting with him. Yet with his heart thundering in his chest, he locked his gaze with hers. Was the overwhelming urge to put his arms around her a trick of the starlight reflected in her eyes?

He cupped her cheek and slid his thumb over her lower lip. Her breath hitched even as his lungs stopped altogether. Madness. He couldn't do this. She was an employee. Completely off limits.

A groan broke loose from her chest, snapping his fraying restraint. Letting his eyes slide shut, he brought his lips to hers. The first kiss he dusted across her incredibly soft mouth, offering her the opportunity to come to her senses. To pull back. To shove him away. She didn't.

To his joyful regret, she leaned into him, pushing up on her toes and driving her lips hard against his. The second kiss escalated fast. While their mouths fused and teeth raked, her fingers combed through his hair, before digging into his skull.

His thoughts became blurry and unreachable as he banded his arm around her waist. Shane slid his other hand into her hair, disrupting the pins holding her updo in place. Curling his fingers around her long, wavy locks, he tugged, changing the angle of her head. She gasped in delight as his tongue slid into her mouth. She welcomed him with a throaty moan that unleashed his desire.

He was on fire for her. A living torch. No longer a cold, dispassionate rock. But an inferno of hunger and lust. The sheer strength of his reaction shocked him into breaking off the kiss. But instead of setting her free amongst a litany of apologies and excuses, he set his cheek against her temple and sucked in several breaths of the chilly mountain air. Her arms went around his waist in a tight hug that he read as affection rather than passion.

A moment later she pushed herself away and raked her fingers through her disheveled hair. She stared at him in wide-eyed amazement for a brief moment before succumbing to an irrepressible grin.

"See," she began, her smoky voice at odds with the delight dancing in her hazel eyes. "I told you. This is the perfect spot for a first kiss."

Four

After yet another mostly sleepless night spent tossing and turning, dawn found Teresa sipping French press coffee at her condo's breakfast bar. She watched rain strike the glass door leading out to her tiny balcony with its peekaboo glimpse of the Sound while her mind replayed last week's shocking revelations on a continuous loop.

She'd contacted Linus's lawyer and confirmed that she now owned a stake in Christopher Corporation. Seven years earlier Linus had been her mentor. Intelligent and successful, kind and encouraging, his advice and guidance had been instrumental in laying the groundwork for what had become Limitless Events.

And if she was honest with herself, her affection for him wasn't solely professional. Teresa had lost her father at a very young age. Could she really be blamed for seeing Linus as a father figure? He'd certainly treated her like the daughter he'd never had. Unfortunately, she'd learned from Liam their closeness had been misinterpreted and created problems with Linus's family. Even though she hadn't re-alized at the time that she'd been the catalyst for his marriage falling apart, Teresa had limited contact with Linus in the years that followed because she was so focused on becoming successful.

Which made his substantial gift to her so much more shocking. While she wanted to get swept up in joy and wonder at the unbelievable upturn in her fortune, the news dealt a fatal blow to the promising new beginning she and Liam had made. She never should've stepped across the line and fallen prey to her passion for the charismatic Seattle billionaire. Doing so had left her open to being damaged by his distrust and bad opinion.

Dwelling on problems she couldn't begin to fix filled Teresa's anxiety well to the top. With only a week until the Richmond anniversary extravaganza was set to begin, dozens of details awaited her attention. Teresa headed into Limitless Events's offices to check in with her staff. Despite having worked closely with most of them on numerous projects, Teresa had a tough time relinquishing control.

She'd never known if this was something she'd learned during the years she'd trained with Mariella Santiago-Marshall of MSM Event Planning or if it had started in childhood. Teresa's mother had been scattered and overwhelmed by the world even before her husband died. It grew so much worse once Talisa had been left alone to raise her two small children. Teresa had grown up too fast, taking care of both her mother and her baby brother.

"Good morning," Teresa said breezily to Corrine, sailing past the mostly empty desks on her way to her office at the back. "I'd like the status meeting to start in fifteen minutes."

That afternoon she was heading to the hotel where the retreat would be taking place and staying there until the event was done. The Opulence was a one-of-a-kind resort perched on a cliff beside a one-hundred-thirty-foot waterfall with sweeping panoramic views of the river and mountains.

"I sent Martha out for treats," Corrine called after her. "I figured we could all use a sugar rush right about now."

Affection rose in Teresa for her efficient assistant. "Good thinking."

Ignoring the couch where she and Liam had made love for the first time, Teresa settled into her desk chair and set up her laptop. Today the soothing ritual of arranging her phone, notepad, pen and coffee cup in a neat line wasn't having its desired effect. Usually creating order forced her to concentrate on what she could control and calmed her.

Confidence swelled in Teresa as she looked over her to-do lists. This she could handle. This she was good at. Being creative and organized.

She noted the employees assigned to various outstanding tasks and noted which giveaway items still needed to be collected. Each attendee would receive a fabulous gift bag filled with the sort of over-the-top luxury items that A-listers took for granted. She'd also suggested to Matt Richmond that they fill the attendees' suites with flowers and welcome baskets. In some cases they'd tailored the goodies to the guests' particular preferences or dietary concerns, utilizing the hotel's excellent concierge, Isabel Withers, to gather information on each person.

Because the people invited to the Richmond retreat were some of the richest people in the world and Matt insisted that each received personalized attention, Teresa had arranged to bring in additional support staff to cater to their every need.

For the first time she noticed the message light blinking on her phone. Her nerves jangled as Liam's betrayed expression filled her thoughts. Although the message could be one of a hundred different things, she greedily hoped Liam had reconciled himself to not blaming her for his father's bequest and was reaching out to let her know.

If Liam chose to blame her for his father's decision to leave her the stock, nothing she could say would convince him otherwise. It would help if she had a genuine answer that would satisfy him, but when she didn't understand Linus's motivation, how could she make a convincing argument?

The corners of her lips drooped as she pondered her hopeless situation with Liam. She couldn't visualize a path back to a place where he trusted her again. Here was a perfect instance where she had no place to turn for help. The Fixer, the man she'd leaned on in the past, certainly couldn't make this right. How did one go about fixing someone else's broken heart?

Was she heartbroken?

Teresa shied away from the emotional question and focused on a concrete issue instead. As much as Liam wanted the shares of his company back, according to the terms of the will, they were stuck with each other for a year.

She was paralyzed at the idea of having to confront his displeasure for the next twelve months while her own treacherous emotions kept replaying memories of their lovemaking.

What if she refused the shares? Would that enable Liam's faith in her to bounce back?

On the other hand, such a large amount could weatherproof her business against future troubles. She'd be a fool to wager her financial security on a long-shot chance that she could have a future with Liam. There was no guarantee that her sacrifice would bring her a happily-ever-after. Those few glorious times she had spent with Liam had obviously been an anomaly.

Sure, they were sexually attracted to each other, but did either of them have what it took to go the romantic distance?

Heaven knew she had a poor track record when it came to intimacy and relationships.

Liam was interesting and irresistible, a combination she found unexpected and intoxicating. He appealed to her mind, body and soul. It was just her luck that so many obstacles stood between them.

Teresa gave an exasperated sigh. She shouldn't waste time bemoaning her past decisions. That's not how she operated her business. It shouldn't be how she handled her personal life. When a problem came up with a client, she took care of the situation, making it right. That sort of confidence didn't follow her into her private life. Like when her brother had been in a jam, she'd reluctantly reached out to the Fixer, thinking the situation beyond her ability to solve. She should've known that someone who took care of problems for the wealthy and elite would expect more than she could afford to pay. And now she owed the man a favor. She shivered with foreboding.

Beyond the tall windows, the gray skies had darkened, making nine in the morning feel more like dusk, matching Teresa's grim mood. She flipped on her desk light and studied the to-do list she'd created that morning, frowning at item five: "Meet with Aspen Wright at two." The hotel's event planner had not appreciated having to take a backseat role with regard to the retreat and had argued with Teresa's decisions at nearly every turn.

Teresa glanced up as several of her staff entered the office, chattering good-naturedly among themselves. At least her staff was upbeat.

The blinking red light continued to demand her attention.

Teresa picked up the handset and dialed her voice mail. The male voice recorded at two that morning wasn't Liam, but her brother Joshua.

"Hey, sis," he said, sounding distracted. Syllables blurring together, he continued. "You're always working so I thought you might be at the office. I need to talk."

To her intense annoyance, the call ended. Questions buzzed through her mind as she hung up the phone. Had he been cut off? Was he in trouble? Was he drunk? Or drugged? He'd claimed he had his "situation" under control. Was that still the case or had he been overly confident in his ability to fix things?

She dialed his phone and rolled her eyes when she was immediately directed to his voice mail. As she muttered curses while his voice directed her to leave a message after the beep, Teresa's thoughts went back to Linus's final gift to her. Though moments earlier she'd pondered refusing it, she might just need the inheritance to get her brother out of trouble. Again.

Which killed any hope of reconciling with Liam. Maybe as painful as it was to give up on him, that was what was best for her. Chances were his trust issues would've ended up breaking her heart.

Then she noted the ache in her chest. Thought about her sleepless nights.

Maybe it was already too late.

Isabel was sending a confirmation email finalizing details for a party of eight that evening at Quintessential Chef when a furious woman in a glittering designer wedding dress stormed into the lobby from the side terrace. The entire wedding party trailed after her in miserable silence.

"You are useless." The focus of the woman's fury was a slender man with a camera. "My entire wedding will be ruined because you haven't gotten a single decent shot."

Predicting there would be bloodletting soon, Isabel raced to intercede. The bride was a stunning twenty-eight-year-old blonde from California with nearly four million followers on YouTube and three million on Instagram. She'd started out five years earlier sharing her thoughts, aspirations and daily inspiration surrounding makeup, food, travel and fashion and parlayed her style into a multimillion-dollar business.

None of her charm or signature confidence was in evidence at the moment. She shook with impatient annoyance.

Isabel boldly stepped between the blogger and the embattled photographer. Although Isabel had briefed the photographer on all the best spots to shoot, the man had obviously not paid attention.

"Excuse me, Ms. Maxwell."

"What?" Stunning blue eyes snapped in Isabel's direction. "Oh, it's you, Isabel."

"I'm sorry you're not getting the photos you want." Isabel whipped out her most winning smile. "I know all the best places on or around the property for you to take photos. Will you let me show you?"

The woman sniffed. "It's hopeless. A complete disaster. I knew I should've gone to Bahia Resort Hotel."

This was the exact sort of thing Isabel wanted to avoid. "I'm a huge fan. I've seen all your posts. I know the sort of places you love to go. Give me a chance."

"I don't know."

"And for your troubles, the hotel would love to offer you and your groom a post-wedding couple's massage tomorrow free of charge."

Isabel knew that Camilla had already enjoyed a romantic welcome basket as well as several complimentary meals, but if the lifestyle blogger was happy, she would rave about the hotel, and that was the best sort of publicity.

"Fine," the blogger grumbled. "Show us where we can get some halfway decent shots."

As soon as she made sure Camilla was happy with the first location, Isabel headed inside to call the spa and set up the massage appointment.

"…And make it free of charge. Thanks." Isabel hung up the phone and jumped when a voice spoke behind her.

"Do you make a habit of handing out free spa treatments?"

Isabel's pulse leaped as she glanced around and saw Tom Busch standing behind her. His scowl told her he wasn't happy.

"When I think it will benefit the hotel." She'd never sucked up to the executive manager the way he preferred and often wondered if that had led him to shut down her ideas for promoting The Opulence as a romantic destination.

"That's not your decision to make," Tom said. "You should ask before comping anything."

"Usually I do." Isabel nodded, but continued to defend her actions. "But today there wasn't time."

"We have procedures for how to do things here."

"I know, but I was trying to smooth over a situation for Camilla Maxwell. She's a lifestyle blogger with almost four mill—"

Tom interrupted. "I don't care who it was for. Don't do it again."

"But—"

"Is there an issue here?"

To Isabel's dismay, Shane had approached while she and Tom had been speaking. Despite his neutral expression, she sensed he'd heard most if not all of the exchange. Being dressed down in front of him brought hot color to her cheeks.

"It's handled," Tom said, turning his back on Isabel in dismissal. "I wasn't expecting you today."

With the men engaged in conversation, Isabel snatched the opportunity to escape. Her blood continued to simmer as she headed toward the side terrace, where she'd left Camilla and her wedding party, but as she admired the picturesque tableau before her, her anger drained away.

The way Camilla and her groom stared at each other ex-
emplified what Isabel worked so hard to achieve.

"Beautiful…" she breathed.

"Do you want to tell me what that was about?"

While she'd been absorbed in what was happening on
the lawn, Shane had exited the building and come to stand
beside her.

"I don't want to talk about it," she murmured. "Look
how perfect this all is. This is what I've been talking about."

"Yes, it's quite nice." Shane might've been discussing
a cup of coffee for all the interest he showed. "Why was
Tom upset with you?"

"Because a crisis arose and I fixed it. Then I offered Camilla and her soon-to-be-husband a free couple's massage
for their trouble." Isabel glanced at Shane's profile, pausing a moment to appreciate his strong nose and bold eyebrows. She caught herself smiling and sighed. "See what's
going on over there?"

"It looks like an ordinary wedding party to me."

"Far from ordinary. That's Camilla Maxwell. She is a
huge lifestyle blogger on social media. I've followed her
for years. She has the most amazing Instagram feed filled
with fashion and travel photos. When she got engaged, I
knew she could go anywhere to get married. So I reached
out to her and pitched her on having her wedding at The
Opulence. When those photos go up on her various online
platforms, the hotel will get tons of publicity."

Isabel paused and turned to Shane. He glanced down at
her, eyes narrowing as their gazes met.

"For the cost of a free spa treatment, The Opulence will
be shown as one of the country's most beautiful spots to
get married." She cocked her head. "Now tell me that's not
worth breaking from procedure to accomplish."

Before Shane could answer, Isabel noticed that the photographer was done shooting this location. She started forward with a glance over her shoulder.

"Are you coming?"

"Coming where?"

"It's a surprise."

"I don't like surprises."

"Some surprises are very nice," she teased, walking backward a few steps so she could keep the conversation going. "You should open yourself up to the prospect of having fun."

Shane started following her. "Do I look like somebody who likes to have fun?"

"No," she admitted, resisting the urge to roll her eyes at him. "But you don't not look like someone who likes to have fun."

The ever-present line between his brows deepened. "What does that even mean?"

"It means you have potential."

After chewing on her comment for several seconds, he seemed disinclined to engage her flirtatious repartee. "Where are we going?"

"To a very picturesque spot so the bride and groom can take romantic pictures with Centennial Falls in the background. You're going to love how they'll look on the website."

Isabel introduced Shane to Camilla Maxwell before leading the way toward the path that ran along the top of the cliff to the falls overlook. Along the way, the photographer snapped the wedding party and the couple against the colorful fall foliage. The bride and groom in formal attire contrasted beautifully with the landscape. With each pause Camilla grew more satisfied with her wedding day photos so that by the time Isabel pitched her final destination, the blogger was eager to go.

"It's a little bit of a hike," Isabel warned. "But totally worth it."

Camilla's Instagram feed, filled with dramatic shots taken on her travels, demonstrated that the blogger was willing to take risks to get the wow shots.

"Lead the way."

They left the wedding party behind and headed down the trail to the bottom of the cliff and the lower viewing site for the falls. The abundant rains over the last few days had increased the river's volume and the falls were in their full glory. Isabel and Shane stood back while the photographer shot frame after frame of the couple with the falls and the resort in the background, muttering appreciative comments as he did so.

Afterward, Isabel escorted the couple to the golf cart she'd summoned to take them back to the resort.

"This was absolutely perfect," Camilla gushed, clinging to her groom's arm. "Exactly what I was hoping for when I booked my wedding here."

"I'm glad you're happy," Isabel said. "I can't wait to see the photos on your website and Instagram feed. And if you wouldn't mind, could the hotel use one or two for our website?"

"Of course."

Feeling victorious, Isabel smiled as she watched the couple go.

"That was nicely done," Shane said, breaking his silence for the first time in over an hour.

Isabel preened at his approval. "Thank you."

His gaze roved over her features, pausing at her lips, before shifting toward the trail. "I suppose we should be heading back."

She was enjoying this time with him too much to agree, but nodded because that was the sensible thing to do. Sensible? It struck her then that while she was trying to inject a little play into his work-focused mindset, he was having a transformative effect on her. Why be practical when what she really wanted to do was drag him to her favorite boulder in the center of the river and have a picture taken of them kissing with the falls as a backdrop?

As they started toward the trail, she snuck a peek at his somber profile and sighed. He was definitely not ready to venture from rock to rock across the river or to be photographed kissing her. Which of course led to her wondering if he'd ever kiss her again.

"So, your ex-girlfriend…" she began, bringing up the awkward situation instead of asking what she really wanted to know.

"What about her?"

"She booked her wedding at The Opulence next October."

"After the way you arranged the romantic proposal, I thought she might."

Warmed by his approving tone, Isabel continued, "I've already started researching the perfect theme for their special weekend. She loves to knit. Both she and Glenn like to run marathons and they have a darling golden retriever named Sunny."

Shane frowned. "How do you know all that?"

"I checked her out on social media."

He looked appalled. "You stalked her?"

"'Stalk' is such an aggressive term," she muttered. "I seek insight from social media cues. When someone contacts me about romantic things to do, or if a guy wants the perfect setting for a proposal."

"Like Glenn…"

"Exactly like Glenn." She beamed at him. "I will go to their Instagram feed or check out their Pinterest boards to see what sort of things they like. You can get a really good idea about people based on what they post online."

"I don't have any social media," Shane said.

"Yes." She nodded ruefully. "I'm well aware of that."

"You've looked?"

"I check out everyone I'm interested in." Her wry smile caused him to raise his eyebrows.

"I guess you're going to have to get to know me the old-fashioned way."

"Is that so," she purred. He was going to let her get to know him. That sounded promising. "I look forward to it."

They hiked in silence for nearly a minute before Shane spoke.

"So, what do you want to know?"

He continued to surprise her.

"Seriously? You'll answer my questions?"

"Possibly." He lifted one broad shoulder and let it fall. "I guess neither one of us will know what I'll answer until you ask."

Five

To Shane's surprise, Isabel didn't take him up on his offer to answer questions during their trek back to the hotel. Even more astonishing was his disappointment. As they drew within sight of the hotel, she paused and put her hand on his arm, stopping him. The touch sizzled through him, heightening his awareness of her soft lips and earnest hazel eyes.

"I want you to know how much I appreciate that you listened to me about my ideas for the hotel," she said. "I tend to lead with my emotions rather than logic. It's both a gift and a curse, and because of that, not everyone finds my ideas valuable."

"Of course." Recalling the scene he'd witnessed between her and Tom Busch earlier, Shane recognized that the executive manager wasn't interested in listening to such a junior employee. No matter how good her ideas might be. "And yet you've done a fine job presenting your ideas."

"In my career I've learned to be more organized." She wrinkled her nose. "It's my personal life where I tend to struggle with impulsive and chaotic urges."

"How so?"

"I love trying new things all the time. I can't tell you how many hobbies have caught my fancy only to end up dropped when something new and shiny catches my attention. I don't imagine you're like that at all."

"I don't have hobbies."

"Nothing? Not even golf or boating or gambling…what is it you do when you're not working?"

"I work out every morning. Running. Weights."

"Working out has 'work' in the title. I don't know if that qualifies it for a hobby. It's more like something you do to keep yourself healthy, like eating well. Unless training is something you feel passionate about."

What did he feel passionate about? His career. That wasn't exactly a hobby. And his drive to be successful was as much about thumbing his nose at his father as it was something that brought him deep satisfaction.

"I don't really have the time or energy to pursue interests beyond work."

"You can't plan to work this hard forever," she said. "Have you ever considered that you might benefit from some balance?"

Did she stop to think he might not appreciate her opinion on his personal life? Shane regarded her in silence for a long moment, before deciding she recognized that she'd overstepped and wasn't worried about it.

"What would you suggest?"

Her wry grin said it all. "I was done an hour ago."

"And you have something in mind that I might find interesting?"

"I might."

Shane didn't wait for her suggestion. "Do you want to have dinner?"

"Dinner?" Her hopeful expression sucker-punched him in the gut. "To discuss how today's photo shoot fits in with my ideas for the resort?"

Whether or not she'd meant to, Isabel had just handed him an out. He wasn't sure why he'd offered the invitation when he was determined not to cross a line with her again. But being with her was proving irresistible.

"We can definitely do that," he said, unable to express the conflicting emotions raging in him.

"That sounds great," she murmured, displaying sudden shy delight at his offer. "There's an Italian restaurant in North Bend that might be up to your standards." The town she mentioned was ten miles south of the hotel. "I need to go home and change. Would an hour from now be okay? I'll bring my laptop along and we can look at the photos from today's shoot. Jason said he'd upload everything right away and send me a link to his gallery."

"I'll see you in an hour."

Shane didn't follow Isabel when she headed into the hotel. Instead, he stood where she'd left him, massaging the back of his neck. What had he just done?

Stepped across the line, that's what. That she possessed a guileless idealism worried him. He'd seen too much. She hadn't seen enough. He had no business inviting her out for dinner.

Yet his instincts told him to stop fighting his interest in Isabel and take a chance for once. They might be as different as night and day, but the chemistry between them intensified with each encounter. He enjoyed her refreshing point of view and the fact that she challenged him to think of something besides his career.

An hour later, he'd exited his car in the parking lot of the Italian restaurant Isabel had suggested and was making his way to the front door when he noticed a bright orange Subaru BRZ wheeling off the highway. He paused to watch the sporty car execute a sharp turn into an open space. A moment later the driver's side door opened and a shapely leg emerged.

While Shane stared in mesmerized fascination, Isabel unfolded herself from the car, slung a tote bag over her shoulder and shut the door. Tonight she wore a snug cobalt dress that bared a great deal of thigh and paired it with a black leather moto jacket. Sexy and confident, she strolled across the pavement in his direction. Her high strappy heels gave her hips a natural roll that caused his heart to hammer. Aware he was gawking, Shane told himself to chill out, but the impact of her sassy smile on his libido couldn't be denied.

A strong urge to sink his fingers into her lush russet locks and bring her lips to his overrode his common sense. As she drew near, her perfume teased his senses. Maintaining a professional distance seemed less important by the second.

"You look great," he murmured.

"You sound surprised," she countered breathlessly, executing a slow pirouette so he could take her in from every angle. "I'm not as unsophisticated as my hotel uniform might suggest."

"I never thought anything like that."

"You did, but I forgive you." Her hazel eyes flashed. "And I'll admit that I dressed like this so you'd see a different side of me."

"You didn't need to." Shane took her arm and guided her toward the restaurant.

Isabel resisted. "What are you trying to say?"

"That I'm interested in you just the way you are."

"You're interested in me?" Her eyebrows climbed. She studied him for several steps. "How am I supposed to take that?"

"Why don't we go inside and find out over a glass of wine?"

But once the hostess settled them in a quiet booth and after ordering a bottle of Syrah from the local winery, the conversation veered toward that afternoon's photo shoot. Isabel slid onto the seat beside Shane and opened her laptop. While she scrolled through hundreds of photos, soliciting his opinion on several, he gave up trying to focus on her words and lost himself in her upbeat tone, her building excitement for the marketing potential and the zing of delight every time her shoulder bumped against his.

He wanted to nuzzle the spot where her dangly earrings bumped against her neck and slide his hand along her silky thigh. Her infectious grin invited him to relax and soak in all of her optimism and passion.

When the food came, she shifted to the opposite side of the booth and put away her computer. Shane immediately missed her proximity and wondered what spell she'd cast over him.

"How's the *costata di agnello*?" she asked, eyeing his rack of lamb with interest.

Shane realized he'd been so absorbed in watching Isabel savor every mouthful of her veal that he'd eaten a third of his dish without tasting a single bite. "Do you want to try it?"

"Please." She reached across the table and snagged a bit of the meat he'd cut. Eyes dancing, she popped the fork into her mouth and groaned. "Delicious."

After watching how much Isabel enjoyed the meal, Shane couldn't wait to see how she reacted to the decadent chocolate dessert the waiter suggested.

"You know, you're pretty young to be the head of a division the size of Richmond Hotel Group," Isabel said, spearing another bite of the flourless torte. "How long have you been with the company?"

"Five years." As he answered, Shane realized Isabel had been deftly interviewing him the entire meal while he knew next to nothing about her. "It's been a combination of hard work and luck."

"'I'm a great believer in luck, and I find the harder I work the more I have of it.' Thomas Jefferson," she said with a decisive nod. "So, where is all your hard work taking you next?"

"What makes you think I'm not perfectly happy with where I'm at?"

She gave that serious consideration for several seconds before asking, "Do you think you'll ever get to a point where you'll want more than what you have now?"

Like a wife and kids? He saw where her thoughts had taken her and decided to shut down that line of inquiry.

"What I have now is everything I need."

"What about sex?"

The blunt question left him choking on the sip of wine he'd just taken. Here he'd been thinking she was a local girl, naive and unworldly, and he the big bad sophisticate from the city. She kept turning the tables on him with her outrageous talk. Was she trying to get under his skin or did she just turn on the charm with everyone?

"What about it? I mean, I'm not a monk."

"So you date?"

"Of course," he said.

With a hint of mockery causing the corners of her lips to curve up, Isabel fixed him with bright curiosity. "How does the evening go?"

What did she want to know? Probably what any sensible woman on a date with a man hoped to hear. That he intended to get to know her before taking her to bed.

"I start with a nice dinner and…" He trailed off. Normally that's all he made time for.

"This is a nice dinner. Very romantic." She pointed to the half-eaten chocolate torte between them.

"You suggested the restaurant," Shane countered, registering his defensive tone.

She cocked her head and regarded him with a curious

half-smile. "You let me eat off your plate and agreed to share a dessert."

He gazed at her baffled wonder. "So?"

"I'm surprised you let me, is all. It shows you're capable of intimacy."

"Intimacy?" He garbled out the word. "I was being polite."

He didn't do intimacy any more than he did romance. What was this woman doing? What was she thinking? Planning? As the questions sped up, his thoughts approached a state of near panic. And then he noticed she was smiling at him in absolute delight.

"When you take these women out that you date, what happens after dinner?" she asked, returning to her earlier line of questioning. "Dancing?"

"Like in a nightclub?" The thought of all that noise and the crush of so many people made him grimace. "No."

"A movie?"

He cleared his throat. "It's been a while since I've been to the theater." Years, in fact. Usually if he caught a popular film it was on TV, months after it left the theater.

"A romantic walk through the city?" Anticipating his dissent, she didn't even wait for him to respond. "So, after dinner you move straight to sex. Do you go back to her place or take her to yours?"

Shane shook his head, regretting that he hadn't stopped her flow of questions before this. A second later it occurred to him that she was looking for reassurance. Despite the way she wore her romanticism like a suit of armor against all that was hard and unkind in the world, Isabel wasn't immune to disappointment or heartbreak. Today's encounter with Tom Busch was proof of that. She'd been visibly rattled by how the executive manager had dressed her down. Her earnest actions had been for the good of the resort and

Tom's inflexibility had landed on her spirits like a ruler across the knuckles, painful and humiliating.

I'm not planning on seducing you, if that's what you're worried about.

That was what she deserved to hear. It was how he felt. He had no intention of taking advantage of her idealistic nature. But perversely this fact wasn't what came out of his mouth.

"It depends."

She popped a forkful of chocolate dessert into her mouth. "On what?"

"On whether I have any interest in seeing her again."

The invitation to attend a marketing meeting at the Richmond Hotel Group's offices in downtown Seattle arrived in Isabel's inbox the day after she and Shane had dinner at the Italian restaurant in North Bend. As he'd escorted her across the parking lot, Shane had made a passing comment about wanting her to present her ideas in person. She'd barely registered his remark because her blood had been rushing through her veins, making her deaf to everything but the music of longing and desire.

Would he kiss her again? Had the chocolate cake and red wine been enough to purge garlic from her breath? Should she invite him back to her place? Would he expect her to? How far was she prepared to take things once she got him alone?

Only the first of these questions received an answer.

To her dismay, Shane had ushered her into her car and retreated with a polite smile, leaving her hormones revved up and her hopes dashed. She drove home, her confidence crushed beneath the weight of disappointment and doubt, and spent the rest of the night dissecting their dinner conversation.

Obviously the kiss on the bridge had been a fluke. A reaction to seeing his ex-girlfriend getting engaged and the manner in which Isabel had stirred him up with her talk of romance and the stage she'd set for a passion-filled encounter. He'd stepped right into her net and she'd been foolish enough to think that was the beginning of something.

In fact, it had been. Just not the something she'd hoped.

Yet, by the time Isabel entered the corporate offices of the Richmond Hotel Group, dressed in a chic black suit with skinny cropped pants and a silky white blouse, she'd shrugged off her initial regret and embraced the opportunity to show off her ideas. The meeting lasted two hours and went better than Isabel could've hoped. By the end, Isabel's best photographs and much of the copy from her original presentation to Shane had been approved for incorporation into the website and updated marketing materials. She was feeling giddy with success as she exited the conference room and shook hands with the marketing staff before making her way through the reception area.

"How did it go?"

Isabel had been so caught up in her thoughts, she didn't notice Shane had come up behind her and now stood with his hands in his pockets, staring at the elevator doors as they slid open. As he gestured for her to precede him, Isabel's heart began to hammer.

"It went great. They are going to make several changes to the website to include weekend romance packages as well as a page promoting the hotel as a romantic destination."

"Great." He pushed the button for the lobby and the doors slid shut. "I bet you feel like celebrating."

Mouth dry, she nodded. "I do."

Two days had passed since they'd had dinner. Two days when she'd obsessively checked her phone for some communication from him. Two days when she'd replayed every remark she'd made, every question and every answer. Had she said the right things? Was he interested? Maybe kissing her hadn't meant anything at all.

"Let's grab a drink."

"Sure." She stared at the descending numbers and tried to keep her expression casual while inside she was shrieking and dancing around like someone who'd won the lottery. "Where do you suggest? I don't know the area all that well."

"I know a spot."

She was certain he did. When they reached the curb, he ushered her into a waiting town car, and she watched downtown Seattle sweep past while her pulse throbbed so hard in her throat she couldn't speak, couldn't ask where they were going or tell him how much she appreciated the opportunity he'd given her.

Ten minutes later, the car stopped and they both slid out. Isabel gazed at the tall buildings around her. There wasn't a bar or even a restaurant in sight. Shane guided her through the doors into a residential building.

"Is this your place?" she croaked as they stood before a bank of elevators. She cursed her unsteady voice.

His eyebrow rose as he picked up on her nervousness. "Is that a problem?"

"Of course not." She wanted this. Wanted him. She didn't question if she was ready to take the next step with him.

Given the way their last evening had ended, the question remained if he was ready to take the next step with her. But surely she should be cheered by the fact that he'd invited her to his home.

"Relax," he murmured as the doors opened on the nineteenth floor. He set his fingers lightly against the small of her back and nudged her forward into the hallway. "We're here for a drink."

"I am relaxed."

One corner of his mouth gave a sardonic twitch as he punched in the key code that unlocked his door. "You look as skittish as a cat at a dog show."

With a single sound of disgust, she sailed past him and entered the unit. The first thing that struck her was the open space and the incredible view.

"Wow!" She set her purse on a table in the entry and headed straight for the wall of windows. Her heels clicked on the polished limestone floors as she took in the view. Off to her left, the setting sun was bathing the skyscrapers in soft gold. "This is spectacular." Her gaze lingered on Mount Rainier. "And the views."

He came to stand beside her. "From the bedroom you can see Elliot Bay."

"I'd like that." She was only half teasing. Her heart raced, making it difficult to keep her tone light. "Lead the way."

"I'll give you a tour later."

Isabel didn't want a tour. She wanted him to take her to bed.

"The sun is setting," she countered, turning to face him. "It might be too late later."

Turning away from the view, he brought the full power of his dark brown eyes to bear on her. The anxiety that had risen in the elevator melted away as the chemistry between them began to bubble. After days of questioning how he felt about her, the penetrating questions in his somber gaze let her know he was interested.

So what was holding him back? She should ask, but for a change her fearless audacity failed her. This wasn't a situation where she took a man to bed for some casual fun. Since laying eyes on Shane a year ago, her heart and body had been laser-locked on him. Sex with him meant something to her. He meant something to her.

"I like that you left your hair down today," he said, the

observation a thrilling peek behind the curtain that hid his thoughts. "It's such a beautiful color. And so soft."

"It's all natural," she said. "I'm all natural."

She had no idea what she meant by the remark, but he took the declaration in stride. His gaze drifted over her features before dipping lower. Isabel wished she'd worn something clingy and revealing instead of the silky blouse and suit jacket that only hinted at her curves.

"How did you get interested in hotel management?"

At the question, she barely stopped herself from rolling her eyes. Surely he hadn't brought her back to his place to ask about her career.

"I wanted to escape Washington and imagined myself living in some of the most exciting cities in the country. Instead, I ended up working for a hotel that isn't more than twenty miles from the small town where I grew up."

No doubt that sounded inexperienced to a sophisticated man of the world like Shane.

"Where did you get your degree?" he asked, strolling toward his big kitchen.

Isabel trailed after him and watched him open a bottle of champagne. He hadn't been kidding about celebrating.

"Washington State University's online hospitality program." She knew he'd graduated at the top of his class from Stanford and hoped he'd think her academic creds passed muster. "WSU is a top online program, and I really didn't have any way of attending school full-time because I needed to work to make ends meet. This way I was able to do all my classwork during my off hours."

After accepting a crystal flute from Shane, she sipped champagne to cover her embarrassment at the way her defensiveness came through loud and clear. Usually she took pride in all she'd accomplished, but when she compared it to so many of the people around her, especially someone like Teresa St. Claire, what she'd done didn't seem all that impressive.

"It took me longer to finish," she continued, "but I graduated without having any school loans."

Even before Isabel's father had left them, there hadn't been a lot of extra money. Most of her clothes had come from thrift stores. Isabel's mother had brought home leftovers from her restaurant job. Anything to stretch a dime. Even now that she could afford it, Isabel lived without a lot of luxuries.

She remembered buying an expensive designer purse for her mother with her first paycheck from The Opulence and how her mother had been so shocked when she'd opened the beautiful box and peered beneath the delicate tissue paper. That her mother had been equal parts awed and appalled had taken some of the joy out of the purchase for Isabel. Right then and there she realized that her mother's thrifty ways had become such an intrinsic part of her that she couldn't begin to appreciate something she didn't absolutely need.

That made Isabel sad. She'd wanted to give everything to the woman who'd raised her and encouraged her. But it had also been a strong reminder that what was truly important was the love and support of those around her.

"And you've been with The Opulence for a year?" Shane asked.

"Yes."

"Any plans for where you'd like to go next?"

"New York, London, Paris, Italy or maybe somewhere in the Caribbean." She gave a breathless laugh. "I'm kidding. I know I don't have enough experience to get my dream hotel yet. And I like what I'm doing right now."

"Don't sell yourself short. I think you're destined for big things."

"I wasn't planning on selling myself short. I think I demonstrated to you that I have a pretty high opinion of myself."

"I have a high opinion of you, too."

Noticing that he hadn't poured a glass of champagne for himself, she set her glass down on the granite countertop. "I'd like a tour of your condo now. All of it. Starting with your bedroom."

Shane shook his head. "I didn't bring you up here for that."

"Then why did you?"

"I wanted to be alone with you." He regarded her through half-lidded eyes.

"Why? If you don't have any interest in sleeping with me."

Something flashed across his features. Something that turned her bones to oatmeal and heated her blood.

"Don't ever think I'm not interested," he growled, his gaze sweeping hungrily over her.

The sudden flare of sexual awareness tore through her, awakening a keen ache between her thighs. Desire pooled in her belly, the pressure a blissful discomfort.

"Then what's the problem?" she demanded, her voice liquid smoke.

"You work for me." With a blink he banked all the heat in his gaze, leaving her short of breath and lacking fulfillment of any kind. "I can't go there."

"Because that would break all sorts of rules." Stepping into his space, she slid her hand against his, rejoicing when he turned his palm to hers. A thousand goose bumps broke out on her skin as he played with her fingers. "And that's not who you are."

"It's all kinds of wrong," he murmured. Lifting his free hand, he drew his knuckles along her hot cheek. "You deserve more than I can give you."

That he hadn't shut her down yet gave her a glimpse

into his soul. He could claim that work consumed his life, but he kept reaching out to her. She offered him something he couldn't bring himself to admit he needed. Fun. Passion. Fantasy.

"You know what your problem is?" she teased. "You're too tense."

The business suit he wore was a set of armor that insulated him from personal relationships. Isabel had no doubt that if she skimmed her hands up his chest and over his shoulders, sweeping the coat down his arms, he would loosen up. Hadn't he kissed her after witnessing Glenn's romantic proposal?

"What do you suggest?"

"We could polish off the bottle of champagne and follow that up with some shots. I'll bet it's been years since you've had too much to drink."

One dark eyebrow rose. "When you're around, I'm better off keeping my wits about me."

"You don't say." Hope flared at his admission. "Why is that?"

"Because you have a knack for making me do things I'll later regret."

"You do say the nicest things," she purred.

His body heat burned through his fine dress shirt as she stripped off his coat. She both heard and felt the sigh that expanded his chest. It was the sound of a man surrendering to the inevitable.

"There, now you look more comfortable," she said, tossing his coat onto a nearby chair and dropping her jacket beside it.

He stood with his hands on his hips, impassively watching her. Only the muscle bunching and relaxing in his jaw gave her any indication that he was at all affected.

"Your tie needs to go," she said, returning to him. She

wrestled with his tie and it followed the path of his coat. "You'll feel much more relaxed when I'm done with you."

"I'm pretty sure where I'm headed is the opposite of relaxed," he muttered.

"You're just so buttoned up." Buttons slipped free beneath her shaking fingers. "You need to let loose."

As more and more skin came into view, Isabel found herself running out of ballsy moves. With more enthusiasm than finesse, she tugged his shirt free of his waistband and attacked the last three buttons. Knees weak with excitement, she parted the shirt and stepped back for a long ogle at his broad, muscular chest, making no attempt to conceal her awe.

"Damn." She gnawed her lower lip and looked him up and down, noting the bulge behind his zipper that said he approved of her decision to take his clothes off. "You're quite something."

He glared at her for several seconds while her heart pounded hard against her ribs. Isabel could see the conflict raging inside him. His nostrils flared as he drew in deep breaths. He gripped the edges of his shirt as if unsure whether to button it back up or tear it off. Tension vibrated in his muscles as he struggled with some internal demon.

"Oh, to hell with this," he growled.

Without warning, he bent down and set his shoulder into her midsection. The next thing Isabel knew, she was hanging upside down and staring at Shane's spectacular ass as he carried her out of the room.

Six

Cursing the string of bad ideas that had brought him to this point, Shane entered his bedroom and set Isabel on her feet beside the bed. Although she claimed she wanted to see the view from his bedroom, her gaze never strayed to the wall of windows where the sun was sinking toward the water.

He shouldn't be doing this. She worked for him. Telling himself that she wanted this as much as he did wasn't an excuse for stepping across the line. Maybe if it was pure lust he could've stopped, but something more than simple physical attraction called to him.

Losing himself in her soft hazel eyes, Shane lifted his hand and brushed his thumb over her lower lip. The edge of her bottom teeth was rough against the pad. Her long lashes drifted downward as he dipped his head and sucked her lower lip into his mouth. Stars exploded behind his eyes, lighting him up in a cacophony of sparks and longing and carnal lust.

Her palm skimmed over his bare chest and latched onto his biceps. She pushed up on her toes, asking for him to deepen the kiss, driving her mouth against his. He responded without hesitation. Holding nothing back. Pushing aside regrets. Reservations.

He slipped his tongue along hers and she met the thrust with raw hunger. He couldn't get enough of her mouth. The sweet taste of her. Eager. Open. Ravenous. He surrendered to the advance and retreat of lips and tongue, nearly losing his mind at the sexy sounds she made when she sucked his lower lip between her teeth and nipped him. The bite sharpened the lust clawing at him, but he tamped down his craving to take her hard and fast.

Recognizing doing decidedly naughty things with someone who worked for him was the height of stupidity, Shane couldn't stop himself from running his hands down her back and over her butt. Flexing his fingers into the soft curves, he lifted her against his growing erection. Her hands clung to his shoulders as he broke off the kiss to let his lips slide down her neck and into the hollow of her collarbone.

"We need to get naked," she declared, her fingertips tracing his abs, sending electrical charges along his nerves.

"We will."

Lifting her into his arms, he carried her the short distance to the bed. He lowered her onto the mattress and followed her down, settling beside her, one hand hooked over her hip, the other combing through her russet waves.

"I love your hair." He smiled down at her. "It feels like silk, and the color is warm and vibrant, just like you."

She blinked at him in blank bemusement for a second before poking him in the chest. "You've been hiding a poet in there."

"You bring that side out of me."

"Damn it, Shane Adams. That's the nicest thing you could've said to me." Her smile was like a sunset, warm and breathtaking as she curved her hand over his skull and pulled him down to her.

And then they were kissing again. Her tongue and teeth devouring him while he let her take the lead. Soon, however, he stole the control back and treated her to a kiss that left them both gasping and breathless.

"I am so turned on right now," she told him, spreading her legs wide so he could settle between them.

"Let's see if we can take that a notch or two higher."

"I'm ready when you are."

He hooked her thigh over his hip, rocking into her. She moaned, eyes closed, head thrown back, fingers busy with the buttons of her blouse. He watched her skin flush and her lips part. Her breathing grew erratic. Each sign of her mounting arousal fascinated him. Tracing her features with his gaze, he noted the placement of each freckle across her nose, the slight tilt to her eyes, the minor twist to her front tooth as it bit down on her plump lower lip.

Although his body ached to get her naked and come inside her, he was content to savor this moment. Letting his passion build while watching hers rise to meet it was astonishingly satisfying. He had no desire to rush.

But then her shirt parted, revealing a lacy white bra and the upper curves of her breasts. A second later she'd popped the front catch, and his mouth went dry at the glorious sight of her fully exposed to him. Murmuring appreciatively, Shane dipped his head, nudged aside the white silk with his chin and slid his lips over her nipple, drawing it into his mouth.

The long, lusty cry that came pouring out of her caused his hips to buck, driving his erection against her. She arched her back, pushed her chest forward and pressed her soft flesh against his mouth. Alternating between sucking and lashing her with his tongue, he cupped his palm over her other breast and kneaded hard. She seemed to like it because she keened in pleasure. He circled his tongue around her tight nipple and grazed his teeth over the sensitive bud.

Her head thrashed and she sank her fingers into his hair, nails digging into his scalp.

A flicker of sanity returned as her fingers eased past his belt, hunting for the part of him that was hot and hard. Groaning as her palm curved over his erection, he eased off her slightly so he could gaze down at her face. The determination in her eyes told him there was no stopping her. The breath he released was ragged and heavy with relief.

"Seriously," she panted, whipping off her shirt and bra before attacking his belt. "We need to get all our clothes off."

"If we do there's no going back."

"Are you trying to be noble?"

"I think I've already failed at that." He shut his eyes to block out her joyful, eager smile. "I need you to be sure you're okay with this."

"I'm completely okay."

He sighed and spoke the phrase that had crowded his thoughts since the first time they'd kissed. "I want you so much."

She kissed his neck and her lush hum tickled his skin, hardening him even more. "That's the best news I've heard in a year."

Returning the favor, he nuzzled her neck, opening his mouth on her sweet skin and sucking gently. "You smell like hot chocolate and pumpkin spice," he murmured, drawing the scent of her into his lungs.

"The idea was to make you want to devour me," she teased as he loosened the button on her pants and lowered the zipper.

Ever helpful, she lifted her hips off the bed so he could slide her pants and underwear off. He trailed his lips over her ribs and the flat plane of her belly, smiling at her sharp inhalation as he deposited kisses along her thighs, then stripped off her shoes and pants, baring her to his gaze.

"Beautiful," he murmured, sliding his palms over her warm, soft flesh, savoring the view of her pale skin. "Absolutely gorgeous."

She shifted onto her knees and avoided his gaze as she reached for his zipper. As she tugged down his pants, he realized his compliments appeared to have had the opposite effect from what he'd intended. Instead of basking in his admiration, she suddenly looked uncomfortable.

"What's wrong?" he asked, sliding off the bed so he could step out of his shoes and pants. He set his fingers beneath her chin and tipped her head until she met his gaze.

"You called me beautiful," she admitted. "I'm just not used to it."

"But you should be." And then he started to understand. "You lavish so much energy on other people's perfect moments that you neglect to create some of your own."

"I guess that's true." Her eyes narrowed as her sparkle returned. "And remarkably insightful."

"Let me make your fantasies come true."

"Oh," she moaned, a truly beautiful noise that made him grin. "That would be nice."

Shane dropped his boxer briefs to the floor and located a condom in his nightstand. After rolling it on, he moved onto the bed and gathered Isabel into his arms. Their eyes met, and Shane glimpsed endless vulnerability and longing in those hazel depths. She was giving him everything and taking a huge risk in the process. Humbled and filled with awe, he kissed her with as much tenderness as his raging body could manage.

She wrapped one arm around his neck and set her palm against his cheek as he slid his hands down her body. Trembling, she opened herself to him, her breath growing shallow and uneven beside his ear as he dipped his finger into her heat. A shudder ripped through her, and he loved that she was so turned on.

"I need you now," she pleaded, tugging his hip and spreading her thighs wider so that he fell into the sexy cradle between them.

Nearly insane with lust, he shifted until he could rub the tip of his erection against her sweet, slippery core. She moaned his name as he pushed forward. Shane hissed out a breath as he entered her in one smooth stroke.

"Wow," he declared, the word ripped from him because she felt so damned good.

"Oh, yes." Her eyes were closed, lips parted, a woman lost in desire. "And more."

Already a snug, wet fit around him, she clenched down even harder as he drew out and filled her once more. Now it was Shane's turn to moan as her cries drove his lust higher. He rocked into her over and over, starting slow, finding a rhythm and pace that she liked. She matched his every thrust, grinding against him, her motions growing bolder and more wild as her own pleasure climbed. And he loved watching her.

Suddenly her eyes snapped open and she smiled when she caught him watching her. "I can handle all you've got," she purred, her voice all sexy smoke and raw vulnerability.

"You sure?" He pushed deeper, stopped and gauged her reaction in the flaring of her eyes and the upward curve to her lips.

She hooked her legs around his back, pulling him tighter, and brought her lips to his ear. "Oh, yes."

So he answered her call, burying himself inside her, thrusting hard until she screamed his name with such fierce determination that he knew she was right on the edge. She rocked into him, finding the perfect friction, and let her pleasure rip. The orgasm blasted through her. She shuddered and shuddered again, squeezing her eyes shut to hold on to it as long as possible.

"I'm coming." Her hoarse shout unleashed his own climax.

The damn thing had snuck up on him as he'd watched Isabel come undone and ripped into Shane with the shock of a lightning bolt. His skin tingled. Pleasure so acute it was painful rolled through him. Shuddering in the midst of his own orgasm, Shane had to bite his lip to keep back the words that wanted to flow out of him.

On the verge of a dangerous confession, he rode the waves of pleasure with his teeth clamped together. As he collapsed onto the mattress beside Isabel, he reached a place of reckoning. Never before had he known a moment like the one he'd just shared with Isabel. It wasn't just great or even fantastic sex. With her, he'd been moved to a whole new level of intimacy and ecstasy.

It terrified him that it had never been that good before.

Because he already knew he wanted more. And more could lead to a situation neither one of them was prepared for.

With four days remaining until the guests would start arriving for the Richmond retreat, Teresa had several items to go over with the hotel's event planner, Aspen Wright. She'd made no secret of resenting that Teresa was calling the shots. No doubt Aspen saw this as management's doubting of her ability. Whatever the case, she was making Teresa's life hell.

"This isn't the setup we discussed," Aspen said, hurtling yet another protest at Teresa.

"Yes, it is," Teresa responded, forcing a smile onto her tight lips. "I said early on that the room will work better for Jessie Humphrey's performance set up with eight rounds."

"The problem is that I'm not sure I have enough tables here at the moment, and with the storm, it's really hard to get deliveries."

Teresa stuck to her guns. "This needs to be done." Her seating chart depended on it.

Although Aspen probably thought she was being unreasonable, the smaller tables of eight offered more intimacy among the party guests.

"Also, I don't know I can if I can do a quick enough turnaround with the linens. At the moment we only have half of what you need."

"You knew what I was requesting," Teresa said. "Why don't you have them?"

"We had a wedding this weekend. Our linen service is delayed because of the storm."

Teresa wanted to shriek. "See what you can do. If we need to change to white linens instead of the ivory then I need to know."

It seemed like a small distinction, but everything needed to be perfect.

"Where are we at with the gold chargers?" Teresa asked, holding her breath.

"We have enough," Aspen said. "But I'll need to see if I have enough mirrors for the centerpieces now that you've changed the number of tables."

I didn't change the number of tables.

"Get it done."

Teresa headed back toward the lobby in a snappish mood that became even more vile as she observed the body language of the couple walking toward the concierge desk. Weeks earlier she'd noticed that Isabel Withers had the hots for the handsome president of Richmond Hotel Group, but figured between Shane's tunnel vision when it came to work and Isabel's vibrant personality, the two would mix like toothpaste and orange juice.

She'd been dead wrong.

To Teresa's surprise, not only was the oh-so-serious Shane Adams showing off his even white teeth in a fond grin while Isabel prattled and gestured, he was behaving even more out of character by ignoring the smartphone ringing in his hand so he could focus on her one hundred percent.

Teresa didn't get it. What was it about Isabel that had transformed Shane into a personable human being? Granted, the woman was pretty, but not really a standout in her severe navy hotel uniform, her russet hair swept into a sleek French twist. Yet this didn't seem to bother Shane in the least. He appeared captivated by Isabel's gregarious smile and playful banter. Her passionate nature had struck the right note with the stoic pragmatist.

Obviously something had transpired between Isabel and Shane. Was it possible that the workaholic had been influenced by the romantic atmosphere of The Opulence and had succumbed to the concierge's abundant charms? If so, it was definitely a demonstration of opposites attracting. From what Teresa had gleaned about the hotel employee and executive, the only trait they shared was that they were both massively organized individuals.

Envy swept through Teresa like an ill wind.

The unfairness of her own failed romance with Liam made her want to stamp her feet and whine like a child denied its favorite candy. Instead, she did something so much worse.

When Shane stepped away to take his call, Teresa approached Isabel.

"I wouldn't go there if I were you," she warned.

"Go where?" Still wearing a smitten half grin, Isabel tore her attention from Shane's retreating figure and looked at Teresa.

"You and Shane. That's a recipe for disaster."

Eyebrows climbing, Isabel asked, "Why would you say that?"

"Because you two aren't the least bit compatible." Teresa recognized that the sorry state of her own love life was not a good reason to give romantic advice to someone who hadn't asked for her opinion.

"We're opposing forces that make up a dynamic whole," Isabel countered lightly, her expression showing more empathy than annoyance.

Teresa exhaled impatiently. Not long ago she'd been over-the-moon happy with Liam. But at the first little hiccup, he'd turned on her. Okay, maybe the huge gift his father had settled on her was more than a little hiccup, but instead of getting to the heart of Linus's motivation, Liam had accused her of lying to him about their relationship.

"What I know," Teresa began, "is that attraction and sex—even great sex—aren't enough to make a relationship work."

"Of course." Isabel agreed amicably. "But chemistry is a good enough place to start. And if you find somebody who you can believe in, someone who every time they smile it gives you butterflies, who makes you feel better just from being with them—isn't it worth the risk?"

Teresa thought about the hundreds of butterflies that had taken flight on the dance floor the first time she and Liam had kissed and the hot rush of passion that had them tearing off each other's clothes that night in her office. The way her heart had stopped when he'd invited her to stay with him during the Richmond retreat and how it had then raced as she realized what a big step it had been for him to ask.

"I don't think that any romance is worth the risk," she grumbled, all too aware that this was not the same song she'd been singing two short weeks ago.

"I guess that's where you and I differ," Isabel said. "If I don't take a risk and open my heart, then I might never be truly happy."

Teresa reeled in her skepticism, reminding herself that Isabel touted herself as a romance concierge. Part of her ability to charm couples was that she threw herself heart and soul into the fairy tale of true love and romance.

"I get goose bumps whenever he comes near me. I wish I could bottle the feeling and sell it in the gift shop." Her engaging grin was like a sunrise, filling Teresa with all things hopeful and optimistic. "I'm tired of being alone," Isabel continued. "I want to have a partner. Have someone to share my success with. I've worked hard this last year and put all my energy into my job. You know what I found out? Success isn't satisfying with no one to share it with."

Isabel's words struck to the heart of what Teresa had realized in the last month. Those moments when she and Liam had started to mesh had made her problems easier to handle and her victories so much sweeter. Unfortunately, it also meant that the crash, when it came, was so much more painful. She wanted to spare Isabel that hurt.

"I can tell you Shane Adams isn't that person."

"You don't know that," Isabel protested.

"I do know it because he's like me. Work consumes him." Teresa took no pleasure in delivering these cold, hard facts, but Isabel needed a reality check. "His career is everything. You're delusional if you think he's going to stop working long hours and make time for you. You deserve someone who's going to get all mushy and romantic. He's not that guy."

"I disagree," Isabel countered, sounding defensive for the first time. "He has promise."

"And don't forget you work for him," Teresa persisted, throwing out more obstacles for Isabel to consider. "He's not going to cross that line."

"What if he did?"

The hint of pink beneath Isabel's fair skin betrayed her. Teresa glanced from the concierge to the tall executive and tried to ignore the stab of envy when she noticed the way Shane's dark gaze lingered on Isabel.

"Look, whatever's going on between you two, the reality is that Richmond Hotel Group is his top priority, and he will always choose to do what benefits the company and his career over what's best for you."

"You might be surprised."

Although they were close to the same age, at this moment Teresa felt world-weary and far too experienced. "For your sake, I hope so."

Seven

Clouds hung low over Tiger Mountain, obscuring the top as Liam drove east along I-90. He kept glancing at them as he ticked off the miles until his exit. These weren't the wispy cirrus or fluffy white cumulus variety that floated serenely across the blue sky, but ominous blankets of nimbus gray that warned of impending storms. Liam felt their oppressive threat like a solid weight on his mood as he pondered what sort of hell the next week would have in store for him.

With the upcoming Richmond retreat set to start in four days, he hadn't expected to be heading up to The Opulence this soon, but with Matt Richmond off the grid with the woman he loved, Liam felt honored to be trusted with the final preparations. The event was important to Matt, and Liam wasn't going to let his best friend down. That this meant he would come into contact with Teresa constantly, Liam was trying to put out of his mind.

He was a professional. He could act like one. Plus, these encounters would let him practice detachment for the next board meeting when he'd have to introduce her as their newest member while keeping his antipathy concealed.

Days earlier he'd visited his lawyer and discovered that contesting the will could make the matter drag on for years and years. Liam had decided the quickest and most efficient way of handling the situation was to have the lawyer draft a document where Teresa would agree to sell him shares at the end of her stint on the board. He intended to present it for her to sign before the end of the retreat.

With the wipers clearing mist from his windshield in an intermittent beat, Liam exited the freeway and began winding his way along the two-lane road twisting through the tree-lined foothills. Despite the tranquil views offered at each new turn, his agitation grew as the distance to the hotel diminished.

Deny though he tried, his emotions were stirred up at the thought of seeing Teresa again. As much as he wished logic and suspicion had dumped ice water over his passion for her, his body and mind remained at odds. Unlike so many women he'd dated in the past, Teresa had burrowed under his skin and was proving difficult to dislodge.

As Liam turned the car into the hotel's driveway, he realized he was grinding his teeth and made a determined effort to relax his jaw before stopping at the lobby entrance. After handing off the car to a waiting valet, he stepped across the threshold, bellhop and luggage in his wake, and briefly paused to gaze about The Opulence's enormous lobby.

He didn't realize he was searching for Teresa until he noticed his disappointment. Much to his dismay, locating her in a room had become second nature to him. The woman had gotten past his guard to such an extent that he thought about her constantly. The memory of her delicate scent clung to his mind like cobwebs. That night on the dance floor when they'd kissed for the first time. The hot, fast coupling on the couch in her office. The slower, leisurely exploration that happened later that night.

He craved the warmth of her fingers against his skin.

The taste of her sweet lips. The sexy sounds she made as she climaxed.

His body stirred, betraying him. Damn it. He had to stop thinking about her like that.

Narrowing his focus, he caught the eye of an attractive redhead at the concierge desk and headed toward her.

Her hazel eyes glinted, indicating recognition. "Hello, Mr. Christopher. Welcome back to The Opulence."

"Hello, Isabel," he said, reading the name tag fastened to her uniform. "Can you take care of checking me in and getting my luggage to my suite?"

"Of course." Isabel typed away on her computer for a few seconds. "Let's see what we have scheduled for you. Looks like you have a dinner reservation at the Overlook tonight at eight."

"That'll work," he said, thinking that would give him time to get an update on the retreat preparations from Teresa and catch up on some work emails. He glanced around the lobby, noting several attractive women eager to make eye contact. Their interest made him smile. It was time he put himself back on the market, and any of them would be a delightful companion. He would grab a drink in the bar later and invite one to dinner.

"And a private dinner for two scheduled for your suite the day after tomorrow at eight."

A private, romantic dinner he and Teresa would've shared. Liam's heart gave an ungainly lurch as he crashed back into the conversation. Before finding out his father had left Teresa shares in Christopher Corporation, he'd been planning to spend at least part of the retreat romancing Teresa.

"You can cancel the dinner in my suite," he said shortly. "My plans have changed. If you could book me a table for two at the Overlook tomorrow at seven instead." He had already confirmed that Shane Adams was free.

Isabel nodded and typed away. "Also, just to confirm that you have a reservation at the spa scheduled Wednesday evening at six."

Apparently his assistant had been quite thorough in orchestrating a romance-filled stay.

"You can cancel all the spa treatments," he told her in a clipped tone. "I'm here to work."

"Of course, but you really shouldn't miss the Turkish Hammam Rub and Scrub followed by our Desert Sage Massage. It's quite a treat. I'm sure you know many of our guests come to stay with us specifically because of the excellence of our spa."

"I really don't need a scrub or a massage," he said, ignoring the way his shoulder muscles protested otherwise.

"Are you sure?" Isabel coaxed, her smile encouraging. "Everyone can use a little pampering now and then."

Liam recalled Matt raving about the quality of the spa here. Although it wasn't usually his thing, maybe a massage would help him relax before the big event. "Fine," he grumbled. "I'll keep the spa appointment."

"Wonderful." Isabel's infectious grin seemed to indicate he'd made the right decision. "Is there anything else I can do for you?"

"I don't suppose you know where Teresa St. Claire might be at the moment."

"I believe Teresa is checking on a delivery for the Richmond retreat. The weather has caused some delays in shipments. How did you find the roads between here and Seattle?"

"Fine." But had they been? Liam cursed silently, realizing he had no idea. He'd been too preoccupied with his thoughts to notice his surroundings. "Manageable," he amended, feeling foolish.

"That's good. We have a lot of people arriving here

over the next few days, and with all the rain we've had, it wouldn't surprise me if a mudslide blocked the highway."

"Let's hope not."

"Do you want me to let Teresa know you're here?"

Did he? Or had he jumped in his car and driven to the hotel in hopes of ambushing her?

Gripped by an urge to do just that, Liam turned down the concierge's offer. He had no prepared contract to deliver to Teresa. So what was he doing here? He could be overseeing everything for Matt from his office in Seattle. Why the overwhelming urge to see her again?

The answer came to him abruptly. He wanted answers. He needed her to convince him all the assumptions he was making were wrong. Beneath this simple explanation, however, lingered a far more complicated motive. Despite his anger with her, his suspicions about what she'd done to convince his father to give her part of the family business, Liam wanted to be near her. To lose himself in her.

"I'm sure she'll be glad to see you," the pretty concierge continued.

On that point they disagreed. "I'm going to grab a drink and check in with my office. If she comes by, send her toward the bar."

Despite being convinced that it was a bad idea to mix alcohol, his volatile emotional state and seeing Teresa again, Liam headed into the bar and settled into a corner with a manhattan and his smartphone. At some point on the drive from Seattle, Matt had sent a text with an attached photo of a romantic shot of him dipping his new bride in a passionate kiss.

She said I Do!

The gorgeous tropical beach. The couple looking so damned happy. Liam stared at the photo for a long time before forcing his fingers to type the obligatory congratulations. Not that Liam begrudged Matt his happiness. Nadia was perfect for him and that they'd found each other was fantastic.

Liam recognized that if his relationship with Teresa had worked out, he might've felt more like celebrating his friend's good fortune. Instead, he was left to grumble that fate wasn't always kind and to wonder if maybe he wasn't cut out for love.

An hour later, he was wrapping up a call to the head of his marketing department when he spotted Teresa crossing the lobby. Classically elegant in a cream pencil skirt and black blouse with a slim gold watch and small hoop earrings, she looked captivating. No plunging necklines, leg-baring hemlines or flamboyant accessories for her. Just consummate professionalism. No one would ever suspect she became an alluring temptress in private.

His heartbeat surged as he watched her pause near the giant flower arrangement at the center space, glaring at the display as if it offended her. It took him a second to realize she wasn't upset with the flowers, but the person she was speaking to on the phone.

Abandoning his second manhattan, Liam headed her way, ignoring the way his nerves jangled in anticipation of being near her again. As he drew within earshot, he noticed her staring at her phone screen as she swore under her breath.

"Something wrong?" Liam asked, pricked by satisfaction when she whirled to face him.

Was it his imagination, or for an instant had she looked pleased to see him? No doubt she believed he'd come here to apologize. If so, that demonstrated just how little she knew him.

"Jessie Humphrey is supposed to be flying in from New York for the party," she explained, "but she's nervous about the weather and I'm not sure if she's going to come. Matt is going to freak if I can't produce a headliner for Saturday night." For a moment her frown deepened, and then, as if realizing what she'd revealed, she shifted topics. "What are you doing here?"

"Matt is on his honeymoon and asked me to keep an eye on things until he gets back."

"Matt and Nadia got married?" She looked shocked and happy and sad all at once. "Wow, that was fast."

"That was my reaction, too," Liam murmured as their gazes came together and locked for the space of a breath. In that moment it was as if they shared a single thought.

That could've been us...

"Well, good for them," Teresa said, shifting her gaze away. Her phone rang and she glanced at the screen. "I have to take this." And without waiting for him to respond, she answered the call. Even before she started to speak, she'd begun shifting her feet in a slow side pass that put space between them. "Hey, Jeannie, thanks for calling me back. Really, the weather isn't that bad here." She gave an awkward little laugh. "It's Seattle. We have rain all the time." A pause while she listened. As she continued to put distance between them, Teresa rubbed her shoulder as if easing an ache. "Please, if you'll reassure her..."

Liam waited until Teresa disappeared down a hallway before pulling out his phone. With his body and mind at war, he dialed a number, all the while telling himself he was acting for Matt's benefit and not because he wanted to help Teresa.

"I have something I need you to do," he told the person who answered. "Jessie Humphrey is supposed to be performing at an event near Seattle, but she's worried about traveling because of the weather. My assistant, Duncan, can get you the details. I need you to make certain she gets here on time."

* * *

"I see your honey is back."

"Really?" Isabel's gaze shot up from the computer screen and raced around the lobby. Her heart and loins pulsed in time, sending her blood pressure skyrocketing.

In the days since she'd spent the night with Shane in Seattle, she'd heard from him once by text, a straightforward response to her announcement that she'd made it back to Centennial Falls in one piece.

Glad you arrived safely. I enjoyed our time together.

Five simple words to fuel her daydreams and spawn a wide variety of fantasies about what would happen when she saw him again.

"Relax," Aspen said, her tone amused. "He's meeting with Teresa to go over the menu for the retreat's opening night cocktail party." The event coordinator shook her head. "Girl, you've got it bad."

Noting the throb between her thighs as she recalled Shane's hands and mouth gliding over her skin, Isabel agreed. "What can I say? The heart wants what the heart wants."

Aspen made a derogatory noise. "Your heart is going to end up flattened like a pancake if you aren't careful. That man isn't going to come within fifty feet of you."

Isabel bit the inside of her lower lip to avoid spilling to her best friend that he already had. In fact, he'd come within her three times. An irresistible smile formed on her lips.

"I appreciate your wisdom," Isabel said, "but you might be underestimating my charm."

"I'm not. You are intelligent and adorable. Any smart single man would snap you up in a second."

"How can you say he's not smart?" Isabel shot her friend a coy smile. "He graduated top of his class from Stanford."

"There's book smarts and then there's street smarts."
Aspen sobered. "That man wouldn't recognize a prize like
you if you were naked and pole dancing for him."

Aspen's vivid imagery sent a spear of lust straight
through Isabel. "He might…"

"He's all business. You don't have a chance." Aspen
squeezed Isabel's arm. "I just don't want to see you get
hurt."

"I know."

Aspen's arguments echoed Teresa's advice, but Isabel
didn't want to focus on the consequences of getting involved with Shane Adams. Being with him was like visit-
ing an amusement park, all thrill rides and sugary treats.
She knew it wouldn't last, but the experience would make
her smile for a long time.

"I'd better get back to work." Aspen sighed. "The Richmond retreat isn't going to set itself up."

Distracted by an email that had popped into her inbox,
Isabel said goodbye to her friend and opened the message.
It was from Tom Busch, the executive manager. He wanted
to see her in his office in an hour. The request was unusual.
Tom preferred to deal with the top rungs in his management
structure. Isabel reported to the front office manager, who
in turn reported to the executive manager.

She thought about the confrontation she'd had with Tom
when she'd comped Camilla Maxwell's couple's massage
and wondered if this was her moment of reckoning.

"Isabel, come on in."

Fighting down a mixture of nerves and annoyance, Isabel pasted on a pleasant smile and perched on one of Tom's
guest chairs. He ignored her for several seconds while he
regarded his computer screen. Isabel guessed the move was
supposed to increase her discomfort. It worked.

At last Tom turned his gaze on her. "How are the preparations going for the guests who will be attending the Richmond retreat?"

She relaxed minutely at the mundane question. "Most everyone attending has responded and we've booked everything they've requested." As she spoke, Tom was nodding his head, not really listening to her answer. "We're prepared to handle anything that comes up at the last minute."

"You're probably wondering why I brought you up here."

Her stomach tightened. "Yes."

"Several weeks ago you came to me with an idea for marketing the hotel as a romantic destination. I've given it some thought and decided that it's a good idea."

Wait…what?

He'd decided it was a good idea?

If he'd brought this up before she'd pitched the idea to Shane, she might feel a rush of satisfaction. But after Shane had arranged for her to meet with corporate marketing, putting his stamp of approval on the romantic destination concept, to hear Tom take credit for what Shane had already decided tied her stomach into knots. Nor could she confront the executive manager about the lie without exposing her personal connection to Shane.

Isabel's cheeks burned as she said, "That's great. I've been working on some ideas—"

"Yes, yes, of course. But I'm really interested in this whole concept of a romance concierge." Tom was smiling now, but he looked through her as if she was a piece of furniture. "I found someone who fits the bill perfectly."

Isabel couldn't believe what she was hearing. It was her idea. She was the romance concierge. Why was he bringing in someone else to do what she was perfectly suited for?

"What?" she demanded, barely able to breathe. "Who?"

"I hired a lifestyle blogger with several million followers. Camilla Maxwell. Apparently she had her wedding here last weekend. Do you know her?"

Did Isabel know her?

"I was the one who reached out to her and suggested she get married at The Opulence." Even as she tooted her own horn, Isabel could see Tom wasn't listening. The unfairness of it all turned Isabel's voice to sandpaper. "But she's a blogger and doesn't know anything about the hotel industry. Why did you choose her?"

"She's featuring her wedding at The Opulence on her blog as well as social media and promoting the hotel as an ideal romance destination. She'll be perfect."

As she listened to Tom, Isabel realized that the executive manager hadn't come to the decision on his own. He'd been told about the change in marketing direction by Shane. "Corporate agrees this concept is a wonderful idea. An influencer like Camilla would bring greater awareness to the hotel."

"I don't understand how it will work," Isabel protested. "Is she moving here?"

"Oh no. She'll be the face of the program. She's a stunning woman, after all. People will believe they're contacting her for their personalized romantic experience." He paused for a beat. "Of course we'll need you to handle all the arrangements."

After she'd poured her heart and soul into the project, someone else was going to swoop in and take credit for it? Worse, Isabel was going to have to do all the grunt work? Outrageous. Nor would she quit. Isabel loved what she was doing. It suited her. But to have her hard work go unrecognized?

"I thought," Isabel murmured, a lump in her throat making her voice sound tinny and raw. "The romance concierge would be my role."

Tom wasn't interested in playing fair when he could take credit for her ideas. "No," he corrected her. "You're the hotel's *concierge*."

Crushing disappointment made her eyes fill with helpless tears. She stared at her clasped hands and struggled
for composure. How could Shane have done this to her?

Corporate agrees.

Suddenly, Teresa's words came back to haunt Isabel.
Shane would always choose what was best for the hotel
over what was good for her. The betrayal cut deep, shaking her confidence in the connection she thought she had
with Shane. So much for believing she was the master of all
things romantic. He'd warned her that he wasn't interested
in such things. His time with her had been about scratching a sexual itch.

"That's all I have for you," Tom said. "You can go back
to your post."

Drowning in humiliation, she fled Tom's office. While
she understood from a marketing standpoint why Shane
would lean toward an influencer like Camilla Maxwell, she
couldn't believe he would do that to her. Almost as devastating was that he'd had Tom break the news…

Before Isabel reached the lobby, she slipped into a quiet
alcove and fought to get her emotions back under control.
Seesawing between anger and despair, she texted Aspen.

Do you have time for a drink after work?

Aspen's answer came immediately.

Always. Where?

Isabel suggested their usual haunt in town. The rustic
bar and grill was a far cry from The Opulence's luxurious ambiance and exquisite cuisine and the perfect place
to complain about their boss. Drained by her heightened
emotions all afternoon, Isabel entered the bar and found
her friend sitting in a booth by the front window. When

she slid into the bench opposite, Aspen looked her over and grimaced.

"What happened?"

Isabel signaled their usual waitress and ordered a dirty martini. "Tom decided to pursue my idea to promote The Opulence as a romantic destination."

"That's great." Aspen noted Isabel's stormy expression and backpedaled. "Or not great. What happened?"

"He shut me out. He hired Camilla Maxwell as the face of The Opulence's romance concierge. Only I get to do all the work."

"And not get any of the credit." Aspen hissed out a breath. "Why would he do that? It was your idea and you're the perfect person to do it. Hell, you've been doing it for the last eight months."

"Tom made it seem like it was his idea, but he had no interest in the whole romance destination idea when I pitched it before." Although now that she thought about it, once Shane brought the idea up, Isabel could see Tom tripping over himself to impress the boss.

"Well, that's not a surprise. The man hasn't had an original idea since he came to the hotel."

"But what if Shane is the one who suggested hiring Camilla because he doesn't think I'm good enough?"

He'd never given her any indication that's what he thought, but how well did she know him, after all? Plus, Teresa and Aspen had reminded her that as an executive, Shane's top priority was the company. And what if Shane thought she'd slept with him to curry favor? Would that make him overlook her for advancement?

"I'm sure he doesn't think that." Aspen gave her a sympathetic head tilt. "He just wants what's best for the hotel. And most of the time executive types like Shane don't even notice the little people like us."

"Shane noticed me," Isabel said, resenting her friend's doubting expression. "He *likes* me."

Aspen's expression went from puzzlement to astonishment in a heartbeat. "Please tell me nothing happened between you two."

"We have a connection." Seeing that she wasn't convincing Aspen, Isabel grew defensive. "I know what you're thinking. I had no business getting involved with Shane."

"Actually, that's not what I was thinking at all." Aspen shook her head sadly.

"Okay," Isabel said. "Maybe that's what I've been saying to myself since meeting with Shane. I thought he was different. I thought I meant something to him."

"Are you going to ask him about it?"

"What if he tells me I wasn't good enough?" Her chest tightened as she was pummeled by a double dose of self-doubt and shame.

Aspen reached across the table and squeezed Isabel's hand. "You're good enough."

"You're my friend so of course you'd say that, but right at this moment I don't feel like I'm ever going to amount to anything."

The urge to drop her head onto her arms and start crying overwhelmed Isabel. She bit the inside of her lip until she'd mastered her emotions.

"So, what are you going to do?"

"I'm tempted to quit." Her spirits plummeted at the thought of leaving the Richmond Hotel Group. She really liked the company and until Tom Busch had become the executive manager, she believed she was making a difference.

"As much as I'd miss you, I've said for a long time that your talents are wasted here. You have all the skills you need to move past a job as a concierge."

"That's exactly what I needed to hear."

She hadn't expected that in the end none of her hard work, innovation or customer service skills would get her noticed. Often her friends had warned her that she was a shade too optimistic, but Isabel had never let adversity slow her down before. So why now? Because what had happened between her and Shane had been personal and remarkable. Or maybe she'd been kidding herself all along.

"You're meant to do bigger things," Aspen told her. "So update your resume and find a job working for someone who will appreciate you."

Images of her time spent with Shane bombarded her, making her heart ache. "I thought I already had."

Eight

After retreating to her hotel suite to kick off her shoes and order a late lunch from room service, Teresa gave herself half an hour to doze in the comfortable armchair. The combination of insomnia, long work days and the cozy warmth of the fireplace's hypnotic flame made her eyelids heavy, and she saw no reason to resist the lure of a twenty-minute nap. Unfortunately, before she fully nodded off, her phone vibrated against the dresser's hard surface, jolting her back to wakefulness.

As the days until the Richmond retreat counted down, Teresa was starting to dread every time her phone buzzed. This happened a lot. On average, at least five things went wrong each hour that required her input.

Although she'd done events for the ultra-wealthy before, nothing had been on quite this scale. Before when she dealt with this level of A-listers, she'd arranged a single event or something over the course of the day. This was a three-day extravaganza, wining and dining and entertaining the sort of people who were used to the finest of everything.

The phone buzzed again, rousing Teresa from her thoughts. This time the call was from Isabel.

"Hey," she said. "What's up?"

"There's a reporter here, looking for you," Isabel said.

Panic flared through Teresa at the news. Had the man who'd threatened her several weeks ago tipped off a reporter about the things Joshua had been up to and the lengths Teresa had gone to hide her brother's illegal activities? Or had Joshua himself let something slip? As much as Teresa loved her brother, she knew he hadn't demonstrated his ability to make good decisions.

"Did they give you a name?" Teresa asked, telling her pounding heart to slow down. The Fixer had done his work and erased all trace of Joshua's bad behavior. If this was a smear campaign there wouldn't be much by way of proof. Or so she hoped.

"She didn't have to," Isabel confided, the smile apparent in her voice. "It's Nicolette Ryan."

"Oh!" For a second Teresa's thoughts froze. She'd known to expect the lifestyle reporter, but in the rush of everything still to do, she'd forgotten today was her arrival date. "Of course. Tell her I'm on my way."

Once Teresa reached the lobby, it was pretty clear where the celebrity stood. The Opulence catered to the sort of people who could afford to charter airplanes and fund lavish weddings, but actors, musicians and other famous people turned into gawking fans just like the rest of the ordinary folks. The beautiful television reporter was signing an autograph for a teenage girl.

Despite the boost from five-inch pumps, Nicolette Ryan was more petite than Teresa expected. She was dressed in a figure-hugging black sheath and stylish cream-colored coat with a shawl collar. Her long black hair framed an oval face with big brown eyes and an engaging smile.

Teresa waited until the beaming girl had raced back to her family before approaching. "Hello, I'm Teresa St. Claire."

"Nicolette Ryan." The two women shook hands. "I'm covering the Richmond fifth anniversary for a lifestyle piece."

"We've been expecting you. Are you checked in?"

"Yes, but I wanted to touch base with you before I headed up to the room."

"What can I help you with?"

"I wanted to make sure everything was ready for us. I was promised a small breakout room we could use to store our camera equipment and conduct interviews."

"Absolutely. It's all set up." Teresa relaxed. She'd double-checked the space that morning. "Do you want to see it now?"

"Sure…" Her phone started ringing. "I have to take this. Can you give me ten minutes?"

When Nicolette walked off, Teresa turned her attention back to Isabel. The day before she'd laid into the younger woman about Shane. It hadn't been any of her business and she needed to apologize.

"Listen," Teresa began, "what I said yesterday about you and Shane was unfair."

Isabel grimaced. "No, you were right."

"Oh dear," Teresa said, tilting her head in sympathy. "I've seen that look before."

Every day in the mirror since she'd spent the night on Liam's yacht. It was the face of a woman dealing with disappointment. One whose romantic dreams had been slapped down. And heart trampled on.

"I think this is the part where you say, 'I told you so,'" Isabel responded, her customary high spirits dampened.

"I don't want to say, 'I told you so.'" Over a glass of wine in her room last night, Teresa had decided to be happy that

Isabel had such faith in what was going on between her and Shane. Being jealous of the other woman's happiness was no excuse for raining on her parade. "I was rude and wrong and I should never have interfered." Although the busy lobby was neither the time nor the place for a heart-to-heart, she liked Isabel and wanted her to know if she needed a shoulder to cry on, Teresa would be there. "Do you want to talk about it? I know I was bitchy and unsympathetic before, but I was wrong."

Isabel's lips tightened as she shook her head. "You weren't wrong. You had Shane figured out. I just didn't want to listen. I wish I had."

"No. I was wrong." The last thing Teresa wanted was for her bad attitude to shadow Isabel's optimism. "I saw you two together. He is completely infatuated with you."

"I don't know about infatuated," Isabel said. "Definitely attracted, but you were right that sex isn't enough and that he's always going to put his career over everything else. Especially a woman he'd only just started getting to know." She looked positively grim as she finished, "And as usual, I moved too fast."

"Don't lose hope," Teresa insisted, wondering at the wisdom of offering romantic advice. "I can't tell you that it will work out between you, but he deserves another shot. It's a lot to expect that Shane would just wake up one morning and be ready for an intense relationship that turns everything he ever thought he wanted and needed on its head."

Yet isn't that what had happened to her? All it had taken was one incredible kiss from Liam to detour her from her carefully mapped-out life.

"Maybe," Isabel said. "But I'm not sure I'll have the chance to find out. I think I'm going to end up leaving the hotel."

That was good news in Teresa's mind. Isabel Withers

had a knack for dealing with difficult people and challenging situations, rivaling Teresa in her ability to find solutions to problems.

Teresa smiled and her expression caught Isabel off guard. "I'm not sorry to hear that."

"I don't understand," Isabel said.

"I've been watching you these last few weeks, and you are one of the most organized and creative people I've ever met. Everything I've needed you've anticipated. In my opinion, your talents are wasted here."

Teresa wondered what it would take to hire the concierge away from the hotel.

"That's really nice of you to say." Isabel looked hopeful. "I don't suppose you'd be a reference for me when I go apply for my next position."

"I'll do better than that. I'll hire you."

"Really?"

"You're the exact sort of person I need. Once we're done with the Richmond retreat, let's grab a drink and talk about it."

"I'd like that." Isabel smiled, her relief showing. "But I can't make any promises. I've been so focused on my romantic destination project for The Opulence, I haven't thought what my next career move will be."

"I get that. And I understand if you change your mind about leaving. Especially if things work out between you and Shane."

"They won't."

Teresa saw the pain that flashed across Isabel's face. "They might."

"I'm not leaving because it didn't work out between us. At least not in the way you think." And then Isabel went into a brief explanation about what transpired with the romance concierge idea. "He knew how important the romance concierge idea was to me, and I just don't know if I can stay while someone else does the job that I created."

"That's crappy," Teresa said, genuinely surprised that Shane had handled things so poorly, especially after the way she'd seen him look at Isabel. "We definitely need to get together and talk next week."

"I'd like that."

Nicolette Ryan approached, a warm smile on her face. "I'm ready if you are."

Teresa led the way toward the breakout room she'd assigned to the news crew. "I've seen you interviewing celebrities on the red carpet," she told the reporter. "You have a knack for asking the right questions and putting them at ease."

"I hope I don't disappoint in person."

"Actually, now that I've met you, I think you're even more remarkable."

The woman's smile became a little self-conscious as if she wasn't used to being flattered. If Teresa had been impressed before, this surprising glimpse of the reporter's true nature turned Teresa into a superfan. No wonder that teenage girl had been beaming.

"You're quite beautiful yourself," Nicolette said. "I hope you'll let me get you on camera. I'd love to get a little behind-the-scenes insight on what goes into putting on an event like this."

"I'd be happy to be interviewed." Wasn't that the truth. Exposure like this could only be good for Limitless Events. Too late she remembered Joshua and the troubles he'd gotten himself into. She couldn't afford to have a reporter finding out what she'd done to help out her brother. Or getting wind of the favor she still owed the Fixer. Something like that could ruin her.

"Wonderful," Nicolette said. "I'll set something up with you in the next few days."

"Great." Teresa smiled, but her heart wasn't in it.

As Teresa and Nicolette parted ways, Teresa tabled the potential threat of a curious reporter asking questions she didn't want to answer.

Although the king-sized bed in Liam's suite was comfortable enough, he had trouble sleeping. Too many thoughts rattled around in his head. Not the least of which was the constant reminder that he'd been planning to share the space with Teresa.

Not long after dawn he was up, showered and heading to the restaurant. He wasn't surprised to spy Teresa seated in the lobby, sipping from a cup and typing on her phone. In the final days before the retreat she'd seemed to be all over the hotel, taking care of the last minute details. Although early on he'd been skeptical of her abilities and had tried to convince Matt to fire her from the event, Liam had to admit he'd been wrong. No matter what had gone on between them, Teresa was a consummate professional and damn good at what she did.

Pushing aside the discomforting flash of admiration, Liam recalled the mission he'd given himself in the days since learning the content of his father's will. At their last encounter, he hadn't made his position known. This time he had no intention of letting her get away until he'd laid out his objectives.

When he drew within ten feet of her, Teresa's attention snapped to him as if aware he was bearing down on her like a tidal wave. Her eyes went wide and her mouth tightened into a flat line as she got to her feet.

"We need to talk about the shares my father left you," he stated, jumping in without polite preliminaries.

Teresa sighed. "What about them?"

"It's important that the shares stay in the family, so I'm having my lawyer draft a contract for you to sign."

"What sort of contract?" Although nothing obvious changed in her body language, her manner became as distant and as cool as a mountain lake.

"A sales contract."

Her eyebrows rose, acknowledging that she had some power in this negotiation. "What if I'm not interested in selling?"

"I will make you a fair offer," he retorted, an edge to his voice. Her willfulness was something he should've prepared for, but hadn't. "As far as I'm concerned, you don't deserve anything from my family."

Now he'd well and truly gotten her back up. "Your father seemed to think otherwise."

Liam ground his teeth in frustration at the position he found himself in. He wasn't accustomed to negotiating with his hands tied. Usually he was operating from a position of strength. Having to come to Teresa when she was obviously up to no good and persuade her to sell to him her shares of stock pained him.

"Look, I don't know what was going on between you and my father—"

"For the last time, nothing was going on—"

"—but for the good of Christopher Corporation, I need control of those shares."

He'd just intimated she wasn't good for Christopher Corporation, and that might not be completely accurate. His father wasn't a fool. He never would've risked the company he'd built by putting it in the hands of someone undeserving.

Unfortunately, Liam wasn't in a place where he could trust anyone. Even the man he'd looked up to every day of his life.

Teresa looked like a thundercloud as she absorbed Liam's censure. "And you thought by coming here and bullying me that I'd happily turn them over?"

"You'll be compensated." This conversation wasn't getting him any closer to his objective, but he couldn't seem to calm the emotions roiling in him.

He didn't want to doubt Teresa. He wanted to sweep her into his arms and find a quiet corner where he could reacquaint himself with all the delightful, impassioned sounds she made when aroused.

"Your father wanted me to have the shares. Aren't you curious why?" She crossed her arms over her chest and looked down her nose at him. "I know I am."

No. Yes.

The question tormented him. He knew his father well. Teresa was a mystery. Yet his father's decision to gift her shares of Christopher Corporation and make her a mandatory board member for a year was beyond Liam's understanding.

"I've been able to think of little else." He made no attempt to hide his suspicion. "I'd very much like to know how you schemed your way into his life. Was it blackmail?"

Far from seeming shocked or angry at his accusation, she shook her head, her entire manner radiating disappointment.

"You can't see the good in anyone, can you?"

Her words acted like a slap, waking him to just how badly he'd overplayed his hand. Any notion of finessing the truth out of her vanished.

"I see the good in lots of people," he countered, all too aware how long it took before he fully trusted those in his orbit.

"Name one," she challenged him.

It wasn't like he thought everyone was out to cheat him, but he tended to expect everyone was working an angle. If they were nice to him he wondered what they wanted. And wasn't it the case that most people were only looking out for number one? He paid his employees well, knowing that money could buy loyalty. When it came to business, he made sure all his contracts were free of loopholes, and he never assumed someone would help them out just to be nice. If he wanted something done, he paid for it. An even, clear-cut exchange, spelled out in black and white, allowed him to sleep nights.

"I'm not playing this game with you." He ignored her I-told-you-so expression.

Her phone rang before she could respond and she glanced at the screen, where Matt Richmond's face was displayed. Worry flickered over her features a second before she answered.

"Hi, Matt," she said in a breezy, competent tone at complete odds with the tension she'd displayed with Liam seconds earlier. "How are you doing?"

She listened and nodded for a few seconds, a genuine smile kicking up one corner of her mouth at whatever news the CEO was relaying. Liam didn't realize he had leaned closer, angling to listen in on Matt's side of the conversation, until Teresa shot him a peevish glance.

The pallor of her skin and the dark circles beneath her eyes spoke to her exhaustion. She wasn't as invincible as she wanted everyone to think. For some reason this stirred his sympathy. With her defenses fraying, he should be going in for the kill. Instead he found himself wanting to pitch in and help.

"Everything is going smoothly here. In fact, we are ahead of schedule."

This lie, told with absolute conviction, rocked Liam back on his heels and reminded him that what came out of her mouth wasn't always the truth.

"You and Nadia have fun," Teresa said, seeing Liam's expression and making a face at him. "Don't worry about anything. I have everything under control." She was smiling at Matt's final words as she ended the call. Without a beat she pointed her finger at Liam. "I know what you're thinking, but don't say it. Matt is on his honeymoon. You don't seriously expect me to burden him with things he can't control, do you?"

"And when he shows up and finds Jessie won't be singing for his guests?"

Teresa tossed her head. "Jessie will come through. She signed a very lucrative contract."

"Yes," he mused. "Money talks."

Teresa shook her head. "You know, before you showed up here with your sales contracts and insults, I was debating whether to accept or refuse what your father left me."

Liam's skepticism must've shown because she sighed heavily and seemed to deflate. Where only a moment ago outrage had enhanced her energy, making her seem invincible, now she looked vulnerable and lost as she scanned his features.

"And now?"

"I only want to make things better for you." She took a half step forward until he could feel the heat of her skin so close, so fragrant, so damned soft. "It's too bad you haven't figured that out yet."

She lifted her hand, the movement slow and dreamy, but before her fingertips could touch his cheek, he caught her wrist. Touching her stirred his blood and roused his emotions. Anger. Lust. Longing. Even as he rejected her sympathy, he wanted to pull her soft curves against his rigid muscles. To kiss her senseless and feel her melt into him. To hear her moan and beg for more.

Somber eyes searched his expression. Did she hope to find pity or mercy? The conflicting emotions in her eyes reflected his pain and confusion. For an instant he was transported back in time. To when their hearts had beat as one. She'd seen through his defenses. Glimpsed the hunger for more than just sex. For connection. For love.

Their gazes locked. Held. Broke away. Each retreating as self-preservation took over.

"I have work to do," she declared breathlessly, turning and rushing off without another word, leaving Liam staring after her, regret dominating his emotions.

Idiot.

He pivoted in the opposite direction, refusing to watch her go, biting down hard on the words that would stop her retreat, bring her back to him.

Nine

Shane prowled through The Opulence's lobby, his attention only partially focused on the phone in his hand. It had been several days since the night he and Isabel had spent together and they'd exchanged only one abbreviated personal text and several professional conversations about the looming Richmond retreat.

Usually few women lingered in his thoughts after a sexual interlude. Mostly he enjoyed their company in the moment and went back to thinking about work. That should've been the case even more so right now with the enormous spotlight being focused on The Opulence thanks to the important event they were hosting for his division's parent company.

Instead, he'd found his thoughts drifting back to the night he'd spent with Isabel at the most inopportune time. This development left him feeling raw and out of sorts, yet dwelling on her made him so damned happy. His seesawing emotions filled him with indecision about how to proceed.

He hadn't intended to complicate his life by sleeping with one of his employees. The fact that he was irresistibly drawn to Isabel wasn't an excuse for such a breach in professionalism. Now that he'd crossed that line, he should man up and tell her that it couldn't happen again.

If only he could trust himself to keep that promise.

"Shane." A male voice broke into his thoughts, turning him in the direction of the hail.

Spying Liam Christopher, Shane extended his hand to his boss's best friend. "How is it going?"

"I'll be doing better once the Richmond party gets going," Liam said. "I imagine you feel the same way."

Shane nodded. "So much is riding on everything going smoothly."

"Do you have time to grab a drink with me?" Liam nodded toward the bar.

"Sure." Out of the corner of his eye, Shane spotted Isabel emerging from the offices behind the front desk. Shane noticed that Isabel wasn't heading toward the concierge desk. On impulse, he decided to intercept her. "Can you give me a couple minutes? I have some business I need to take care of first."

"I'll see you in there."

Although Isabel was moving with purpose, Shane's long strides let him draw near with very little effort. She looked surprised and not too pleased that he'd slipped through the employee-only exit behind her.

"Are you getting out of here?" he asked, matching her pace, wondering why she didn't stop or even slow.

"Yes," she said. "I'm done for the day."

"I just agreed to have a drink with Liam. Would you have time for dinner later?"

"I'm going out with a friend."

Shane noticed a definite chill in the air and thought he knew the reason. "Look, I'm sorry I haven't been in touch—"

The glance she shot his way was full of reproof. "Do you really think I'm that childish?"

"No." Maybe he was missing something. "Of course not. It's just that I've been busy this week and you probably expected me to call…"

"While it would've been nice to hear from you, I understand that you have a lot going on with the upcoming retreat."

If he took what she said at face value, then why was she so annoyed with him? "What about dinner tomorrow?"

That stopped her. She swung around to face him, her beautiful hazel eyes narrowing as she regarded him. Whatever she saw made her lips tighten.

"I just can't do this with you right now," she said. "I have to go."

Before Shane could sort out what had gone wrong between them since their passionate goodbye kiss a few days earlier, Isabel turned and marched off down the corridor. More puzzled than annoyed, Shane retraced his steps and headed toward the bar.

Liam sat at a table near the window, watching raindrops run like tears down the glass. His drink was nearly empty, and as Shane entered, he signaled to the waitress to bring him a scotch and ordered another round for Liam.

"Everything okay?" Shane asked as he took the seat opposite the head of Christopher Corporation.

"Is this rain ever going to stop?"

"The forecast isn't looking good." Shane wondered if Liam's melancholy had to do with the persistent storm or the recent loss of his father.

"Matt's going to be pissed if this affects turnout for the retreat. He wanted to go big for the fifth anniversary."

Shane had been thinking the same thing. "Have you heard from him?"

Liam finished his drink before answering. "He and

Nadia got married on a beach somewhere in the Caribbean. He sent me this." Liam showed Shane a picture of Matt sweeping his lovely bride into a romantic kiss.

All Shane could think as he stared at the photo was that Isabel would've loved how that unexpected romance had turned out. "She was his assistant."

"Yep." Liam turned the phone around and stared morosely at the picture.

"Seems like he crossed a line professionally."

"I guess."

The waitress set drinks down in front of the two men and scooped up Liam's empty glass. The interruption gave Shane several seconds to ponder this development.

"He must've figured she was the one for him," Shane continued, unable to stop himself from musing out loud. "But how did he know?"

Liam was contemplating the ice in his drink, his frown making it appear as if he was only listening with half his attention. "I've been wondering the same thing myself since I got the news. I never imagined Matt was looking to settle down. And now that he has…"

"What about you?" Shane asked, remembering Isabel mentioning that a certain event planner had caught Liam's eye. "It seems like you and Teresa St. Claire were hitting it off."

"That's over." Liam spun his glass on the table. "She wasn't the person I thought she was."

"Sorry to hear that." And to Shane's surprise, he did feel bad for Liam.

It occurred to Shane that ten days ago he never would've given any relationship a second thought, failed or successful. He'd been one hundred percent focused on the portfolio of hotels managed by his division. Now, he caught himself daydreaming about an idealistic redhead who'd disrupted his usually organized thoughts with flights of fancy.

"Are you involved with anyone?" Liam asked in turn, but Shane wasn't sure if it was out of politeness or curiosity.

"No time," Shane said, offering his stock answer.

"You should make time." Startling advice coming from a guy as known to be allergic to romantic entanglements as Liam Christopher.

"You can say that after your thing with Teresa didn't work out?"

Liam shrugged. "It was great while it lasted."

"So you're thinking you'll be more open to a relationship next time around?"

"I wouldn't go that far." Liam smirked, but the smile never touched his eyes. "Right now all I'm thinking about is the Richmond event and the announcement I'm set to make Saturday morning."

"Sure." With a nod, Shane let the thread drop.

In fact, he had no idea why he'd pursued the topic for as long as he had. It's not like he was thinking about getting married and looking for reasons why he should keep seeing Isabel. A wife and kids were a distraction his career couldn't afford. Maybe he'd be open if she was the sort of woman who would be satisfied with financial security and the perks of being an executive's wife. Someone who'd accept his ridiculous hours and not make undue demands on his time.

That was not Isabel Withers. From the beginning, she'd been bossy, cajoling, impossible to ignore. She'd keep on influencing every aspect of his life, from what he ate to how he exercised. She'd encourage him to take up hobbies. Suggest activities they could do together. She enjoyed hiking. No doubt they'd hit the trails on the weekends. To take in the scenery. To relax. He could see them getting a dog. Yet another thing to make demands on his attention.

Shane didn't have time for any of that. He was on a mission to make his father eat his words. And Isabel was in the way. Getting involved with her had already put his career in jeopardy. The smart move would be to end things before any permanent damage was done.

Seeing that Liam's attention had drifted to the rain-filled evening outside, Shane picked up his phone and sent a text.

We need to talk.

Jacked up on caffeine and frustration, Teresa tapped her foot as she waited for her coffee order to be filled. Her phone buzzed as texts poured in. With two days until the retreat began, she should've been completely focused on the event, but found herself in a state of near constant distraction because of Liam's presence at the hotel.

It seemed as if fate conspired to put him in her path at every turn. She recognized that made sense since he was acting as Matt's right hand while the Richmond Enterprises CEO was enjoying his honeymoon, but every time she ran into him, she recalled her behavior during their last encounter.

Had she really been so naive as to think that letting him glimpse how much she cared about him might make all his animosity and mistrust go away? Worse, she'd been surprised when he'd rejected her olive branch. Then there was the impending contract he'd insisted she sign, promising to sell him her shares in the company at the end of a year. She continued to vacillate over what to do about that.

With Liam at the helm and thanks to the deal he'd recently made with Richmond Enterprises with the joint venture, the Sasha project, it sounded as if Christopher Corporation was going to become even more successful than it already was. Part of her wanted to keep the shares and grow wealthy beyond what she'd ever imagined possible.

On the other hand, her financial problems clamored for her to sell the shares to Liam. The money could then be used to help her brother, who seemed to be constantly in debt. Then too, a single signature could vanquish those nagging fears that she was one calamity away from bankrupting her company.

She took her coffee and thanked the barista. Her knotted shoulder muscles loosened somewhat as she pondered having a financial cushion. How wonderful it would be to have the flexibility to take only those clients who appreciated her talent and expertise and the benefit to her business if she could focus on what she did best.

With a sigh, Teresa brought her attention back to the text one of her staff had sent. The florist ordered the wrong shade of lilies. They're pink not yellow. This was a fall event. She'd wanted the guest room bouquets to reflect the glorious autumn tones of the maples, oaks and aspens. Why couldn't anything in her life go smoothly? Her phone picked that moment to ring. Glancing at the familiar number, she braced herself before answering.

"Tell me it's good news for a change," she said to Isabel Withers.

"Jessie Humphrey just arrived!" The concierge's wild exuberance came through loud and clear. Isabel had proclaimed herself a huge fan when Teresa asked her to be on the lookout for the singer.

"I'm on my way."

With the steady sheets of rain falling outside, the activity at the front desk had ground to a halt, allowing all three staff members to cluster before a lean, sexy woman wearing jeans and a gray sweater beneath an oversized black trench coat. Although Jessie was known for her impeccable taste in heels, today she wore sensible black boots, perfect for traveling in that day's drenching downpour.

Teresa approached the new arrival, admiring the woman's perfect caramel-colored skin and lustrous dark brown curls piled atop her head before introducing herself.

"I'm so glad you made it," Teresa added, wondering what miracle had changed Jessie's mind about traveling in the terrible weather. "Did you have any trouble getting here?"

"I was a little worried about traveling by helicopter," Jessie said, sliding off her dark glasses, her white smile flashing. "But then I realized that the coast guard uses them all the time to rescue people during storms. And the pilot was so confident that I relaxed."

"That was so smart of you to hire a helicopter," Teresa said, wondering how many other guests would arrive that way. After all, the hotel was an hour's car ride from Seattle, but the roads would be challenging to navigate during the storms.

"It wasn't me. The arrangements were made by Christopher Corporation. I understand they have something to do with the event this weekend."

Teresa's brain felt sluggish as she absorbed this information. "Liam Christopher?"

"I believe that's right." Jessie gave a little shrug. "Do you know him?"

Did she? Obviously not as well as she thought.

"Yes." Her throat seized up. Liam had arranged for Jessie to arrive on time and safely. Had he done it for her or to keep Matt from being disappointed? More likely the latter since he hadn't said anything to her about it. Should she be annoyed with him or grateful? "I'll let him know you've arrived. After you settle into your suite, I'll show you where you will be performing. Meanwhile, if there's anything you need, Isabel is our concierge." Teresa cracked a smile. "And a huge fan."

Teresa was feeling far more hopeful by the time she'd returned to the concierge desk. Maybe things were starting to take a turn for the better. "Well, that's certainly a relief."

Isabel smiled at her. "You know, I think there's a spa appointment with your name on it tonight at six."

"Oh, I couldn't." But the thought of taking a couple hours off to be pampered was almost more than she could resist.

"If you don't slow down you'll burn out before the retreat even starts."

"I couldn't possibly…" But Teresa could feel herself weakening. She gripped her smartphone until her fingers cramped. So many details awaited her attention. "I really shouldn't…"

Before she could offer another weak protest, Isabel pushed an appointment card across the desk in her direction.

"Six o'clock," the concierge repeated. "You'll be getting an oxygenating facial followed by our famous Desert Sage Massage. Don't be late."

Fresh off the spa's Turkish Hammam ritual, Liam stepped into a room with the dual massage tables and shut the door behind him. He hadn't known what to expect from the rub and scrub experience, but found the Turkish water treatment unusual but enjoyable. He'd lain face down on a hot marble bed while water had been poured over his legs and back. A couple of rounds of soapy scrub had followed, and then a shower of water waved back and forth had rinsed him clean. After drying off and donning his robe, he'd been escorted to this room.

Soothing music filled the candlelit space. Staged beside the wall to his left sat two comfortable chairs with a round table between. A champagne bottle chilled in a bucket with two flutes beside it. One empty. One filled. Lifting the full glass to his lips, he tossed back half the liquid, feeling the prickle of bubbles exploding against the back of his throat.

He stripped off his robe and let it fall across the arm of one of the chairs. Naked, he approached the nearest massage table, noting the tightness in his shoulders put there since reading his father's will. Caught up in his thoughts,

Liam didn't realize the second bed was occupied until he neared the sheet-shrouded tables.

Two massage beds.

Champagne with two flutes.

What the hell? Had he been directed to the wrong room?

In his confusion he must've made a sound because the mound beneath the linens shifted. A woman's bare arm appeared, hand clutching the linen covering to her chest. She awkwardly shifted onto her elbow to prop up her upper body. Familiar features shifted from shock to dismay as Teresa spied him.

She squeaked and recoiled, but trapped by the sheets and her unwillingness to risk exposure, she had nowhere to go. "What the hell are you doing here?"

The full impact that they were both naked and very much alone landed a direct punch. He swallowed hard. "I'm here for a massage." His voice came out more husky than he liked.

His explanation sent her gaze roaming over his bare torso. His lower half was mostly hidden by the massage table, but part of him was slowly rising into view as his lust awoke with a gleeful howl.

Teresa stared at him, her mouth working but no sound coming out. Her fixation on his body only increased the rush of blood to his groin. The impulse to leap across the table and haul her into his arms grew stronger with each thunderous beat of his heart. What kept him in place wasn't his suspicions about her relationship with his father or her earlier refusal to sell him the Christopher Corporation shares, but the knowledge that they could be interrupted at any moment.

"You can't be," she said in a breathless rush. "I'm here for a massage. You must be in the wrong room."

"No," he countered, sensing mischief at work. The hotel functioned too efficiently for this to have been a mistake.

"This is where I was directed. Obviously someone thought we might enjoy a couple's massage."

"Don't be ridiculous. We're the farthest thing from a couple."

And then he recalled that he'd intended to romance her during the Richmond retreat before finding out about his father's will and had never ordered his assistant to cancel the arrangements.

Annoyed at the absurd situation, he lifted the top sheet. "You've got that right."

Still…now that he was here…

Sliding between the sheets, he settled onto the table, biting back a groan as the warmth from the heated bed enveloped him in a comfortable embrace. Despite the hotel's air being a perfect balance of temperature and humidity, the rainy November weather seemed to have worked its chill into his bones and muscles.

"What do you think you're doing?" Teresa demanded. "You can't stay here."

"I told you. I'm here for a massage." He turned his head and regarded her with a half smile. "If that makes you uncomfortable, feel free to leave."

Of course, she'd have to parade her naked body past him to reach her robe, which he'd belatedly realized was hanging from a hook on the back of the door, and he'd definitely lift his head to watch the show.

"Look," he said, "It's just a massage."

"A couple's massage," she fumed.

He ignored the interruption. "I think both of us could use a little relaxation right about now." With a muted huff, she settled back down, and over the tinkling chimes and water sounds coming from the stereo speakers, he heard the shuffling sounds of her straightening the linens.

Seconds later a soft knock sounded on the door and a pair of women entered. They introduced themselves as

Diane and April. Soon, the scent of lavender and bergamot filled the air as the massage therapists began working essential oils into their skin.

To Liam's relief, the pair worked in silence, offering him a chance to fully immerse himself in the pleasure of strong fingers digging deep into his tight muscles. As he lost himself to Diane's competent hands it became possible to put Teresa out of his mind and let himself float, but when the time came to turn onto his stomach, he couldn't help but glance her way to see how she was enjoying the experience.

Was it a coincidence that she'd brought her attention to bear on him at the exact same moment? Their gazes collided and sparks raced along his nerve endings. He spied the turmoil in her eyes, noted a similar uproar pushing aside his earlier tranquility.

Craving her. Distrusting her. Fighting emotions that should've died when she inherited the Christopher Corporation shares. His body and mind were at complete odds. But it was his heart—unreliable, traitorous organ—that he couldn't control.

Ten

Teresa tore her gaze away from the questions roiling in Liam's eyes, unable to believe she was lying naked on a massage table a mere three feet away from him. For the last half an hour she'd been kicking herself for staying. Why hadn't she gotten up and left the room? She couldn't blame modesty. The man had seen her naked before. Plus, she could have wrapped herself in the sheet and avoided flashing him.

She'd stayed out of sheer stubbornness. Unwilling to give him the satisfaction of having driven her away. Refusing to let him know how strongly he affected her.

It wasn't fair that he stirred her body and made her heart seize with longing. Her whole body ached that she'd chosen a man whose distrust flared at the slightest provocation. And yet, had she chosen him?

Did her yearning for Liam Christopher make any sense?

Sure, she admired his business acumen and appreciated his incredible body. His charisma had bowled her over, but she was sensible enough to resist any of those things. What had gotten to her was the way he'd jumped in and helped her brother without being asked. He hadn't needed to get involved. He wasn't trying to win her over or seduce her. Unlike the Fixer, there'd been no demand of a future payment or expectation that she owed him a favor in return. Nor did she doubt that he'd taken on just such a thing on her behalf.

The massage therapist dug strong fingers into Teresa's tight shoulders and the delicious pain made her bite back a moan. Until April started working on her back, Teresa hadn't realized just how knotted up she'd become. When was the last time she'd treated herself to a massage? A year? Why couldn't she bring herself to take time to relax? Because she was always chasing the win, never quite believing that her work would be good enough.

Teresa forced away thoughts of Liam and work and concentrated on letting her muscles unwind. She was almost asleep by the time the hour was up and the two women slipped from the room. Loathing the return to reality, but recognizing that the Richmond event wasn't going to organize itself, Teresa sighed. Although the massage therapists said there was no immediate need to evacuate the room, dozens of details still awaited her attention.

The swoosh of the champagne bottle sliding free of its ice bath disrupted the soothing music that had been playing during the massage. Teresa's eyes flew open. How had she forgotten that she wasn't alone? Clutching the sheet to her bare chest, keenly aware of her nakedness, Teresa levered onto one elbow and watched Liam refill both flutes.

"I'll close my eyes if you want to get up."

Unsure if he was being gallant or sardonic, Teresa glared at him while resentment rumbled. He certainly hadn't been shy about showing off his own body, and she envied his confidence. It would serve him right if she paraded past him in glorious nudity, and before she could question the impulse, she tossed aside the sheet and slid off the massage table.

Head held high, pointedly ignoring him, she ambled over to her robe, lifted it off the hook and slipped into it. Despite the adrenaline hit to her earlier tranquility, her boldness both amazed and pleased her. Buoyed by confidence, she knotted the belt and turned in Liam's direction rather than follow her instincts and bolt out the door.

"Champagne?" he asked smoothly, extending one of the flutes in her direction.

"Thank you." Proud of her unruffled tone, Teresa stepped close enough to take the drink. She lifted it to her lips and took a leisurely sip, debating her next move. "For five minutes, can we pretend that nothing exists outside this room?"

Liam's eyes narrowed and he regarded her with a mixture of wariness and curiosity. "What did you have in mind?"

Something crazy and reckless.

The man's suspicious nature had brought things to an end before she'd been ready to let go. The shock of his rejection had left her floundering with a dozen declarations unsaid. Their last night together had been ripe with promise and she'd been eager to take their relationship in the direction of deeper intimacy. In the aftermath of that fateful evening, she'd been angry and confused, but mostly she'd been frustrated because while he might have received closure that night, she'd been too busy defending herself to have the same.

Teresa set her glass on the table, hoping she hadn't misread his signals. "What I had in mind…" she said, avoiding his gaze lest she see something reflected in his eyes that stopped her cold. Heart thumping vigorously against her ribs, she narrowed the distance between them. With fingers that shook, she raked her nails into his hair in the way she knew he liked. "…is this."

The tension knotted in her stomach as he set aside his glass and wrapped his arms around her, stopping her breath. Tears burned her eyes that he hadn't rejected her advance. The hard embrace gave her no space and no chance to re-inflate her lungs before his lips crashed down on hers.

Moaning beneath the delicious hunger of his kiss, she opened to his questing tongue and met his passion with fierce joy. No matter what else was wrong between them, this all-consuming desire would always burn white-hot and pure.

When his hand slipped between them and tugged open her robe, she didn't protest. His palm skimmed over her hip and rode the indention of her waist to her breast. Lowering his head, he took one nipple into his mouth and sucked. She gasped as the sexy tug sent a bolt of electricity straight through her. Her world shimmered with pleasure from that alone, but then his hand was sliding between her thighs and he was dropping to his knees before her.

His lips skimmed over the twitching muscles of her abdomen and moved lower. "You are so beautiful," he muttered, his tone reverent, as he ran his palms along the backs of her thighs.

He kissed her legs with such adoration that Teresa wanted to cry out from that alone. All of the arguments and anger melted away as she plummeted into a world of white-hot desire.

"I have to taste you," he murmured against her skin. "I haven't been able to stop thinking about you. Let me. Just let me do this for you."

Teresa couldn't say no to that request. Especially not after the way he asked. The husky, aching throb in his voice left her wet and achy and hot. Earlier, while the massage therapist had worked lotion over her skin, she'd imagined it was Liam's hands stroking her shoulders and sliding along her legs. Nearly purring with pleasure, she'd taken the fantasy one step further and pictured his fingers easing into the dampness between her thighs, stroking her the way she loved.

The hunger aroused by the vision had been almost too much to bear. She'd never imagined he'd ever want to touch her like that again. Yet here he was, tending to her needs as if he'd read her mind and teased forth all her imaginings.

Her knees buckled as his tongue slid across where she wanted him most. He gripped her hips, anchoring her while she threaded her fingers through his hair. She gasped his name as he deepened the masterful stroke of his tongue. Shaking, lit up like a Fourth of July celebration from the pleasure of his deft touch, she moaned and murmured, encouraging him while waves of pleasure pummeled her.

"You taste so good," he whispered before returning to her slick heat, lapping at her clit, turning her world upside down with jolt after jolt of sharp, blissful sensation.

Shamelessly, she grabbed his head, pulling him closer. Her pleasure tightened and escalated, intensifying to such an extent that she rocked her hips into his face, pressing herself against his mouth, while a soft frantic keening escaped her parted lips. He seemed to understand that she was close because he pulled her even tighter against him, fingers digging into her soft bottom, touching off the electric spark that started the chain reaction of her climax. Oblivious that the massage room was neither isolated nor soundproof, she held nothing back. Her wild cries sounded frantic and desperate as shockwaves rolled over her.

Gasping for air, her legs trembling so badly she could scarcely stand, she relaxed her fingers and stroked Liam's dark head in appreciation. He set his forehead against her abdomen, hands continuing to coast from the back of her knees to the small of her back, tender caresses so unlike the heated tight grip on her moments earlier.

"That was amazing," she rasped, making no attempt to hide her admiration. Wanting to return the pleasure, she began to sink down. "Let me do that for you."

"No." He lunged to his feet and grabbed her arms beneath the elbows, keeping her upright. He wouldn't meet her eyes as he growled, "This was a mistake."

She wanted to scream denials at him. To insist that the only mistake was that he doubted her. But humiliation pressed on her vocal chords, muting her. She could only shake her head, denying his claim.

"Liam…"

"I can't keep doing this," he said, cutting her off.

"Keep doing what?" His declaration left her reeling. How could he be like this after what had just happened between them? After the care he'd taken with her pleasure?

"Encounters like this aren't good for either of us. We have to move on."

As if she'd been pushed into icy water, she began to shake. After tearing her arms from his grasp, Teresa snatched her robe together and fumbled with the belt.

That's what she'd been trying to do. To close a door. One last kiss goodbye.

"Don't you think I want to?" she countered, knowing how ridiculous she sounded. She'd made the move on him, practically begged him for a kiss. No wonder he was confused.

"I don't know what you want."

I want you.

But she recognized that even if she spoke the words out loud he wouldn't care. He'd made up his mind about her and no amount of arguing would change his opinion. Instead of making an even bigger fool of herself, she slumped into the nearby chair in miserable silence while Liam headed for the door. The idealistic part of her that couldn't stop believing they were meant to be together wanted to call out, to ask him not to go, but she bit her lip and stubbornly held

her tongue. As much as she longed to recapture the connection that had been growing between them before they'd
discovered the terms of his father's will, Teresa wasn't sure
that was possible.

Isabel stood at the bathroom sink of her tiny cabin and
stared at the text Shane had sent her the previous night. She
could guess what was on his mind. This has been fun, baby,
but I don't have time for you. Although it wasn't in her nature to play games, the brusque message had vexed her and
so she was taking her time responding. The delay hadn't en-
abled her to calm down and think rationally, but no matter
how angry, it went against her nature to be bitchy and rude.

I'm off at four.

She'd debated beating him to the punch and ending
things via text, but wanted to see his face as he dropped
his bomb on her. On the heels of her reply came another
message.

Are you available for dinner tonight?

Outrageous. How could he act as if the whole Camilla
Maxwell situation wasn't eating her alive? After the lengths
she'd gone to, showing him the candlelit proposal on the
bridge and the romantic photo shoot in front of the falls, he
should've known she'd be devastated to be passed over. He
deserved to get a lengthy lecture on how people deserved
to be treated, and that required time and privacy.

Sure. I'll cook.

She followed up with her address and brief directions.
Hosting him at the cabin she rented was strategic. She

wanted privacy to speak her mind, and if he needed to escape, it would be less awkward if he didn't have to stick around to settle the bill.

In the hours that followed, Isabel had waffled between anxiety and righteous frustration. After work she'd shopped for groceries and did some last-minute tidying up while practicing her impassioned lecture. As the clock ticked past seven and the rain continued to drench the area, Isabel wondered if Shane had sensed the hell storm he was about to walk into and changed his mind about coming, or if he was merely having trouble finding the place. A mixed bag of relief and annoyance rushed through her as she spied headlights winding up her driveway.

Heart drumming in time with the downpour, she went to the door and flung it open to watch him approach. Raindrops sparkled on his dark hair and the shoulders of his trench coat as he took her porch steps in two easy bounds and came to stand before her. His enticing lips bore no sign of a smile. Despite the bottle of wine he extended toward her, he looked as if he was approaching tonight's dinner as a business meeting.

"Did you have trouble finding the place?" she asked, her dread twisting in her stomach as she fell back and motioned him inside.

"I missed the turn the first time," he said. "You're pretty isolated here."

"I love being surrounded by all the trees." She forced a smile. "It means I don't have a view, but I really enjoy the solitude."

"You strike me as the sort who would rather be in the thick of things in the middle of town."

Against her better judgment, his remark warmed her. He'd been thinking about her. She liked that far too much.

"Let me take your coat."

While she hung the trench coat on a hook near her door,

he surveyed the pine-covered walls, tiny living room and ancient but clean kitchen. His expression gave no clue what he thought of the deer antler side tables, the worn couch covered by one of her mother's quilting projects or the cheery fire crackling in the stone fireplace. While the ambiance might not be up to his standards, the meal she'd prepared was one from her favorite food blogger and destined to impress.

"Something smells really good," he remarked, his keen gaze on her as she moved into the kitchen.

Satisfaction bloomed. She was eager to demonstrate her skills to him once again. In the wake of her meeting with Tom, Isabel wanted Shane to realize he'd made a mistake in choosing Camilla Maxwell over her as romance concierge.

"It's a standing rib roast," she told him.

"Can I help you with anything?"

He dominated her small space with his tall, muscular form and powerful personality. Tonight he'd exchanged his expensive business suit for worn jeans and a navy sweater.

In the grip of an awkward bout of nerves, she gestured to the bottle. "You can open the wine."

She pulled out a corkscrew and handed it over. She watched him work while Jessie Humphrey's voice flowed from a Bluetooth speaker in the living room. The romantic music was a mistake. Her phone was on the counter and she tapped to skip the song.

As many times as she'd seen the star performing on TV, for some reason now that she'd met Jessie, Isabel perceived a whole new level of nuance in Jessie's performance. She sang like her soul had been shredded. Like each word held deep personal meaning. And perhaps they did. For all her fame and fortune, the pain in Jessie Humphrey was real and palpable. Isabel's heart ached in sympathy.

Shane looked up from pouring the wine. "Why'd you change the song?"

Isabel wished she dared tell him the real reason. That she felt betrayed and regretted the feelings she'd developed for him over the last year. "I wasn't in the mood."

One dark eyebrow rose. "It seems like the way she puts her whole heart in every one of her songs would be right up your alley."

"Songs with that much emotion are born out of heartache." And too raw for how she was feeling at the moment. "Every time I listen to her I wonder who she's writing about."

"Hmm," Shane mused. "Another topic you're knowledgeable about. Among your many talents, are you a songwriter, too?"

"No." Isabel reached for a glass of wine and took a hearty gulp to dull a sudden flare of pain. "My father was. He wrote all his own stuff."

"What sort of music?"

"Alternative rock, mostly."

"Would I recognize the group?"

"I doubt it. His band never broke out, but they had a small but loyal following. Sometimes I think it would've been better if they'd either hit it big or failed completely." Isabel wasn't sure why she felt suddenly compelled to share such a painful part of her life. "My dad was gone all the time, traveling all over the country, mostly playing smaller venues."

"Why would it have been better if he'd made it big or failed?"

"If he'd failed, my mother could have convinced him to give it up. If he'd succeeded he wouldn't have felt so desperate to keep going. He and his bandmates were constantly chasing the next big opportunity. It consumed my father."

She stopped speaking, recalling those complicated days before her father had stopped coming home to his wife and daughter altogether.

"I know what it's like to work too hard, chasing something that doesn't exist," Shane said, his eyes on a distant place, a muscle jumping in his jaw. "Ever since I graduated from college and my dad told me I wasn't good enough to join the family business, I've sacrificed everything to prove him wrong."

"Seems to me that you accomplished what you set out to do. No one looking at you and seeing all you've done would be anything but proud of you."

"Yet that's not the case. My dad will never see me as anything but the screwup I was all through high school and into college."

"I can't imagine that's true. The *Seattle Business Journal* named you one of the city's rising stars. Surely he saw the article."

"Oh, he saw it. My uncle made certain of that. But he never said a word to me."

Despite his stoic expression, Shane's pain came through loud and clear. Impulsively, Isabel reached for his hand. When Shane squeezed her fingers in return, Isabel found in him a sympathetic soul.

"The night my dad left for good, I heard him tell my mother how he wished I'd never been born." The confession surprised Isabel. It was something she'd only ever shared with her closest friends.

"Come here." Shane pulled her into his arms and dropped his cheek against the top of her head.

When she'd pictured how the night would go, she'd never

expected that sharing her story with Shane and hearing his in return would take some of the sting out of her father's leaving. Nor had she intended to end up in his arms. The ache in her throat impressed on Isabel how complicated their situation was. Shane had the power to ruin her career and damage her heart.

"I guess we should both give up on our fathers ever loving us the way we want," she murmured against his chest, telling herself to stop being a fool. She shouldn't be taking solace from past hurts in Shane's arms after the way he'd let her down about the romance concierge position. At last she rallied her willpower and pushed away. "I can't do this."

"Do what?" When she didn't immediately answer, Shane tried again. "Look, if you're upset about what's been going on, you don't need to be."

How could the man act like replacing her as The Opulence's romance concierge was a nothing event? Did he seriously think he could encourage her ideas, invite her to pitch those ideas to corporate marketing, give her the most amazing night of her life and then act like it was okay to steal what she'd developed?

"I don't need to be upset?" Isabel couldn't believe what she was hearing. "You've got to be kidding."

"Okay." Peering at her from beneath his ridiculously long lashes, he raked his fingers through his hair, disrupting the waves. The dishevelment only increased his appeal. "I'll admit I'm not good at this."

Was this some sort of master manipulation to make her look like the crazy, unreasonable one? He couldn't possibly be as perplexed as he appeared. This sheepish charm had to be a device he used to twist situations to his advantage, right? Except he hadn't shown himself to be anything less than completely straightforward with her.

"Oh, I think you're plenty good at it," she muttered, refusing to be fooled. "In fact, it seems to me that you've mastered the art of doing exactly this."

"You're wrong." The sound he huffed out sounded like a rusty chuckle. "I've spent my life doing the exact opposite."

Eleven

With tension stretching his nerves to the point of discomfort, Shane watched as Isabel's lush mouth tightened into a grim line. Despite her unhappy expression, she looked so damned adorable in her bare feet, snug jeans and dark green sweater bringing out the forest green in her eyes. He was almost overwhelmed by the impulse to take her to bed and let the dinner burn. But they were in the midst of something that couldn't be solved with hot, sweaty sex.

The problem stemmed from that we-need-to-talk text, signaling that he didn't want to pursue her further. The instant it had left his phone he regretted sending it because as soon as he'd taken steps to shut things down between him and Isabel, Shane recognized that was the last thing he wanted to do. Worse, unaccustomed to owning his emotions, he'd been reluctant to send a follow-up text, explaining his dilemma.

Thus, he'd been overjoyed when she'd agreed to have dinner, hoping maybe she hadn't taken the text the way he'd meant it. But from the way she was reacting right now, his struggle to communicate with Isabel had led to him mucking things up.

"What are you talking about?" she demanded, annoyance bleeding into confusion.

"What am I talking about?" Shane countered, sensing he was walking blindfolded through a minefield. "What are you talking about?"

"Like you don't know." Isabel set her hands on her hips and glared at him.

"I really don't think I do." He leaned back against the kitchen counter and crossed his arms over his chest. "Can you tell me what's going on with you?"

Her scowl grew even more pronounced as she began. "Yesterday, Tom told me that he thinks promoting the hotel as a romance destination has merit and wants to go ahead with it."

"It'll be a huge benefit." Shane nodded, recalling how enthusiastic his marketing department had been. "You were right about that."

"And the romance concierge position?"

"What about it?"

She tossed her head, causing her silky russet locks to drift and resettle. "Are you kidding me?"

A bad feeling grew in his gut. "What's wrong?"

"I'm not going to be The Opulence's romance concierge."

"You're not?" He could see she was unhappy about this. "What's changed?"

"What's changed?" she echoed bitterly. "Like you didn't know that Tom hired Camilla Maxwell to be the face of all things romantic and trendy at the hotel."

This news was a blow Shane didn't see coming. Holy hell. No wonder she was so upset. He lifted his hand, intending to touch her, but she backed out of reach.

"I didn't," he assured her, not convinced she believed him. "And she's a blogger. How would that even work?"

"It'll work because I'm the one who will continue to do the actual work of making the guests' experiences perfect." Isabel's disillusionment ground into Shane like broken glass. "How could you…" she broke off and dashed her knuckles beneath the corners of both eyes.

"How could I what?"

Her breath came and went in huge, unsteady gulps. "Tom said that corporate agreed."

Now he understood why she'd been avoiding him. A string of curses flowed through Shane's thoughts. "I assure you I knew nothing about it."

"You didn't tell him to?" Her misery lost its sharp edges as hope reentered her gaze.

"Of course not." Shane frowned. "And anyway, it doesn't matter."

"And why not?" She shot back. Obviously it mattered to her.

"Because you're not going to be working for The Opulence much longer." Seeing the panic in her hazel eyes, he rushed to explain. "Your talents are wasted on a single hotel. I want to bring you to corporate headquarters. I'd like you to look at every one of the hotels Richmond manages and come up with a romantic plan for each one."

Her eyes opened wide. "That sounds amazing. I never imagined…" She broke off and shifted her gaze away. "This isn't because…"

"Because?"

"We're sleeping together."

"I'd already decided to offer you the position before anything happened between us." That wasn't quite true. When he'd kissed her that first time, he hadn't been thinking of promoting her. He'd just given into the overwhelming urge to taste her. "I'm bringing you to corporate because you sold me on your ideas and the marketing department thought you were brilliant."

She considered this for a long moment before asking, "So, how will this affect things between us?"

Shane didn't have a ready answer. Not only did he recoil from going public about dating one of his employees, but also the way Isabel whipped up his emotions pushed him past his comfort zone. The smart thing would be to end their personal relationship here and now. They'd both slipped up—him more than her. No reason to compound the mistakes by persisting with their sexual relationship. Yet he couldn't bring himself to say goodbye.

"Teresa St. Claire offered me a job with her company," she said into the silence between them.

He wasn't surprised someone else had tried to snap her up. "Do you want to take it?"

Shane could see where the event planning business would be a good fit for Isabel. And if she no longer worked for Richmond, he could pursue her without either of their careers being affected. This simple solution should've brought an end to his concern. Instead, it highlighted a new issue.

Was he ready for his life to change if he continued to date Isabel?

"I'm not sure," she said, her gaze shifting away. "It might be time to try something new. And it would be a lot less complicated…for us."

Her hesitation was a plea for him to reassure her that he was interested in something that extended past these next few days. As strongly as he believed in Isabel's talent and abilities, Shane couldn't honestly say if he'd been motivated to offer her a job at corporate so he'd have an excuse to stop seeing her. It might have been bad form to date a lowly concierge at one of his hotels, but they could've kept that under wraps. Promoting her into the Seattle office put extreme pressure on their relationship.

"Let's get through the Richmond retreat," he said. "We can discuss this more on the other side."

Disappointment chased across Isabel's features before she nodded. "Sure. Of course."

With his entire body alive with energy and lust, Liam forced himself to exit the massage room. Grappling with the painful act of turning his back on the woman he'd left spent and lethargic in the aftermath of her stunning orgasm, he marched toward the locker room, where he'd left his clothes. Teeth clenched against the pounding, urgent longing to return and take back his bitter rejection, Liam's hands shook as he changed into gray slacks and a black sweater before striding out of the spa without a backward glance.

Any relaxation he might've gained from the massage vanished in the aftermath of what had followed. Now, his jacked-up pulse sent waves of heat surging through his veins. His skin burned. Adrenaline whipped his nerve endings into a frenzy. He couldn't bear to head up to his empty suite and face the long night alone. Instead, he bypassed the bank of elevators, ignored the siren call of the bar's excellent selection of scotch and headed straight out the lobby doors into the night.

Rain-drenched wind lashed at his face but didn't slow him down. Distantly Liam noted the valet asking if he wanted his car, and he shook his head a second before stepping from beneath the entrance canopy into the downpour. Icy sheets of cold water struck him, plastering his hair to his head, penetrating the cotton fibers of his sweater and instantly banishing all heat from his skin. But even as his core temperature dipped, the rain did little to eliminate his emotional uproar.

What the hell had he just done? He promised himself he would not go there again. But all she had to do was crook a finger at him and he was on his knees, worshipping her.

Damn it.

What made it so much worse was that he wanted to do it all over again. And then to take her up on her offer to do the same to him. Just the thought of her mouth on him made his blood run wild and hot.

Half-blinded by the downpour, Liam headed away from the hotel, following a sign that indicated the trail to the falls lay ahead. Calling himself all sorts of idiot, Liam strode onto the path, fighting the urge to shout curses at the top of his lungs. With the wind at his back, hastening him along, he reached the overlook at the top of the falls. Palms flat atop the stone wall, the thunder of the falls a concussive roar filling his ears, Liam lifted his voice in a series of savage curses at the woman who'd wronged his family and at himself for his inability to resist her.

The rain eased as his turmoil bled away. With each drop that struck him, he grew calmer and awakened to his foolishness. In fact, by the time he retraced his steps, he wished he'd never ventured out into the rain. Chilled and shivering, he reflected that a better response to the encounter with Teresa might have been to sit in the bar beside a roaring fire, sip an excellent twenty-five-year-old scotch or manhattan and size up various single women he'd noted days earlier.

Unfortunately, he couldn't summon the enthusiasm for a night of uncomplicated sex with a beautiful stranger. Since meeting Teresa, his focus had narrowed to one woman. One scheming, lying female who haunted him day and night.

Liam retreated back down the trail, feeling like an idiot as he entered the hotel through a side door, avoiding the lobby. Reluctant to have to explain his sodden clothes to anyone, he found the stairwell and jogged up the five flights of stairs. The exercise warmed him after the chill of outdoors. Relieved to have encountered no one, he opened the door his suite and stepped inside.

After shedding his sopping clothes on the bathroom

floor, he stepped into the shower and turned the taps to blazing hot, and in moments the chill had left his skin. Dressed in gray slacks and a black crew neck sweater, he exited the suite once more. This time, when he approached the lobby, he wrapped himself in cool disdain and headed to the bar for a late dinner and a much-needed drink.

He was perusing the bar menu when a beautiful brunette approached his table.

"Hello, you're Liam Christopher, right?"

"Yes." He surveyed her slender figure, admiring the shapely legs bared by her figure-hugging black dress and made to look even longer by the stiletto heels she wore. A detached part of Liam appreciated the sexy beauty while wishing he could summon the enthusiasm to pursue her. "I'm sorry, you look familiar…"

She flashed an engaging grin. "Nicolette Ryan." She put out her hand and he automatically took it. "I do lifestyle reporting. I'm here to cover the Richmond retreat, where I understand your company is making a big announcement."

"Of course." Memory triggered, he recalled Matt telling him that she was invited because she knew how to respect a guest's privacy if they didn't want to be interviewed or shown on camera. "Would you like to join me for a drink?"

"Actually…" Her gaze strayed toward the bar's entrance. "I'm waiting for someone. But I'd love to sit down with you tomorrow if you have time."

He pulled up his calendar. Most of the day was booked. "How about four o'clock?"

Her high-wattage smile was intended to make him feel like the most important person in the room. "That would be perfect."

The heat he should've been feeling at being the focus of such a beautiful woman's attention never manifested. Instead, movement near the bar's entrance caught his notice. He glanced over in time to catch Teresa's entrance.

His mouth went dry.

Like Nicolette, she wore a snug black dress with lace-covered cutouts that enhanced her sex appeal. Her long blond hair cascaded in a silky curtain over one shoulder. Her composure didn't slip at all as she spied him speaking with Nicolette. In fact, her gaze swept past him and lingered on the reporter. Nicolette noticed his attention had wandered and glanced over her shoulder. Something passed between the two women before Nicolette gave a quick nod and turned back to Liam.

"I'll leave you to enjoy the rest of your evening," she said. "See you tomorrow at four."

And then she headed over to join Teresa at a quiet table in the back, leaving Liam to wonder what the two women could possibly have to discuss.

Twelve

With the Richmond retreat set to receive its first official guests the next day, Isabel and Shane stole away to her cabin for a late dinner. Something had changed between them since the night of their big talk. Although Shane had become Isabel's dream lover, when he wasn't making love to her with tenderness or raw passion, she found herself dreading the moment when he dropped the bomb, ending their fling.

Maybe that's why she devoted so much of their time together to getting him naked and ravishing him. It was easy to pretend she was in a perfect relationship while passion consumed them.

"Hear that?" Isabel asked, leaning over Shane's shoulder as he fed fresh logs onto the fire. She caressed his ear with her lips in the way she'd learned drove him crazy.

"What?"

"The wind has really picked up." Its howling stirred her blood, making her feel wild and untamed.

Shane got to his feet and glanced at the window. "Maybe I should head back to Seattle."

"Or…" She drew him toward the couch and gave him a firm shove. He dropped into the cushions with a startled grunt.

"Or?"

"You could spend the night here." As she spoke, she hiked up her full skirt and straddled his lap, letting her heat and the wetness that had slicked her panties drive his arousal hard. She curved her hands over his shoulders, savoring the power in his muscles.

His dark eyes heated as he curved his long fingers over her butt. "Are you sure you're not getting sick of me?" He bucked his hips upward, driving himself into her.

With a lazy smile she rode the motion, giving her hips a little grinding twist that earned her a hoarse moan. She loved that sound and didn't want to face never hearing it again.

"I like having you around, but if you think we're spending too much time together…" She made as if to get up. "I'll get your coat."

Before she could do more than shift her weight, his fingers bit into her hips, keeping her right where she was.

"Don't bother," he said, his voice husky. "I like being here with you."

"But how should we spend our time?" she purred, raking her nails through his hair.

"We could play a game."

The wind gusted, slapping rain against the windows. The whole cabin seemed to shudder at the impact. Or maybe that was just the storm surge of despair battering her heart as she realized that with the Richmond retreat starting tomorrow, this might be their last night together.

She rocked her hips, grinding herself against him. "What sort of a game?"

"I'm thinking of a number between one and ten. If you get it wrong, you take something off."

"I like this game." And the fact that he grew playful in her company. She leaned down and blew in his ear. "Four."

"Nope, sorry. The number was five."

"Damn," she murmured, shivering as he stripped her T-shirt over her head. Her nipples pebbled as his fingers grazed over her lace-covered breasts. "Your turn. Guess a number."

"Three."

"Nope, sorry," she said. "The number was seven."

She stripped off his dress shirt and hummed in appreciation as she trailed her palms over the smooth flesh of his shoulders and chest.

"Two," she crowed, his startled expression making her laugh. "What?"

"How'd you know that was the number I was thinking of?"

"First of all…" She pointed to her breasts. "And second, you do realize the point of this game is all about getting us naked, right?"

"Yes." He drew the word out, obviously not getting her point.

She grinned. "It's okay to cheat."

"Right," he murmured. "The number was five. You guessed wrong."

"Again?" She reached behind her and popped the clasp on her bra. "I guess this needs to go."

She tossed her lingerie aside and gave her head a vigorous shake, sending her hair spilling over her shoulder and setting her breasts to jiggling enticingly.

"You are gorgeous," Shane muttered, his voice hoarse with desire. He gathered her breasts into his hands. "These are gorgeous."

Smiling in appreciation, she gave her hips another rocking twist and heard a rush of air through his parted lips. She liked that it was easy to turn him on. Her confidence bloomed still more as he cursed before dipping his head to capture one nipple in his mouth. As his tongue worked over the hard bud, he curved his hands over her hips, fingers biting into her flesh while she worked a sexy bump and grind on him.

Leaning forward, she rubbed her cheek against his stubble, enjoying the sandpaper feel of it against her skin. It was a stark contrast to the softness of his wavy black hair that caressed her fingers as she drove them through the silky waves. Her senses awakened to his every micromovement. The bunch of his leg muscles against her inner thighs. The subtle hitch in his breath beneath the rumbling encouragement pouring from his throat. The dip of his lashes as he tried to read her.

"Kiss me," he said, his tone as much request as demand.

"My pleasure."

She crushed her lips to his, drinking in his low moan of satisfaction. The hard kiss told him she intended to own the moment. Her fingers curved around his head, as she parted her lips and sent her tongue questing forward. She'd never been interested in stuff like this with other guys she dated. Mostly because they'd been more interested in their pleasure than hers.

In contrast, Shane gave and gave and gave before he took his own pleasure. Having a man hanging on your every moan was incredibly sexy. The other way he'd surprised her was how he was okay with her taking the lead from time to time. With someone who liked control as much as Shane, she'd expected he would prefer to be in charge all the time. Instead, she'd discovered that her aggressiveness turned him on.

Which was good for her and better for him. She liked him fully aroused. Insanely hungry. Mad with anticipation. And tonight, she intended to blow his mind.

Isabel broke off the kiss. "It's your turn. Pick a number," she panted, kissing her way down his chest. Her hand had already trailed over his abs and made its way south of his belt.

"Sex!" The word shot out of him as she molded her fingers over the hard length of him pushing against his zipper. "Six." He cursed. And then laughed.

"Wrong," she crowed, shifting off his lap in order to get at his pants.

"Where are you going?" He sounded half-desperate and that made her smile.

"I'm not going anywhere." She made quick work of his belt and zipper. "But these are."

Once he was down to his boxers, she stood and set her hands on her hips, taking him in while giving him time to ogle her lean, fit body. She'd worked hard to earn all the muscles on display and was gratified to see approval in his eyes. His anticipatory grin made her greedy for more.

Even as his eyes grew hot and his erection tented his boxers, she became aware of an equally insistent pulse between her thighs. She wanted him. Inside her. Driving hard and fast toward his climax. Taking her with him. Making her pant and moan and even scream. She caught her lips between her teeth as a growl of pleasure rattled out of him.

"The underwear next," he said, his raspy tone and greedy gaze driving her pleasure higher. "I want to see all of you."

She liked being told by Shane what to do during sex. That he shared his needs with her, described what felt good, what turned him on. All this gave their lovemaking an unexpected intimacy. For a man who kept his cards close to his chest, she knew more about him than she'd ever dreamed.

"What else do you want?" she asked him, turning and sliding her panties off one hip and then the other. She glanced back at him and, seeing she had his full attention, bent forward at the waist to slide her underwear down her legs.

His curse left her smiling. To further drive him crazy, she caressed her fingertips up her thighs and over the curves of her butt, imagining how she'd feel when Shane's hands made the same journey.

"You have a spectacular ass, did you know that?"

"What? This old thing?" Straightening, she gave herself a little spank before turning around. "I've had it forever."

"I wouldn't mind having it forever," he said, holding out his hand. "A man could die happy with such a beautiful thing in his life."

Isabel didn't know what to make of his words, so she decided not to think too much. She planned to imprint every second of their time together in her mind. He was a man worth remembering long after their paths diverged.

"I don't think you need these any longer." With a sassy smile, she leaned forward and hooked her fingers into the waistband of his boxers. Her sharp downward yank made him grunt in surprise, but a moment later he was grinning.

As his erection appeared, she licked her lips in anticipation. The heavy pulse between her thighs thundered mercilessly as she knelt between his long legs. Plying him with hands and mouth, she intended to drive him crazy, and then leave him shattered and spent.

"Isabel?"

She dipped her head and flicked him with her tongue, smiling at the raw expletive that tore loose from him. "Like that?" she teased, going back for a second, longer lick.

A husky groan rattled free as he slouched back and gave himself completely over to her ministrations. Yet as relaxed and open as he appeared, his sable eyes remained a bit wary.

"I want this to be good for you," she said. "Let me."

She wrapped her hand around the base of his shaft and slowly settled her mouth over him. He tasted salty and sexy and a wildness spread through her blood. The low sounds of pleasure rattling in his chest boosted her confidence and Isabel glanced at his face.

He'd closed his eyes and was breathing hard. Concentration mingled with awe suffused his expression. His fingers were clenched in a death grip on a throw pillow and Isabel realized now was the time to turn up the heat. She worked her mouth over him, combining tantalizing swirls of her tongue with coordinated movements of her lips and hand.

"You're killing me," he muttered as she took him as deep as possible.

She answered by increasing the pace just enough to make him moan her name, and then his fingers threaded through her hair, guiding her head.

He exhaled raggedly. "Feels amazing."

Isabel had more surprises up her sleeve and shifted her free hand to cup his balls. His body jerked in surprise at her light squeeze and his fingers tightened on her scalp. A moment later, whereas up until now he'd been still and nearly docile beneath her, he began lifting his hips and rocking forward into her.

From the sounds he was making and the near agony of his expression, Isabel knew what he needed. And wanted to give him a moment he'd never forget. So, she gave him her mouth and made herself a willing receptacle for his pleasure.

As he realized what she'd offered, his eyes went wide. She met his gaze and offered him a wicked half smile. A second later he shuddered and began thrusting. The power of his joy intensified her own pleasure and she raked her nails across his skin. The minor pain acted like a torch, setting him on fire.

His thighs began to tremble. His body quaked. No shout or loud groan accompanied his orgasm. In fact, she thought he stopped breathing as he came.

TAKEN BY STORM

In the aftermath, she sat back on her heels and grinned. "Okay?"

He cracked his eyes open. "Okay?" A weak chuckle sounded. "Hell, no. I'm not okay. You've ruined me."

His reaction was all she could hope for and more. "Sorry."

"You aren't one bit sorry." Shane reached down and hauled her up and forward until she lay sprawled across his naked body. His fingers cupped her cheek. "You loved that and I loved that."

She went all shivery inside at his use of the word *loved*. Something rattled loose in her chest. As much as she'd tried to protect herself from being hurt by staying focused on the red-hot sex between them, Isabel conceded she'd already lost that battle. Dozens of times a day the *L*-word leaped into the front of her mind. It had become as relentless as the downpour outside.

"And you trusted me," he continued. "Let me do it hard." He brought his lips to hers and it was a reverent kiss. "Thank you." A pause. "For the trust."

She tensed a little as he brought up the tricky subject. While it was true that she trusted him with her body, believed he'd treat her carefully, what remained undefined between them gave her frequent anxious moments.

Burying her face in the spot where his shoulder and neck came together, Isabel murmured, "Of course I trust you."

Normally the view out the main ballroom's twenty-foot wall of windows was nothing short of spectacular. Today, driving rain obscured the manicured lawn and the pine-covered mountains far beyond. At the edge of the stone terrace that ran alongside the building, wind hammered tall, ancient trees. Their branches whipped back and forth with each gust.

The storm mirrored the turmoil Teresa felt inside. It

wasn't just the looming party that was agitating her or the problems presented by the storm, but what had happened between her and Liam at the spa. She was still kicking herself for going there with him again. Why couldn't she just accept that they were done? In the coming months she would be sitting on Christopher Corporation's board and she needed to start treating him like a professional colleague.

Yet she couldn't shake that after what had happened between them in the spa, all her hastily built defenses were little more than scattered piles of rubble. Nor could she blame Liam for the destruction. After all, she'd handed him the sledgehammer. How did she proceed with him going forward? Fantastic sex wasn't going to fix what was broken between them no matter how often they gave it their all. The reality was that he didn't trust her. Or couldn't. No, in fact, he didn't want to.

Teresa peered past the rain pounding the ballroom's windows, gaze tracing the curving paths that crisscrossed the lawn while she assessed the planting beds that bordered them. Would anything be left of the lush foliage after this storm had passed? As she watched, a lounge cushion tumbled past on its way toward the river and the one-hundred-thirty-foot drop.

With the storm intensifying, flooding and wind damage threatened the party preparations. Florists were supposed to be arriving from Seattle today with truckloads of stunning arrangements to fill every suite in The Opulence. Navigating the winding roads in this sort of weather would be treacherous. What if they refused to make the journey? Or couldn't?

Teresa grimaced. She had to stop focusing on what-ifs and maybes.

So what if she didn't have flowers? She had the well-stocked welcome baskets to distract them as well as the incredible gift bags each retreat attendee received. At least she'd made sure those items arrived early. Her staff was delivering the baskets even now and making sure each suite was personalized to the attendee.

The sheer rage of the storm drew Teresa closer to the glass. She couldn't believe the violence of the wind and rain. She'd never seen anything like it in the Pacific Northwest. It was unusual. More than unusual—it was once in a lifetime. She shivered. If this kept up, the party was going to be…

Even as her mind went there, something large moved outside. A dark shape began toppling toward her. Buffeted by the wind, one of the oak trees at the edge of the terrace had given up its battle. The volume of rain they'd received over the last week combined with the violent winds had loosened the roots in the ground. It was falling. Teresa watched it come down in slow motion. It didn't occur to her to step back until she could identify the individual leaves shivering as they advanced.

Her mind started shrieking at her. *Run!* As Teresa turn to flee, the lights went out. Disoriented, her heel snagged on the carpet and a red-hot spike ripped through her ankle. Her head clipped the back of a chair as she fell to her knees. Dizzy, she heard the sound of shattering glass behind her. The storm roared like a beast freed and a hard blow landed on her shoulder from behind. Icy water drenched her as the heavy weight drove her to the ground and trapped her beneath its wet, leafy mass.

Liam was having a drink in the bar with Nicolette Ryan when he heard a distant boom and noticed several hotel employees racing through the lobby. The lights blinked out, but within twenty seconds the backup generator clicked on. Never one to sit by when something was going wrong, he excused himself to the reporter, jumped to his feet and followed.

"A tree crashed through the ballroom's windows and a woman's trapped," a man in a gray shirt and pants called as he passed Liam. "We'll need a chainsaw to get her out."

"Does anybody know who's trapped?" Liam asked as he moved through the crowd that had gathered to view the devastation.

"Teresa St. Claire was meeting with Aspen here a few minutes ago," one of the waitstaff said. "It might be either one of them."

Liam bolted across the room toward a familiar blond head half-hidden by the autumn-brown leaves of one of the ancient oaks. Nearly a third of the tree had crashed through the wall of windows. Heedless of the rain-soaked carpet, Liam dropped to one knee beside Teresa, appalled that she didn't seem to be moving. The roaring storm hadn't let up at all and the voices behind and around him faded as he reached for her.

The wind blew water into his eyes as Liam touched her cheek, feeling the chill beneath his fingers. *She can't be dead. Don't let her be dead.* Even as these thoughts chased through his head, she gave a slight moan and her lashes fluttered. Liam didn't realize how afraid he'd been until his heart gave a huge bump against his breastbone.

"Teresa. Teresa, can you hear me?"

"What…?"

Her fingers dug into the carpet like she was trying to crawl out from beneath the weight bearing down on her. He grabbed the branch pinning her to the ground and applied all this strength, but couldn't budge it. There was nothing for him to do but wait for reinforcements and the helplessness ate at him.

"Don't try to move," Liam told her. "You have a tree on top of you."

"A tree?" She blinked and that seemed to clear her thoughts. Fear widened her eyes.

Frustrated, Liam glanced around and noted all the people standing around, including Nicolette Ryan, who'd followed him from the bar. As much as he wanted to scream at them to do something, keeping Teresa calm was his first priority.

"We're working to get you out. Maintenance is coming with a chainsaw. Hang in there."

It was the most agonizing ten minutes of his life as he waited for the guy to return. When he did, the maintenance man came with reinforcements and Liam was grateful that The Opulence operated with such smooth efficiency. Working together, the men had the limb cut and Teresa freed in short order. She shifted into a sitting position and picked dead leaves from her clothes as Liam knelt beside her.

"Are you okay?" He stroked her damp hair away from her face and surveyed her features.

"My shoulder is sore." She shifted her feet under her, preparing to rise, and winced, grabbing at her left ankle. "And I think I might've twisted my ankle as I tried to get out of the way."

Liam didn't wait for her to say another word. He carefully lifted her into his arms and carried her out of the ballroom, conscious that his dramatic gesture was drawing everyone's attention. Including the reporter, who had her cell phone up and a pleased smile on her face as she watched him walk past.

It might be ridiculous to feel so protective about a woman he claimed that he was done with. If she hadn't been hurt he might've been able to keep that promise. Seeing her lying beneath that tree had made him realize that she still got to him, but he had no idea how to move past all the doubts and recriminations.

He carried her into his suite and set her down on the

couch. "I'll get you some ice." He found a plastic bag in one of the kitchenette drawers and poured ice into it.

She winced as he applied the cold bag to her ankle. "Thanks."

"You should get out of those wet clothes."

Despite her obvious pain and although she still looked shaken by her ordeal, one slim eyebrow rose in a mocking salute. Realizing how she'd taken what he'd meant as a practical suggestion, he frowned.

"I can find something of mine for you to wear." He suddenly noticed his own damp clothing. "I think we both need to get dry."

"You could just take me back to my room," she said, but didn't sound as if she wanted to go.

"I think someone should keep an eye on you."

She gave him a sad smile. "And you're volunteering?"

"I'll get you some dry clothes."

When he returned, she was reviewing the contract his lawyer had sent over for Liam to review. It had been sitting on the coffee table. She wore a frown as she scanned the document. As he dropped a T-shirt and his pajama bottoms beside her, Teresa glanced up.

"Why is it so hard for you to trust?"

"I grew up believing that I shouldn't give anyone the benefit of the doubt."

"Why?"

"My mother has always been convinced that people were out to get her, and she had plenty of examples that proved it." While he'd offered a straightforward answer to her direct question, admitting such a profound failing about someone he loved felt like the bitterest betrayal.

"I didn't know her that well, but she was nothing but polite to me. Even when she thought I was sleeping with her husband."

"She's very good at making her fears seem rational.

Maybe if she raved about conspiracies it would've been easier to dismiss her claims." For several seconds Liam closed his eyes. "It got worse after she and my father divorced. Over and over she urged me to question whether my friends had my back. But even when it was obvious they did, a tiny voice in the back of my mind always doubted."

"I get it," Teresa said. "While I couldn't do what I do without my team, I'm always checking up on them, rarely giving them the freedom to do their job without being second-guessed by me."

"It drove my dad crazy. That's why he divorced my mom."

"Do you think it will always get in the way of us…?" She faltered and stared at the contract in her hands. "Of us working together?"

Liam didn't think she'd started out asking about their professional relationship.

"When it comes to business, I've hired the best people and trust them to do what needs to be done. I take steps to make sure I know all the information I need before making a decision. It's my personal life I struggle with." Especially in light of the way Teresa was keeping the truth from him regarding her relationship with his father. "How do I know if I can fall in love and not be hurt?"

"How do any of us know?" Teresa set aside the document. "I guess we're a pair. Like you, I've wrapped myself up in growing my business because it's safe and use work as an excuse for why I don't date. But the truth is, you're the first man I've wanted to be with in a long, long time."

"I want to be with you, as well," Liam said, surprising himself with the admission. "I just don't know how to get past everything that's between us."

Teresa nodded. "Neither do I."

Thirteen

Gasping for breath, Isabel fell onto her back, too spent to lift her arm and clear the strand of hair away from her sweat-soaked skin.

"Damn, you're good at that," she murmured. "I don't think I'll ever be able to move again."

Shane chuckled…*chuckled*…as he headed into the bathroom to dispose of the condom. Lots and lots of sex obviously agreed with him. Everyone at the hotel had been commenting on how relaxed he looked despite all the problems brought on by the days of rain and high winds. And every time one of her coworkers wondered why he looked so happy, Isabel had to hide a smile.

No one knew they'd been sneaking around. They'd been very careful to keep their interaction at the hotel to a minimum and when they did speak, neither one of them behaved in anything less than a professional manner. For Isabel's part, she knew how much Shane valued his reputation. Nor did she want anyone to view his offer of promotion as anything other than something she'd earned because of the solid work she'd done for the hotel.

Isabel grinned at the joy humming through her. She had a lot to be happy about at the moment. Great sex with Shane. Her career taking off. But the bulk of her pleasure came from the transformation of this logical workaholic into a man driven by his passionate need for her and his willingness to open up about things he'd long kept bottled up.

A string of curses flew through the open bathroom door, each one more biting than the last, and intruded on her blissful glow. Isabel lifted onto her elbows and stared toward the source of the sounds.

"What's wrong?" she asked, imagining all sorts of issues that could've come up given the way the rain lashed at the windows.

Shane appeared in the doorway. Backlit by the bathroom's light, his face in shadow, the power of his naked body took her breath away. She'd traced his chiseled muscles with her fingertips and lips. Felt the impact of his lean strength as he pressed her into the mattress. Such tactile experiences had been amazing, but she could spend the rest of her life staring at his broad shoulders, lean hips and corded muscles without ever growing tired of the sight.

"The condom had a tear," he growled, raking his fingers through his hair, the gesture reflecting acute worry and annoyance. "Damn it. This can't be happening."

"Oh." She absorbed this information and ran it through a series of filters. While the development wasn't great, it wasn't exactly dire. First off was the issue of safety. She hadn't had a lot of partners and was always very careful and assumed Shane was, as well. "We should be okay."

"Okay?" he demanded. Advancing toward the bed, he clicked on the bedside light. "It's not okay. The condom broke. That's a problem."

"You don't have to worry about catching anything from me," she explained, rushing to reassure him.

"I'm not worried about catching anything," he said, his brown eyes cold and distant as he gazed at her. "I'm worried about getting you pregnant."

"You don't need to be." Before she could elaborate that she was on the pill because of her irregular periods, Shane started grabbing up his clothes and putting them on.

"There's a morning-after pill or something, isn't there? Do you need a prescription or is it something you can get over the counter? Is there a drugstore nearby that's open at this hour?"

He was so busy peppering her with questions while he dressed that he hadn't yet noticed she was frowning at him. She'd never seen him so distraught. He was positively frantic.

"Let me look up some information on that." He grabbed his phone and began tapping away. "Okay, it says here that you can get it over the counter." He glanced at the window as a gust of wind threw rain against the glass. "Damn it. We probably shouldn't go anywhere in this." He glanced back down at his phone. "Maybe we'll be okay." Shane's breath gusted out as the last bit of information calmed him down somewhat. "If this information is correct, it's ninety-five percent effective if you take it within 24 hours."

If his blind panic hadn't felt a lot like stinging rejection, Isabel might've found the whole thing amusing. But she was falling in love with this man, and his horror over her potential pregnancy had been authentic and intense. This eye-opening glimpse of him was completely at odds with the solid, dependable man she'd come to know, and ice settled into her bones at the mistake she'd made in opening herself up to him.

Which was probably why she didn't resist the need to strike back.

"If you're so paranoid about getting a woman pregnant, perhaps you should check the expiration date on your condoms." Her voice shook as she vented her humiliation and grief. "And while you're at it, maybe stock up on the morning-after pill so if things like this happen in the future, you'll be able to eliminate the threat before it has a chance to become a problem."

His gaze whipped to her, and Isabel immediately regretted her words and tone. Of course he was worried about the future havoc a broken condom could have on his life. Had he not spent enough time warning her that his focus was solely on his career? He didn't want to make time for a relationship, much less a child.

"Isabel…"

Heart breaking, she flung up both her hands. "Oh, please don't."

And then, to her profound relief, his phone began to ring.

"I can't…" Shane began, unsure how to proceed.

He couldn't what? Offer her a future? Handle more than a few blissful days of great sex? He'd done what he'd sworn to avoid and let himself get tangled up in her. They'd never discussed where things went beyond these few days. The fact remained that she was his employee. A valuable one. He didn't want to lose her. In business. Or in his personal life. The fact that he'd put himself in a place where he would be forced to choose inspired a string of condemnations to run through his mind.

"This is all going really fast," he continued. "I don't know how you fit in my life."

The devastated expression on Isabel's face was like a knife through Shane's heart. Damn it. He'd never promised her anything, but from what she'd said, it was obvious that he'd mishandled the situation. Explaining to her that he'd only been concerned for her welfare would fly as well as a plane without wings. He hadn't once asked her if she was okay or even let her join him in being anxious.

Instead, she'd sat as cool and composed as always and watched him fall apart.

Now she glanced at his ringing phone. "I think you'd better answer that call. If someone is trying to get ahold of you at this hour, it must be important."

Stomach twisted in knots, he accepted the call. "What?"

At first there was silence on the line and then a man spoke. "It's Benny Jacobs. I'm with maintenance at The Opulence." He sounded worried and more than a little nervous.

Rubbing the back of his neck, Shane tempered his tone. "Sure, Benny. What can I do for you?"

"There's a problem here at the hotel. A big one. And we can't get ahold of Tom Busch."

"What happened?" Shane asked, startled to find that for the first time in his life, he wanted to avoid a work-related crisis.

His gaze followed Isabel as she got out of bed and started pulling on jeans and a long-sleeved blouse. Her motions were jerky and her features wore a hard, determined look he'd never seen before. The implications created a ball of dread in his gut.

"One of those old trees fell and punched a big hole in the main ballroom." Benny went on to explain how they were handling things. "The storm has the guests pretty stirred up."

"I'll be there as soon as I can." He hung up the phone and turned to Isabel. "I have to go back to the hotel." He quickly explained the situation.

"I'm coming with you. If the guests are upset, the more staff on hand, the better."

"Thanks." Grateful for her help, Shane headed out of the bedroom. He paused just outside the doorway. "And later we should talk."

"Let's just worry about the guests for now."

That he'd made a mess of things was abundantly clear
as they raced out to his car. Nor did he get any time to figure out what to say to make things better. The three-mile
drive back to the hotel should've taken less than ten minutes, but with downed branches littering the road and the
heavy winds blowing blinding rain and debris at them,
visibility had diminished so he could barely see three feet
ahead of his front bumper. Shane was forced to creep along
lest he hit something or miss a place where the road had
washed out.

Deciding to take only his vehicle might have been a
blessing or a curse. Granted, it was one fewer car on the
road, but the only time Isabel spoke during the half-hour
trip was to warn him of obstacles in their path. After a dis-
agreement like they'd had, another woman might've taken
the enforced proximity to hammer at him with her anger.
Isabel was unique. She'd obviously set aside her unhappi-
ness in order to cope with the current crisis. This allowed
Shane the space he needed to focus on the road and made
him admire her all the more.

She was a romantic idealist, filled with fantastic plans
for how to make people happy. Her eloquent passion had
touched his cold, dead heart, bringing him to life like a
magical kiss from a princess. Was it any wonder that her
favorite animated movie was *Beauty and the Beast?* With
him cast as the beast to her beauty?

Yet the joy she'd brought into his life hadn't completely
transformed him. When duty called, he was happy to turn
his back on a woman who'd needed to be reassured of his
strong feelings for her. He'd prioritized his career over his
personal life so many times that it was second nature. It
was safe.

Putting out fires. Fixing problems. Maximizing potential. All these things were activities within his con-

trol. They required order and logic. And filled him with satisfaction.

Or they had until he'd let himself be charmed by Isabel's smiles and fanciful ideas of love and romance.

Seeing her smile. Hearing her cry out in passion. Losing himself in her heat. With her he felt invincible and more vulnerable than he ever had. He'd placed the power to tear him apart into her soft, tender hands, and then, like a stubborn fool, he'd snatched it back. No doubt she forgave him for playing games with her, understanding that his behavior was based in fear.

Before she got out of the car she turned to him. "What are we doing?" Even before she finished the question, she was shaking her head. "Never mind," she said, disappointment making her brisk as she fumbled for the door handle. "Forget I asked."

But her velvety hazel eyes begged him to tell her what she meant to him.

He wanted to be honest with her, but fell back on tired platitudes instead. "I never think about my future in terms of a relationship."

That wasn't what he meant to say—not at all. But the thought of her pregnant left him confronting the possibility that he could be a dad. The panic returned, twisting him up and rendering him frozen and searching for answers. What if he didn't have the temperament for parenthood? He sure as hell didn't have a good role model to draw inspiration from.

His instincts told him to rely on Isabel. She'd drawn him to the edge of a cliff, shown him a world of adventure and delight waiting for him to explore. He only had to take a risk and follow her past his comfort zone. Let himself walk beside her into the unknown.

But instead of trusting her to help him, Shane stumbled back.

Gutless bastard.

She deserved to know how she made him feel. Confused. Enthusiastic. Ravenous. All things foreign to a man who ruled his emotions with iron control.

But he wasn't an adventurer, someone who reached for the stars while balanced on the top rung of a wobbly ladder, one step above the sign that warned: This Is Not a Step. Which was exactly why he needed her to inspire him to take risks so he could feel alive.

"I'm sorry. I shouldn't have asked. I told myself not to put you on the spot." Isabel gave a funny, awkward laugh. "It's the weather. All the wind and rain. It has everyone stirred up."

"It's not the weather," he growled.

Although he didn't deserve it, she put her free hand against his cheek and gave him a heartbreaking smile of sympathy and acceptance. "It's okay. Really. I'm a die-hard romantic. I see happy endings for everyone. It's a curse."

"It's a gift," he countered, his tone brooking no argument. He recognized that she often regressed into self-mockery to ease a tense situation, but he couldn't allow her to downplay her greatest strength. "You're a gift."

Her eyes widened at his husky declaration and her throat worked. "Thank you."

And then she was throwing open the car door and flinging herself into the rain-drenched night, leaving their single umbrella behind for him. Thoughts a tumultuous mess, Shane watched her hunched figure disappear through the lobby doors.

What if she was pregnant?

Such a thing would cause his entire life to unravel.

Children deserved green space to run and play, so he'd have to move out of his bachelor pad in downtown Seattle and find a house in the suburbs with a yard and a longer commute because he'd chosen a neighborhood with the best schools. He'd buy a sensible car based on its good safety ratings.

His son or daughter would also demand more of his time, forcing him to rebalance his life, taking fewer business trips, spending less hours at the office, eating dinner at home.

But beyond the physical changes that would affect his home and career, something subtler would take place, as well. He'd no longer be focused on himself. Both Isabel and the child would become permanent fixtures in his world. Any decisions he made would be with them in mind.

In a sudden flash, Shane saw himself sitting on the floor while his child played with building blocks. He pictured himself getting up in the middle of the night to soothe a crying baby, letting Isabel catch up on some much-needed sleep. Side by side they would cheer at soccer games and clap enthusiastically at school plays, take prom photos and team up on game night.

How did he know this was how he'd behave? Because it was the exact opposite of what his father had done.

With his future spooling through his mind like a sentimental TV commercial, the grievances Shane had clung to fell away. He'd sacrificed his twenties to proving his father wrong, burying himself in work to advance his career. His friends had gotten married and started families and he'd drifted away from them, cynically believing that his choices were the right ones. Every promotion, every pay raise had demonstrated that he was the successful one. Never once had he questioned if that was true.

Enough.

The time had come to make some changes in his life. Starting with a certain free-spirited redhead who'd struck a spark and brought him to life.

* * *

Dimly aware that Teresa had left at some point before dawn to check on the ballroom's broken windows, Liam was brought to full wakefulness by the alarm on his phone around seven. He opened his eyes to face an empty suite and the realization that, based on the wild storm the night before and the damage to the hotel, it was pretty clear the Richmond retreat would have to be postponed. Due to her ankle, Teresa had spent the majority of the night on her phone, controlling the chaos from his suite, while Liam had talked to Matt several times, giving him hourly updates.

He had just finished a long hot shower when his phone rang. It was his private investigator.

"Hey," he said, tossing aside the towel he'd been using on his hair. "What's going on? Did you find anything out that connects Teresa and my father?"

"Nothing new. It doesn't seem as if they had any connection in the years between when your parents divorced and when you started seeing her."

Liam greeted this information with a mix of relief and frustration. "There has to be something. My dad wouldn't just give away twenty-five percent of his stock without a damn good reason."

"Well, there is one thing. Did you know that Teresa's father, Nigel St. Claire, worked for Christopher Corporation twenty years ago?"

This was news to Liam. "Doing what?" he asked, remembering that she'd lost her father when she was around six years old.

"He'd been active on some projects. I wasn't able to find out too much because of how spotty the records were from back then."

"And why is this just coming up now?"

"When I couldn't find anything about Teresa, I started looking at her parents."

"And you're sure it was Teresa's father?"

"Positive. He interned during college and then came on full-time once he graduated. There was a note in his file that he'd taken a leave of absence to deal with some family issues and never came back. Do you want me to dig further? See what sort of projects he was working on?"

Did he? A chill of premonition chased down Liam's spine that he quickly dispelled. Chances were his father hadn't known some low-level staffer. The whole thing was nothing more than a coincidence.

"See what you can find out," Liam said before hanging up with the PI.

Why hadn't Teresa ever mentioned that her father had worked for Christopher Corporation? Surely she'd known. Could this explain why his father had given her the stock?

Liam had just completed his packing when his phone rang a second time that morning.

"Tell me it isn't true," his mother demanded.

"Tell you what isn't true?" Liam countered, wishing he hadn't picked up the phone. "Do you know anything about Teresa's father working for Dad?"

His mother seemed confused by the question. "Why would I know anything about that?"

"I thought maybe that explained why Dad would've left her the shares."

"Your father made a fool of himself where that girl was concerned. And so are you." Catherine sounded aggrieved. "Oh, Liam, how could you?"

He decided not to play dumb. "My personal life is my business."

"And mine. What you do affects me." Her voice broke. "I can't have their affair coming up in public."

"There was no proof that they had an affair," Liam corrected her, annoyed that she kept bringing this up. He didn't want to confront his own doubts on the matter. "That was all a misunderstanding."

"And now you're sleeping with her, too."

"It's over."

"Not according to the story I'm reading."

"What story?" Gut twisting in dismay, he flashed back to the meeting between Teresa and Nicolette in the bar.

"And it's not just a story. There are pictures, as well."

Liam closed his eyes and counted to ten. "I'll look into it."

Fourteen

In the wake of the storm, Teresa navigated the chaotic lobby on the crutches the doctor had given her last night, dead smartphone clutched in her hand. People clustered in knots, buzzing about the damage in the aftermath of the storm, making plans to get away as soon as the roads cleared. So much had gone wrong. All her careful planning up in smoke.

Not even Jessie Humphrey at the piano, giving an impromptu concert, could fix what ailed her. As she hobbled past unhappy guests and stressed hotel staff, two things struck her at once. Foremost in her mind was the reality that she urgently needed a new venue for the Richmond retreat. Yet despite the blow to the event and potential damage to her career, she was happier than she'd been in weeks.

Liam had opened up to her in a way she'd never imagined possible following his anger at her for being included in Linus's will. That he'd shared his private concerns about his mother's behavior had touched Teresa's heart. The admission hadn't been easy for him to make and demonstrated that he might be able to move past his distrust of her. As to why that had such a disconcerting impact on her spirits, Teresa wasn't ready to scrutinize.

Approaching the concierge desk, Teresa held up her phone. "I've misplaced my charger. Do you have anywhere I can plug this in?"

Isabel gave her usual affirmative nod and held out her hand. As she plugged in Teresa's phone, the landline on the concierge desk began to ring. Showing no sign of her obvious fatigue from the previous night's wild weather, Isabel offered a bright greeting to the caller. After listening for several seconds, she caught Teresa's eye and mouthed the words *Matt Richmond*.

"Yes, it was a crazy evening," Isabel said. "But no one was seriously hurt, and Shane rallied the troops to get tarps in place over the damaged areas and has already spoken with the insurance adjusters."

When Teresa raised her eyebrows at how much information Isabel possessed regarding Shane's activities, a rosy color bloomed on the concierge's cheeks, but there was no sign of her usual happy smile.

"That's because her cell phone died at some point last night," Isabel explained. "She's standing right here. I can put her on." Isabel extended the phone to Teresa.

"Hello, Matt," Teresa began, bracing herself for the conversation to come.

"I've gathered from Liam and Shane's reports that things are under control, but still chaotic." The CEO sounded tense and on edge.

"Shane is on top of everything having to do with the property." Teresa glanced toward the front doors, where a woman was berating a valet for the dent her car sustained during the storm. Before things spiraled out of control, Shane arrived on the scene and calmed the woman within minutes. "And he's been smoothing things with the guests. Everyone is pretty upset."

"Obviously the party will have to be postponed."

"I'm afraid so. I've already started looking for a new venue." She didn't add that the first three places she'd contacted were booked solid for the next two months.

"I appreciate your quick response to the situation."

"Of course." After all, this party's success was going to give her company a major boost. "Do you have a date in mind for the retreat to be rescheduled?"

"Not at the moment. Perhaps we can schedule a meeting at my office to discuss it after you settle everything there."

"Sure. I was planning on heading back to Seattle tomorrow." Meanwhile she'd get Corrine to start a list of potential locations.

"I'm sorry I'm not there to deal with my guests. Nadia and I are still planning to arrive this morning," Matt said, surprising Teresa with the apology. "It was my party. You shouldn't have to bear the brunt of everyone's displeasure over how things turned out."

His concern touched her. "I appreciate that, but dealing with problems is part of what you hired me to do."

"Still, I want you to know that I understand the difficult position I put you in."

"Thank you." The conversation gave her hope that whatever challenges she faced next during her scramble to pull together a whole new event, he wouldn't judge her too harshly. "I'll let you know when I get back to Seattle. Hopefully I'll have a replacement venue by then."

She hung up the phone and glanced at her cell. Enough battery life had been replaced to wake the phone. Without unplugging it, she cued up her main screen and noticed she had a dozen missed calls. Surprised it wasn't more, Teresa checked to see who'd tried to get ahold of her.

Joshua had called her five times last night. Five! Teresa's

heart contracted in fear. Nothing for weeks and now this sudden flurry of calls. That couldn't be good. She dialed his number and fumed when the call rolled to his voice mail. She left a brief explanation of the storm and told him to call her back. Then she went to the messages to see if he'd left her a voice mail, only to see he hadn't.

Panic and annoyance fought for domination as she wondered what had inspired his urgent attempts to get ahold of her. The last time she'd spoken with Joshua, he said he had everything under control. Guilt threaded through her anxiety. Her chest tightened, making breathing difficult. Joshua was her brother. Her responsibility. And now she couldn't reach him.

Teresa glanced at her phone, debating whether to reach out to the Fixer again. She already owed him one favor. Could she afford two? She certainly couldn't ask Liam for help again. The battery indicator glowed red with warning. How much time did she have to deal with this new problem? She shivered, remembering her turmoil when she believed her brother had been kidnapped. That hoax reminded her to question everything about her brother's current situation.

That realization sparked a new revelation. Her cynicism gave her new insight into Liam's knee-jerk reactions. When the truth has been twisted over and over, how do you know what to believe? She'd only been dealing with Joshua's latest escapades for a few weeks. What would it be like to spend your entire life forced to sort out conflicting stories from people you loved and trusted?

As if her thoughts had drawn him to her, Teresa spied Liam striding in her direction. The shifting crowd filling the hotel lobby made his path irregular and offered Teresa ample time to survey his tall form. Her spirits executed a familiar somersault as their gazes met, but just as quickly she picked up on his tension and her skin prickled with uneasiness. She recognized that grim look, having seen it all too often in the last several weeks.

"We have to talk," he said, tension compressing his tone into a growl.

Isabel barely noticed when the wind and rain stopped around dawn. Operating by the glow of the emergency lights, she'd spent the night making herself useful wherever she could from dealing with the guests who'd come to the front desk demanding to know when the power was going to come back on, to pitching in with room-to-room checks to make sure people were okay.

Later, she and Aspen had huddled in a corner of the ballroom and stared at the devastation as the maintenance guys did their best to remove the tree and tack tarps over the massive hole. In her friend's eyes, Isabel glimpsed the grim reality that months and months of events would have to be canceled. All Aspen's hard work and planning plus the stress for the brides who could no longer look forward to their dream weddings at the hotel as well as the revenue the hotel would lose from corporate events.

Through the night and into the morning, while Isabel worked, her thoughts were never far from Shane. The last week had been a whirlwind. She'd never imagined Shane would be so good for her career or her personal life. He made her happier than she'd ever known. She'd fallen in love with him despite his being a stubborn, disciplined realist. In fact, it was his inflexibility and tunnel vision when it came to work that proved just how much he needed her.

But now that she'd glimpsed his sharp resistance to the things she wanted for her future, could she stay with him? Should she? Her heart told her he could change his mind. In less than two weeks he'd already become a less controlled, more lighthearted version of himself. Was it possible he could fully transform into the man she'd glimpsed over the last few days? The one who communicated and was considerate of her needs. Who smiled more and bent the rules.

Yet Teresa's warning about Shane had planted a seed that sent deep roots of doubt into her soul. In the aftermath of how he reacted when the condom broke, could she ever fully trust that he wouldn't wake up one day and regret that their time together had distracted him from what he believed was important?

Isabel recognized that it wasn't like her to go dark when so many things about life filled her with joy and enthusiasm, but had she ever been out on a ledge as far as she let herself go with Shane Adams? He obviously wasn't going to stop being the man he was. She'd been a fool to think she could sway him with a few romantic walks in the woods and some good food. What if she was little more than a brief distraction?

Still, part of her rebelled at the thought of giving up on him. It wasn't like her to ignore a challenge. Even when that challenge made her feel the same frightened panic as when she'd overheard her father regret that he'd ever had a family? Those words were burned into her six-year-old psyche. Even though she'd fought to rise above the harsh sentiment, despite dedicating herself to all things good and fun and romantic and fantastic, her father's scorn was always in the back of her mind.

Shane didn't have her coping skills. He'd spent much of his adult life shutting down his emotions. He might never be open to love. Could she live with that?

She recalled his text in the wake of her career tailspin after learning Camilla Maxwell was going to become the hotel's romance concierge. We need to talk. Had they ever had the conversation he initiated? She'd hijacked the discussion with what Tom had told her. What had followed had involved lots of amazing sex and that dreamy isolation all new lovers fall into.

So, what had he intended to discuss with her?

Shane strolled into The Opulence's lobby to get a fresh cup of coffee. He'd lost track of how much caffeine he'd consumed since arriving at the hotel last night. Matt Richmond was en route to the hotel to survey the situation, but in the meantime, the staff was dealing with their anxious guests and trying to ensure that word got out to those who hadn't yet arrived that the whole retreat had been canceled.

The mood among the guests had brightened as the storm moved on, aided by the impromptu concert being given by Jessie Humphrey. The star sat at the piano, running through her vast repertoire, her gorgeous voice filling the lobby with tales of big love and excruciating loss. As the lyrics flowed over him, Shane mulled over what had occurred over the last couple of weeks that had led to the changes currently taking place in his perception.

The catalyst for his transformation stood near a pillar, listening with all her heart to Jessie Humphrey. Shane headed her way. The expression on her face was so beautiful that his heart flipped in his chest. He simply couldn't wait another second to tell her the impact she'd made on his life.

"Listen," he began, stopping beside her. "About earlier."

She shook her head vigorously. "Not now. I'm in the best place I could be right at the moment. This is my favorite song of Jesse's. I just want to listen to her sing."

Shane noted this bit of data into the mental file where he cataloged Isabel's favorite things. Never before had he paid such keen attention to what a woman wanted or needed. Isabel was different. She did so much for everyone else. He wanted to return the favor. To create special moments for her. So, instead of intruding, he stood beside her, resisting the urge to seek physical contact, and listened with his heart wide open.

When applause broke out at the end of the song, Isabel turned to him. "Last night you didn't give me a chance to explain." Beneath her calm, reasonable tone was a thread of pain. "You didn't give me a chance to get a word in edgewise. Instead you just went on and on about how horrible it was that I might be pregnant, insinuating that you might be forced to have me in your life longer than you'd anticipated."

"That's not what I meant at all."

Isabel shook her head, not letting him sidestep with excuses. "I'm not a fool. I know real panic when I see it. You can handle anything that gets thrown at you in your career, but one broken condom…" Her words came quickly as angry color rushed into her cheeks. She sucked in a breath and let it out slowly. "One broken condom sends you into a tailspin."

Shane resented the depiction of his reaction, but she deserved to be angry. For several seconds he'd been blind with panic. "I'm sorry," he said. This was being in a relationship. Listening and respect. "You had something to say. I didn't give you the chance."

"I didn't freak out." She crossed her arms over her chest and jut out her chin, wordlessly challenging whether he was ready to hear her out. "Because I'm not going to get pregnant."

A familiar worry rose in him, but pushed it down. He couldn't react to data and make decisions without considering how it might emotionally impact the next person. He needed to hear her out and discuss what was bothering him.

"How is it that you know?"

"Because I'm on the pill. I have been for years. I have heavy periods and became anemic because of them. The doctors recommended birth control." She assessed his reaction through narrowed eyes. "I'll spare you the explanation how that works."

Shane decided most men would be uncomfortable when confronted by talk of periods and bleeding so he kept his response to an understanding nod.

"I probably should've said something early on," she continued, "but we didn't know each other that well and condoms are always a good idea."

Utilizing nonverbal cues to communicate that he was following her was the perfect decision. Better that he not speak until he was clear what would make him sound intelligent and supportive.

"So you don't have to worry." She paused, and her grief struck him like a bat to the gut. "Because I know what a big deal that would be for you. It would just destroy your life."

Although her inflection hadn't changed, her words told him that his behavior had damaged her trust. And he suspected that he'd have to go to great lengths to repair it.

"It would change my life," he agreed, taking her hand, relieved when she didn't pull free. "But I'd be open to it."

"Since when?" she grumbled. Hope flickered in her eyes and was quickly extinguished.

"You put a spell on me," he said.

"That's…" She looked nonplussed. "I wasn't trying to."

"Weren't you?" He'd thought about this long and hard. "Your whole plan was to make me fall in love with you. The marketing strategy was nothing but a ploy."

She gaped at him for several seconds before sputtering, "That's not true." But the way her gaze dodged away from his said there was more to it than that.

"You played like you were appealing to my business side because if you'd told me that you were out to seduce me, I would've run like hell." He paused to offer her a chance to deny it. "Right?"

"Me, seduce you?" She laughed. "As if I could."

After everything that had happened between them, she really had no sense of her appeal. "Why would you doubt how much I want you?"

"You made it pretty clear you thought I needed to broaden my horizons. I knew I wasn't the sort of sophisticated woman you're used to." As if suddenly aware that they were holding hands, she tried to tug free.

Shane tightened his hold and brought their clasped hands to his chest. "So, what did you think we were doing?"

"I guess I thought it was a fling while you were in the area for the Richmond retreat." She stared at his chin. "I mean, you were pretty clear about your priorities."

He wasn't sure he was fully buying her claim of a fling. Then again, it hadn't occurred to Shane until that moment that Isabel might not feel as strongly about him as he did about her. After all, the reason she'd been angry with him once before had been due to Tom's handling of the romance concierge situation. That time, Shane had thought she was mad because he hadn't called her after their first time together.

"Then why did you get angry at how I reacted to the condom breaking?"

She gave an exasperated sigh. "Because I thought you'd just drift out of my life. Stop calling. That I could've handled. Watching a man panic at the thought of having gotten her pregnant is not any woman's idea of a great way to end an evening."

"Is that what you want?" As he asked the question, white-hot agony invaded his chest. "For me to drift out of your life? Stop calling?"

"Of course not." She stared at their clasped hands. "But maybe where we are now is a good place to call it quits."

She was giving him an out. All he had to do was agree

and they could part as friends. He could go back to business as usual. Long hours. Lots of travel. Eating alone.

The lifestyle he'd embraced because he wanted to prove his dad wrong. Stupid. He shouldn't care what that sorry excuse for a parental authority thought about him. Shane took in the woman standing before him, remembering all the times her gaze had reflected joy and passion and respect for him. Did he really believe there was a better mirror in the world than Isabel's gorgeous hazel eyes?

"I don't want to call it quits," he growled, throat seizing at the thought of ever losing her. "Not now. Not ever."

A tear caught on her lashes as she glanced up at him. "Don't say it unless you mean it," she whispered. "I couldn't take it."

Not giving a damn who saw, he swept his arm around her waist and brought her tight against him. Cupping her cheek, he brought his lips to hers and kissed her with all his heart and soul. She made a sound like a sob and opened herself to him. Joy radiated from her, flooding his senses. Pieces clicked into place inside him. He was whole for the first time in forever.

Filled with absolute peace and belonging, he broke off the kiss and nuzzled her ear. "I love you."

She jerked back and raked his expression with her doubts. After several rapid heartbeats, disbelief morphed into astonishment.

"You do," she murmured, placing her palm against his cheek. "You really do. I love you, too. I've been falling for you for a year. I just never imagined…" Her words faded into a husky chuckle. "You love me."

"How could I not? Thanks to you I no longer want to bury myself in work and avoid the things that could truly make me happy, like you and our future together. I may not always be comfortable sharing my emotions, but you are the perfect woman to help me with that."

"But, Shane, after all the time and energy you've put into building your career with Richmond Hotel Group, can you just decide to have a personal life?"

He saw the point she was trying to make and the reassurance she needed. "I've given enough to the company. I want to make time for myself. For us."

"Us," she repeated, her smile blooming. "I really like the sound of that."

"So, how do we begin our new life together?"

"I have some vacation time I still need to use up before the end of the year," she said. "Maybe I can come to Seattle and we can play house for a week. I'll be your fifties housewife, waiting at home to greet you, wearing a flowered apron and carrying chilled martinis."

"Or you could pick your top fantasy destination and we could go there."

Wonder bloomed on Isabel's face, causing Shane's heart to pound. Making her happy was going to become a top priority for him. Now he understood why she took such satisfaction from giving other people their dream moments. The joy came right back.

"You'd do that for me?" She wrapped herself around his arm, giddy with delight. "You'd take time off?"

"I'd do that for us." He dipped his head and kissed her lips. "We're a team from now on. I just want to make you happy."

She slid her fingers into his hair and held him close. "You already do."

Epilogue

Teresa recoiled from Liam's displeasure. What had gone wrong? His tight gaze raked over her face, leading her to suspect something had blown up and he distrusted her again. How could he do this to her after last night? Was he regretting giving her a glimpse into his troubled past? In the cold light of day, was the vulnerability too much for him to bear?

As if in slow motion, she could see what was coming. He was poised to take it all back. To push her away. To reject their intimacy. To retreat into skepticism and doubt.

This time, she was not having it. She could not bear to have Liam toss her aside again. He didn't get to hold all the cards. To dictate the ebb and flow of their relationship. To give and withhold affection because he was angry or hurt or suspicious. To take her needs and emotions for granted.

Hiding her pain and longing behind annoyance, she held up her hand. "Let me start. You don't have to say a word, Liam. Last night was crazy. We connected on a new level, but that doesn't mean it's going anywhere." As she shrugged offhandedly, Teresa knew she was giving the greatest performance of her life. "We're good in bed together and as fun as it's been, I'm really not looking for more."

Liam's eyes widened as her words landed. This was clearly not the reaction he'd anticipated and shutters slammed down over his expression. Obviously he wasn't relieved that she'd beaten him to the punch. No doubt she'd dented his pride. Teresa felt a sick rush of satisfaction followed almost immediately by despair. This wasn't her. She didn't save her dignity by making situations worse. She fixed problems. Made people feel joy and delight.

Still, a hint of uncertainty made her second-guess her reaction. Wouldn't she have done a better job of handling things if she'd let him have his say before throwing their fledgling romance under the bus?

Her phone buzzed and, hoping it was her brother trying to reach out to her again, Teresa glanced down at the screen. To her dismay, the message was from Corrine and carried an urgency she couldn't ignore.

911

Grinding her teeth in irritation at being interrupted during a key moment of personal discovery and transformation, Teresa nevertheless couldn't resist the pull of responsibility. She keyed up the message and stared at the link Corrine had shared.

The headline stopped her breath.

MOGUL'S TORRID AFFAIR WITH FATHER'S MISTRESS ENDS AFTER HER SURPRISE INHERITANCE REVEALED.

"Did you do this?" She held up her phone so Liam could read the screen. From his lack of surprise, she realized this is what he'd come to talk to her about. "No, this isn't your style," she corrected herself. "But you think I was somehow involved."

"I saw you talking to Nicolette Ryan."

Her first impulse was to explain that part of her job involved coordinating with reporters who were covering newsworthy events like the Richmond retreat.

"You know what, I don't have time for this. You think I'm untrustworthy, but I think you're afraid that we were starting to make a connection." Distantly Teresa realized that her impassioned words contradicted the declaration she'd made seconds earlier about it being all hot sex and nothing more between them. "Intimacy scares the hell out of you because you don't like feeling exposed and out of control. Well, that's your stuff to deal with. I'm done trying to prove myself to you. From here on out, the only contact I want to have with you is about my shares in Christopher Corporation."

And with that, she pivoted on her heel and walked away before he glimpsed the hot tears that flooded her eyes, turning her world into an indistinguishable, uncertain mess.

* * * * *

THE BILLIONAIRE'S BARGAIN

NAIMA SIMONE

To Gary. 143.

One

Delilah. Jezebel. Yoko. Monica.

According to past and recent history, they were all women who'd supposedly brought down a powerful man. Isobel Hughes silently snorted. Many of the people inside this North Shore mansion would include her name on that tarnished list.

Swallowing a sigh, she started up the stairs of the pillared mansion that wouldn't be out of place in the French countryside. Sitting on acres of meticulously landscaped grounds, the structure screamed decadence and obscene wealth. And though only a couple of hours' travel separated it from her tiny South Deering apartment, those minutes and miles might as well be years and states.

I can do this. I have no choice *but to do this.*

Quietly dragging in another deep breath, she paused as the tall, wide stained-glass doors opened to reveal an imposing gentleman dressed in black formal wear. His tuxedo might fit him perfectly, but Isobel didn't mistake him for who, or what, he was: security.

Security to protect the rarefied elite of Chicago high society and keep the riffraff out of the Du Sable City Gala.

Nerves tumbled and jostled inside her stomach like exes battling it out. Because she was a member of the riffraff who would be booted out on her common ass if she were discovered.

Fixing a polite but aloof mask on her face, she placed the expected invitation into the guard's outstretched hand as if it were a Golden Ticket. As he inspected the thick ivory paper with its gold engraved wording, she held her breath and resisted the urge to swipe her damp palms down the floor-length black gown she'd found at a consignment shop. Once upon a time, that invitation would've been authentic. But that had been when she'd been married to Gage Wells, golden child of the Wells family, one of Chicago's oldest and wealthiest lineages. When she'd believed Gage had been her handsome prince, the man who loved her as much as she'd adored him. Before she'd realized her prince was worse than a frog—he was a snake with a forked tongue.

She briefly closed her eyes. The present needed all of her focus. And with Gage dead these past two years and her exiled from the social circle she'd never belonged in, the present required that she resort to deception. Her brother's highly illegal skills were usually employed for forged IDs such as driver's licenses, birth certificates and passports for the city's more criminal element, not counterfeit invites to Chicago's balls. But he'd come through, and as the security guard scanned the invitation and waved a hand in front of him, she whispered a thanks to her brother.

The music that had sounded subdued outside seemed to fill the space here. Whimsical notes of flutes and powerful, bright chords of violins reverberated off the white marble walls. Gold tiles graced the floor, ebbing out in the shape of a flowering lotus, and a huge crystal-and-gold chande-lier suspended from the glass ceiling seemed to be a deli-cate waterfall over that bloom. Two sets of staircases with gilded, intricate railings curved away from the walls and ascended to the next level of the home.

And she was stalling. Ogling her surroundings only de-layed the inevitable.

And the inevitable awaited her down the hall, where music and chatter and laughter drifted. All too soon, she approached the wide entrance to the ballroom, and the glass doors opened wide in invitation.

But instead of feeling welcomed, nausea roiled and shud-dered in her belly.

You can still turn around and leave. It's not too late.

The tiny whisper inside her head offered a lifeline she desperately wanted to grasp.

But then an image of her son wavered across her mind's eye, invoking an overwhelming swell of love. The thought of Aiden never failed to grasp her heart and squeeze it. He was a gift—*her* gift. And she would do anything—suffer anything—for him.

Including seeking out her dead husband's family and throwing her pride at the feet of the people who despised her. She'd committed the cardinal sins of being poor and falling for their golden child.

Well, she'd paid for that transgression. In spades.

Over the last couple of years, she'd reached out to her husband's family through email and old-fashioned snail mail, sending them pictures of Aiden, offering updates. But every email bounced back, and every letter was returned to the sender. They hadn't wanted anything to do with her or with the beautiful boy they considered her bastard.

She wanted nothing more than to forget their existence, just as they'd wiped hers out of their minds. But to keep a roof over Aiden's head, to ensure he didn't have to shiver in

the increasingly chilly October nights or go to sleep hungry
as she debated which overdue bill to pay, she would risk
the wrath and derision of the Wells family.

The mental picture of her baby when she'd left him tonight—safe and happy with her mom—extinguished her
flare of panic. Because it wouldn't do to enter these doors
scared. The guests in this home would sense that weakness. And like sharks with bloody chum, they would circle
and attack. Devour.

Inhaling yet another deep breath, she moved forward.
Armored herself with pride. Ready to do battle.

Because she could never forget. This was indeed a battle.
One she couldn't afford to lose.

Hell no. It can't be.

Darius King tightened his fingers on the champagne
flute in his hand, the fragile stem in danger of snapping.

Shock and disbelief blasted him like the frigid winds
of a Chicago winter storm, freezing him in place. Motionless, he stared at the petite brunette across the ballroom as
she smiled at a waiter and accepted her own glass of wine.
Though he'd only met her a couple of times, he recognized
that smile. Remembered the shyness in it. Remembered
the lush, sensual curve of the mouth that belied that hint
of coy innocence.

Isobel fucking Hughes.

Not Wells. He refused to honor her with the last name
she'd schemed and lied to win, then defiled for the two
years she'd been married to his best friend. She didn't deserve to wear that name. Never had.

Rage roared through him, incinerating the astonishment
that had paralyzed him. Only fury remained. Fury at her
gall. Fury at the bold audacity it required to walk into this
mansion as if she belonged here. As if she hadn't destroyed

a man and dragged his grieving, ravaged family to the very brink of destruction.

"Oh, my God." Beside him, Gabriella Wells gasped, her fingers curling around his biceps and digging deep. "Is that…"

"Yes," Darius growled, unable to soften his tone for Gage's sister, whom he cared for as if she were his own sibling. "It's her."

"What is she doing here?" Gabriella snarled, the same anger that had gripped him darkening her lovely features. "How did she even manage to get in?"

"I have no idea."

But he'd find out. And asses would be kicked when he did. The security here was supposed to be tighter than that of the goddamn royal family's, considering the people in attendance: politicians, philanthropists, celebrities, the country's wealthiest business people. Yet evidence that the security team wasn't worth shit stood in this very room, sipping champagne.

"How could she dare show her face here? Hell, *in Chicago*?" Gabriella snapped. "I thought we were rid of her when she left for California. No doubt whatever sucker she attached herself to finally got tired of her and kicked the gold-digging bitch out. And she's probably here to suck Dad and Mother dry. I swear to God…" She didn't finish the thought, but charged forward, her intentions clear.

"No." He encircled her arm, his hold gentle but firm. Gabriella halted, shooting him a let-me-go-now-dammit glance over her shoulder. Fire lit the emerald gaze that reminded him so much of Gage's. At twenty-four, she was six years younger than her older brother, and had adored him. And though she'd been in college, studying abroad for most of her brother's marriage, tales of her sister-in-law had reached her all the way in England, and Gabriella despised the woman who'd hurt Gage so badly.

Darius shook his head in reply to her unspoken demand of freedom. "No," he repeated. "We're not causing a scene. And running over there and confronting her will do just that. Think of your parents, Gabriella," he murmured.

The anger didn't bleed from her expression at the reminder, but concern banked the flames in her eyes to a simmer, and the thin, grim line of her mouth softened. Neither of them needed to voice the worry that Darius harbored. Gabriella and Gage's father, Baron Wells, had suffered a heart attack the previous year. Nothing could convince Darius that it hadn't been grief over his son's death in a sudden car accident that had precipitated the attack, added to long work hours, poor eating habits and a lax exercise regimen.

The last several months had finally seen the return of the imposing, dignified man Darius had known and admired all of his life. Still, a sense of fragility stubbornly clung to Baron. A fragility Darius feared could escalate into something more threatening if Baron glimpsed his dead son's widow.

"I'll go and find security so they can escort her out," he said, the calm in his voice a mockery of the rage damn near consuming him. "You can locate your parents to make sure they don't realize what's going on."

Yes, he'd have Isobel Hughes thrown out, but not before he had a few words with her. The deceitful, traitorous woman should've counted herself lucky that he hadn't come after her when she'd skipped town two years ago. But with the Wells family shattered over their son and brother's death, they'd been his first priority. And as long as Isobel had remained gone, they didn't have to suffer a daily reminder of the woman who'd destroyed Gage with her manipulations and faithlessness. In spite of the need to mete out his own brand of justice, Darius had allowed her to disappear with the baby the Wells family doubted was their grandson and nephew. But now…

Now she'd reappeared, and all bets were off.

She'd thrown down the gauntlet, and fuck if he wouldn't enjoy snatching it up.

"Okay," Gabriella agreed, enclosing his hand in hers and squeezing. "Darius," she whispered. He tore his attention away from Isobel and transferred it to Gabriella. "Thank you for…" She swallowed. "Thank you," she breathed.

"No need for any of that," he replied, brushing a kiss over the top of her black curls. "Family. We always take care of one another."

She nodded, then turned and disappeared into the throng of people.

Anticipation hummed beneath his skin as he moved forward. Several people slowed his progress for meaningless chatter, but he didn't deter from his path. He tracked her, noting that she'd moved from just inside the entrance to one of the floor-to-ceiling glass doors that led to a balcony. Good. The only exit led out onto that balcony, and the temperature of the October night had probably dropped even more since he'd arrived. She wouldn't venture through those doors and into the cold. He had a location to give security.

It was unfair that a woman who possessed zero morals and conscience should exhibit none of it on her face or her body. But then, if her smooth, golden skin or slender-but-curvaceous body did reveal any of her true self, she wouldn't be able to snare men in her silken web.

Long, thick, dark brown hair that gleamed with hints of auburn fire under the chandelier's light flowed over one slim shoulder and a just-less-than-a-handful breast. Dispassionately, he scanned her petite frame. The strapless, floor-length black gown clung to her, lifting her full curves so a hint of shadowed cleavage teased, promised. A waist that a man—not him—could span with his hands flowed into rounded hips and a tight, worship-worthy ass that he didn't need to see to remember. Even when he'd first met her—as the only witness and friend at her and Gage's quickie court-house marriage—it'd amazed him how such a small woman could possess curves so dangerous they should come with a blaring warning sign. Back then he'd appreciated her curves. Now he despised them for what they truly were—an enticing lure to trap unsuspecting game.

Dragging his inspection up the siren call of her body, he took in the delicate bones that provided the structure for an almost elfin face. One of his guilty pleasures was fantasy novels and movies. Tolkien, Martin, Rowling, King. And he could easily imagine Arwen, half-Elven daughter of King Elrond in *The Lord of the Rings*, resembling Isobel. Beautiful. Ethereal. Though he couldn't catch the color of her eyes from this distance, he clearly recalled their striking color. A vivid and startling blue-gray that only enhanced the impression of otherworldly fragility. But then there was her mouth. It splintered her air of innocence. The shade-too-wide lips with their full, plump curves called to mind ragged, hoarse groans in the darkest part of night. Yeah, those lips could cause a man's cock to throb.

He ground his teeth together, the minute flare of pain along his jaw grounding him. It didn't ease the stab of guilt over the sudden, unexpected clench of lust in his gut. He could hate himself for that gut-punch of desire. Didn't he, more than anyone, know that a pretty face could hide the black, empty hole where a heart should be? Could conceal the blackest of souls? His own ex-wife had taught him that lesson, and he'd received straight fucking A's. Yeah, his dick might be slow on the uptake, but his head—the one that ruled him, contrary to popular opinion about men—possessed full disclosure and was fully aware.

Isobel Hughes was one of those pretty faces.

As if she'd overheard her name in his head, Isobel lifted her chin and surveyed the crowded ballroom. Probably searching for Baron and Helena. If she thought he'd allow her within breathing space of Gage's parents, she'd obviously been smoking too much of that legalized California weed. He'd do anything to protect them; he'd failed to protect Gage, and that knowledge gnawed at him, an open wound that hadn't healed in two years. No way in hell would this woman have another shot at the people he loved. At his family.

The thought propelled him forward. Time to end this and escort her back to whatever hole she'd crawled out of.

Clenching his jaw, he worked his way to the ballroom entrance. Several minutes later, he waited in one of the side hallways for the head of security. Glancing down at his watch, he frowned. The man should've arrived already...

Darkness.

Utter darkness.

Dimly, Darius caught the sound of startled cries and shouts, but the deafening pounding of his heart muted most of the fearful noise.

He stumbled backward, and his spine smacked the wall behind him. Barely able to draw a breath into his constricted lungs, he frantically patted his jacket and then his pants pockets for his cell phone. Nothing. *Damn.* He must've left it in the car. He never left his phone. Never...

The thick blackness surrounded him. Squeezed him so that he jerked at his bow tie, clawing at material that seconds ago had been perfectly comfortable.

Air.

He needed air.

But all he inhaled, all he swallowed, was more of the obsidian viscosity that clogged his nostrils, throat and chest.

In the space of seconds, his worst, most brutal nightmare had come to life.

He was trapped in the dark.

Alone.

And he was drowning in it.

Two

*B*lackout.

Malfunction. Doors locked.

Remain calm.

The words shouted in anything but calm voices outside the bathroom door bombarded Isobel. Perched on the settee in the outer room of the ladies' restroom, she hunched over her cell phone, which had only 2 percent battery life left.

"C'mon," she ordered her fingers to cooperate as she fumbled over the text keyboard. In her nerves, she kept misspelling words, and *damn autocorrect*, it kept "fixing" the words that were actually right. Finally she finished her message and hit send.

Mom, is everything okay? How is Aiden?

Fingers clutching the little burner phone, she—not for the first time—wished she could afford a regular cell. But with her other responsibilities, that bill had been one of the first things she'd cut. Constantly buying minutes and battling a battery that didn't hold a charge presented a hassle, but the prepaid phone did the job. After seconds that seemed like hours, a message popped up on the screen.

He's fine, honey. Sleeping. We're all good. Stay put. It's a blackout and we've been advised to remain inside. I love you and take care of yourself.

Relief washed over Isobel in a deluge. If she hadn't already been sitting down, she would've sunk to the floor. For the first time since the world had plunged into darkness, she could breathe.

After several moments, she located the flashlight app and aimed it in the direction of where she believed the door to be. The deep blackness seemed to swallow up the light, but she spied the handle and sighed. Without ventilation, the area was growing stuffy. The hallway had to be better. At the very least, she wouldn't feel like the walls were closing in on her. Claustrophobia had never been a problem for her, but this was enough to have anyone on edge.

She grabbed the handle and pulled the door open, the weak beam illuminating the floor only feet in front of her. As soon as she stepped out into the hall, the light winked, then disappeared.

"No, not yet," she muttered, flipping the phone over. But, nope, the cell had died. "Dammit."

Frustration and not-a-little fear scrabbled up her chest, lodging there. Inhaling a deep breath and holding it, she forced herself to calm down. Okay. One thing her two years in Los Angeles had granted her was a sense of direction. The ballroom lay to the left. Follow the wall until it gave way to the small alcove and the side entrance she'd exited.

No problem. She could do this.

Probably.

Maybe.

Releasing that same gulp of air, she shuffled forward, hands groping until they knocked against the wall. Step one down.

With halting steps, she slid along, palms flattened, skimming. The adjacent corridor shouldn't be too far…

Her chest bumped into a solid object seconds after her hands collided with it. A person. A big person, if the width of the shoulders and chest under her fingers were anything to go by.

"Oh, God. I'm sorry." She snatched her arms back. Heat soared up her neck and poured into her face. She'd just felt up a man in the dark.

Horrified, she shifted backward, but her heel caught on the hem of her dress, and she pitched forward. Slamming against that same hard expanse of muscles she'd just molested. "*Dammit*. I—"

The second apology drifted away as a hoarse, ragged sound penetrated the darkness and reached her ears. For a long moment, she froze, her hands splayed wide over the stranger's chest. It rapidly rose and fell, the pace unnatural. She jerked her head up, staring into the space where his face should've been. But she didn't need to glimpse his features to understand this man suffered some kind of distress. Because those rough, serrated, *wounded* sounds originated from him.

The urge to comfort, to stop those god-awful moans overrode all embarrassment at having touched him without his permission. At this moment, she needed to touch him. To ease his pain.

As she slid one palm over his jackhammering heart, she swept the other over his shoulder and down his arm until she enclosed his long fingers in hers. Then she murmured, "Hi. Talk about an awkward meet cute, right? Citywide blackout. Get felt up in the hallway. Sounds like the beginning of a rom-com starring Ryan Reynolds."

The man didn't reply, and his breathing continued to sough out of his lungs, but his fingers curled around hers, clutching them tight. As if she were his lifeline.

Relief and determination to tow him away from whatever tormented him swelled within her. It didn't require a PhD in psychology to figure out that this man was in the throes of a panic attack. But she had zero experience with how to handle that situation. Still, he'd responded to her voice, her presence. So she'd continue talking.

"Do you know who Ryan Reynolds is?" She didn't wait for his answer but kept babbling. "*The Green Lantern*? *Deadpool*? I'm leading with those movies, because if you're anything like my brother, if I'd have said *The Proposal*, you would've stared at me like I'd suddenly started speaking Mandarin. Well…that is, if you *could* stare at me right now." She snickered. "What I wouldn't give for Riddick's eyes right now. To be able to see in the dark? Although you could keep Slam City and, ya know, the murder. Have you ever seen *Pitch Black* or *The Chronicles of Riddick*?"

This time she received a squeeze of her fingers and a slight change in the coarseness of his breathing. A grin curved her lips. Good. That had to be a positive sign, right?

"*The Chronicles of Riddick*? I enjoyed watching Vin Diesel for two hours, but the movie? Meh. *Pitch Black*, though, was amazing. One of the best sci-fi movies ever. Only beat out by *Aliens* and *The Matrix*. Although I still maintain that *The Matrix Revolutions* never happened, just as *Dirty Dancing 2* is a dirty rumor. They're like Voldemort. Those Movies That Shall Not Be Named."

A soft, shaky chuckle drifted above her, but seemed to echo in the dark, empty hallway like a sonic boom. Probably because she'd been aching to hear it. Not that she'd been aware of that need until this moment.

An answering laugh bubbled up inside her, but she shoved it back down, opting to continue with what had been working so far. Talking. The irony that this was the longest conversation she'd indulged in with a person outside of her family in two years wasn't lost on her. Cruel experience had taught her to be wary of strangers, especially those with pretty faces wielding charm like a Highlander's claymore. The last time she'd trusted a beautiful appearance, she'd ended up in a loveless, controlling, soul-stealing sham of a marriage.

But in the dark…

In the dark lived a kind of freedom where she could lose her usual restrictions, step out of the protective box she'd created for her life. Because here, she couldn't see this man, and he couldn't see her. There was no judgment. If he were attending the Du Sable City Gala, then that meant he most likely came from wealth—the kind of wealth that had once trapped her in a gilded prison. Yet in this corridor in the middle of a blackout, money, status, lineage traced back to the Mayflower—none of that mattered. Here, they were only two people holding on to each other to make it through.

"My next favorite sci-fi is *Avatar*. Which is kind of funny, considering the famous line from the movie is 'I see you.'" She couldn't smother her laughter. And didn't regret the display of amusement when it garnered another squeeze of her hand. "Do you have a favorite?"

She held her breath, waiting. Part of her waited to see if his panic attack had finally passed. But the other part of her wanted—no, *needed*—to hear his voice. That part wondered if it would match his build.

Being tucked away in a mansion's dark hallway in a blackout…the insane circumstances had to be the cause of her desire. Because it'd been years since she'd been curious about anything regarding a man.

"The Terminator."

Oh. Wow. That voice. Darker than the obsidian blanket that draped the city. Deeper than the depths of the ocean she sorely missed. Sin wrapped in the velvet embrace of sweet promise.

A dangerous voice.

One that invited a person to commit acts that might shame them in the light of day, acts a person would revel in during the secretive, shadowed hours of night.

Her eyes fluttered closed, and her lips parted, as if she could breathe in that slightly abraded yet smooth tone. As if she could taste it.

As if she could taste him.

What the hell?

The inane thought rebounded against the walls of her skull, and she couldn't evict it. Her eyes flew open, and she stared wide into nothing. For the second time that evening, she thanked God. At this moment, she offered her gratitude because she couldn't be seen. That no one had witnessed her unprecedented, humiliating reaction to a man's *voice*.

"A classic." She struggled to recapture and keep hold of the light, teasing note she'd employed with him BTV. Before The Voice. "But I take your *Terminator* and one-up you with *Predator*."

A scoff. "That wasn't sci-fi."

Isobel frowned even though he couldn't see her disapproval. "Are you kidding me?" She dropped her hand from his chest and jammed it on her hip. "Hello? There was a big-ass alien in it. How is that not sci-fi?"

A snort this time. "It's horror. Using your logic would mean *Avatar* was a romance."

Okay, so this guy might have the voice of a fallen angel tempting her to sin, but his movie knowledge sucked.

"I think I liked you better when you weren't talking," she grumbled.

She was rewarded with a loud bark of laughter that did the impossible. Made his voice even sexier. Desire slid through her veins in a slow, heady glide.

She stiffened. No. Impossible. It'd been years since she'd felt even the slightest flicker of this thing that heated her from the inside out.

If she harbored even the tiniest shred of common sense, she'd back away from this man now and blindman's bluff it until she placed some much needed distance between them. Desire had once fooled her into falling in love. And falling in love had led to a heartbreaking betrayal she was still recovering from.

No, she should make sure he was okay, then leave. With moving back to Chicago, raising her son as a single mother and working a full-time job, she didn't have the time or inclination for something as mercurial as desire.

You're sitting here in the dark with him, not dating him. One night. Just one night.

She sighed.

And stayed.

"Is something wrong?" A large hand settled on her shoulder and cupped it. She gritted her teeth, refusing to lean into that gentle but firm hold.

"Nothing. Just these shoes," she lied, bending and slipping off one and then the other to validate the fib. "They're beautiful, but hell on the feet."

He released another of those soft chuckles that sent her belly into a series of tumbles.

"What's your name?" His thumb stroked a lazy back-and-forth caress over her bare skin, and she sank her teeth into her bottom lip. Heat radiated from his touch. Until this moment, she hadn't known her shoulder was an erogenous zone. Funny the things she was finding out in the dark.

What had he asked? Right. Her name.

Alarm and dread filtered into her pleasure, tainting it.

Gage had done a damn good job of demonizing her to his family, and then his family had made sure everyone with a willing ear and flapping gums knew Isobel as a lying, greedy whore. It'd been two years since she'd left Chicago, but the insular ranks of high society never forgot names when it came to scandals.

Again, she squeezed her eyes shut as if she could block out the scorn and derision that had once flayed her soul. She still yearned to be known as more than the cheap little gold digger people believed her to be.

"Why do you want my name?" she finally replied.

A short, but weighty pause. "Because I need to know who to thank," he murmured. "And considering we've known each other all of ten minutes, 'sweetheart' seems a little forward."

"I don't mind 'sweetheart,'" she blurted out. His grasp on her shoulder tightened, and a swirl of need pooled low in her belly. "What I mean is we don't need names here. In the dark, we can be other people, different people, and I like the idea of that."

The bit of deception plucked at her conscience. Because she had no doubt that if he was familiar with her name, he would want nothing to do with her. And selfish though it might be, she'd rather him believe she was some coy debutante than the notorious Widow Wells.

That large hand slid over her shoulder, up her neck and cradled the back of her head. A sigh escaped her before she could contain it.

"Are you hiding, sweetheart?" he rumbled.

The question could have sounded inane since it seemed like the whole city was hunkered down, cloaked in darkness. But she understood what he asked. And the lack of light made it easier to be honest. At least in this.

"Yes," she breathed, and braced herself for his possible rejection.

"You're stiffening again." The hand surrounding hers squeezed lightly, a gesture of comfort. "Don't worry, your secrets are as safe with me as you are." He paused, his fingertips pressing into her scalp. "Just as I am with you."

Oh, God. That...vulnerable admission had no business burrowing beneath skin and bone to her heart. But it did.

"Keep your name, but, sweetheart—" he heaved a heavy sigh, and for an all-too-brief moment he pressed his forehead to hers "—thank you."

"I..." She swallowed, a shiver dancing down her spine. Whether in delight or warning, she couldn't tell. Probably both. "You're welcome. Anyone would've done the same," she whispered.

Something sharp edged through his low chuckle. "That's where you're wrong. Most people would've kept going, only concerned with themselves. Or they would've taken advantage."

She didn't answer; she wanted to refute him but couldn't. Because the sad fact was, he'd spoken the truth. Once she'd been a naïve twenty-year-old who'd believed in the good in people, in the happily-ever-after peddled by fairy tales. Gage had been her drug. And the withdrawal from him had nearly crushed her into the piece of nothing he'd constantly told her she was without him.

Shaking her head to get him out of her mind, she bent down and swept her hands along the floor, seeking the purse she'd dropped. Her fingertips bumped the beaded clutch, and with a small sound of victory, she popped it open and withdrew the snack bar she'd stashed there before leaving her apartment. With a two-year-old, keeping snacks on hand was a case of survival. And though her son hadn't joined her at the gala, she'd tossed the snack in out of habit. Now she patted herself on the back for her foresight.

Unbidden, a smile curved her lips. If Aiden could see

her, he would be holding out his chubby little hand, demanding his "eats."

She pinched the bridge of her nose, battling back the sting in her eyes. Obtaining help for her son had driven her to this mansion, and she'd failed. It would be easy to blame the blackout for her not locating and approaching the Wellses. But she couldn't deny the truth. She'd left the ballroom and headed to the restroom to convince herself not to leave. The plunge of the city into darkness had snatched the decision out of her hands, granting her a convenient reprieve from facing down the people who'd made it their lives' purpose to ensure she understood just how unworthy and hated she was.

But it was only that—a reprieve. Because when it came down to a choice between her pride and providing a stable environment for her son, there wasn't a choice.

When the blackout ended, she still had to face the Wellses.

"Did I lose you?" His softly rumbled question drew her from her desperate thoughts.

Clearing her throat, she settled on the floor, tucking her legs under her. She tugged on the hem of his pants, and he accepted her silent invitation, sinking down beside her. When the thick muscles of his leg brushed her knee, she reached out and skated a palm down his arm until she located his hand. She pressed half the cereal bar into it.

"What is this?" His low roll of rich laughter slid over her skin, and she involuntarily tightened her grip on her half.

"Dinner." Isobel bit into the snack and hummed. The oats, almonds and chocolate weren't caviar and toast points, but they did the job in a pinch. And this situation definitely qualified as a pinch.

"I have to say this is a first," he murmured, amusement still warming his voice.

God, she liked it. A lot. No matter how foolish that feeling might be.

"So, you don't want to share your name," he continued. "And I'll respect that. But since I'm sharing a cereal bar with you, I feel like I should know more about you besides your predilection for sci-fi movies. Tell me something about you."

She didn't immediately reply, instead nibbling on her snack while she figured out how to dodge his request. She didn't want to give him any details that might assist him in figuring out her identity. But another nebulous reason, one that she felt silly for even thinking, flitted through her head.

Giving him details about herself...pieces of herself... meant she couldn't get them back.

And she feared that. Had been taught to fear that.

Yet...

She bowed her head, silently cursing herself. What was it about this man? She'd never seen his face, didn't know his name. And still, he called to her in a way that electrified her. If she'd learned anything from the past, she would shield herself.

"I'm a grudge-holder," she said, the words escaping. *Damn it.* "I'll never let my brother off the hook for burning my Christmas Barbie's hair to the scalp when I was seven. I still give Elaine Lanier side-eye, whenever I see her, for making out with my boyfriend in the eleventh grade. And I will never, ever forgive Will Smith for *Wild, Wild West*."

A loud bark of laughter echoed between them, and she grinned. The sound warmed her like the sun's beams.

She tapped his leg. A mistake on her part. As she settled her hand back in her lap, she could still feel the strength of his muscle against her fingertips. Good God. The man was *hard*. She rubbed her fingertips against her leg as if she could erase the sensation. "Now your turn," she said, forcing a teasing note into her voice. "Tell me something about yourself."

He hesitated, and for a moment, she didn't think he would answer, but then he shifted beside her, and his thigh pressed closer, harder against her knee. Her breath snagged in her throat. Heat pulsed through her from that point of contact, and she savored it. For the first time in years, she... embraced it.

"I love to fish," he finally murmured. "Not deep sea or competitive fishing. Just sitting on a dock with a rod, barefoot, sun beating down on you, surrounded by quiet. Interrupted only by the gently lapping water. We would vacation at our summer home in Hilton Head, and my father and I would spend hours at the lake and dock behind the house. We'd talk or just enjoy the silence and each other. We even caught fish sometimes."

His low chuckle contained humor, but also a hint of sadness. Her heart clenched at the possible reason why.

"Those were some of my best memories, and I still try to visit Hilton Head at least once a year, although I haven't been in the last two..."

His voice trailed off, and unable to resist, she reached out, found his hand and wrapped her fingers around his, squeezing. Her heart thumped against her chest when his fingers tightened in response.

"I have the hugest crush on Dr. Phil. He's so sexy."

He snorted. "I cook the best eggplant parmesan you'll ever taste in your life. It's an existential experience."

Isobel snickered. "I can write with my toes. I can also eat, brush my teeth and play 'Heart and Soul' on the piano with them."

A beat of silence passed between them. "You do know I recognize that's from *The Breakfast Club*, right?"

Laughter burst from her, and she fell back against the wall, clutching her stomach. Wow. She hadn't laughed this hard or this much in so long. It was…freeing. And felt so damn good. Until this moment, she hadn't realized how much she'd missed it.

At twenty, she'd met Gage, and within months, they'd married. She'd gone from being a college student who worked part-time to help pay her tuition to the wife of one of Chicago's wealthiest men. His family had disapproved of their marriage and threatened to cut him off. Initially, Gage hadn't seemed to care. They'd lived in a small one-bedroom apartment in the Ukrainian Village neighborhood of Chicago, and they'd been happy. Or at least she'd believed they had been.

Months into their marriage, the charming, affectionate man she'd wed had morphed into a spoiled, emotionally abusive man-child. Not until it'd been too late had she discovered that his fear of being without his family's money and acceptance had trumped any love he'd harbored for Isobel. Her life had become a living hell.

So the last time she'd laughed like this had been those first four months of her marriage.

A failed relationship, tarnished dreams, battered self-confidence and single motherhood had stolen the carefree from her life, but here, stuck in a mansion with a faceless man, she'd found it again. Even if only for an instant.

"Hey." Masculine fingers glanced over her knee. "You still with me?"

"Yes," she said, shaking her head. "I'm still here."

"Good." His hand dropped away, and she missed it. Insane, she knew. But she did. "It's your turn. Because you phoned it in with the last one."

"So, we're *really* not going to talk about how you know the dialogue to *The Breakfast Club*?" she drawled.

"Yes, we're going to ignore it. Your turn."

After chuckling at the emphatic reply, she continued, "Fine. Okay, I…"

Seconds, minutes or hours had passed—she couldn't tell in this slice of time that seemed to exist outside of reality. They could've been on another plane, where his delicious scent provided air, and his deep, melodic voice wrapped around her, a phantom embrace.

And his touch? His touch was gravity, anchoring him to her, and her to him. In some manner—fingers enclosing hers, a thigh pressed to hers, a palm cupping the nape of her neck—he never ceased touching her. Logic reasoned that he needed that lodestone in the blackness so he didn't surrender to another panic attack.

Yet the heated sweetness that slid through her veins belied reason. No, he wanted to touch her…and, God, did she want to be touched.

She'd convinced herself that she didn't need desire anymore. Didn't need the melting pleasure, the hot press of skin to skin, of limbs tangling, bodies straining together toward that perfect tumble over the edge into the abyss.

Yes, she missed all of it.

But in the end, those moments weren't worth the disillusionment and loneliness that inevitably followed.

Here, though, with this man she didn't know, she basked in the return of the need, of the sweet ache that sensitized and pebbled her skin, and teased places that had lain dormant for too long. Her nipples furled into tight points, pressing against her strapless bra and gown. Sinuous flames licked at her belly…and lower.

God, she was hungry.

"You've gone quiet on me again, sweetheart," he murmured, sweeping a caress over the back of her hand that he clasped in his. "Talk to me. I need to hear your beautiful voice."

Did he touch all women this easily? Was he always this affectionate? Or was it the darkness? Did he feel freer, too? Without the accountability of propriety?

Or is it me?

As soon as the traitorous and utterly foolish thought whispered through her head, she banished it. Yes, these were extraordinary circumstances, and she was grabbing this slice in time for herself, but never could she forget who she was. Because this man might not know her identity, but he still believed her to be someone she absolutely wasn't—wealthy, a socialite…a woman who belonged.

"Sweetheart?"

That endearment. She shivered. It ignited a curl of heat in her chest. It loosed a razor-tipped arrow at the same target. No one had ever called her "sweetheart." Or "baby" or any of those personal endearments. Gage used to call her Belle, shortening her name and because he'd met her in her regular haunt, the University of Illinois's library, like a modern-day version of the heroine from *Beauty and the Beast*. Later, the affectionate nickname had become a taunt, a criticism of her unsophisticated and naïve nature.

She hated that name now.

But every time this man called her sweetheart, she felt cherished, wanted. Even though it was also a stark reminder that he didn't know her name. That she was lying to him by omission.

"Can I ask you a question?" she blurted out.

"Isn't that kind of our MO?" he drawled. "Ask."

Now that she could satisfy the curiosity that had been gnawing at her since she'd first encountered him, she hesitated. She had no right—never mind it not being her business—to probe into his history and private pain. But as hypocritical as it made her, she sought a piece of him she sensed he wouldn't willingly offer someone else.

"Earlier, when I first bumped into you…you were having a panic attack," she began. He stiffened, tension turning his body into a replica of the marble statue adorning the fountain outside the mansion. Sitting so close to him, she swore she could feel icy waves emanate from him. Unease trickled through her. *Damn it*. She should've left it alone. "I'm sorry…" she rasped, tugging on her hand, trying to withdraw it from his hold. "I shouldn't have pried."

But he didn't release her. Her heart stuttered as his grip on her strengthened.

"Don't," he ordered.

Don't what? Ask him any more questions? Pull away? How pathetic did it make her that she hoped it was the latter?

"You're the only thing keeping me sane," he admitted in a voice so low that, even in the blackness that magnified every sound, she barely caught the admission.

A thread of pain throbbed through his confession, and she couldn't resist the draw of it. Scooting closer until her thigh pressed against his, she lifted the hand not clasped in his to his hard chest. The drum of his heart vibrated against her palm, running up her arm and echoing in her own chest.

She felt and heard his heavy inhale. And she parted her lips, ready to tell him to forget it. To apologize again for intruding, but his big hand covered hers, halting her words.

"My parents died when I was sixteen."

"God," she breathed. That hint of sadness she'd detected earlier when he'd talked about fishing with his father… She'd suspected, and now he'd confirmed it. "I'm so sorry."

"Plane crash on their way back from a business meeting in Paris. Ordinarily my mother wouldn't have been with my father, but they decided to treat it as an anniversary trip. They were my foundation. And I…" He paused, and Isobel waited.

She couldn't imagine… Her father had been a nonfactor in her life for most of her childhood, but her mom… Her mother had been her support system, her rock, even through the years with Isobel and Aiden's move to California and back. Losing her…she closed her eyes and leaned her head against his shoulder, offering whatever comfort he needed as he relayed the details of the tragedy that had scarred him.

"My best friend and his family took me in. I don't know what would've happened to me, where I would be now, without them. But at the time, I was lost. Adrift. In the months afterward, I'd skip school or leave my friend's house in the middle of the night to go to the building where we'd lived. The penthouse had been sold, so I no longer had access to my home, but I would sneak into the basement through a window. It had a loosened bar that I would remove and squeeze through. I'd sit there for hours, just content to be in the building, if not in the place where I'd lived with them. My best friend—he followed me one night when I sneaked out, so he knew about it. But he never told."

Another pause, and again she didn't disturb him. She wanted to hug that best friend for standing by the boy-now-man. She'd had girlfriends in the past, but none that would've—or could've, given their own family situations—taken her in as if she were family. This friend of his, he must've been special.

"About four months after my parents' death, I'd left school again and went to the basement. I'd had a rough night. Nightmares and no sleep. That's the only reason I can think of for me falling asleep in the basement that day. I don't know what woke me up. The noise? The heat?" His shoulder rose and fell in a shrug under her cheek. "Like I said, I don't know. But when I did, the room was pitch-black. I couldn't even see my hands in front of my face. I heard what sounded like twigs snapping. But underneath that, distant but growing louder, was this dull roar. Like engines revving in a closed garage. I'd never been in one before, but somehow I knew. The building was on fire, and I was trapped."

"No," she whispered, fingers curling against his chest.

"I couldn't move. Thick black smoke filled the base-

ment, and I choked on it, couldn't breathe. I can't tell you
how long I laid there, paralyzed by fear or weak from inhaling smoke, but I thought I was going to die. That room—it
became my tomb. A dark, burning tomb. But then I heard
someone shouting my name and saw the high beam of a
flashlight. It was my friend. I found out later that he'd heard
about the fire on the news, and when I hadn't shown up at
his house after school, he'd guessed where I'd gone. The
firemen had believed they'd cleared the entire building, but
he'd forced them to go back in and search the basement.
He should've stayed outside and let them come find me,
but he'd barreled past them and entered with only his shirt
over his face to battle the smoke, putting his life in danger.
But if he hadn't... He saved my life that day."

"Oh, thank God." Sliding her hand from under his, she
wrapped her arm around his waist, curving her body into
his. She'd known him for mere hours, and yet the thought
of him dying, of being consumed by flames? It bothered
her in a way that made no sense. "He was a hero."

"Yes, he was," he said softly. "He was a good man."

Was a good man. No. It couldn't be... Horror and disbelief crowded up her throat. "He's gone, too?"

"A couple of years now, but sometimes it seems like
yesterday."

"I'm so sorry." Isobel shifted until she knelt beside him.
She stroked her hand up his torso, searching out his face.
Once she brushed over his hard, faintly stubbled jaw, she
cupped it and lowered her head, until her forehead met his
temple.

His fingers drifted over her cheek, and after a moment's
hesitation, tunneled into her hair. Her lungs seized, shock
infiltrating every vein, organ and limb. Only her heart
seemed capable of movement, and it threw itself against
her sternum, like an animal desperate for freedom from
its cage.

Blunt fingertips dragged over her scalp. A moan clawed its way up her throat at the scratch and tug of her hair, but she trapped the sound behind clenched teeth. She couldn't prevent the shudder that worked its way through her. Not when it'd been *so long* since she'd been touched. Since pleasure had even been a factor. So. Long.

"I need to hear that lovely voice, sweetheart," he rumbled, turning and bowing his head so his lips grazed the column of her throat as he spoke. Sparks snapped under her skin as if her nerve endings had transformed into firecrackers, and his mouth was the lighter. "There are things I want to do to your mouth that require your permission."

"Like what?" Had she really just asked that question? And in that breathy tone? What was he doing to her?

Giving you what you're craving. Be brave and find out, her subconscious replied.

"Find out if it's as sweet as you are. Taste you. Savor you. Learn you," he murmured, answering her question. He untangled their clasped fingers and with unerring accuracy, located her chin and pinched it. Cool but soft strands of hair tickled her jaw, and then her cheek, as he lifted his head. Then warm gusts of air bathed her lips. She could taste him, his breath. Something potent with faint hints of lemon, like the champagne from earlier. But also, underneath, lay a darker, enigmatic flavor. Him. She didn't need to pinpoint its origin to know it was all him. "Then I want to take your mouth. Want you to take mine."

"I…" Desperate, aching need robbed her of words. Of thought.

"Give me the words, sweetheart." He didn't breach that scant inch of space between them, waiting on her consent, her permission.

When so much had been ripped from her in the past, choices not even offered, that seeking of her agreement squeezed her heart even as his words caused a spasm to roll through her sex.

"Yes," she said. Then, as if confirming to herself that she was indeed breaking her self-imposed rules about caution and recklessness, she whispered again, "Yes."

With a growl, he claimed that distance.

She expected him to crush his mouth to hers, to conquer her like a wild storm leveling everything in its path. And she would've thrown herself into the whirlwind, been willingly swept up. But his tenderness was as thorough in its destruction as any tornado.

His lips, full, firm yet somehow soft, brushed over hers. Pressed, then withdrew. Rubbed, cajoled, gave her enough of him, but waited until she granted him more. On the tail end of a sigh she couldn't contain, she parted for him. Welcomed the penetration of his tongue. Slid into a sensual dance with him. It was she who sucked him, licking the roof of his mouth, sampling the dark, heady flavor of his groan. She who first brought teeth into play, nipping at the corner of his mouth, raking them down his chin, only to return to take just as he'd invited her to do.

She who crawled onto his lap, jerking her skirt up and straddling his powerful thighs.

But it was he who threw oil onto their fire, ratcheting their desire from a blaze into a consuming inferno.

With a snarl that vibrated through his chest and over her nipples, he tugged her head back and opened his mouth over her neck. She arched into the hot, wet caress of tongue and teeth, her hands shifting from his shoulders to his hair and holding on. Every flick and suck echoed low in her belly, between her thighs. Fleetingly, the thought that she should be embarrassed at how drenched her panties were flitted through her head. But the clamp of his hand on her hip and the roll of his hips, stroking the hard, thick length of his cock over her sex, obliterated every rationalization.

Think? All she could do was *feel*.

Pleasure, its claws tipped with greed, tore at her. She whimpered, clung to him.

"Again," she ordered. Begged. Didn't matter. As long as he did it *again*.

"That's it," he praised against her throat, licking a path to her ear, where he nipped the outer curve. Hell, when had *that* become an erogenous zone? "Tell me what you want, what you need from me. I'll give it to you, sweetheart. You just have to ask."

Keep turning me inside out. Keep holding me like I'm wanted, cherished. Keep making me forget who I am.

But those pleas veered too close to exposing that part of her she'd learned to protect with the zeal of a dragon guarding a treasure.

So instead she gave him what she could. What she'd be too embarrassed to admit in the light of day. "Here." With trembling, jerky movements, she yanked down the top of her dress, drew him to her bared breasts. "Kiss me. Mark me."

He followed through on his promise, giving her what she'd requested. His tongue circled her nipple, lapped at it, swirled before sucking so hard the corresponding ache twinged deep and high inside her. She tried to hold in her cry but couldn't. Not when lust arrowed through her, striking at the heart of her. He murmured against her flesh, switching breasts, and treating her other peak to the same erotic torture. Skillful fingers plucked and pinched the tip that was damp from his mouth.

"More," she gasped. "Oh, God, more."

"Tell me." The hand on her hip tightened, and he delivered another slow, luxurious stroke to her empty, wet sex. "Tell me once more. I want your voice, your words."

Frustration, the last stubborn remnants of shyness and passion warred within her. Her lips moved, but the demand *make me come* that howled inside her head refused to emerge. Finally she grabbed the hand at her waist and slid it over her hiked-up dress, down her inner thigh and between her legs. She pressed his palm to her, moaning at the temporary relief of him cupping her.

"You're cheating," he teased, but the almost guttural tone had her hips bucking against him. As did his, "You're soaked. For me."

"Yes," she rasped. "For you. Only for you." Truth. That piece of herself, she offered him. She'd never been this hungry, this desperate before. Not even for—*no!*

She flung herself away from the intrusive thought. Not here. In this hall, there was only room for her and this nameless, faceless man, who nonetheless handled her like the most desirable, beautiful creature he'd ever held. Or at least that's what she was convincing herself of for these stolen moments.

"Touch me," she whispered, grinding down against his hand. "Please touch me."

The fingers still sweeping caresses over her nipple abandoned her flesh to cradle her face. He tipped her head down until their mouths met. "Don't beg me to touch you," he said, his lips grazing hers with each word. "You'll never have to beg me to do that."

He sealed the vow with a plunge of his finger inside her.

She cried out, tossing her head back on her shoulders as pleasure rocked through her like an earthquake, cracking her open, exposing her.

"Damn," he swore. "So damn tight. So damn…" He bit off the rest of his litany, slowly pulling free of her, then just as slowly, just as tenderly thrusting back inside. But she didn't want slow, didn't want tender. And she told him so with a hard, swift twist of her hips, taking him deeper.

"Sweetheart," he growled, warned.

"No," she panted. "I need to… Please." He'd said she

didn't need to plead with him, but if it would get her what she craved—release, oblivion—she wasn't above it.

With a snarl, he crushed his mouth to hers, tongue driving between her lips as he buried himself inside her. She moaned into his kiss, even as she spread her legs wider, granting him deeper access to her body. And he took it. He withdrew one finger and returned to her with two, working them into her flesh, working *her*.

Something snapped within her, and she rode his hand, rode the exquisite storm he whipped to a frenzy with every stroke, every brush of his thumb over her clit, every curl of his fingertips on that place high and deep in her sex. He played her, demanding her body sing for him. And God, did it.

With one last rub over that, before now, untouched place, she splintered, screaming into his mouth. And he swallowed it, clutching her to him, holding her tight as she crashed headlong into the abyss, a willing sacrifice to pleasure.

Isobel snuggled under her warm blanket, grabbing ahold of those last few moments of lazy sleepiness before Aiden cried out, demanding she come free him from his crib and feed him. She sighed, curling into her pillow...

Wait. Her pillow wasn't this firm. Frowning, she rolled over...or tried to roll over. Something prevented the movement...

Oh, hell.

Not something. Some*one*.

She stiffened as reality shoved the misty dredges of sleep away and dragged in all the memories of the night before. Gala. Blackout. Finding a mysterious man. Calming him. Laughing with him. Kissing him...

She jerked away, her lashes lifting.

Weak, hazy pink-and-orange light poured in through the large window at the end of the hall. Morning, but just barely. So maybe about six o'clock. Still, the dawn-tinged sky provided enough light to realize the warm blanket was really a suit jacket. Instead of a mattress, she perched on a strong pair of muscular thighs. And her pillow was a wide, solid chest covered in a snow-white dress shirt.

Heart pounding like a heavy metal-drum solo, she inched her gaze up to the patch of smooth golden skin exposed by the buttons undone at a powerful throat. Her belly clenched, knots twisting and pulling tight as she continued her wary, slow perusal.

A carved-from-a-slab-of-stone jaw dusted with dark stubble.

An equally hard chin with just the faintest hint of a cleft.

A beautiful, sensual mouth that promised all kinds of decadent, corrupting pleasures. Pleasures she had firsthand knowledge that he could deliver. She clearly remembered sinking her teeth into the bottom, slightly fuller curve.

Suppressing a shiver that he would surely feel, as they were pressed so closely together, she continued skimming her gaze upward past a regal, patrician nose and sharp, almost harsh cheekbones.

As she raised her scrutiny that last scant inch to his eyes, his dense, black, ridiculously long lashes lifted.

She sucked in a painful breath. And froze. Except for her frantic pulse, which reverberated in her head like crashing waves relentlessly striking the shore. Deafening her.

Not because of the striking, piercing amber eyes that could've belonged to a majestic eagle.

No. Because she recognized those eyes.

It'd been two years since they'd coldly stared at her over a yawning, freshly dug grave with a flower-strewn mahogany casket suspended above it. But she'd never forget them.

Darius King.

Gage's best friend.

The man who blamed her for Gage's death.

The man who hated her.

Hated her... Hated her... As the words—and the throbbing pain of them—sank into her brain, her paralysis shattered. She scrambled off him, uncaring of how clumsy her backward crab-walk appeared. She just needed to be away from him. From the shock that quickly bled from his gaze and blazed into rage and disgust.

God, no. How could she have kissed...touched... Let him...

You're fucking him, aren't you? Admit it, goddamn you. Admit it! You're fucking my best friend! You whore!

The memory of Gage's scream ricocheted off the walls of her skull, gaining volume and power by the second. Darius hadn't been the first man he'd thought she'd been cheating with—not even the third or fifth. But she'd never seen him as enraged, as out-of-control at the thought of her being with this man. Gage had never physically abused her during their marriage, but that night... That night she'd truly been afraid he would hit her.

Afterward she'd made a conscious effort to not look at Darius, not be alone in the same room with him if she couldn't avoid him altogether. Even after he'd married an iceberg of a woman, she'd maintained her distance.

And now, not only had she laughed and talked with him, but she had allowed him inside her body. She'd allowed him to bring her the most soul-shattering pleasure.

Meeting his stare, she could read the condemnation there. The confirmation that she was indeed the whore Gage had called her.

Humiliation, hurt and fury—at him and herself—barreled through her, propelling her to her feet. Snatching up her purse and shoes, she clutched them to her chest.

"Isobel." The voice that had caressed her ears with its deep, melodious tone, that had stirred desire with explicit words, now caused ice to coat her veins. Gage used to take great delight in telling her how much his friend disliked her. Though she now knew when her husband's lips were moving, he was lying, hearing Darius's frigid disdain directed at her, meeting his derisive gaze… She believed it now, just as she had then.

"I-I…" She dragged in a breath, shaking her head as she backpedaled. "I need to go. I'm sorry," she rasped.

Hating that she'd apologized, that she sounded scared and…broken, she whirled around and damn near sprinted down the thankfully empty hallway, not feeling the cold marble under her feet. Or the stone as she escaped the mansion. None of the valets from the night before appeared, but she'd glimpsed the direction in which they'd driven off and followed that path.

Twenty minutes later, with keys snatched from the valet stand and car successfully located, she exited onto the freeway. Though with every mile she steadily placed between her and the mansion—and Darius—she couldn't shake the feeling of being pursued.

Couldn't shake the sense that she could run, but couldn't hide.

But that damn sure wouldn't stop her from trying.

Three

Darius stood outside the weathered brick apartment building, the chill of the October morning not having evaporated yet.

At eight thirty, the overcast sky didn't add any cheer to this South Deering neighborhood. The four rows of identical windows facing the front sported different types of shades, and someone had set potted plants with fake flowers by the front entrance, but nothing could erase the air of poverty that clung to this poor, crime-stricken section of the city. Foam cups, paper and other bits of trash littered the patch of green on the left side of the apartment complex. Graffiti and gang tags desecrated the side of the neighboring building. It sickened him that only thirty minutes away, people lived in almost obscene wealth, a good many of them willingly choosing to pretend this kind of poverty didn't exist. He'd been born into those rarefied circles, but he wasn't blind to the problems of classism, prejudice and ignorance that Chicago faced.

Still... Gage's son was growing up here, in this place that hovered only steps above a tenement. And that ate at Darius like the most caustic acid.

Stalking up the sidewalk, he approached the front entrance. A lock sat above the handle, but on a whim, he tugged on it, and the door easily opened.

"You have to be kidding me," he growled. Anyone off the street could walk into the building, leaving all the residents here vulnerable where they should feel safest. Aiden being one of the most vulnerable.

Darius stepped into the dimly lit foyer, the door shutting behind him. Rectangular mailboxes mounted the wall to his right, and to his left, the steel doors to an elevator. In front of him, a flight of stairs stretched to the upper floors. With one last glance at the elevator doors, he headed for the stairs. He wasn't trusting the elevator in a building this damn old.

According to the information his investigator had provided, Isobel lived on the third floor. He climbed several flights of stairs and entered the door that led to her level. Like the lobby, the hallway was clean, even if the carpet was threadbare. Bulbs lit the area, and the paint, while not fresh, wasn't as desperately in need of a new coat as the downstairs. The broken lock on the front door notwithstanding, it appeared as if the landlord, or at least the residents, cared about their home.

Seconds later, he arrived in front of Isobel's apartment door, standing on a colorful welcome mat depicting a sleeping puppy. It should've seemed out of place, but oddly it didn't strike him that way. But it did serve to remind him that a young boy lived behind the closed door. A boy who deserved to live in a home where he and the puppy could run free and play. A place with a yard, a swing set.

A safe place.

Anger rekindled in his chest, and raising his fist, he

knocked on the door. Moments passed, and it remained shut. He rapped on the door again. And still no one answered.

Suppressing a growl, he tucked his hands into the pockets of his coat and narrowed his gaze on the floor.

"Isobel, I know you're home. I can see the shadow of your feet. So open the door," he ordered.

Several more seconds passed before the sound of locks twisting and disengaging reached him, and then she stood in the entrance.

He deliberately inhaled a calming breath. For the entire drive from his Lake Forest home, he'd tried to prepare himself for seeing her again. It'd been a week since the night of the blackout. A week since he'd suffered a panic attack, and she'd held his hand and dragged him back from the edge with her teasing, silly conversation and lilting laughter. A week since he'd feasted on her mouth, experienced the tight-as-hell grip of her body spasming around his fingers, and her greedy cries of pleasure splintering around his ears.

A week since he woke and the piercing anticipation of finally glimpsing the face of the mysterious woman he'd embraced faded into a bright, hot anger as he realized her true identity.

Yes, he'd tried to ready himself for the moment they'd face each other again. And staring down at her now, with all that long, thick hair tumbling over her shoulders, framing a beautiful face with fey eyes that should have existed only within the pages of a fantasy novel, his attempt at preparation had been for shit. Even in a faded pink tank top and cotton pajama pants, with what appeared to be fat leprechauns and rainbows, she knocked him on his ass.

And he resented her for it. Hated himself more.

Because no matter how he tried, he couldn't forget how she'd burned in his arms that night. Exploded. Never had a woman been that uninhibited and hot for him. She'd scorched him so that even now—even a week later—he still felt the marks on his fingers, his chest, his cock. He had an inkling why his best friend had been driven crazy because of her infidelities.

Because imagining Isobel aflame like that with another man had a green-tinted anger churning his own gut.

Which was completely ridiculous. Gage had tortured himself over this woman. It would be a breezy spring day in hell before Darius allowed himself to be her next victim.

"What do you want?" Isobel asked, crossing her arms under her breasts. Her obviously braless breasts.

"To talk," he said, trying and failing to completely keep the snap out of his voice. "And I'd rather not do it out in the hallway."

Her delicate chin kicked up, and even though she stood almost a foot shorter than his own six feet three inches, she continued defiantly standing there, a female Napoleon guarding her empire. "We don't have anything to talk about, so whatever you came here to say should be a very short conversation. The hallway is as good a place as any."

"Fine." He smiled, and it must have appeared as false as it felt because her eyes narrowed on him. "But the private investigator I hired to find you also spoke with your neighbors. Including a Mrs. Gregory, who lives across the hall. A lovely woman, from what he tells me. Seventy-three, lives alone, never misses an episode of the *Young and the Restless* and is a terrible gossip. At this very moment, she probably has her ear against the door, trying to eavesdrop on our conversation. So if you don't mind her finding out where you spent the night of the blackout—and *how* you spent it—I don't either."

Her head remained tilted at that stubborn angle, and the flat line of her mouth didn't soften. But she did slant a glance around him to peek at the closed door across the hall. Whatever she saw made her lips flatten even more.

"Come in." She stepped back, allowing him to pass by her. When he moved into the tiny foyer, she called out, "Good morning, Mrs. Gregory," and shut the door. "I swear that woman could tell the cops where Jimmy Hoffa is buried," she muttered under her breath.

Humor, unexpected and unwelcome, rippled through his chest. He remembered this about her from the night of the blackout. Funny, self-deprecating, charming. Given everything he knew of Isobel's character, the side she'd shown him in the darkness must've been a charade.

Her shock and horror the following morning had been real, though.

He gave his head a mental shake. He wasn't here to rehash the colossal mistake he'd committed in the dark. He had a purpose, an agenda. And before he left this morning, it would be accomplished.

Making resolve a clear, hard wall in his chest, he moved into the living room. Well, *moved* was generous. The change in location from foyer to the main room only required two steps.

Jesus, the whole apartment could fit into his great room—three times. The living room and dining room melded into one space, only broken up by a small counter that separated it from the equally small kitchen. A cramped tunnel of a hallway shot off to the left and led to what he knew from floorplans of the building to be a miniscule bedroom, bathroom and closet.

At least it was clean. The obviously secondhand couch, coffee table and round dining table wore signs of life—scratches, scuff marks and ragged edges in the upholstery. But everything was neat and shined, the scent of pine and lemon a pleasant fragrance under the aroma of brewing coffee. Even the colorful toys—blocks, a plastic easel, a colorful construction set and books—were stacked in chaotic order in one corner.

A hard tug wrenched his gut to the point of pain at the sight of those symbols of childhood. A tug that resonated with yearning. Aiden had been only six months old the last time Darius had seen him. That'd been at Gage's funeral. How much had the boy changed in the two years since? Had his light brown hair darkened to the nearly black of Gage's own color? As he'd matured, had he grown to resemble his mother, or had he inherited more of his father's features?

That had been the seed of Gage's and the family's doubts regarding the baby's parentage. The boy had possessed neither Gage's nor Isobel's features, except for her eyes. So they'd assumed he must look like his father—his true father. That Isobel had refused a paternity test had further solidified their suspicions that Gage hadn't been Aiden's father. And then, out of spite, she'd made Gage choose—his family or her. Of course, out of love and loyalty, and foolish blindness, he'd chosen her, isolating himself from his parents and friends. Till the end.

Selfish. Conniving. Cold.

Except maybe not so cold. Darius had a firsthand example of how hot she could burn...

Shit.

Focus.

Unbuttoning his jacket, he turned and watched Isobel stride toward him. She did another of those chin lifts as she entered the living room. Jesus, even with suspicion heavy in those blue-gray eyes, they were striking. Haunting. Beautiful.

Deceitful.

"You're not going to ask me to have a seat?" he drawled, the dark, twisted mix of bitterness and lust grinding relentlessly within him.

"Since you won't be staying long, no," she replied, crossing her arms over her chest again. "What do you want?"

"That's my question, Isobel." Without her invite, he lowered to the dark blue, worn armchair across from the couch. "What do you want? Why were you at the gala last week?"

"None of your business."

"See, that's where you're wrong. If you came there to pump the Wellses for money, then it is most definitely my business," he said. Studying her, he caught the flash of emotion in her eyes. Emotion, hell. Guilt. That flash had been guilt. Satisfaction, thick and bright, flared within him. "What happened, Isobel? Did whatever fool you sank your claws into out there in Los Angeles come to his senses and kick you out before you sucked him dry?"

She stared at him, slowly uncoiling her arms and sinking to a perch on her sofa. "The *poor fool* you're so concerned about was my Aunt Lila, who I stayed with to help her recover from a stroke," she continued, derision heavy in her voice. "She died a couple of months ago from another massive stroke, which is why I'm back here in Chicago. Any more insults or assumptions you want to throw out there before finally telling me why you're here?"

"I'm sorry for your loss," he murmured. And he was sorry. He, more than anyone, understood the pain of losing a loved one. But that's all he would apologize for. Protecting and defending his family from someone who sought to use them? No, he'd never regret that. "Now… What do you want with the Wells family? Although—" he deliberately turned his head and scanned the tight quarters of her apartment, lingering on the pile of envelopes on the breakfast bar before returning his attention to her "—I can probably guess if you don't want to admit it."

Her shoulders rolled back, her spine stiffening. Even with her just-rolled-out-of-bed hair and clothes, she appeared…regal. Pride. It was the pride that clung to her as closely as the tank top molding to her breasts.

"What. Do. You. Want. With. Them?" he ground out, when she didn't answer.

"Help," she snapped, leaning forward, a matching anger lighting her arctic eyes. "I need their help. Not for me. I'd rather hang pictures and lay a welcome mat out in a freshly dug hole than go to them for anything. But for the grandson they've rejected and refused to acknowledge, I need them."

"You would have the nerve to ask them for help—no, let's call it what it is—for *money* and use your son to do it? The son you've kept from them for two years? That's low even for you, Isobel." The agony and helplessness over Gage's death, the rage toward the woman who was supposed to have loved him, but who had instead mercilessly and callously broken him, surged within him. Tearing through him like a sword, damn near slicing him in half. But he submerged the roiling emotions beneath a thick sheet of ice. "The answer is no. You don't get to decide when they can and can't have a relationship with the grandson who is the only part they have left of the son they loved and lost. You might be his *mother*, and I use that term loosely—"

"Get out." The quiet, sharp words cut him off. She stood, the fine tremor shivering through her body visible in the finger she pointed toward the door. "Get the hell out and don't come back."

"Not until we discuss—"

"You're just like them," she snarled, continuing as if he hadn't even spoken. "Cut from the same golden but filthy cloth. You don't know shit about me as a mother, because you haven't been there. You, Baron or Helena. So you have zero right to have an opinion on how I'm raising my son. And for the record, I didn't try to keep them from Aiden. They didn't want him. Didn't want to know him. Didn't even believe he was their grandson. So don't you dare walk in here, look at this apartment and judge me—"

"Oh, no, Isobel," he contradicted her, slowly rising to his feet as well, tired of her lies. Especially about the people, the *family*, who'd taken him in when he'd lost his own.

Who'd accepted him as their own. "I judged you long before this. Your actions as a wife—" he spat the word out, distasteful on his tongue "—condemned you."

"Right." She nodded, a sneer matching his own, curling her mouth. "I was the money-grabbing, social-climbing whore who tricked Gage into marriage by getting knocked up. And he was the sacrificial lamb who cherished and adored me, who remained foolishly loyal to me right up until the moment of his death."

"Don't," he growled, the warning low, rough. He'd never called her a whore; he detested that word. Even when he'd discovered his ex-wife was fucking one of his vice presidents, Darius had never thrown that ugly name at her. Yet to hear Isobel talk about Gage in that dismissive manner when his biggest sin had been loving her... "You don't get to talk about him like that."

"Yes." Her harsh crack of laughter echoed in the room. "That's right, another rule I forgot from my time in my loving marriage. I don't get to speak until I'm spoken to. And even then, keep it short before I embarrass him and myself. Well, sorry to break it to you, but this isn't your home. It's mine, and I want you out—"

"Mommy." The small, childish voice dropped in the room like a hand grenade, cutting Isobel off. Both of them turned toward it. A toddler with dark, nearly black curls and round cheeks, and clad in Hulk pajamas, hovered in the entrance to the living room. Shuffling back and forth on his bare feet, he stuck his thumb into his mouth and glanced from Isobel to Darius before returning his attention to her.

Aiden.

An invisible fist bearing brass knuckles landed a haymaker against Darius's chest. The air in his lungs ejected on a hard, almost painful *whoosh*. He couldn't breathe, couldn't move. Not when his best friend's son dashed across the floor and threw his tiny but sturdy body at his mother, the action full of confidence that she would catch him. Which she did. Kneeling, Isobel gathered him in her arms, standing up and holding him close.

Over his mother's shoulder, Aiden stared at Darius with a gaze identical to Isobel's. A hand roughly the size of a toddler's reached into his chest and squeezed Darius's heart. Hard.

Christ.

He'd expected to be happy or satisfied at finally seeing Aiden. But he hadn't been prepared for this…this overwhelming joy or fierce protectiveness that swamped him, weakened his knees. Gage's son—and there was no mistaking he was indeed Gage's son. He might have Isobel's eyes, but the hair, the shape of his face, his brow, nose, the wide, smiling mouth… They were all his best friend.

The need to protect the boy intensified, swelled. Darius would do anything in his power to provide for him… raise him the way Gage didn't have the opportunity to do. Resolve shifting and solidifying in his chest, his paralysis broke, and he moved across the room, toward mother and son.

"Hello," he greeted Aiden, the gravel-roughened tone evidence of the emotional storm still whirling inside him.

Aiden grinned, and the tightening around Darius's ribcage increased.

"Aiden, this is Mr. King. Can you tell him hi?" Isobel shifted so she and Aiden faced Darius. Her voice might've been light and cheerful, but her eyes revealed that none of the anger from their interrupted conversation had abated. "Tell Mr. King, hi, baby," she encouraged.

"Hi, Mr. King," he mimicked. Though it actually sounded more like, *Hi, Mih Key.*

"Hi, Aiden," he returned, smiling. And unable to help himself, he rubbed the back of a finger down the boy's warm, chubby cheek.

A soft catch of breath reluctantly tugged his attention away from the child. He glanced at Isobel, and she stared at him, barely blinking. After a moment, she shook her head, turning her focus back to her son.

What had that been about? He studied her, trying to decipher the enigma that was Isobel Hughes.

There's no enigma, no big mystery. Only what she allows you to see.

As the reminder boomed in his head, he frowned. His ex-wife had been an expert at hiding her true self until she'd wanted him to glimpse it. And that had only happened toward the end of the relationship, when both of them had stopped pretending they shared anything resembling a marriage. Not with her screwing other men, and Darius refusing to play the fool or pay for the black American Express card any longer.

"Want milk," Aiden demanded as Isobel settled him on the floor again. "And 'nana."

She brushed a hand over his curls, but the hair just fell back into his face. "You want cereal with your milk and banana?" she asked. Aiden nodded, smiling, as if congratulating her for understanding him. "Okay, but can you go play in the room while I fix it?"

Aiden nodded again, agreeing. "Go play."

She took his hand in hers and led him back down the hall, talking to him the entire time until they disappeared. Several minutes later, she returned alone, the adoring, gentle expression she gave her son gone.

"I have things to do, so…" She waved toward the front door, but Darius didn't move. "Seriously, this is ridiculous," she snapped.

"He's Gage's son," he murmured.

Fire flared in her eyes as they narrowed. "Are you sure? You can tell that from just a glance at him? After all, I've been with so many men. Any of them could be his real father."

"Don't play the victim, Isobel. It doesn't fit," he snapped. "And I'm not leaving until we talk."

"I repeat," she ground out. "We have nothing to—"

"We're getting married."

She rocked back on her bare heels as if struck. Shock rounded her fairy eyes, parted her lips. She gaped at him, her fingers fluttering to circle her neck. He should feel regret at so bluntly announcing his intentions. Should. But he didn't.

He'd had a week to consider this idea. Yes, it seemed crazy, over-the-top, and he'd rejected it as soon as the thought had popped into his head. But it'd nagged at him, and the reasons why it would work eventually outweighed the ones why it wouldn't. Of all the words used to describe him, *impetuous* or *rash* weren't among them. He valued discipline and control, in business and in his personal life. His past had taught him both were important. It'd been an impromptu decision that had robbed him of both his parents, and an impulsive one that had led him to marry a woman he'd known for a matter of months. The same mistake Gage had made.

But this…proposition was neither. He'd carefully measured it, and though just the thought of tying himself to another manipulative woman sickened him, he was willing to make the sacrifice.

Whatever doubts might've lingered upon walking up to her building, they had disintegrated as soon as he'd laid eyes on Aiden.

"You're crazy," she finally breathed.

He smiled, and the tug to the corner of his mouth felt cynical, hard. "No. Just realistic." He slid his hands into the front pockets of his pants, cocking his head and studying her pale, damnably lovely features. "Regardless of what you believe, I'm not judging you on the neighborhood you live in or your home. But the fact is you aren't in the safest area of Chicago, and this building isn't a shining example of security. The lock on the front door doesn't work. Anyone could walk in here. The locks on your apartment door are for shit. There isn't an alarm system. What if someone followed you home and busted in here? You would have no protection—you or Aiden."

"So I have a security system installed and call the landlord about the locks on the building entrance and my door. Easy fixes, and none of them require marriage to a man I barely know who despises me."

"If they were easy fixes," he said, choosing to ignore her comment about his feelings toward her, "why haven't you done them?" He paused, because something flickered in her gaze, and a surge of both anger and satisfaction glimmered in his chest. "You have contacted your landlord," he stated, taking her silence as confirmation. "And he hasn't done a damn thing about it." He stepped forward, shrinking the space between them. "Pride, Isobel. You're going to let pride prevent you from protecting your son."

Lightning flashed in her gaze, and for a moment he found himself mesmerized by the display. Like a bolt of electricity across a morning sky.

"Let me enlighten you. Pride became a commodity I couldn't afford a long time ago. But in the last two years, I've managed to scrape mine back together again. And neither you nor the Wellses can have it. I'm not afraid to ask for help. That's why I was at the gala. Why I was willing to approach Baron and Helena again. *For my son*. But you're not here to offer me help. You're demanding I sell my soul to another devil, just with a different face and name. Well, sorry. I'm not going to play your game. Not when it won't only be me losing this time, but Aiden, as well."

"Selling your soul to the devil? Not playing the game?"

he drawled. "Come now, Isobel. A poor college student nabbing herself the heir to a fortune? Trapping him with a pregnancy, then isolating him from his family? Cry me a river, sweetheart. I was there, so don't try to revise history to suit your narrative."

"You're just like him," she whispered.

Darius stifled a flinch. Then cursed himself for recoiling in the first place. Gage had been a good man—good to her.

"You have two choices," he stated. "One, agree to marry me and we both raise Aiden. Or two, disagree, and I'll place the full weight of my name and finances behind Baron and Helena to help them gain custody of Aiden."

She gasped and wavered on her feet. On instinct, he shifted forward, lifting his arms to steady her. But she backpedaled away from him, pressing a hand against the wall and holding up the other in a gesture that screamed *stop right there*.

"You," she rasped, shaking her head. "You wouldn't do that."

"I would," he assured her. "And I will."

"Why?" She straightened, lowering both arms, but the shadows darkening her eyes gathered. "Why would you do that? Why would they? Baron and Helena...they don't even believe Aiden is Gage's. They've wanted nothing to do with him since he was born. Why would they seek custody now?"

"Because he *is* their grandson. I'll convince them of that. And he deserves to know them, love them. Deserves to learn about his father and come to know him through his parents. Aiden is all Baron and Helena have left of Gage. And you would deprive them of that relationship. I won't let you." The unfairness of Isobel's actions, of her selfishness, gnawed at him. She hadn't witnessed the devastation Gage's death had left behind, the wreckage. Baron had suffered a heart attack not long after, and yes, most of it could be attributed to lifestyle choices. But the loss of his only son, that had definitely been a contributing factor.

Yet if they'd had Aiden in their lives during these last two difficult years...he could've been a joy to them. But Isobel had skipped town, not even granting them the opportunity to bond. If she'd stayed long enough, Baron and Helena would've done just what Darius had—taken one look at the child and *known* he belonged to Gage.

"And I won't let you make Aiden a pawn. Or worse, a substitute for Gage. *He won't become Gage.* I refuse to allow you and the Wellses to turn him into his father. I'll fight that with every breath in my body."

"He would be lucky to become like the man his father was," Darius growled. "To be loved by his parents. They welcomed me into their home, raised me when I had no one."

She didn't get to smear the family that had become his own. Gage had been his best friend, his confidante, his brother. Helena had stepped in as his mother. And Baron had been his friend, his mentor, his guiding hand in the multimillion-dollar financial-investment company Darius's father had left behind for his young, inexperienced son.

So no, she didn't get to malign them.

"I'm his mother," she said.

As if that settled everything.

When it didn't.

"And they're his grandparents," he countered. "Grandparents who can afford to provide a stable, safe, secure and loving home for him to thrive and grow in. He'll never want for anything, will have the best education and opportunities. Aiden should have all of his family in his life. You, me, his grandparents and aunt. He should enjoy a fulfilled, happy childhood, with the security of two parents and without the weight of struggle. With you marrying me, he will."

And the Wellses would avoid a prolonged custody battle that could further tax Baron's health and possibly endanger his life. His recovery from the heart attack was going well, but Darius refused to add stress if he could avoid it.

Besides, as CEO and president of King Industries Unlimited, the conglomerate he'd inherited from his father, not only would Aiden be taken care of, but so would Isobel. She would want for nothing, have all the money available to satisfy her every materialistic need. He had experience with bearing the albatross of a greedy woman with Faith, his ex-wife, and though it galled him to have to repeat history, he'd rather take the financial hit than allow Isobel to extort more money from the Wellses. They'd protected him once, and he would gladly, willingly do the same for them.

"No." Isobel stared up at him, shoulders drawn back, hands curled into fists at her side. Though she still wore the evidence of her worry, she faced him like one general standing off against another. A glimmer of admiration slipped through his steely resolve. She'd reminded him of Napoleon earlier, and she did so again. But like that emperor, she would fail and eventually surrender. "I don't care how pretty you wrap it up, blackmail is still blackmail. And I'm not giving in to it. Now, for the last time, get out of my house."

"Call it what you want to help you sleep at night," he murmured. He reached inside his suit jacket and removed a silver business card holder. He withdrew one as he strode to the breakfast bar, and then set it on the counter. "Think carefully before you make a rash decision you'll regret. Here's where you can reach me."

She didn't reply, just stalked to the front door and yanked it open.

"This isn't anywhere near over, Isobel," he warned, exiting her apartment.

"Maybe it isn't for you. But for me, I'm going to forget all about you as soon as you get out." And with that parting shot, she closed the door shut behind him. Or more accurately, in his face.

He didn't immediately head down the hallway, instead pausing a moment to stare at the door. And smile.

He'd meant what he'd told her. This wasn't over.

And damn if he wasn't looking forward to the next skirmish.

Four

A week later, Isobel drove through the winding, tidy streets of Lake Forest. During the hour and fifteen minutes' drive from South Deering, the inner-city landscape gave way to the steel-and-glass metropolis of downtown, to the affluent suburb that made a person believe she'd stepped into a pretty New England town. The quaint ice cream shop, bookstore, gift shop and boutiques in the center of the town emanated charm and wealth. All of it practically shouted history, affluence and *keep the hell out, riffraff!*

She would be the aforementioned riffraff. Discomfort crawled down her neck. Her decade-old Honda Civic stuck out like a sore thumb among the Aston Martins, Bugattis and Mercedes Benzes like a poor American relation among its luxurious, foreign cousins. Her GPS announced her upcoming turn, and she returned her focus to locating Darius's home.

Minutes later, Siri informed her that she'd reached her destination.

Good. God.

She didn't know much about architecture other than what she retained from the shows on HGTV, but even she recognized the style of the three-story home as Georgian. Beautiful golden bricks—not the weathered, dull color of her own apartment building—formed the outside of the huge structure, with its sloped roof and attached garage. It curved in an arc, claiming the land not already seized by the towering maple trees surrounding the property. Black shutters framed the many windows that faced the front and bracketed the wide wine-red door.

"You are not in South Deering anymore," she murmured to herself.

No wonder Darius had scrutinized her tiny apartment with a slight curl to his lips. He called this beautiful, imposing mansion home. Her place must've appeared like a Hobbit hole to him. A Hobbit hole from the wrong side of the Shire tracks.

Sighing, she dragged her attention back to the reason she'd driven out here.

She had a marriage bargain to seal.

After climbing the three shallow steps that led to the front door, she rang the bell. Only seconds passed before it opened and—instead of a housekeeper or butler—Darius stood in the entryway.

It wasn't fair.

His masculine beauty. His affect on her.

She was well versed in the danger of handsome men. They used their appearance as a lure—a bright, sensual lure that entranced a woman, distracted her from the darkness behind the shiny exterior. And by the time a woman noticed, it was way too late...

Even though she was aware of the threat he presented, she still stared at him, fighting the carnal thrall he exuded like a pheromone. His dark brown hair waved away from his strong brow, emphasizing the slashing cheekbones, patrician nose, full lips and rock-hard jaw with the faint dent in the chin. And his eyes...vivid, golden and piercing. They unleashed a warm slide of heat in her veins, even as she fought the urge to duck her head and avoid that scalpel-sharp gaze.

With a quick glance, she took in the black turtleneck and slacks that draped over his powerful shoulders, wide chest and muscular thighs. It didn't require much effort to once again feel those thighs under hers or recall the solid strength of his chest under her hands. Her body tingled with the memory, as if he'd imprinted himself in her skin, in her senses, that night. And no matter how she tried, she couldn't evict him.

"Isobel." The way that low, cultured drawl wrapped around her name was indecent. "Come in."

She dipped her chin in acknowledgment and moved forward. Doing her best not to touch him, she still couldn't avoid breathing in his delicious scent—cedar and sun-warmed air, with a hint of musk that was all male. All him. She'd tried her best to forget the flavor of him from that night, too. Epic fail.

The heels of her boots clacked against the hardwood floor of the foyer, and she almost bent to remove them, not wanting to make scuff marks. She studied the house, not even attempting to hide her curiosity. Yes, the inside lived up to the splendor of the exterior. A wide staircase swept to an upper level, and two airy rooms extended from each side of the entryway. Huge fireplaces, furniture that belonged in magazines and rugs that could've taken up space in museums. And windows. So many windows, which offered views of acres of land.

But she examined her surroundings for hints into the man who owned the home. Framed photos lined the mantel in one of the living rooms, but she couldn't glimpse the images from this distance. Were they of the parents he'd told her about during the blackout? Were they of Gage, when they were teens? Around the time he'd saved Darius's life? Did the photographs contain images of the Wellses?

Her survey swept over the expected but beautiful portraits of landscapes and zeroed in on a glass-and-weathered-wood box. A step closer revealed a collection of antique pocket watches. She shifted her inspection to Darius, who watched her, his expression shuttered. Oh, there had to be a story there.

But she wasn't here to find it out.

"You know why I'm here," she said. "I'd like to get this over with."

"We can talk in the study." He turned, and after a moment of hesitation, she followed.

They entered the massive room, where two walls were floor-to-ceiling windows and the other two were filled with books. A large, glossy black desk dominated one end, and couches, armchairs and an immense fireplace claimed the rest. It invited a person to grab a book and settle in for a long read. She couldn't say how she knew, but she'd bet her last chocolate bar that Darius spent most of his time here.

"So, you've come to a decision." He perched on the edge of his desk and waved toward one of the armchairs. "Please, have a seat."

"No, thank you," Isobel murmured. "I—" She swallowed, for an instant unable to force the words past her suddenly constricted throat. A wave of doubt assailed her, but she broke through it. This was the right decision. "I'll agree to marry you."

She expected a gloating smile or a smirk. Something that boasted, *I win.*

Instead his amber gaze studied her, unwavering and intense. Once more she had the inane impression that he could see past her carefully guarded shields to the vulnerable, confused and scared woman beneath. Her head argued it was impossible, but her heart pounded in warning. His figuring out her fears and insecurities when it came to the situation and *him* would be disastrous.

"What made you change your mind?" he asked.

No way was she telling him about arriving home with Aiden after work one night last week to find the police staked out in front of her building because of a burglary and assault. It'd only nailed home Darius's warning about the unsafety of her environment—for her and for Aiden.

Instead she shrugged. "Does it matter?"

"This was a hard decision for you, wasn't it?" he murmured.

Anger flared inside her like a struck match. "Why would you say that? Maybe I just held out longer so you wouldn't guess how giddy I am to have a chance at all your money? Or maybe I was hoping you would just offer more. I'm a mercenary, after all, always searching for the next opportunity to fill my pockets." His mouth hardened into a firm line, but she didn't care. She was only stating what they both knew he thought of her character. Straightening from the chair, she crossed her arms over her chest and hiked her chin up. "Like I said, I'll agree to marry you, but I have a few conditions first. And they're deal breakers."

He nodded, but the slight narrowing of his eyes relayed his irritation. Over her sarcasm or her stipulations, she couldn't tell, but in the end, neither mattered. Just as long as he conceded.

"First, you must promise to place Aiden, his welfare and protection above anything else. Including the Wellses' needs and agenda."

Another nod, but this one was tighter. And the curves of his mouth remained flattened, grim. As if he forced himself to contain words he wanted to say. If that were the case, he controlled it, and she continued.

"Second, I'm Aiden's mother, and since he's never known a father, you'll fill that role for him. If you don't, I won't go through with this. If you can't love and accept him as if he's your own blood, your son, then we're done. I won't have him hurt or rejected. Or worse, feel like he doesn't belong." Like she had. The soul-deep pain of being unworthy had wounded her, and she still bore the scars. She wouldn't subject Aiden to that kind of hurt. Even if it meant going to court.

"He *is* my blood," Darius said, and she blinked, momentarily stunned by his fierceness. "Gage and I might not have shared the same parents, but in all other ways we were brothers. And his son will be mine, and I'll love Aiden how his father would have if he'd lived and had the chance."

Satisfaction rolled in, flooding her and sweeping away the last of her doubts surrounding that worry. Even if Darius knew next to nothing about the man he called his brother. She believed him when he said he'd love Aiden how Gage *should have*.

"Which brings me to my next concern. I'm Aiden's mother and have been making all decisions regarding him since he was born. I'm not going to lie and claim including you will be an easy adjustment, but I promise to try. But that said, we're his parents, and we will make those decisions together. Us. Without interference from the Wellses."

"Isobel," he growled, pushing off the desk. He stalked a step closer to her, but then drew to an abrupt halt. Shoving a hand through his hair, he turned his head to stare out the window, a tic pulsing along his clenched jaw.

Cursing herself for doing it, she regarded the rigid line. That night when they'd been two nameless, faceless people in the dark, she hadn't needed sight to tell how strong and hard his jaw had been. Her fingers and lips had relayed the information.

God, she needed to stop dwelling on that night. It was

gone, and for all intents and purposes, it didn't happen. It'd disappeared as soon as the morning light had dawned.

"Isobel." He returned his attention to her, and she braced herself for both the impact of his gaze and his words. "I agree with your conditions, but they are his grandparents. And you need to understand that I won't keep him away from them."

Like you have. The accusation remained unsaid, but it screamed silently in the room.

"I emailed Baron and Helena pictures of Aiden after I left for California. And when every one of those messages bounced back as if I'd been blocked, I mailed them, along with letters telling them how he was doing and growing. But they came back unopened, marked 'return to sender.' So I didn't keep him from them. They kept themselves out of his life."

Darius frowned. "Why would they lie about that?"

"Yes. Why would they lie about that?" She shook her head, holding up a hand when his lips parted to what would, no doubt, be another defense of his friend's family. "I have one last condition."

She paused, this one more difficult than the previous ones. Demanding things on Aiden's behalf proved easy for her. But this one... This one involved her and Darius. And it acknowledged that something had happened between them. That "something" being he'd made her body sing like an opera diva hitting notes high enough to shatter glass.

"What is it?" Darius asked when she didn't immediately state the added rule.

"No sex," she blurted out. Mentally rolling her eyes at herself, she inhaled a deep breath and tried it again. "This arrangement is in name only. No sex."

He stilled, his powerful body going motionless. Shadows gathered in his gaze, broiling like a storm building on a dark horizon.

"I guess I need to applaud your honesty," he drawled. "This time around, you're being up front about your plans to betray your husband with another man."

Fury scalded her, and as unwise as it was, she stalked forward, until only inches separated them. "You're so damn sure of yourself. It must be nice to know everything and have all the answers. To be so sure you have all the facts, when in truth you don't. Know. A. Damn. Thing," she bit out.

He lowered his head until their noses nearly bumped, and his breath coasted across her mouth. She could taste his kiss, the sinful, addictive flavor of it.

Memories bombarded her. Memories of his lips owning hers, taking, giving. Of his hands cupping her breasts, tweaking the tips that even now ached and taunted beneath her bra. Of his fingers burying themselves inside her over and over, stroking places inside her that had never been touched before.

Of his cock, so hard and demanding beneath her...

"So you don't care if I take another woman?" he pressed, shifting so another inch disappeared.

An image of him covering someone else, moving over her, straining against her...driving into her, filled her head. A hot wave of anger swamped her, green-tipped claws raking her chest. Her fingers curled into her palms, but she shook her head. Whether it was to rid herself of the mental pictures or in denial of the emotion that smacked of jealousy—a jealousy she had no business, no right, to feel— she didn't know.

"No," she lied, retreating. "Just respect my son and me."

The corner of his mouth tipped into a scornful half smile. "Of course," he said, the words containing more than a hint of a sneer. "Now I have a couple of conditions. The first, we marry in three months. That should give you plenty of time to become accustomed to the arrangement, me and condition number two. You and Aiden are going to move in with me."

Oh, hell no. "No, not happening."

He nodded. "Yes, you are," he contradicted, the flint in his voice echoed in his eyes. "That's my deal breaker. One of my reasons for this whole arrangement is for Aiden to be raised in a safe, secure environment. He'll have both here."

"Okay, fine. I understand that. But why do we need to live with you. We could find an apartment or home in Edison Park or Beverly—"

"No," he stated flatly, cutting her protest off at the knees. "You'll both live here, and Aiden will know a home with two parents. This isn't a point for discussion, Isobel."

Shit. Living under the same roof as Darius? That would be like Eve sleeping under the damn apple tree. Temptation. Trouble. But what option did she have? Sighing, she pinched the bridge of her nose. Okay, she could do it. Besides, this house was huge. She didn't even have to occupy the same side as Darius.

"Fine," she breathed. "Is there anything else?" She had the sudden need to get out of the house. Away from him. At least until she had no choice but to share his space.

"One last thing," he said, his tone deepening, sending an ominous tremor skipping up her spine. "Say my name."

She stared at him, not comprehending his request. No, his order.

"What?"

"Say my name, Isobel," he repeated.

Tilting her head to the side, she conceded warily. "Darius."

Heat flashed in his eyes, there and gone so fast, she questioned whether she imagined it. "That's the first time you've said my name since that morning."

He didn't need to specify to which morning he referred. But the first time... That couldn't be true. They'd had several conversations, or confrontations, since then... Then again, if it were true...

"Why does it matter?" she asked, something dark, complicated and hot twisting her stomach, pooling lower. "Why do you want to hear me say your name?"

He stared at her, the silence growing and pulsing until its deafening heartbeat filled the room. Her own heart thudded against her sternum, adding to the rhythm.

"Because I've wanted to know what it sounds like on your tongue," he said, his voice quiet.

But so loud it rang in her ears. *On your tongue.* The words, so charged with a velvet, sensual promise, or threat—she couldn't decide which—ricocheted against the walls of her head.

She shivered before she could check her telltale reaction. And those eagle eyes didn't miss it. They turned molten, and his nostrils flared, his lips somehow appearing fuller, more carnal.

Danger.

Every survival instinct she possessed blared the warning in bright, blinking red. And in spite of the warmth between her legs transforming to an aching pulse, she heeded it.

Without a goodbye, she whirled around and got the hell out of there.

Maybe one day she could discover the trick to outrunning herself.

But for now, escaping Darius would have to do.

Five

Darius passed through the iron gate surrounding the Wellses' Gold Coast mansion and climbed the steps to the front door. The limestone masterpiece had been in their family for 120 years, harkening back to a time when more than the small immediate family lived under its sloped-and-turreted slate roof. As he twisted his key in the lock and pushed the heavy front door open, he considered himself blessed to be counted among that family. Not by blood, but by choice and love.

After entering the home, he bypassed the formal living and dining areas, and moved toward the rear of the home, the multihued glow from the stained-glass skylight guiding his way. This time of day, a little after five o'clock, Baron should have arrived home from the office. Since his heart attack, he'd cut his work days shorter. Helena and Gabriella should also be home, since they served dinner at six o'clock sharp every evening. In the chaotic turns Darius's life had suffered, this routine and the surety of family tradition had been—and still was—a reassurance, one strong, steady stone in a battered foundation.

But tonight, with the news he had to deliver, he hated potentially being the one taking a hammer to them.

"Darius," Helena greeted, rising from the feminine couch that had been her domain as long as he could remember. The other members of the family could occupy the armchairs or the other sofa, but the small, antique couch was all hers, like a queen with her throne. "There you are."

She crossed the room, clasping his hands in hers and rising on her toes. Obediently, he lowered his head so she could press her lips to one cheek and then the other. Her floral perfume drifted to his nose and wrapped him in the familiarity of home. "I have to admit we've all been discussing you, wondering what it is you have to talk to us about. You're being so mysterious."

She smiled at him, and her expression only increased the unease sitting in his gut. He'd called to give them a heads-up without relaying the reason. This kind of information—about his impending marriage—required a face-to-face conversation.

"Hi, son." Baron came forward and patted him on the shoulder, enfolding Darius's hand in his. Warmth swirled in his chest, as it did every time the man he admired claimed him. "Sit and please tell us your news. Helena and Gabriella have been driving me crazy with their guessing. Do us all a favor and put them out of their gossipy misery."

"Oh, it's just been us, hmm?" Gabriella teased, arching an eyebrow at her father. She turned to Darius and handed him a glass of the Remy Martin cognac he preferred. "He wasn't exactly tuning out over the gossip about the blackout. It seems several people have leveled suits against Richard Dent, the tech billionaire who owns the mansion, for emotional distress. Apparently his apology for trapping people in overnight wasn't enough." She shook her head. "I didn't see him, but I even hear Gideon Knight was there. Can you imagine being caught in the dark with *him*?"

"I've met the man," Darius said, referring to the financial genius who'd launched a wildly successful start-up a couple of years ago. "He's reserved, but not as formidable as people claim."

He accepted the drink, bending to brush a kiss across Gabriella's cheek. She clasped his other hand in hers, squeezing it before releasing him to sit on a chair adjacent to her mother. He sank onto one across from her, while, with a sigh, Baron lowered to the largest armchair in the small circle.

Darius shot him a glance. "How're you feeling, Baron?"

"Fine, fine." He waved off the concerned question. "I'm just old," he grumbled.

After studying him for another few seconds, Darius finally nodded, but his worry over causing Baron more stress with his announcement doubled. Even so, he had to tell them, rather than have them discover the truth from another source.

"You already know Isobel Hughes has returned to Chicago."

All warmth disappeared from Helena's face, her gaze freezing into emerald chips of ice, her lips thinning. Gabriella wore a similar expression, but Baron's differed from the women in his family. Instead of furious, he appeared... tired.

"Yes," Helena hissed. "Gabriella told us Isobel showed up at the gala. How dare she?" she continued. "I would've had her arrested immediately."

"Attending a social event isn't a punishable offense, honey," Baron said, his tone weary.

His wife aimed a narrow-eyed glare in his direction, while Gabriella shook her head. "She's lucky the blackout occurred. Criminal or not, I would've had her escorted from the premises."

Leaning forward and propping his elbows on his spread knees, Darius sighed. "I have an announcement, and it concerns Isobel…and her son. I've asked her to marry me, and I'll become Aiden's stepfather."

A heavy silence plummeted into the room. They gaped at him, or at least Helena and Gabriella did. Again, Baron's reaction didn't coincide with his wife's or daughter's. He didn't glare at Darius, just studied him with a measured contemplation, his fingers templed beneath his chin.

"Are you insane?" Gabriella rasped. She jolted from the chair as if propelled from a cannon. Fury snapped in her eyes. But underneath, Darius caught the shivering note of hurt and betrayal. "Darius, what are you thinking?"

"You saw for yourself what she did to Gage, how she destroyed him. How could you even contemplate tying yourself to that woman?" Helena demanded, her voice trembling.

Pain radiated from his chest, pulsing and hot, with the knowledge that he was hurting the two women he loved most in the world. "I—"

"He's doing it for us," Baron declared, his low baritone quieting Helena's and Gabriella's agonized tirades. "He's marrying her so we can have a relationship with the boy."

"Is this true?" Helena demanded. Darius nodded, and she spread her bejeweled hands wide, shaking her head. "But why? He's not even our grandson."

"He is," Darius stated, his tone brooking no argument. "I've seen him," he added, softening his tone. "He's definitely Gage's son."

Gabriella snorted, crossing her arms over her chest. "You'll forgive us if we don't trust her lying, cheating words."

"Then trust mine."

He and Gabriella engaged in a visual standoff for several seconds before she spun on her heel and stalked across the room, toward the small bar.

"Gabriella's right," Helena said. "Sentimentality could be coloring your opinion, have you seeing a resemblance to Gage because you want there to be one." She paused, her pale fingers fluttering to her throat. "That she refused to have a DNA test done after his birth solidified that he wasn't Gage's son, for me. If he was, she wouldn't have been afraid to have one performed. No." She shook her head. "She's caused too much harm to this family," Helena continued. "I can't forget how she isolated Gage from us, so he had to sneak away just to see us. She destroyed him. I'll never forgive her. Ever."

"And no one asked you to be our sacrificial lamb," Gabriella interjected. "What about your life, marrying someone you love?" she rasped. Clearing her throat, she crossed the room and handed her mother a glass of wine before returning to the chair she'd vacated. "There's a very reasonable solution, and it doesn't require you shackling yourself to a woman who's proven she can't be trusted. If by some miracle the child is really Gage's, then we can fight for custody. We would probably be more fit guardians than *her* anyway."

"Take a small boy away from the only parent he's ever known? Regardless of our opinion concerning her moral values, I've seen her with him. She adores him, and she's his world. It would devastate Aiden to be removed from her." And it would kill Isobel. Of that, Darius had zero doubt. "Isobel wouldn't give up custody without a hard battle, which would be taxing on all of you, too. No, this is the best solution for everyone." He met each of their eyes. "And it's done."

Several minutes passed, and Darius didn't try to fill the silence, allowing them the time to accept what he understood was hard news. But they didn't have a choice. None of them did.

"Thank you, Darius," Baron murmured. "I know this wasn't an easy decision, and we appreciate it, support you in it. Bringing the boy into his family—it's what Gage would've wanted. And we will respect Isobel as his mother…and your wife."

Helena emitted a strangled sound, but she didn't contradict her husband. Gabriella didn't either. But she stood once more and rushed from the room.

"Just be careful, Darius. I've lost one son to Isobel Hughes. I don't think I could bear it if I lost another," Helena pleaded, the pain in her softly spoken words like jagged spikes stabbing his heart. Rising, she cradled his cheek before following Gabriella.

"They'll be fine, son," Baron assured him.

Darius nodded, but apprehension settled in his chest, an albatross he couldn't shake off. His intentions were to unite this family, return some of Helena and Baron's joy by reconciling them with their son's child.

But staring at the entrance where Helena and Gabriella had disappeared, he prayed all his efforts wouldn't end up destroying what he desired to build.

Six

Isobel leaned over Aiden, gently sweeping her hand down his dark curls. After the excitement of moving into a new home and new room jammed with new toys and a race car bed he adored, Aiden had finally exhausted himself. She'd managed to get him fed, bathed and settled in for the night, and all while avoiding Darius.

It'd been a week since she'd agreed to the devil's bargain, and now, fully ensconced in his house, she could no longer use Aiden as an excuse to hide away. With a sigh, she ensured the night-light was on and exited the bedroom, leaving the door cracked behind her. She quietly descended the staircase and headed toward the back of the home, where the kitchen was. She would've preferred not to come downstairs at all, but her stomach rumbled.

The room followed what appeared to be the theme of the home—huge, with windows. Top-of-the-line appliances gleamed under the bright light of a crystal chandelier, and a butcher block and marble island dominated the middle of the vast space. A breakfast nook with a round table and four chairs added a sense of warmth and intimacy to the room. Isobel shook her head as she approached one of the two double-door refrigerators.

She should be grateful. But even now, standing in a kitchen her mother would surrender one of her beloved children to have, she couldn't escape the phantom noose slowly tugging tighter, strangling her. Powerlessness. Purposelessness. Futile anger. The emotions eddied and churned within her like a storm-tossed sea, pitching her, drowning her.

She'd promised herself two years ago that she'd never be at the mercy of another man. Yet if she didn't find some way to protect herself, maintain the identity of the woman she'd come to be, she would end up in a prison worthy of *Architectural Digest*.

Minutes later, she had the makings of a ham-and-cheese sandwich on the island. Real ham—none of that convenience-store deli ham for Darius King—and some kind of gourmet cheese that she could barely pronounce but that tasted like heaven.

"Isobel."

She glanced up from layering lettuce and tomatoes onto her bread to find Darius in the entrance. Her fingers froze, as did the rest of her body. Would this deep, acute awareness occur every time she saw him? It zipped through her body like an electrical current, lighting every nerve ending.

"Darius," she replied, bowing her head back over her dinner.

Though she'd removed her gaze from him, the image of his powerful body seemed emblazoned on her mind's eye. Broad shoulders encased in a thin but soft wool sweater, the V-neck offering her a view of his strong, golden throat, collarbone and the barest hint of his upper chest. Jeans draped low on his hips and clung to the thick strength of his thighs. And his feet...bare.

This was the most relaxed she'd ever seen him, and that he'd allow her to glimpse him this way…it created an intimacy between them she resented and, God, foolishly craved. Because as silly as the presumption might be, she had a feeling he didn't unarm himself like this around many people.

Remember why you're here, her subconscious sniped. *Blackmail and coercion, not because you belong.*

"Did you want a sandwich?" she offered, the reminder shoring up any chinks in her guard.

"Thank you. It looks good." He moved farther into the room and withdrew one of the stools lining the island. Sitting down across from her, he nabbed the bread bin—because what else would one store freshly baked bread in?—and cut two thick slices while she returned to the refrigerator for more meat and cheese. "I'm sorry I had to leave earlier. I didn't want to miss Aiden's first night in the house. There was a bit of an emergency at the office."

"On a Saturday?" she asked, glancing at him.

He shook his head, the corner of his mouth quirking in a rueful smile. "When you're the CEO and president of the company, there's no such thing as a Saturday. Every day is a workday."

"If you let it be," she said. But then again, she understood the need to work when it called. As a single mom with more bills than funds, she hadn't been able to turn down a shift at the supermarket or tell her mom she would skip helping her clean a house.

"True," he agreed, accepting the ham she handed him. "But then I've never had a reason to dial back on the work. I do now," he murmured.

Aiden. He meant Aiden and being a stepfather. She silently repeated the words to herself. But they didn't prevent the warm fluttering in her belly or the hitch in her breath.

"How old are you?" she blurted out, desperate to distract herself from the completely inappropriate and stupid heat that pooled south of her belly button. "I don't mean to be rude, but you don't seem old enough to run a company."

"Thirty," he replied. She could feel his weighty gaze on her face like a physical touch as she finished preparing his meal. "My grandfather started the business as one corporation, and my father grew it into several corporations, eventually folding them all under one parent company. When he died, my father left King Industries Unlimited to me, and I started working there when I was seventeen, in the mail room. I went from there to retail sales associate to account manager and through the ranks, learning the business. By the time I stepped in as CEO and president at twenty-five, and with the guidance of Baron, I had been an employee for seven years."

"Wow," she breathed. "Many men would've just assumed that position as their due and wouldn't bother with starting from the bottom." She hesitated, but then whispered, "I can only imagine your father would've been proud of your work ethic."

With his amber eyes gleaming, Darius nodded. "I hope so. It's how he did it, and I followed in his footsteps."

Their gazes connected, and the breath stuttered in her lungs. Her pulse jammed out an erratic beat at her neck and in her head.

Clearing her throat, she dropped her attention to her sandwich, and with more effort than it required, sliced it in half and did the same to his. "Tell me more about your work?" she requested, cursing the slight waver in her voice. Her biggest mistake would be letting Darius know he affected her in any manner. *Get it together, woman*, she scolded herself. "Was it hard suddenly running such a huge company?"

Over ham-and-cheese sandwiches, they spoke about his job and all it required. Eventually the conversation curved into more personal topics. He shared that his home had been his parents', one they'd purchased only months before they'd died. And the pocket watch collection had been his father's, and like the family company, Darius had taken it over and continued to add to it. She told him about her family, leaving out the part about her brother's lucrative but illegal side business. Even her mother pretended it didn't exist and refused to accept any money earned from it. Isobel also added amusing stories about Aiden from the last two years.

"He took one look at Santa and let out the loudest, most terrified scream. I think the old guy damn near had a heart attack." She chuckled, remembering her baby's reaction to the mall Santa. "He started squirming and kicking his legs. His foot caught good ol' Saint Nick right in the boys, and they had to shut down Winter Wonderland for a half hour while, I'm sure, Santa iced himself in his workshop."

Darius laughed, the loud bark echoing in the room. He shook his head, shoulders shaking. His eyes, bright with humor, crinkled at the corners, and his smile lit up his normally serious expression.

An unsmiling Darius was devastatingly handsome.

A smiling Darius? Beyond description.

Slowly, as they continued to meet each other's gazes, the lightness in the room dimmed, converting into something weightier, darker. A thickness—congested with memories, things better left unspoken and desire—gathered between them. Even though her mind screamed caution, she didn't—couldn't—glance away. And if she were brutally honest? She didn't want to.

"You're different from how I remember you," he said, his gaze roaming over her face. Her lips prickled when that intense regard fell on her mouth and hovered for several heated moments. "Even though it was only a couple of times, you were quieter then, maybe even a little timid and withdrawn. At least around me. Gage said you were different around your family."

"I trusted them." She knew they wouldn't mock her just because she didn't use the proper fork or couldn't discuss politics. They accepted her, loved her. She'd never feared them.

Darius frowned, leaning forward on the crossed arms he'd propped on the marble island. "You didn't trust your husband?"

She paused, indecision about how much to share temporarily muting her. But, in the end, she refused to lie. "No," she admitted, the ghostly remnants of hurt from that time in her life rasping her voice. "I didn't."

How could she? Gage had been a liar, and he'd betrayed their short marriage. He'd promised her Harry and Meghan and had given her Henry VIII and wives one, two and five.

To gain his family's sympathy after marrying Isobel, he'd thrown her under the proverbial bus, accusing her of tricking him into marrying her by claiming she'd been pregnant. She hadn't been, though it'd happened shortly after their marriage. At first, they'd been happy—or at least she'd believed they'd been. True, they'd lived in a tiny apartment, living off her small paycheck from the grocery store while he looked for work since his family had cut him off, but they'd loved one another. After she'd refused to take a paternity test at the demand of his parents, things had changed. Subtly, at first, he'd isolated her from family and friends. He'd claimed that since his family had disowned him, it was just the two of them—soon to be the three of them—against the world. But that world had become smaller, darker, lonelier…scarier.

Gage had been a master gaslighter. Unknown to her, he'd thrown himself on his parents' mercies, spewing lies— that she'd demanded he abandon his family, that she was cheating on him. All to remain in the family fold as their golden child and maintain their compassion and empathy by making Isobel out to be a treacherous bitch he couldn't divorce and turn back out on the street. In truth, he'd been a spoiled, out-of-control child who hadn't wanted her but didn't want anyone else to have her either.

"He was your husband," Darius said, his tone as low as the shadows already accumulating in his eyes.

"He was my jailor," she snapped.

"Just like this is a prison?" he growled, sweeping a hand to encompass the kitchen, the beautiful home. "He gave you everything, while giving up his own family, his friends—hell, his world—for you. What more could he have possibly done to make you happy?"

Pain and anger clashed inside her, eating away any trace of the calm and enjoyment she'd found with Darius during the past hour. "Kindness. Compassion. Loyalty. Fidelity."

"It's convenient that he isn't here to defend himself, isn't it? Still, it's hard to play the victim now when we all know how you betrayed him, made a fool of him. In spite of all that, he wouldn't walk away from you." Fire flared in his eyes. The same fierce emotion incinerating her, hardened his full lips into a grim line. "I saw him just before he died. I begged him to walk away, to leave you. But he wouldn't. Even as it broke him that he couldn't even claim his son because of the men you'd fucked behind his back."

Trembling, Isobel stood, the scratch of the stool's legs across the tiled floor a discordant screech. Flattening her palms on the counter, she glared at him, in this moment, hating him.

"I broke him? He broke me! And destroyed whatever love I still had for him when he looked at our baby and called him a bastard. So don't you dare talk to me about being ungrateful. You don't know what the hell you're talking about."

Refusing to remain and accept any more accusations, she whipped around the island and stalked toward the kitchen entrance. Screw him. He didn't know her, had no clue—

"Damn it, Isobel," he snapped, seconds before his fingers wrapped around her upper arm.

"Don't touch—" She whirled back around and, misjudging how close he stood behind her, slammed into the solid wall of his chest. Her hands shot up in an instinctive attempt to prevent the tumble backward, but the hard band of his arms wrapped around her saved her from falling onto her ass.

The moment her body collided with his, the protest died on her tongue. Desire—unwanted, uncontrollable and greedy—swamped her. Her fingers curled into his sweater in an instinctive attempt to hold on to the only solid thing in a world that had constricted then yawned endlessly wide, leaving her dangling over a crumbling edge.

"Isobel." Her name, uttered in that sin-on-the-rocks voice, rumbled through her, and she shook her head, refusing to acknowledge it—or the eruption of electrical pulses that raced up and down her spine. "Look at me."

His long fingers slid up her back, over her nape and tunneled into her hair. She groaned, unable to trap the betraying sound. Not when his hand tangled in the strands, tugging her head backward, sending tiny prickles along her scalp. She sank her teeth into her bottom lip, locking down on another embarrassing sound of pleasure.

"No," he growled, pressing his thumb to the center of her abused lip and freeing it. With a low, carnal hum, he rubbed a caress over the flesh. "Don't hold back from me. Let me hear what I do to you."

Oh, God. If she could ease her grip on his shirt, she'd clap her palms over her ears to block out his words. She hadn't forgotten how his voice had aided and abetted his touch in unraveling every one of her inhibitions the night of the blackout. It was a velvet weapon, one that slipped beneath her skin, her steel-encased guards, to wreak sensual havoc.

"Look at me, sweetheart," he ordered again. This time she complied, lifting her lashes to meet his golden gaze. "Good," he murmured, giving her bottom lip one last sweep with his fingers before burying them in her hair so both hands cupped her head. "Keep those fairy eyes on me."

Fairy eyes.

The description, so unlike him and so reminiscent of the man in the dark hallway weeks ago, swept over her like a soft spring rain. And then she ceased to think.

Because he proceeded to devastate her.

If their first kiss in the dark weeks ago started as a gentle exploration, this one was fierce. His mouth claimed and conquered, his tongue demanding an entrance she willingly surrendered. Wild and raw, he devoured her like a starving man intent on satisfying a bottomless craving. Again and again, he sucked, lapped, dueled, demanding she enter into carnal battle with him.

Submit to him. Take him. Dominate him.

With a needy whimper that should probably have mortified her, she fisted his shirt harder and rose on her toes, granting him even more access and commanding more of him. Angling her head, she opened her mouth wider, savoring his unique flavor, getting drunk on it.

But it wasn't enough. Never enough.

"Jesus Christ," he swore against her lips, nipping the lower curve, then pressing stinging kisses along her jaw and down her throat.

Kisses that echoed in her breasts, sensitizing them, tightening the tips. Kisses that eddied and swirled low in her belly. Kisses that had her thighs squeezing to contain the ache between her legs. Already a nagging emptiness stretched wide in her sex, begging to be filled by his fingers, his cock. Didn't matter. Just as long as some part of him was inside her, branding her.

The thought snuck under the desire, and once it infiltrated, she couldn't eject it. Instead it rebounded against her skull, loud and aggressive. *Branding me. Branding me.*

And Darius would do it; he would imprint himself into her skin, her body until she couldn't erase him from her thoughts…her heart. Until he slowly took over, and she ceased to exist except for the sole purpose of pleasing him…of loving him.

No. No, damn it.

Never again would she allow that to happen.

With a muted cry, she shoved her palms against his chest, lunging out of his embrace, away from his kiss, his touch.

Their harsh, jagged breaths reverberated in the kitchen. His broad chest rose and fell, his piercing gaze narrowed on her like that of a bird of prey's, waiting for her to make the slightest move so he could swoop in and capture her.

Even as her brain yelled at her to get the hell out of there, her body urged her to let herself be caught and devoured.

"No," she whispered, but not to him, to her traitorous libido.

"Then you better go," Darius ground out as if she'd spoken to him. *"Now."*

Not waiting for another warning, she whipped around, raced down the hall and bounded up the stairs. Once she closed the bedroom door behind her, she stumbled across the floor and sank to the mattress.

Oh, God, what had she done?

The no-sex rule had been hers. And yet the first time he'd touched her, she'd burned faster than kindling in a campfire.

Desire and passion were the gateways to losing reason, control and, eventually, independence.

Those who forget the past are condemned to repeat it.

She'd heard the quote many times throughout her life. But never had it been so true as this moment.

She'd made this one mistake.

She couldn't afford another.

Seven

An ugly sense of déjà vu settled over Isobel as she stared at the ornate front door of the Wellses' home. It'd been a slightly brisk October evening just like this one four years ago when she'd arrived on this doorstep, arm tucked in Gage's, excited and nervous to meet his family. She'd been so painfully naïve then, at twenty, never imaging the disdain she would experience once she crossed the threshold.

The differences between then and now could fill a hoarder's house. One, she was no longer that young girl so innocently in love. Second, she fully expected to be scorned and derided. And perhaps the most glaring change.

She stood next to Darius, but with Gage's son riding her hip.

Her stomach clenched, pulling into knots so snarled and tight, they would need Houdini himself to unravel them.

"There's no need to be nervous," Darius murmured beside her, settling a hand at the small of her back. The warmth of his hand penetrated the layers of her coat and dress, and she steeled herself against it, wishing he'd remove it. When about to enter the lion's den, she couldn't allow her focus and wits to be compromised by his touch. "I've already talked to them about us, and I'll be right here with you."

Was that supposed to be a reassurance? A pep talk? Well, both were epic fails. She wore no blinders when it came to Gage's family. Nothing—no talk or his presence—would ever convince them to accept her. She'd robbed them of their most precious gift. There was no forgiveness for that.

"This night is about Aiden," she said more to herself than him. "All I care about is how they treat him."

The weight of his stare stroked her face like the last rays of the rapidly sinking sun. She kept her attention trained on the door. It'd been almost a week since she'd moved into his home—since the night they'd kissed. And in that time, she'd become a master of avoidance. With a house the size of a museum, it hadn't proven to be difficult. When he spent time with Aiden, she withdrew to her room. And when she couldn't evade him, she ensured Aiden remained a buffer between them. A little cowardly? Yes. But when engaged in a battle for her dignity and emotional sanity, the saying "by any means necessary" had become her motto.

"They'll love him," he replied, with certainty and determination ringing in his voice.

Before she could respond, the door opened and Gabriella, Gage's sister, stood in the entranceway. The beautiful, willowy brunette, who was a feminine version of her brother, smiled, stepping forward to press a kiss to Darius's cheek.

An unfamiliar and nasty emotion coiled and rattled in Isobel's chest. Her grip on Aiden tightened, while her vision sharpened on the other woman.

Whoa.

Isobel blinked. Sucked in a breath. What the hell was

going on? No way could she actually be...*jealous*. Not by any stretch of the imagination did Darius belong to her. And even if in some realm with unicorns and rainbows where he was hers to claim, Gabriella was like a sister to him.

Get a grip.

If this overreaction heralded the evening's future, it promised to be a long one. Long and painful.

"It's about time you arrived," Gabriella said, laying a hand on his chest. "Mother and Dad are climbing the walls."

"Now, that I'd pay money to see," he drawled.

So would Isobel.

"Gabriella, you remember Isobel." Darius's hand slid higher, to the middle of her back, and just this once, she was thankful for it.

The other woman switched her focus from Darius to Isobel. Jade eyes so like her brother's met hers, the warmth that had greeted Darius replaced with ice. Isobel fought not to shiver under the chill. *She can't hurt you. No one in this house can hurt you*, Isobel reminded herself, repeating the mantra. Hoping it was true.

"Of course," Gabriella said, her tone even, polite. "Hello, Isobel." She shifted her gaze to Aiden, who hugged Isobel's neck, his face buried against her coat. Unsurprisingly, he had a thumb stuck firmly in his mouth. Isobel didn't blame him or remove it. Hell, she suddenly wanted to do the same. "And this must be Aiden."

"Yes, it is." Darius removed his hand from Isobel's back and reached around to stroke a hand down her son's curls. Curls that were the same nearly black shade as Gabriella's. "Aiden, can you say hi?"

Shyly, Aiden lifted his head and whispered, "Hi," giving Gabriella a small wave.

The other woman stared at the toddler, her lips forming a small O-shape. Moisture brightened her gaze, and she blinked rapidly. "Hi, Aiden," she whispered back. Drawing in an audible breath, she looked at Darius. "He looks like Gage."

Anger flared to life in Isobel's chest. She wanted to snap, *Of course he does*, but she swallowed it down. Yet she could do nothing about the flames still flickering inside her.

Part of her wanted to say screw this and demand Darius drive them home. But the other half—the half that wanted the Wells family's derision toward her regarding Aiden's paternity laid to rest—convinced her to remain in place. She still resented their rejection of her son, but if they were willing to meet her halfway so Aiden could know them, then she could try to let it go.

Try.

"Come in." Gabriella stepped backwards, waving them inside, her regard still fixed on Aiden.

Minutes later, with their coats turned over to a waiting maid, they all strode toward the back of the house and entered a small parlor. Helena, lovely and regal, was perched upon the champagne-colored settee like a queen surveying her subjects from her throne. And Baron occupied the largest armchair, his salt-and-pepper hair—more salt now than the last time she'd seen him—gleaming under the light thrown by a chandelier.

Their conversation ended when Gabriella appeared with Darius, Aiden and Isobel in tow. Slowly, Baron stood, and Isobel just managed to refrain from frowning. Though still tall and handsome, his frame seemed thinner, even a little more…fragile. And perhaps the most shocking change was that the hard, condemning expression that had been his norm when forced to share the air with her was not in attendance. By no means was his gaze welcoming, but it definitely didn't carry the harshness it formerly had.

But the censure his demeanor lacked, Helena's more than made up for. She rose as well, her scrutiny as frigid and sharp as an icicle. Her mouth formed a flat, disapproving line, and for a moment Isobel almost believed she'd stumbled back in time. Gage's mother had disliked her on sight, and like a fine wine, the dislike had only aged. Into hatred.

Suddenly Isobel's arms tightened around Aiden, flooded with the need to shield him, protect him. And herself. He was her lodestone, reminding her that she was no longer that timid, impressionable girl from the past.

"Darius." Baron crossed the room, his hand extended. Darius clasped it, and they pulled each other close for a quick but loving embrace. Then the older man turned toward her, and even with his lack of animosity, she braced herself. "Isobel, welcome back to our home." He stretched his hand toward her, and after a brief hesitation, she accepted it, her heart pulsing in her throat. His grip squeezed around her fingers, rendering her speechless, the gesture the most warmth he'd ever shown her. "And this is Aiden."

Awe saturated his deep baritone, the same wonder that had filtered through his daughter's in the foyer. His nostrils flared, his fingers curling into his palms as if he fought the need to reach out and touch her son. Clearing his throat, Baron switched his gaze back to Isobel.

"He has your eyes, but his features… It's like looking at a baby picture of my son," he rasped. "May I…?" He held his arms out toward Aiden.

Nerves jingled in her belly, but the plea in the man's eyes trumped them. "Aiden? Do you want to go to Mr. Baron?" She loosened her grip on her son and tried to hand him, but the child clung harder to her as he shook his head. "I'm sorry," she murmured, feeling regret at the flash of disappointment and hurt in the man's gaze. "He's a little shy around new people."

"A shame," Gabriella murmured behind her.

Isobel stiffened, a stinging retort dancing on the tip of her tongue. But Darius interceded, tossing a quelling glance toward Gage's sister over his shoulder. With an arched eyebrow and open hands, he silently requested to take Aiden. Dipping her chin, she passed her son to Darius, who practically launched himself into the man's arms. Aiden popped his thumb back into his mouth, grinning at Darius around it.

"Well, how about that," Baron whispered. "He certainly seems to have taken to you."

Darius shrugged, sweeping a hand down Aiden's small back. "It doesn't take long for him to warm up. And once he does, he'll talk your ear off." He poked Aiden's rounded tummy, and the boy giggled.

The cheerful, innocent sound stole into Isobel's heart, as it'd had done from the very first time she'd heard it.

"I have to admit, he does resemble Gage," Helena said, appearing at her husband's side, studying Aiden. "Isobel." She nodded, before dismissing her and turning to Darius, an affectionate smile thawing her expression. "Darius." She tilted her head, and he brushed a kiss on her cheek. "I haven't seen you in days. But it seems you have time for everyone else." She tapped him playfully on the chest. "Beverly Sheldon told me how she saw you at the Livingstons' dinner party. And how Shelly Livingston couldn't seem to keep her hands to herself." Helena chuckled as if immensely amused by Shelly Livingston's grabby hands.

Isobel fought not to react to the first shot fired across the bow. It hadn't taken long at all. She thought Helena or Gabriella would've at least waited until after drinks before they got in the first dig, but apparently the "you're an interloper and don't belong, darling" portion of the evening had begun.

Yet her purpose—letting Isobel know that Darius had attended a social event without her on his arm, probably out of shame—had struck true. Which was as inane as that flash of jealousy with Gabriella. Pretending to be the newly engaged, loving couple hadn't been a part of their bargain.

He could do as he wanted, escort whom he wanted, flirt with whom he wanted...sleep with whom he wanted. It didn't matter to her.

Liar.

Flipping her once again intrusive, know-it-all subconscious the middle finger, she shored up the walls surrounding her heart.

"Beverly Sheldon gossips too much and needs to find a hobby," Darius replied, frowning. "It was an impromptu business dinner, not a party, and I'm sure Shelly's fiancé, who also attended with her father, would've had some objections if she 'couldn't seem to keep her hands to herself.'"

Helena waved his explanation off with a flick of her fingers and another laugh. "Well, you're a handsome man, Darius. It's not surprising women flock to you."

"Helena," Baron said, a warning heavy in her name.

"Now, don't 'Helena' me, Baron." She tsked, brushing her husband's arm before strolling off toward the bar across the room. "Would anyone like a drink?"

Good God. This was going to be a really long evening.

"Have you decided on whether or not you'll acquire SouthernCare Insurance?" Baron asked Darius, reclining in his chair as one of the servants placed an entrée plate in front of him.

Isobel let the business talk float over her, as she had most of the discussions around the dinner table. If the topics weren't about business, then it was Helena and Gabriella speaking about people and events Isobel didn't know anything about, and neither woman had made the attempt to draw her into the conversation. Not that she minded. The less they said to each other, the better the chance of Isobel making it through this dinner without emotional injuries from their sly innuendoes.

Still, right now she envied her son. By the time dinner

was ready to be served, Aiden had been nodding off in Darius's arms. He'd taken Aiden to one of the bedrooms and settled him in. Aiden had escaped this farce of a family dinner, but she hadn't been as lucky.

Mimicking Baron, Isobel shifted backward, granting the servant plenty of room to set down her plate of food. When she saw the food, she barely managed not to flinch. Prime rib, buttered asparagus and acorn squash.

Gage's favorite meal.

She lifted her head and met Helena's arctic gaze. So the choice hadn't been a coincidence. No, it'd been deliberate, and just another way to let Isobel know she hadn't been forgiven.

Nothing had been forgotten.

Message received.

Picking up her fork—the correct fork—and knife, Isobel prepared to eat the perfectly cooked meat that would undoubtedly taste like ash on her tongue.

"I was leaning toward yes before the trouble with their vice president leaked." Darius paused, murmuring a "thank you" as a plate was set in front of him. "One of their employees came forward about long-time, systematic sexual harassment within the company, and their senior vice president of operations is one of the key perpetrators. No," he said, shaking his head, tone grim. "I won't have King Industries Unlimited tainted with that kind of behavior."

Unlike the rest of the conversation surrounding business, Darius's comment snagged her attention, surprising her so much, she blurted out, "You would really base your decision on that?"

Silence crackled in the room. In the quiet, her question seemed to bounce off the walls. Everyone stared at her, but she refused to cringe.

It was Darius's scrutiny she resolutely met, ignoring

the others'. And in his eyes, she didn't spy irritation at her interruption. No, just the usual intensity that rendered her breathless.

"Of course. I don't condone it, and I won't be associated with any business or person who does. Every person under my employ or the umbrella of my company should have the expectation of safety and an environment free of intimidation."

"Your employees are lucky to work for you then," she murmured.

More and more companies were trying to change their policies and eliminate sexual harassment—or at least indulge in lip service about removing it. But the truth couldn't be denied—not everyone enjoyed that sense of fairness or security. Even at the supermarket, the supervisor didn't think anything of calling her honey or flirting with her, going so far as to occasionally say how "lucky" her man was. She'd never bothered to correct him, assuming if he knew she didn't have a "man" at home, the inappropriate behavior would only worsen.

That Darius would turn down what was most likely a multimillion-dollar deal because of his beliefs and out of consideration for those under him… It was admirable. Heroic.

"I like to hope so," he replied just as softly.

A sense of intimacy seemed to envelop them, and she couldn't tear her gaze away from his. Her breath stuttered in her lungs, her heart tap-dancing a quick tattoo at the heat in those golden depths.

"Of course his employees are fortunate," Gabriella interjected, shattering the illusion of connection. "Darius is a good man. He doesn't brag about it, but he's founded—and often single-handedly funded—several foundations that provide scholarships for foster children, housing for abused women coming out of shelters, and literacy and job-placement programs for under-privileged youth. And those are just some of his...projects."

The strategic pause before "projects" let Isobel know Gabriella considered *her* to be one of those charity cases. If passive-aggressiveness was a weapon, Gabriella and Helena would own codes and security clearances.

"It's wonderful to know Aiden will have an admirable role model in Darius," Isobel said, voice neutral. Silence once more descended in the room, but Isobel didn't shrink from it. The scared, quiet girl they had known no longer existed; the woman she was now wouldn't stand mutely like a living target for their verbal darts.

Darius glanced at her, and once more she found herself trapped in his gaze. Something flickered in the golden depths. Something that had her lifting her glass of wine to her lips for a deep sip.

"If Gage couldn't be here to raise him, he would've wanted family to do it," Darius finally said to the room, but his eyes... His eyes never wavered from her.

"Still," Helena pressed, not looking at Darius but keeping her attention firmly locked on Isobel. "A boy should know his father. Tell me, Isobel, since you claim Aiden is Gage's, have you showed him pictures? Does he know who his real father is?"

"Helena," Darius growled a warning.

"Darius, darling," Helena replied, tilting her head to the side. "We all commend you for your sacrifice in this difficult situation, but I think you'd agree that a child deserves to know who his true parents are, right?"

A muscle jumped along Darius's jaw, but Isobel set her glass down on the table, meeting Helena's scrutiny.

"I've always shown Aiden pictures of Gage, since he is Aiden's father, as well as talked to him about Gage. And he understands who his *real father* is, as much as a two-year-old can."

"Hmm," came Helena's noncommittal, *condescending* answer.

"Aiden looks so much like Gage when he was that age," Baron added from the head of the table, aiming a quelling glance at his wife.

But Helena didn't respond, instead turning to Gabriella and asking about a function she was supposed to attend that week.

Pain and humiliation slashed at Isobel, but she fought not to reveal it. Not only did she refuse to grant them that pleasure, but she didn't have anything to be ashamed of. They accused *her* of cheating, when the opposite had been true.

But what would be the point in trying to explain the truth to his family? They would never believe her. Not after they'd always accepted every utterance from Gage as the gospel.

And with him dead, he was even more of a saint.

And she would always be a sinner.

Eight

Darius poured himself another glass of bourbon. This would be his third. Or maybe fourth. Didn't matter. He wasn't drunk yet; he could still think. So whatever number he was on, it wouldn't be his last. He'd keep tossing it back until the unease and anger no longer crawled inside him like ants in a colony.

Tonight had been a clusterfuck. Oh, it'd been frigidly polite, but still… Clusterfuck.

After crossing the study, he sank down onto the couch and took a sip of the bourbon. Clasping the squat glass, he slid down, resting his head on the couch's back, his legs sprawled wide.

Jesus, when would the forgetful part of this begin?

He hated this sense of…betrayal that clung to him like a filthy film of dirt. And no matter how hard he tried to scrub it clean with excuses, it remained, stubborn and just as grimy.

When he'd asked Isobel to the Wellses' house that night,

he'd promised her they would be civil, and she would be in a safe space, be welcomed. Baron had, but Helena and Gabriella, they'd made a liar of him. He understood their resentment—even now, when he thought of Gage, that mixture of anger and grief still churned in his chest, his gut. But tonight had been about Aiden, about them connecting with the boy, and that meant forging a fragile truce with his mother. Showing her respect, at least.

Hours later, the disappointment, the disquiet continued to pulse within him like a wound, one that refused to heal.

Isobel had definitely been enemy number one when she'd been married to Gage. All of them believed Gage had moved too fast, married too young. Darius had been equally confused when he'd cut them all off for almost a year. None of them could understand why Gage hadn't divorced her, especially when he started confiding in them about her infidelity. As far as Darius could tell, his friend had genuinely been in love with his wife, and her betrayals had destroyed him.

Still. Remembering the woman he'd shared a hallway with in the dark... The woman who loved her son so selflessly... The woman whose family rallied around her, supported her and her son unconditionally... That Isobel didn't really coincide with the one the Wellses detested.

But if he were brutally honest—and alcohol had a way of dragging that kind of truth forth—it hadn't only been this evening that had unnerved him.

She did.

Everything about her unsettled him.

From the thick dark hair with the hints of fire to the delectable, curvaceous body that tempted him like a red flag snapping in front of a bull.

Earlier, when she'd thrust her chin up in that defiant angle, he'd had to force himself to remain in his seat instead of marching around the table and shocking the hell out of everyone by tugging her head back and claiming that beautiful, created-for-sin mouth.

Another truth he could admit in the dark with only bourbon for company.

He wanted her.

Fuck, did he want her.

Maybe if the past had stayed in the past, he could have convinced himself their space of time in the hallway had been just that—a blip, an anomaly. But once he'd kissed her again, once he'd swallowed her moans, once he'd felt her slick, satiny flesh spasm around his fingers as she came... No, he craved this woman with a need that was usually reserved for oxygen and water.

Even knowing that she'd betrayed Gage just as Faith had cheated on Darius, he still couldn't expunge this insane, insatiable desire.

So, what did that say about him? About his dignity? His fucking intelligence?

He snorted, raising his glass to his lips for a deep sip.

It said that, as much as he'd claimed to the contrary, his dick had equal partnership with his brain.

Yet...he frowned into the golden depths of the bourbon. The more time he spent with Isobel, the more doubt crept into his head, infiltrating his long-held ideas about her, about the woman he'd believed her to be. But for him to accept that she was not the woman who'd betrayed her husband in the past, it would mean that Gage had consciously—and maliciously—lied to Darius's face. And to his family. And to all of their friends. It would mean Darius's best friend, the man who'd been closer to him than a brother, had intentionally destroyed Isobel's reputation.

And that he couldn't believe.

Could Gage have somehow misinterpreted her actions? Or maybe there was more to the story that Gage hadn't shared with his family before his death?

"Darius?"

He glanced in the direction of the study's entrance, where the sound of his name in *her* voice had originated.

And immediately wished he hadn't.

Now the image of her standing in the doorway, barefoot, her long, toned legs exposed by some kind of T-shirt that hit her midthigh, and hair a sexy tumble around her beautiful face would be permanently branded onto his retinas.

"What are you wearing?" he growled.

Hell, he hadn't intended to vocalize that question. And with his bourbon-weakened control, no way in hell could he prevent the lust careering through him.

She peeked down at herself, then returned her fairy eyes to him. "What?" she asked. "This is what I sleep in. Excuse me if it's not La Perla enough for you, but I didn't exactly expect to bump into anyone."

La Perla. Fox and Rose. Agent Provocateur.

His ex-wife had insisted on only purchasing the expensive, luxury lingerie for herself, and they'd shown up regularly on his credit card statements, which was the only reason he recognized the brands.

But damn. Now, staring at her body with those lethal curves, he would love to put that useless-until-now information to work. To drape her in the softest silk and the most delicate lace. To personally choose corsets, bras and panties to adorn a woman who didn't need anything to enhance her ethereal beauty and earthy sensuality. And still he wanted to give them to her. To see her in them.

To peel them from her.

Taking another sip, he wrenched his gaze from the temptation in cotton.

"What do you want, Isobel?" he rasped.

She stepped into the room, the movement hesitant. It should be. If she had any idea of the need grinding inside him like a relentlessly turning screw, she'd leave.

"I was headed toward the kitchen and saw the light on in here. I thought you'd gone to bed." A pause. "Are you okay?"

"I'm fine," he said automatically. *Lie.*

"I'm sorry for you," she said, gliding farther into the room and halting a small distance from him. As if unsure whether or not she should chance come any closer.

Smart woman.

The way the alcohol and lust coursed through him like rain-swollen rapids, he should warn her away, bark an order to get out of the study. Instead he watched her, a predator silently waiting for his prey to approach just near enough for him to pounce.

"Sorry for me," he repeated on a serrated huff of laughter. "Why?"

"Because I went there tonight knowing I wouldn't be welcome. I wasn't surprised by anything that happened. But you were shocked…and hurt. And for that, I'm sorry."

He lifted his head, stared at her, astonishment momentarily robbing him of speech.

Discomfort flickered across her features, and she shrugged a shoulder. "Anyway… Your relationship with them isn't my business…"

"You weren't hurt?" He ground his teeth around a curse. He hadn't intended to snap at her. Dragging in a deep breath, he held it, then exhaled. "You weren't hurt by what they said, how they acted?"

She studied him for a long second, then slowly shook her head. "No, Darius. For me, it was business as usual. For the two years I was married, I was never good enough. Smart enough. Sophisticated enough. Just never…enough."

"I can't believe that," he snapped, banging his glass on the table and surging to his feet. Tunneling his fingers through his hair, he paced away from her. He *couldn't.*

Because then what did that say about the past, about what he'd believed?

What would it say about the family he idolized?

"It's not that you can't believe it. You won't," she contradicted, her voice low, laced with an unmistakable thread of resignation. As if she hadn't expected much from him. Certainly not for him to accept her truth. "And you never will. You won't allow yourself to even consider that the brave man who saved you from a burning building, the honorable man who became your brother when you lost your parents could've changed. Or at the very least, had one side with you and another with his wife, who he grew to resent almost from the moment he said 'I do.'"

"No," Darius rasped, stalking closer and eliminating the small space between them. "He went against his family's wishes to have you, risking everything for you…"

"And he came to hate me for it," she whispered, tilting her head back to meet his gaze. "Just like you eventually will. You said you're going through with this engagement and marriage for Baron, Helena and Gabriella. What happens when they force you to choose between your pretend wife and them? Because it'll happen. They've earned your love, your loyalty, but you've given your word to me. Oh, yes." She nodded, shadows swirling in her lovely, haunted eyes. "In the end, you'll resent me, too."

He squeezed his eyes closed, his jaw so hardened, so tense, the muscles along it twinged. Emotion. So much emotion howled and whistled inside him, he feared one misstep, one wrong-placed touch, and he would shred under the power of it.

"I already resent you, Isobel," he ground out, forcing himself to meet her gaze. Her scent—delicate like newly opened rose petals and intoxicating like the bourbon he'd been drinking—wrapped around him with phantom arms. Heat emanated from her petite body, and he wanted to curl against it. "And it has nothing to do with tonight or a future emotional tug-of-war. I hate that I can't get you out of my head. Can't stop replaying a night that should've never happened. I can still *feel* you. Your lips parting for mine. Your skin under my hands. Your tight, soaking-wet flesh gripping my fingers so hard, it almost bruised me. You just won't get out of my goddamn head."

Lust churned his voice to the consistency of gravel. "I hate that I know who you are, and I still want to fuck you. I hate that I can't tell if you're the sweet, giving woman from that dark hallway or the conniving one who was married to my best friend." He shifted that scant inch forward and brought his chest to hers, his thighs to hers. His breath to hers. "I hate that I want to find out."

Her labored pants broke across his mouth, and he slicked his tongue across his lips, seeking to taste that hard puff of breath. Her scrutiny followed the movement, and like clouds moving in over a blue sky, lust darkened her gaze. God, why didn't she close those beautiful eyes? Shield both of them from the knowledge that she craved him as he did her? He placed the responsibility on her, because he was the weaker one. She had to be the strong one and save them both.

"Turn around and walk out of here, Isobel," he warned her, his voice so guttural, he almost winced. "I'll break your condition. I'll put my hands and mouth on you. I'll finish what we started in the dark if you don't."

A small, muted whimper escaped her. Almost as if she'd tried to trap the needy sound but hadn't been fast enough.

"You're not running, sweetheart." He lifted his hand, let it hover over her cheek for a weighty moment, granting her time to evade it. But she remained still, and he swept the pad of his thumb over her cheekbone, then lower, across the lush curve of her bottom lip.

"No," she whispered. "I'm not."

"Your rule," he whispered back.

"Break it... Break me."

The request, uttered on a trembling breath, snapped the already tattered ropes on his control, and with a groan, he crushed his mouth to hers. When her heady taste hit his tongue, that groan morphed into a growl. Delicious. Addictive. He drove his fingers into her hair, tipping her head back so he could gorge on her. Yeah, he was committing the sin of gluttony, and resigned himself to hell for it.

Her palms slid over his sides and up his back, curling into the backs of his shoulders. The bite of her nails sent pleasure sizzling through him like an electrical charge, arrowing straight for his cock. He shifted, pressing harder against her, giving her full, undeniable disclosure to what she did to him.

Abandoning her hair, he dropped his arms, molding his hands to her ass, cupping the curves. He bent his knees, then abruptly straightened, hiking her into his arms. A bolt of carnal satisfaction struck him when her legs wrapped around his waist and her arms encircled his neck, holding on to him. Her mouth clung to his, that wicked tongue twisting and tangling, dancing and dueling. Damn, he wanted that talented mouth on his skin, on every part of him.

After quickly striding back to the couch, he sank down to the cushions, arranging her so she straddled his thighs. He broke their kiss long enough to fist the hem of her shirt and yank it over her head. All that hair tumbled down around her shoulders, back and chest, transforming her into a seductive siren. He wanted to crash himself against her and drown in pleasure.

"You're going to take me under, aren't you?" he murmured, voicing his thoughts.

"Are you afraid?" she asked.

He shifted his enraptured gaze from her hair to her eyes. *Yes.*

The reply erupted inside him, ringing with certainty,

but he didn't vocalize it. Instead he cradled the nape of her neck and drew her forward until their lips brushed, pressed, mated.

Impatient, he stroked a caress over her shoulders, down her chest and finally reacquainted himself with the flesh he'd dreamed about before waking up, hard and hurting. He cupped her, squeezed…and it wasn't enough. Ripping his mouth free of hers, he bent his head, trailed his lips over the soft swell of her breast, then circled his tongue around the taut, dusky peak.

Her cry rebounded off the walls and windows, and her arms clasped him to her. Her scent, rich and deep, filled his nostrils, and he licked it off her skin. In response, her hips rolled, rocking her lace-covered folds over him. The pressure against his erection had him hauling in a breath and bracing himself against the stunning pleasure barreling through him. He shifted beneath her, sliding down a fraction so his length notched firmly against her. He dropped a hand to her hip, encouraging her to continue riding him. Continue stoking the fire between them until it consumed them.

"You're so sweet." He lapped at her nipple, then drew it into his mouth, suckling on her, tormenting her as she was doing to him. "Dangerous," he admitted.

Her only response was to buck those slim hips. It was the only response he needed. Switching to her neglected breast, he worshipped it, losing himself in the taste, texture and wonder of her.

"Let me," she panted, gripping his hair and tugging his head up. He resisted, but spying her flushed cheeks, swollen lips and glazed eyes, he relented. "I want to…need to…"

She didn't finish the thought, but with trembling fingers, plucked at his shirt buttons. Too impatient, he replaced her attempt with a hard yank. The buttons flew, scattered, and he tore off the offensive material.

"God," she breathed, flattening her palms to his chest. He shuddered, the sensation of being skin to skin almost too sharp. "You're beautiful. So...beautiful."

Another shiver rippled through him, just as intense, but it was the result of her words rather than her touch. Or rather the stark truth in her words. When they were clothed, minds and bodies not warped by passion, he didn't trust her. But here...with their bodies stripped...honesty existed between them. The honesty of lust and pleasure. She couldn't hide from him, couldn't lie to him. Not when the evidence of her desire soaked her underwear and his pants.

He loosened a hand from the soft ropes of her hair and slid it down her back, over her hip and between her legs. She stiffened a second, and he paused, imprisoning a groan as her wet heat singed him. But only when she melted against him, her whispered, "Please" granting him permission to continue, did he slip underneath the plain but sexy-as-hell underwear to the soft, plush flesh beneath.

She jerked, whimpered as he glided through the path created by her folds, ending his journey with a firm circle over her clit. The little bundle of nerves contracted and pulsed under his fingertip, and he teased it. She straightened, her hands clutching at his shoulders, her back arched, surrendering to his touch.

She was the most goddamn beautiful thing he'd ever seen.

"I love how wet you get for me," he rasped, stroking her hair away from her face, studying her pleasure-stricken expression. Dipping his hand lower, he rimmed her tiny, fluttering entrance. "You have more for me, sweetheart?"

He didn't wait for a reply but drove a finger inside her. Her cry caressed his ears even as her silken sex clutched at him, convulsed around him. He growled, loving her response to him. Hungry for more. Withdrawing, he slid in another finger, stretching her, preparing her to take him so he wouldn't inadvertently hurt her. And the selfish side of him reveled in the tight clasp of her body, in the soft undulations of her flesh that relayed her pleasure and impatience. Impatience for him, for what he was giving her. For what he was promising her.

"Can you take another?" he murmured, pulling free again.

"Yes." Her fingernails denting his skin. "Please, yes."

Leaning forward, he opened his mouth over the pulse throbbing like a snare drum at the base of her throat as he slowly buried three fingers inside her. She bucked her hips, twisting like a wild thing on his lap. Jesus, she was gorgeous in passion—sexy, uninhibited and burning like a blue flame. Her desire scorched him.

Grinding out a curse, he lifted her off his thighs and set her beside him. Ignoring her disappointed cry, he shed her of the underwear, leaving her bare before him. With his gaze fixed on her lovely nakedness, he removed his wallet from his pants. Then he snatched out a condom and shoved his pants down his legs, too desperate to be inside her to completely strip them off.

With hands he prayed were gentler than the maelstrom of greed tearing at him, he repositioned her over him. He couldn't prevent the shiver that worked its way through him as he fisted the base of his cock, notching the tip at the entrance to her body. Perspiration trickled down his skin as he slowly—so damn slowly—lowered her over him.

God. Every muscle in his body tightened, with the control it required not to plunge himself inside exacting its toll.

Hot.

Tight.

Ecstasy.

Fire raced up and down his spine, snapping and crackling. It rolled and thundered through his veins, transforming his blood to pure, undiluted pleasure. Already she consumed him, and he hadn't even seated himself fully inside her. And though razor-sharp need sliced at him, he didn't rush it. He'd rather suffer before hurting Isobel. Even now those tiny muscles rippled and fluttered over his flesh, adjusting to his penetration. Tremors quaked through her petite frame, and whimpers slipped past her lips.

"Shh," he soothed, pausing. Keeping one hand braced on her hip, he cupped her cheek with the other, tipping her head down. "Your pace, sweetheart. Tell me what you need, and it's yours," he said against her lips.

"Kiss me."

She tilted her head, opening for him, and he twisted his tongue with hers, sucking on it. She joined in the duel, thrusting and parrying. Pursuing and eluding. It turned wild, raw.

Before the kiss ended, she sat fully and firmly on his cock.

With a snarl, he tore away from her, tipping his head back against the couch. She was…perfect.

"Isobel," he growled, raising his head again, unable to *not* see what she did to him. How she took him.

Cradling her hips, he lifted her, stared in rapt fascination as she unsheathed him, leaving his length glistening with the evidence of her desire. Then when just the head remained inside her, he eased her back down, still watching as she parted for him, claiming him.

Branding him.

"After that night in the hallway," he gritted out, pulling free again. "I regretted not taking you. Not knowing how it felt to bury myself inside you. But now," he rasped, lowering her. "Now I'm glad I didn't. Because then I would've missing seeing how you so sweetly spread for me. And that, sweetheart…that would've been a crime."

"Darius," she whispered, and the sound of his name on her lips tattered the remnants of his control.

He drove inside her, snatching her down to him. Not that he needed to. She rode him, fierce and powerful, and in that moment, she was the one doing the claiming. And he surrendered, letting her incinerate him. And he held on, thrusting, giving, willingly being rendered to ash.

"Please," she begged, her body quaking. She clung to him even as she surged and writhed against him. "Please, Darius."

He didn't need her to complete the thought; he already knew what she wanted. Reaching between them, he stroked a path down her belly and between her legs. Murmuring, he rubbed the pad of his thumb over her swollen clit. Once. Twice...

Before he could reach three, her sex clamped down on him, a strangling, muscular vise that dragged a grunt out of him. She exploded, seizing his cock, spasming and pulsing around him as she flew apart in his arms.

He rode her through it, thrusting hard and quick, ensuring she received every measure of the release that gripped her. Only when the quakes eased into shivering did he let go.

Pleasure—powerful, intense and brutal—plowed into him. His brain shorted, his vision grayed as he threw himself into an orgasm like a willing sacrifice, wanting to be consumed, obliterated, reshaped.

But into what? The unknown terrified him.

Then, as the darkness submerged and swamped him, he didn't think.

Couldn't think.

Could only feel.

And then, not even that.

Nine

Isobel released a weary sigh as she pulled into an empty spot in the four-car garage.

Darius had moved one of his luxury vehicles so she could have a parking space, and had invited her to drive one of them. But she had yet to take him up on the offer. She'd already invaded his house, and she and Aiden were living off his money. Taking one of the cars as if she owned it edged her one step closer to being the gold-digging creature she'd been called. So no, she'd continued driving her beat-up but trusty Honda Civic. Even if parking it next to his Bugatti Chiron seemed like blasphemy.

Climbing out of her car, she inhaled the early evening air. Though she'd left work at the grocery store without wearing her jacket, she now drew it around her, the black collared shirt and khakis of her uniform not fighting off the nippy breeze.

Glancing down at her watch, she picked up her pace and strode toward the front door of Darius's home. It was just nearing five o'clock, and like the previous days, she was hoping she'd beat him home from work. Since she no longer had to work a second shift with her mother to make ends meet, she'd switched her hours at the store. Four days a week, she left the house at eight to arrive for her nine-to-four shift. Isobel liked the nanny, Ms. Jacobs, just fine. She was grateful for her, because her presence allowed Isobel to continue working even when she couldn't ask her mom to watch Aiden. Still, she missed her son fiercely when she left.

And yet over the last few days, she'd been thankful for her job. Concentrating on customers, price checks and sales prevented her from obsessively dwelling on…other things.

Other things being the cataclysmic event of sex with Darius.

A flush rushed up from her chest and throat, pouring into her face. She loosened her collar as the memories surged forth, as if they'd been hovering on the edges of her subconscious, waiting for the opportunity to flood her.

Her step faltered, and she stumbled. "Damn," she muttered.

No matter how many times those mental images flashed across her brain, they never failed to trip her up—literally and figuratively. She vacillated between cringing and combusting. Cringing at the thought of her completely abandoned and wild reaction to him.

Combusting as she easily—too easily—recalled how his mouth and hands had pleasured her, marked her. How he'd triggered a need in her that eclipsed any previous sexual experience, rendering all other men inconsequential and mediocre.

He'd spoiled her for anyone else.

And she'd committed a fatal error in letting him know just how much she craved him.

So yes, she'd been avoiding him, trying to reinforce her emotional battlements. And surprisingly he'd allowed her to evade him. The few times they'd been in the same room since That Night, he'd treated her with a distant politeness that both relieved and irritated her. Pretending as if they'd never shook in each other's arms, him buried inside her to the hilt.

Pinching the bridge of her nose as she entered the house, she deliberately slammed the door on those memories, and not just locked it but threw three dead bolts just for good measure.

"Where have you been?"

She skidded to a halt in the foyer at the furious demand, her head jerking up. Shock doused her in a frigid wave, and she stared at Darius. Anger glittered in his amber gaze, tightened the skin over his sharp cheekbones and firmed the full curve of his mouth into a flat line.

"Hello to you, too, Darius," she drawled with acid sweetness.

"Where. Have. You. Been?" he ground out, his big body vibrating with emotion. It flared so bright in his eyes, they appeared like molten gold.

"At work, although I don't see how that's any of your business," she snapped. "Which is becoming a common refrain between us. I might be in your home, but no clause in that contract mandated me having to run my every movement by you."

A snarl curled the corner of his lips, and he shifted a step forward but stopped himself. "I beg to disagree with you on that, Isobel. When it has to do with Aiden's care and no one knows where the hell you've been for hours, and you don't answer your cell phone, then it most definitely. Is. My. Business." He pivoted away from her, the action sharp, full of anger. His fingers plowed through his hair, fisting it, before he turned back to her. "Aiden started coughing and became irritable, and when Ms. Jacobs took his temperature, he had a low-grade fever. She tried to call you to see if you wanted her to make a doctor's appointment for him. When she couldn't reach you, she called me. Damn it, Isobel," he growled. "I didn't know if something had happened to you or if you were in trouble or hurt…" Again, he glanced away from her, a muscle ticking along his clenched jaw. "No one could find you," he finally growled.

Worry for her son washed away her annoyance and propelled her forward. "Is he okay? I can take him to an after-hours clinic…"

"He's fine. I had a doctor come out and examine him. He has a virus, probably a twenty-four-hour bug, but nothing serious. I've just looked in on him, and he's sleeping."

Relief threaded through her concern, but didn't get rid of it. As a cashier, she wasn't allowed to have a cell phone on the floor. When her mother had been watching Aiden, this hadn't been a problem, as she'd trusted her mother to handle anything that came up. Not to mention that the store had been minutes from her mom's place. Maybe she should've given Darius her work schedule, or told him she was continuing to work at the store, period. And she'd just told Ms. Jacobs she was going to be out.

Damn. She turned toward the staircase, her thoughts already on her baby. But Darius's voice stopped her.

"I'll be in the library, Isobel. After you look in on him, come find me. This conversation isn't finished." The "don't make me come find you" was implicit in the order, but she ignored it, instead rushing up the stairs to her son.

Fifteen minutes later, after she'd satisfied herself that he was resting and breathing easily, she headed toward the library. Her heart thudded against her chest, her blood humming in her veins. Returning to the scene of the crime. She'd barely glanced at the entrance to the room since she'd last left it, and now she had to reenter it. Maybe sit on the same couch where she'd lost her control, her pride and possibly her mind.

She hated having to enter this room again and be reminded of how she'd come apart. Of how she'd cemented his belief that she was an immoral whore who would screw anyone. After all, she'd claimed not to want him, but at his first touch, she'd surrendered.

Break it... Break me.

Hadn't those been the words she'd uttered as she begged him? *Break the no-sex rule she'd instituted. Break her with his passion.*

Briefly, she closed her eyes, attempting to smother the humiliation crawling into her throat, squatting there and strangling her.

Deliberately keeping her gaze off the couch, she strode into the room and located Darius, who was in front of his desk, with his arms crossed and his eagle-eyed scrutiny fixed on her.

"Isobel."

"Can we get this over with so I can return to Aiden?"

He didn't move, but she could practically *see* him bristle. "How is he?" he asked, surprising her once more with his concern for her son.

"Sleeping, as you said," she murmured. "He's still warm, but he seems to be resting okay." Drawing in a breath, she mimicked his pose, crossing her arms over her chest. "I'm sorry you couldn't reach me. That was my fault. I was at work, and management doesn't allow us to have our cells on us. And I didn't even notice I had missed calls when I left. So I apologize for worrying…everyone."

"Work?" he asked, his voice dropping to a low rumble. "What 'work'?"

"I'm sure the private investigator you hired included my job in his or her report," she said, sarcasm dripping from her tone. "If not, you might want to request a refund for his shoddy performance."

He shook his head, dropping his arms to slash a hand through the air. "Don't tell me you're still going to that supermarket?"

"Of course I am," she replied. "That contract didn't require me to give up my job."

"Why?" he demanded. "You don't need the job, especially when it pays basically pennies. And yes, I do know how much you make, since my investigator's report included not only where you work but how much you're paid," he added.

"There's nothing wrong with ringing up groceries. It's good, honest work." She thrust her chin up. "Maybe you're so far removed from that time in the mail room, you don't remember what that's like."

"No, there's nothing wrong with your job." He frowned, cocking his head to the side. "But what do you need it for, Isobel? If there's something you want, why don't you just come to me and ask?"

His obvious confusion and—hurt?—smoothed out the ragged edges of her anger. How could she make him understand?

After his parents had died, he might've lived with the Wellses, but he'd never been totally dependent on them. Not with a multibillion-dollar empire waiting on him. Not with homes scattered around the country and money in bank accounts. He didn't know the powerlessness, the helplessness of being totally reliant on someone else's generosity... or lack of it.

She'd learned that particular lesson the hard way with Gage. Yes, she might've held down the job when she'd been married, but Gage had considered his role to be manager of their finances. And he'd been horribly irresponsible with them. And later, when his parents had parceled out sympathy money to him, he'd stingily doled that out to her, holding money for things like groceries and diapers over her head.

Never again would she be at the mercy of a man.

And if that meant keeping a low-paying job with good hours so she could maintain a measure of independence, then she would do what was necessary. If it meant losing some time with Aiden while she squirreled away her wages, well, then sacrifices needed to be made. She needed to be able to provide for them when Darius's charity finally reached its limits.

She was a mother first. And any good mother did what needed to be done.

"Then enlighten me, Isobel. Because I don't understand. You have a home. You don't have to pay any bills. You even have cars at your disposal if you'd stop being so damn prideful and use them—"

"No, you're wrong," she interrupted, her voice quiet but heavy with the emotion pressing against her sternum. Frustration, irritation and sadness. "*You* have a home. *You* have cars at your disposal. *Your* money pays the bills. None of this is mine. Even after we sign that marriage certificate and exchange vows, it still won't be. If you put me out, I couldn't leave with any of it. Couldn't lay claim to it. And you could put me out at any time, on any whim, because of any conceived sin on my part. And I would be on the street, homeless, with no money or resources for me and my son. No." She shook her head. "I won't allow that to happen."

He stared at her, shock darkening his eyes. His lips parted, head jerking as if her words had delivered a verbal punch.

"I would never abandon you or Aiden like that," he said, the words uttered like a vow.

She knew only too well how vows could be broken.

"I know you believe you wouldn't. But minds change,

feelings change," she murmured. Then, suddenly feeling so tired that her limbs seemed to weigh a hundred pounds, she sighed, pinching the bridge of her nose. "Are we done here? I need to get back to Aiden."

"No," he said, the denial firm, adamant. As if it'd pushed through a throat coated in broken glass. "You don't believe me."

"I wanted to return to college. Did you know that?" she asked softly. Without waiting for him to reply, she continued, "One of my regrets is that I quit school. I would've been the first one in my family to earn a degree if I'd stayed. So graduating from college was a dream of mine, but when I broached it with Gage, he convinced me to wait until after the baby was born. At the time, I thought him wanting that time for the two of us was sweet. So I agreed. But after Aiden came, I couldn't go back. Working a full-time job, being a mom…" She shrugged. "College would've been too much, so I had to place it on the back burner. But I've always wanted to go back. To obtain that degree. To have a career that I love. And when Aiden is older, I'll show him that no matter how you struggle, you can do anything you desire."

Scrubbing her hands up and down her arms, she paced to the wide floor-to-ceiling window and stared sightlessly at the view of his Olympic-size pool, deck and firepit. Her admission made her feel vulnerable, exposed.

"Did Gage support your dream?" Darius asked quietly.

She didn't turn around and face him. Didn't let him see the pain and anger she couldn't hide. Darius didn't want to hear the truth. Wasn't ready to hear it. And he wouldn't believe her anyway. College, money for tuition—those had been givens in his and Gage's worlds. He wouldn't understand or see how his friend would begrudge his wife that same experience.

"Gage had specific ideas about the wife he wanted," she

whispered instead. "A wife like his mother." One to cater to him. Be at his beck and call. Place him as the center of her universe, at the exclusion of everyone else.

Images from that time flashed across her mind, and she deliberately shut them down, refusing to tumble back into that dark time when she'd been so helpless and powerless.

Silence descended on the room, and she swore she could feel Darius's confusion and disbelief pushing against her.

"If what you say is true, how—"

She'd expected him not to believe her. But she *hadn't* expected the dagger-sharp pain to slice into her heart. Uttering a sound that was somewhere between a scoff and a whimper, she turned, unable to stand there while he doubted every word that came out of her mouth. This is what she got for opening up and letting him in even a little.

Lesson learned.

"Wait. *Damn it, Isobel*," he growled, his arms wrapping around her, his chest pressing to her spine. His hold, while firm, wasn't constrictive, and it was this fact that halted her midescape. "That came out wrong. Just give me a minute. Don't I have the right to ask questions? To try to understand?"

A pause—where the only sound in the room was the echo of their harsh breaths. He loosened his arms, releasing her and taking his warmth with him. Turbulent emotions surged up from the place deep inside her that remained wounded and bruised. The place that cried out like a heart-sore child for satisfaction, for someone to hear her, for acceptance. That place urged her to lash out, to hurt as she'd been hurt.

But flashes of Darius being so affectionate with Aiden, of him upset on her behalf after the dinner with the Wellses, of him kissing and touching her—those flashes filled her head. And it was those flashes that tempered her reply.

"Love blinds us all."

Unable to say any more, unable to hear him defend his friend and family, she left the study and climbed the stairs to return to Aiden.

How they could ever forge a peaceful, if not loving, marriage when the past continued to intrude?

And to that question, she didn't have an answer.

Ten

"No, Mommy!"

Darius heard Aiden's strident, high-pitched objection before he stepped into the doorway of the boy's room. Isobel sat on one of the large beanbag chairs, Aiden curled on her lap, reading a book. Well, Isobel was reading anyway, Darius mused, humor bubbling inside him.

"No," Aiden yelled again, stabbing a chubby finger at one of the pages. "Nose." He twisted around and declared, "Eye," nearly taking out hers with his enthusiastic poke. "Nose," he repeated, squishing his with the same finger.

Isobel laughed, dropping a kiss on his abused nose. "You're right, baby. Nose. Good job!"

"Good job," he mimicked, clapping.

Warmth slid through Darius's veins like liquid sun. The previous evening had left him confused, and the maddening cacophony of questions lingered.

Gage had specific ideas about the wife he wanted.

She'd made it sound like she hadn't met Gage's standard.

If so, had there been consequences? What had those consequences been? Had he and Gage's family been so fixated on Gage's side that they'd missed clues about the truth of Gage's marriage?

Darius closed his eyes, but when the image of Isobel's face, filled with sadness, hurt and resignation, just before she left the study, flashed across the back of his lids, he opened them again.

Nothing could excuse breaking one's marriage vows. But if her dreams had been crushed, if her marriage had been less than what she'd expected, if her husband had changed, was that why she'd turned to other men? Had she been seeking the affection and kindness she believed her husband hadn't given her?

Darius longed to ask her, because these questions tortured him.

"Darry!" Aiden shrieked, jerking Darius from his dark jumble of thoughts. Catching sight of him, Aiden scrambled out of Isobel's lap and dashed on his little legs toward him.

Joy unlike anything he'd ever experienced burst in his chest as he scooped the boy up and held him close. His heart constricted so hard, so tight, his sternum ached. But it was a good hurt. And not just because Aiden had thrown himself at Darius with the kind of confidence that showed he knew he would be caught. But also because, for a moment, Aiden's garbled version of his name sounded entirely too close to *Daddy*. And as selfish as it might be, he yearned to be Aiden's father. Already he fiercely loved this boy as if they shared the same blood and DNA.

He kissed Aiden's still-warm forehead. "How's he feeling this morning?" he asked Isobel.

For the first time since he'd entered the room, she met his gaze. He noted the wariness reflected in her eyes. Noted and shared it. He might have been knocked on his ass by her confession the previous night, but he still didn't—couldn't—trust her. No matter how much his body craved hers. Actually, that grinding need only cemented why he had to be cautious with her. He'd shown in the past he could be led around by his dick, and he would never be that foolish again. Especially with a woman who had already betrayed her vows of fidelity.

And that was the crux of the war waging inside him.

Though it was difficult to reconcile the materialistic gold digger with the woman he was living with—the doting, sacrificing mother, the proud fighter—loyalty came down to family.

They'd earned it.

Isobel hadn't.

"He's still running a small fever, but it's lower than yesterday, and he has more energy. As you can tell," she added dryly.

He nodded, poking Aiden in his rounded stomach and chuckling at the child's giggling and squirming. Setting the boy on his feet, Darius straightened, finding Isobel's stare again.

"Can I see you downstairs for a moment?"

"Fine," she said after a brief hesitation, rising from the floor and setting Aiden's book on his bed.

"I'll wait for you in the living room." Not waiting for her response, he retraced his earlier path down the hallway and staircase. He'd purposefully chosen the living room. Right now the study contained too many memories.

Minutes later, Isobel entered the room, and though he resented his reaction to her, his blood sang and his pulse drummed, the throb echoing in his cock. This was what she did to him by simply breathing. How did he armor himself against her?

God forbid she discovered his weakness.

"You wanted to see me," she said.

"Yes." He picked up a manila envelope from the mantel over the fireplace and offered it to her.

Frowning, she strode forward and gingerly accepted it. "What is this?"

"Open it, Isobel."

Flicking him a glance, she reluctantly acquiesced. He studied her as she withdrew the thin sheaf of papers and scanned the contract and bank documents. Bewilderment, shock and finally anger flitted across her face in rapid-fire succession. Her head snapped up, and her eyes narrowed. She pinned him with a glare.

"What. Is. This?" she repeated, her tone as hard as stone.

"Exactly what it looks like," he replied evenly, unsurprised by her response. "An addendum to our original contract. For entering our agreement, you receive one million dollars that will be deposited in an account under your name alone, as the bank documents reflect. It's yours free and clear. Even if you seek a divorce, it will still be yours."

"Like a signing bonus?" she drawled, the words acerbic.

He dipped his head. "If that's what you want to call it."

"No." She dropped the papers and the envelope on the glass table next to them as if they burned her fingers. "Hell no."

"Isobel—"

But she slashed a hand through the air, cutting off his explanation. "Is this about last night?" She shook her head so hard, her hair swung over her shoulders. "I didn't tell you that to make you feel guilty. If you hadn't pushed me, I wouldn't have said anything. At. All. But I damn sure won't take pity money from you now. If you wanted me to have that money—" she jabbed a finger in the direction of the papers "—then you would've included it during our original *negotiations*."

"You're right," he growled, and from her silence, he surmised his admission shocked her. "But at the time, I didn't want to hear anything except a yes. But now I want you to have it. And I can't unhear your fears or your dreams." Or the other things hinted at but left unsaid. "Maybe I need to give you what you missed. Your education. A father for your son. Help raising him. Time with him. Let me try to give it back to you, Isobel."

The only time in his life that he'd ever begged anyone for anything was when he'd pleaded with God to return his parents to him. But here, he came damn close.

She stared at him, and he battled the urge to turn away and evade that fey gaze that cut too deep and saw too much.

"Okay," she murmured.

He paused, her capitulation rendering him momentarily speechless. "Okay," he repeated. "And I'm not asking you to quit the supermarket or not replace it with something else. You can return to college, or I can arrange an entry-level position in a company or field of your choice that will allow you to get your foot in the door of your career. Or both college and the job. I don't want to steal your independence, Isobel. I don't want to be your jailor."

"Well, I really didn't want to ask my current manager for a reference anyway." A small smile flirted with her mouth. "Thank you, Darius."

"You're welcome," he said, his fingers suddenly tingling with the need to brush a caress over those sensual lips and feel that smile instead of just seeing it.

Silently, they stood there, snared in each other's gazes. She was the first to break the connection, and he bit back a demand for her to return to him, to give him her thoughts.

"I was going to bundle Aiden up and take him to see my mom. She's been calling nonstop since yesterday. I think she just needs to lay eyes on him." She halted, her eyes again meeting his. "Did you… I don't know if you'd like to…" Her voice tapered off, red staining the slashes of her cheekbones.

She was inviting him to come with her to visit her mother. Considering they didn't have a traditional relationship, introducing him to her family hadn't occurred. But she was offering that to him. It…humbled him.

"Why don't you invite her here instead since his fever isn't completely gone? I can send a car for her. Or go get her myself. Whichever she prefers. If you'd like, she can spend the day here with you and Aiden."

She blinked. "A-are you sure?" she stammered. "This is your home. You don't have to…"

"No, Isobel," he contradicted, injecting a thread of steel in the words. "This is our home. And it is always open to your mother, to your family."

She didn't agree with him—but she didn't refute him either.

And for today at least, it was a start.

Eleven

Isobel removed her earrings and dropped them into the old wooden jewelry box that had been a gift from her mom for her thirteenth birthday. Closing the lid, she picked up her brush and dragged it through her hair, meeting her own gaze in the mirror of the vanity. A smile curved her lips, and she didn't try to suppress it. Even if she looked like a dope wearing a silly grin for no reason.

Well, that wasn't true. She had a reason.

A wonderful day with her mom, Aiden…and Darius.

She carefully set the brush down as if it were crafted out of fragile glass instead of durable plastic. When truthfully, she was the one who felt delicate…breakable.

Inhaling a deep breath, she splayed her fingers low on her belly in a vain attempt to stifle the chaotic flutter there.

Once the car bringing her mother had arrived, she'd expected Darius to retreat to his study or even head to his office. He'd done neither. Instead Darius had stayed with them, warmly welcoming her mother and melting her re-

serve toward him with his graciousness and obvious adoration of Aiden. They'd watched movies, played with Aiden,
cooked, ate and laughed. She'd glimpsed another side of
Darius that day. Charming. Relaxed.

Like his gift of the contract addendum and the bank
account with more money than she'd ever see in five life-
times. She shook her head. She still couldn't believe that.
Not only had he handed it over to like it'd been change in a
car ashtray, but he'd given it to *her*, the woman he considered a money-grubbing user. When she thought on it, the
shock returned, and she had to stop herself from pinching
her skin like some kid.

She could take care of Aiden.

She didn't have to work at the supermarket.

She could return to college.

She had no-strings-attached options.

A whirl of electric excitement crackled inside her. In the
space of minutes, her world had expanded from the size of
a cramped box to a space without walls, without ceilings.

He'd done that for her. For her son.

Isobel spun on her heel, charged out of the bedroom and
marched down the hall before she could change her mind.
Seconds later, she knocked on the door of Darius's room.
Already cracked, it swung further open under her hand.

"I'm sorry," she apologized, wincing as she shifted into
the opening. "I didn't…know…it…"

The words dried up on her tongue, along with all the
moisture in her mouth.

Good. Lord.

Darius stood in the middle of the room, naked to the
waist. Miles and miles of golden, taut skin stretched over
muscle like barely leashed power. Wide, brawny shoulders,
strong arms roped with tendon and veins that seemed to
pulse with vitality and strength. A solid chest smattered
with dark brown hair that her fingers knew was springy

to the touch. It thinned into a silky, sexy line that bisected his rock-hard stomach. Her gaze trailed that line, following it with complete fascination as it disappeared beneath the loosened belt and unbuttoned jeans.

Face heating, she jerked her head up, her stare crashing into his whiskey-colored one. Whiskey. Yes. She'd always compared it to an eagle's gaze, but whiskey was more accurate. Especially considering the punch it delivered and the heat it left behind.

"I'm sorry," she apologized again, inwardly cringing at her hoarse tone. Like sandpaper smoothed with jagged rock. "I didn't mean to interrupt…" She waved a hand up and down, encompassing his towering frame. "I'll just go," she said, already whirling around.

"Isobel." Her name halted her escape. No, it was the swell of arousal low in her belly that froze her. "Come here."

No "I'll meet you downstairs." Not "it's fine. Let me get changed and we'll talk later." Not even "come back." But, *come here*.

It was a warning. An invitation.

A threat. A seduction.

"Come here," he repeated, and she surrendered, her feet shifting forward, carrying the rest of her with them until she stood in front of him.

His heat, his cedar-and-musk scent, his almost tangible sensuality called out to her, enticed her to eliminate those scant few inches and bury her face against his chest. Inhale him *and* feel him. Somehow she resisted. But just. And even now that resistance was pockmarked, and so thin one touch would shred it.

"What do you want?" he asked, the sharp blades of his cheekbones and the hewn line of his jaw only emphasizing the blaze in his eyes. "Why did you come in here?"

"To thank you for today," she murmured. "For...everything."

"You're welcome," he rumbled, and as if in slow motion, he lifted a hand and rubbed the back of his fingers down her cheek. "Now tell me why you really came to find me."

She parted her lips to deliver a stinging reply, but it didn't come. Before she could contain it, the truth that she hadn't even acknowledged burst free.

"For you. I want you."

Another blast of flames in his eyes, and then her world tipped upside down. In one breath, she stood trembling before him, and in the next her back met his mattress, and Darius loomed over her. Her world narrowed to his big body and starkly beautiful face.

He tunneled his fingers through her hair, the blunt tips pressing against her skull. His gaze burned into hers, capturing her. Not that she wanted to be anywhere but here—his breath tangling with hers, his chest and legs covering hers, his cock branding her stomach through their clothes.

"Take it back," he ordered. When she stared up at him, confused, he lowered more of his weight onto her. She felt claimed. His flesh ground into her, teasing her with the promise of the pleasure only he was capable of delivering. "Take back your condition. Tell me you don't want me to fuck anyone else," he growled. "Tell me the thought of me touching another woman would drive you insane. Tell me I'm allowed to have you and only you."

She dug her nails into his shoulders, the words he demanded to hear crowding the back of her throat.

"Isobel," he growled.

The sexy, primal rumble unlocked her voice. "You can't touch another woman except me. You're not allowed, because it would drive me crazy," she finished on a gasp, with the word *crazy* barely out of her mouth before he swallowed it, his tongue thrusting forward past her parted lips and taking her in a kiss so blatantly carnal, so wild and possessive, it propelled the breath from her lungs.

But that was okay, because he gave her his.

He devoured her. It was wild, a clash, an erotic battle where both seized and neither lost. An ache opened wide in her, like a deep chasm that could never be filled. And yet she would never stop trying.

Did it register somewhere underneath the turbulent, consuming need that he hadn't asked her to make the same request? Yes. Did it also occur to her that he didn't ask because he didn't believe she would honor his demand of faithfulness? Yes. Did it hurt like a nagging, old wound? God, yes.

But right now, with his mouth working hers like he owned it, she didn't dwell on the pain. She submerged it beneath the waves of passion crashing over her. Later, when his hands didn't tilt her head back to receive more of him, that's when she'd think on it. But not now.

Darius abruptly straightened, tugging her up with him. With hurried hands, he balled the hem of her sleep shirt and yanked it over her head, leaving her clad only in a plain pair of black boy-short panties. Definitely not the expensive, seductive lingerie he was probably used to, but as he stared down at her, unchecked desire lighting his amber gaze, it didn't matter. Not when, without uttering a word, he told her he wanted her with a hunger that rivaled the need grinding her to dust.

Slipping a hand behind his neck, she drew his head down to her as she arched up to meet him. This time their kiss was slower, wetter. Somehow hotter.

He eased her back to the bed, his chest pressed to hers, and she undulated under him, rubbing her breasts over him, dragging her nipples across the solid wall of muscle. Correctly interpreting her message, he tore his mouth away from hers and blazed a path down her neck to the flesh that tightened in anticipation of his wicked attention.

As he cupped one breast, he nuzzled the other. She cradled his head, silently demanding he stop toying with her. And with a rumble that vibrated against her abdomen, he obeyed, parting his lips over her and drawing her in. She cried out, bowing so hard, her back lifted off the mattress. The strong pull of his mouth set off sparks behind her closed eyelids and matching spasms deep inside her. *God*, the ache. She wrapped her legs around his hips and ground against his cock, shuddering at the swell of pain-tinged pleasure. Whimpering, she repeated the action. Coupled with the mind-twisting things his mouth was doing to her breasts, she teetered close to the edge of release. So close…

"Not yet, sweetheart," he rasped against her skin.

Treating her nipple to one last kiss, he trailed his lips down her stomach, pausing to lap at her navel before continuing to the drenched center of her body. With an abrupt tug, he had her panties down her legs and tossed behind him.

Mortification didn't have time to sink its sharp nails in her as he lodged himself between her thighs, which were perched on his shoulders. She didn't have the opportunity to inform him that she'd never cared for oral sex, had never understood the allure of it. Didn't have a chance to tell him she'd just rather have him inside her because she didn't want to disappoint him.

No, she didn't say any of that because the second his mouth opened over her sex, shock and searing pleasure robbed her of the ability to think, to form coherent sentences.

"Oh, God," was all she could squeeze out of her constricted throat. He stroked a path through her folds, lapping at her, his growl humming against her. Grasping his head, she fisted his hair, to hold on and to keep him right there. He circled her clit, blowing on the pulsing knot of nerves, then he tortured her with short stabs and long sweeps. She writhed against his worshipping lips. Bucked into each stroke. Begged him to suck harder, faster, slower and gentler. She went wild.

And when release rushed forward in a flood so strong, so sharp, so potent, she didn't fight it. She surrendered to the undertow with a loud, piercing cry, chanting his name like an invocation.

Dimly, she registered the mattress dipping. Heard the soft shush of clothing over skin. Caught the crinkle of foil. Didn't have enough energy to turn her head and investigate. But when Darius reappeared over her, his big, beautiful body crouched over her like the gorgeous animal he was, desire rekindled in her veins, burning away the post-orgasm lassitude. It was unbelievable. She'd just come hard enough to see stars, and now, when it should've been impossible, her sex trembled and clenched, an emptiness deep inside her begging to be filled.

She lifted her arms to him, and without hesitation, he came down over her, one hand curving behind her head and the other cupping the back of her thigh, holding her open. With her eyes locked on to his, she waited, her breath trapped in her throat. Even when he pushed forward, penetrating her, stretching her, she didn't look away. The inexplicable but no less desperate need to see his face, his eyes, gripped her. She longed to see if they reflected the same awe, rapture and relief that surged within her. To determine if she was alone on this tumultuous ride.

His full, sensual lips firmed into a line. His nostrils flared, the skin across his cheekbones tightened and in the golden brown depths of his eyes…there, she saw it. The flare of surprise, then the blazing hungry heat and something shadowed, something…more.

No, she wasn't alone. Not in the least.

Wrapping her arms tighter around his neck, she burrowed her face in the strong column, throwing herself into the ecstasy, the burn, the passion—into him. Opening her mouth over his skin, she tasted his tangy, musky flavor, mewling as he burrowed so deep inside her, she wondered how far he would go, how much he would take.

Not enough. The answer quivered in her mind. *It won't ever be enough.*

A trill of alarm sliced through her, but it was almost immediately drowned out by the carnal havoc he created within her body. After sliding his hands down her back, he palmed her behind and held her for his long strokes. He forged a path that only he could travel, dragging his thick length in and out of her and igniting tremors with each thrust. She savored each one, rolling up to meet each plunge.

"With me, sweetheart," he murmured in her ear. Tunneling his fingers into her hair, he gripped the strands and tugged her head back. His eyes so dark with lust that only flickers of gold remained, he grated through clenched teeth, "I'm not going alone. Get there and come with me."

The words, so arrogant and commanding, but strained with lust and drenched in need, were like a caress over her flesh. Clawing at his back, she slammed her hips against his, and his cock rubbed against a place high inside her, forming a catalyst, a detonator to her pleasure.

She shattered.

Screaming, she threw her head back against the pillows, propelling herself into the orgasm that claimed her like a ravenous beast, devouring her, leaving nothing. Above her, Darius rode her through it, until he stiffened and quaked. The throbbing of his flesh triggered another orgasm, rolling into the previous one like an unending explosion of ecstasy.

Darkness swept over her, pulling her under, but not before a seed of worry sprouted deep in her head. In the heat of passion, they'd become something new tonight.

But what? *Who?*

And would they survive it?

Twelve

Darius stared at his computer monitor, but he didn't see the report on the possible acquisition. Too many other thoughts crowded his mind. No, he had to be honest with himself.

Isobel.

Isobel crowded his mind, not leaving room for anything else.

Who was this woman? The selfish, devious conniver he'd believed her to be these past years? Or the woman he'd come to know since the night of the blackout? Just a week ago, he would've said both. That maybe single motherhood and being on her own had matured her from the person she'd been. But now…

Now doubts niggled at the back of his mind; perhaps he'd been wrong all along.

The things Isobel had hinted at—the controlling nature of her marriage, the lack of independence, the chameleon nature of the man Darius had called friend and she'd called husband—as well as the things she'd left unsaid. Working at a neighborhood grocery store even though she resided in one of the wealthiest zip codes in the state.

But if he believed Isobel—and God help him, he was starting to—then that meant Gage had concealed a side of himself from his family. What else had he hidden? Was it possible that Darius's best friend could've lied to them, to him? And if so, how could he have been so blind? He couldn't have been...right?

The urge to unearth the truth swelled within him, and he reached for the phone. He could have the company PI investigate for him. Contact Gage and Isobel's old neighbors or employees that had worked with Isobel at the time. It'd been years, but maybe they could give him some insight...

Just as his fingers curled around the receiver, the desk speaker crackled, and his executive assistant's voice addressed him.

"Mr. King, Mrs. Wells is here to see you."

Darius pressed the intercom button. "Thank you, Charlene," he replied. "Please let the marketing team know we're going to move our one o'clock meeting to one thirty."

"Yes, sir."

Darius rose from his chair and was already halfway across his spacious office when Helena opened his door and strode in. In spite of his unsettled thoughts, pleasure bloomed inside him at the unexpected but welcome visit. Several weeks had passed since the disastrous dinner at her home. Since then, he'd visited them several times, but without Isobel and Aiden. Though they'd asked about the boy and when they could spend time with him, Darius hesitated. First, he'd promised from the beginning that he wouldn't make arbitrary decisions about Aiden without consulting Isobel. And that included taking him to see his grandparents without her permission, even if he longed for them all to build a loving relationship.

Helena, regal in a black dress that wrapped around her still-slender figure, met him with outstretched arms.

"What brings you here today?" He led her to his office sitting area, lightly clasping her elbow.

She arched a dark, elegant eyebrow. "Do I need a reason to come see family? Especially when he's been a bit of a stranger lately?"

Darius laughed as he helped her settle on the black leather couch and then took a seat beside her. "That was subtle," he drawled. "Like a claw hammer to the head."

She smiled, but her point was well-taken. True, he hadn't been by the Wellses' home as often as he'd visited in the past. In the past weeks, he, Isobel and Aiden had settled into a cautious but peaceful routine. A truce that included Isobel in his bed, where they fucked until neither could move. God, she stripped him of his control, and that both terrified and thrilled him. Intimidated him and freed him.

It was the terror and intimidation that kept his mouth sealed shut when she slipped out of his bed in the dark, early mornings, returning to her room and leaving him alone. She never slept the night through with him. That bothered and relieved him.

Relieved him because the intimacy of sharing a bed smacked of a relationship, a vulnerability he wasn't ready to reveal to her. He'd given that trust to one woman, and she'd screwed him, literally and figuratively.

Bothered him because her sneaking out like he was her dirty secret didn't sit well with him.

"So you're here because you miss me?" he teased, deliberately dismissing his disquieting thoughts.

Helena's smile dimmed just a fraction, taking on a faintly rueful tinge. "Of course I do, darling. We all do. But I have another reason for coming to you. Next week is Thanksgiving. What are your plans?"

He stifled a sigh. Him joining them for the holidays was a tradition. But this year, it wasn't only him.

"I haven't discussed it with Isobel yet. She might want to spend the holiday with her family. And if that's her choice, I can come by the house afterward."

Anger flashed in her eyes, and she thinned her lips. "I see," she finally said. "You have a new family, whose wishes come first."

"Helena—"

"No." She sliced a hand through the air. "I'm glad you said that, it makes my next reason for being here easier to say." Her chin hiked up. "I want a DNA test for Aiden."

Shock whipped through him, and he stiffened under the blow of it. "What?"

"We want a DNA test," she repeated. "Yes, Aiden does resemble Gage, but that's not enough. In order for us to erase any doubt, we need to know he's Gage's son. And that can only be answered with a paternity test." Her features softened, and she settled a hand over his knee, squeezing lightly. "I need this, Darius."

His first reaction had been to flat-out refuse, but then reason crept in. Would having a DNA test done be so wrong? It would cement that Aiden was indeed Gage's son, and once the Wellses had the truth, they could finally lay this issue to rest and move on. He could give them that; he owed them that.

Isobel. He briefly closed his eyes.

Isobel wouldn't agree, just as she hadn't years ago. She would view it as an insult, but if it could facilitate healing… Yes, she would be angry about him going behind her back, but the results…how could she argue with the results when it meant the Wellses laying down their swords and Aiden having all of his family in his life, without doubts?

Meeting Helena's gaze, Darius nodded. "I'll arrange it."

Satisfaction flared in the blue depths. "Thank you, Darius. Another thing? Let's keep this between us for now. Baron doesn't know I'm here, and I don't want this impacting his health. So when you have the results, please contact me."

Unease over the further request for secrecy ate at him, but again he nodded.

"I should go," she murmured, standing. But then she hesitated, staring at him. "You're like a son to me, Darius," she said, steel entering her tone, belying the sentimental words. "And I love you, which is why I believe I have the right to say this to you. Gage fell for Isobel's sweet, innocent act, and look how he ended up. Betrayed, broken, angry...and dead. I would want to die myself if she did the same to you. So please, Darius, be careful, and don't succumb to the same game. Just...be aware, because Isobel is not who she pretends to be."

Darius didn't stop Helena as she left his office. After the door shut with a soft click, he slowly rose, her words of caution whirling inside his head.

Please be careful, and don't succumb to the same game... Isobel is not who she pretends to be.

He shook his head as if he could dislodge them, but they clung to him like burrs. Anger continued to dog him the rest of the day, nipping at him. He'd refused to play the fool again. But with Helena's warning ringing in his head, he couldn't shake the thought that her words had come a little too late.

Darius shoved open the front door to his house, the usual peace it brought him as he stepped into the foyer absent. His day had gone from hell to shit. By the time he left, hours earlier than his usual time, his employees had probably tossed confetti in the air as the elevator doors closed behind him. And if he were honest, he wouldn't blame them. His mood had been dark ever since Helena's impromptu visit, and even now, shutting the door behind him, he couldn't shake it loose.

He needed a drink. And time alone. Then, he mused, heading toward his study, he'd go find Aiden and Isobel. It wouldn't be fair to inflict his attitude on them.

What the fuck?

He slammed to a halt in the doorway of the study, shock winding through him like frigid sleet.

Gage fell for her sweet, innocent act, and look how he ended up. Betrayed, broken, angry... Please be careful, and don't succumb to the same game... Isobel is not who she pretends to be.

As they had all day, Helena's words tripped through his brain, growing louder and louder with each pass.

Isobel sat on the couch in his study, with her head bent close to the man perched next to her.

On the same couch where she'd straddled him, and he'd pushed into her body for the first time.

Jealousy, ripe and blistering, ripped through him. The power of it rocked him, and it was only the unprecedented intensity that unlocked its grip on him. Dragging in a breath, he forced the destructive emotion under a sheet of ice.

As if she'd heard his deep inhale, her head lifted, and their eyes met.

Surprise rounded her eyes, and an instant later, a smile started to curve her mouth, but that stopped as she scanned Darius's face. It shifted into a frown, before smoothing into a carefully blank expression.

"Darius, I didn't hear you arrive," she finally said, voice neutral as she rose to her feet.

What did that expression hide?

Isobel is not who she pretends to be.

"Obviously," he drawled, then shifted his attention to

the tall man who now stood beside her. Handsome, wearing an expensive gray suit and about Darius's age. Green-tinged acid ate at his gut.

Faith used to wait until he'd left for the office, then sneak men into their house. Their bed had been a favorite location for her trysts. She'd gleefully thrown that information at him. Part of her pleasure had been in knowing that, at night, Darius would lie in the same bed where she'd fucked other men.

And here Isobel stood with some stranger. Playing the same game? After all, she hadn't expected him home from work this early. He studied her. Seeking signs of deceit, of guilt, but not expecting to find any. She was more of an expert than that.

"Where's Aiden?" he asked.

Translation: *Where is Aiden while you're down here... entertaining?*

From the narrowing of her eyes, she didn't require a translator. "He's upstairs, taking a nap. Ms. Jacobs is with him," she replied, tone flat. Turning to the man beside her, she waved a hand in Darius's direction. "Ken, let me introduce you to Darius King. Darius, Ken Warren."

"Nice to meet you, Mr. King," the other man greeted, striding forward with his hand outstretched. "Ms. Hughes speaks highly of you."

"Does she now?" he murmured, and after a pause in which he stared down at the extended palm, he clasped it. "A shame I can't say the same."

"Thank you, Ken," Isobel said, walking forward and shooting Darius a look that possessed a wealth of *fuck you*. "I appreciate you coming all the way out here. I bet house calls are rare in your profession."

"Not as much as you'd think." He chuckled. "Call me if you have any questions." Nodding at Darius, he said, "Again, nice to meet you."

She ushered him out of the room, and Darius moved into the study, stalking toward the bar. He poured Scotch into a glass and then downed it, welcoming the burn.

With his back to the door, he didn't see her reenter the room, but he felt it. The air seemed to shift, to shimmer like steam undulating off a hot sidewalk after a summer shower. That's how aware he was of her. He could sense the moment she entered a damn room.

Pivoting, he leaned a hip against the edge of the bar, taking another sip of the alcohol as he watched her approach.

"You are an asshole," she hissed, the anger she'd concealed in front of Ken Warren now on vivid display. It flushed her cheeks and glittered in her eyes like stars as she stalked to within inches of him. "I don't know what happened at the office, but you had no right to be so rude to him and to me. What the hell is wrong with you?"

"What's wrong is that I came home to find a strange man in my house, with my soon-to-be-wife, sitting on the same couch where I've fucked her," he drawled. "So forgive me if my mood is a little…off."

"I knew it," she murmured. For a long moment, she studied him as if trying to decipher a code that baffled her. "I *knew it*," she repeated, a soft scoff accompanying it. "I took one look at your face and could've written a transcript of your thoughts. *I caught her with her latest screw. In* my *house. I knew she wouldn't be able to keep her legs closed for long.* Am I close?" The sound that escaped her lips was a perversion of laughter. "You're so predictable, Darius."

She whipped around and stalked to the couch. Leaning over the arm, she picked up a small, dark brown box and marched back to him.

"Here." She thrust the case at him. "Ken is the husband of one of the moms I met at the Mommy Center Aiden and I go to on Tuesdays and Thursdays. When I found out he was a jeweler, I thought of you. Take it," she ordered, shoving the item at him again.

A slick, oily stain spread across his chest and crept up his throat as he accepted the box. As soon as he did, she moved backward, inserting space between them that yawned as wide as a chasm.

He clenched his jaw, locking down the need to reach for her and pull her back across that space. Instead he shifted his attention to the case. It sat in the middle of his palm. A jeweler. She'd said Ken Warren was a jeweler.

With his heart thudding dully against his sternum, he pried the top off. And it ceased beating at all as he stared down at the gold pocket watch nestled on a bed of black silk. A detailed rendering of a lion was etched on the face of it, the amber jewels of its eyes gleaming, its mouth stretched wide as if in midroar. Awed, he stroked a fingertip over the excellent craftsmanship and artistry.

It was…beautiful.

"When I saw it, I knew it was yours. A lion for both your first and last names. *Darius*, which means royalty, and then *King*," she murmured. "I thought it would be a perfect addition to your and your father's collection."

He tore his gaze away from the magnificent piece and met her eyes. Awe, gratefulness, regret and sadness—they all coalesced into a jumbled, thick mass that lodged in his throat, choking him.

She'd bought a gift for him, had chosen it with care and thoughtfulness.

And he'd returned that kindness with suspicion and scorn.

He'd fucked up.

"Thank you," he rasped. "Isobel…"

"Save it." She took another step back. "You're sorry now. Until the next time when I fail some test or, worse, pass it. Is this what I have to look forward to for however long this *agreement* lasts? I spent two years walking on eggshells. At least give me a handbook, Darius. Tell me now so I can avoid the condescending comments, the scathing glares and condemning silences."

"I'm sorry," he said, trying again to apologize. "You didn't deserve that."

"I know I didn't," she snapped. "But the truth is, you can say those two words, but you obviously believed I did. You convicted me without even offering me the benefit of the doubt. Of course, me sitting with a man couldn't be innocent. Not Isobel 'The Gold Digger' Hughes."

Suddenly the anger leaked from her face, from her body. Her shoulders sagged, and a heavy sadness shadowed her eyes. The sight of it squeezed his heart so hard, an ache bloomed across his chest.

"I just wanted to do something nice for you. To show you how much I appreciate all you've done for Aiden, show you all that you…" She trailed off, ducking her head briefly before lifting it. *Finish it*, he silently yelled. *Finish that sentence.* "I'm fighting a losing battle here, and Darius, I'm tired. Tired of trying to change your mind, of proving myself, of paying the price for a sin I never committed. I'm…" She shrugged, lifting her hands with the palms up in surrender. "Tired."

Slowly, she turned and headed toward the study entrance.

"Isobel," he called after her, her name scoring his throat. But she didn't pause, and desperation scratched him bloody, demanding he *stop her*. Give her the truth he'd kept from her. Pride and honesty waged a battle inside him. Self-preservation and vulnerability. "Stop. Please."

She'd jerked to a halt at his "please." Probably because she'd never heard him utter the word before. Still, her back remained to him, as if he had mere seconds before she bolted again.

Shoving a hand through his hair, he thrust the other in his pants pocket and paced to one of the walls of windows. "I don't remember you at the wedding, but you might recall that I married. Her name was Faith." He emitted a soft scoff. "When we first met, her name had seemed like a sign. Like fate or God sending me a message that she was the one. I'd wanted what my parents had, and I thought I'd found that with Faith.

"She'd reminded me of my mother. Not just beautiful and elegant, but full of life and laughter. Faith had a way of dragging a smile out of you even when everything had gone to hell. Dad used to call it the ability to 'charm the birds right out of the trees.'" In spite of the ugly tale he was about to divulge, a faint smile quirked a corner of his mouth. He couldn't count how many times his father had lovingly said that about his mom, usually after she'd used said charm to finagle something out of him. "Faith and I only dated several months, but the Wellses loved and approved of her, and I believed we would have a long, happy marriage... I was wrong."

Isobel's scent, delicate and feminine, drifted to him seconds before she appeared at his side. She didn't touch him but stood close enough that he could feel her.

"Within six months, I realized I'd made a mistake. The affectionate, witty woman I'd known turned catty, cold and spiteful. Especially if I said no to something she wanted. I discovered a little too late that she didn't love me as much as she loved what I could afford to give her. As much as the lifestyle I offered her." He clenched his jaw. The despair, disillusion and anger that had been his faithful companions back then returned, reminding him how foolish he'd been. "But even then, I'd still been determined to salvage our relationship. Hoping she'd change back into the woman I'd married. Then..." He paused, fisting his fingers inside his pants pockets. "Then I came home a day early from a business trip. Since it'd been late, I hadn't called to let her know I was arriving. I walked into our bedroom and found her. And one of my vice presidents. I froze. Stunned. And in so much goddamn pain, I couldn't breathe. By this time, our marriage was hanging on by a thread, but I was still hopeful. Of all the things she could do—had done—I hadn't expected this betrayal. Didn't think she was capable of it."

Again, he paused, his chest constricting as the memories of that night bombarded him, the utter helplessness and grief that had grounded his feet in that bedroom doorway, rendering him an unwilling voyeur to his wife's infidelity.

A delicate hand slipped into his pants pocket and closed over his fist. He tore his sightless gaze away from the window and glanced at Isobel. She didn't face him, keeping her own stare focused ahead, but the late afternoon light reflected off the shiny track of tears sliding down her cheek.

She was crying.

For him.

Clearing his throat, he looked away, that tightness in his chest now a noose around his neck. He forced himself to continue. To lance the wound.

"I filed for divorce the next morning. We'd only been married a year and a half. A year and a half," he repeated. "I felt like a failure. Still do. I was so ashamed, I hid the truth from Baron, Helena and Gabriella. They still don't know why Faith and I divorced."

His admission echoed inside him like a clanging church bell. He'd never voiced those words aloud. Didn't want to admit that his disastrous marriage continued to affect his life years after it had ended. Thank God he hadn't been so lovestruck that he'd forgone a prenup. He wouldn't have put it past Faith to try to clean him out just from spitefulness.

"Why?" Isobel asked, her voice gentle but strong. "You made a mistake. It doesn't make you a failure. Just human.

Like all of us mortals. Wanting to believe in a person, wanting to believe in love, doesn't reflect on your intelligence or lack of it. It speaks volumes about your integrity, your honor, your heart. Just because that other person didn't have the character or dignity to respect their vows, to cherish and protect your heart, doesn't mean you're a fool or a disappointment. She didn't respect your relationship, you or herself. That's her sin, not yours. But, Darius," she turned to him, and he shifted his gaze back to her. "It's your decision, but you should forgive her, let it go."

He frowned. "I have forgiven her, and obviously I've moved on. I'm not pining for her." Hell no. That bridge had not only been burned, but the ashes spread.

"No, you haven't," she objected. "Forgiveness isn't just about cutting someone off or entering new relationships. It's deciding not to allow that person or that experience to shape your decisions, your life. It's not giving that person power over you even though they're long gone. And when your choices, your views, are influenced by past hurt, then those betrayals do have power over you." Her mouth twisted into a rueful smile. "I should know. I've fought this battle for two years. But understand—this is what I've had to come to grips with—forgiveness isn't saying what that person did was okay. It's just choosing to no longer let that poison kill you."

"Who have you forgiven, Isobel?" he murmured, but his mind already whispered the answer to him.

She didn't immediately answer, but seconds later she sighed and dipped her head in a small nod.

"Every day when I get up, I make the choice to forgive Gage. It's a daily process of letting go of the pain and anger. Especially since he's Aiden's father. I refuse to taint that for him with my own bitterness. And I refuse to be held hostage by it. Gage isn't here any longer. I'm never going to hear 'I'm sorry' from him. And even though Faith is very much alive, you most likely won't receive an apology from her either. So, what do we do? Forgive ourselves for the guilt and blame that isn't ours. But as long as we hold on to the past, we can never grab ahold of the future and all it has for us."

He stood still, her words sowing into his mind, his heart. By her definition, had he really released Faith, the past? He bowed his head, pinching the bridge of his nose.

"What about wisdom, Isobel? Only a fool or a masochist doesn't learn from his mistakes."

She slowly removed her hand from his and stepped back. He checked the urge to reach for her, to claim her touch again.

"Wisdom is applying those lessons, Darius. It isn't judging someone based on your own experiences. It isn't allowing the past to blind you to the reality even when it's staring you in the face." She lifted her hands, palms up. "Today you walked in here and jumped to the conclusion that I was sneaking behind your back with another man. That I had brought him into your home like your ex-wife. It's easier for you to be suspicious than to believe that maybe I'm not like her."

She inhaled and tilted her chin up, with defiance in the gesture, in the drawing back of her shoulders.

"I did not cheat on Gage, Darius. I never betrayed him— he betrayed me. He was the cheater, not me."

Before he could object, question her accusation or deny it—maybe all three—she pivoted on her heel and exited the room. Minutes passed, and when she returned, he remained standing where she'd left him, too stunned by her revelation. *Gage cheated? No. Impossible.* He'd loved Isobel. Hell, sometimes it'd seemed he'd loved her to the point of obsession. He couldn't, *wouldn't have*, taken another woman to his bed. Not the man Darius had known.

Did you really know him?

The insidious question crept into his brain, leaving be-hind an oily trail of dread and doubt.

"Here." She extended a cell phone to him. He reached for it before his brain sent the message to ask why. "It's my old phone, the one I had when I was married to Gage. I saved it for the pictures I'd taken of him for Aiden when he was older. But I want you to read this."

She pressed the screen and a stream of text messages filled the screen.

From Gage.

He tore his attention away from her solemn face to the phone.

I should divorce you. Where would you be then? Back in that dirty hole I found you. It's where you belong.

You'll never find someone better than me. No one would want you, anyway. I don't even know why I bother with you either. You're not good enough for me.

Don't bother waiting up for me. I'm fucking her tonight.

And below that message, a picture of Gage maliciously smiling into the camera, his arm wrapped around a woman.

Bile raced up from the pit of Darius's stomach, scorch-ing a path to his throat. He choked on it, and on the rage surging through him like a tidal wave. Swamping him. Dragging him under.

She hadn't deserved the kind of malevolent vitriol con-tained in those texts. No woman did. And that his friend, one of the most honorable, kindest men he'd ever known, had sent them to his *wife*... The woman he'd proclaimed to love beyond reason...

Had Gage been that great of an actor? And to what end?

The questions plagued him, drumming against his skull, not letting up. Because he needed answers. He needed to understand. His heart yearned to reject the idea that Gage could've been that spiteful...an abuser.

"Tell me," he rasped. "All of it."

After a long moment, her soft voice reached him.

"I was twenty when we met. And he was handsome, charming, funny and, yes, wealthy. I didn't—still don't—understand why he chose me. And I didn't care—I loved him. Becoming pregnant so soon after we married was a little scary, but seemed right. He'd started becoming a little moody and irritable a few months after we married, but soon after the baby arrived, and I refused the paternity test, he completely changed. I didn't understand then, but now I see he hated being poor, regretted being cut off from his family and blamed me for it. Resented me. That's when the isolation started. He needed to know where I went, who I was with. He decided my every move, from who I could spend time with to what I wore. Since I just wanted to please him, I gave in. But then I couldn't see my family because they were a 'bad influence.' And if I spoke to a man for too long, or smiled at one, I was cheating. The little money I earned, and the money his parents started giving him, he controlled that, as well. If I needed anything—from personal hygiene items to new clothes for Aiden—he bought them, because he couldn't trust me to spend wisely. I was trapped. A prisoner. And my husband was my warden."

"Why did you stay?" Darius asked, desperate to understand. To punch something. "Why didn't you leave?"

"Love," she murmured. "At first, love kept me there. I foolishly believed it could conquer all. But then that fairy tale ended, and fear and insecurity stepped in. I'd left school, had no degree. A minimum wage job. At that point, the unknown seemed far more terrifying than the known. And I never stopped believing that if I learned the proper way to act and speak, if I could get Gage to love me again like he used to, everything would be okay. His family would love and accept me, too." She shook her head, letting loose a hollow chuckle that bottomed out Darius's stomach. "And I wanted our child to have a two-parent home like I didn't. So I stayed longer than I should've. The night I told Gage I wanted a divorce is the night he…"

Grief tore through Darius. And, still clutching the phone with its offensive messages, he turned and stalked away from Isobel. His thigh clipped the edge of his desk, and he slammed his palms on the top of it, leaning all of his weight on his arms.

It was a death.

A death of his belief in a man he'd called brother. The demise of his view of him. Whom had Darius been defending all these years? How could he still love Gage…?

Her arms slid around him. Her cheek pressed to his back.

The comfort—the selfless comfort—nearly buckled his knees.

"It's okay to love him," she murmured, damn near reading his mind. Her voice vibrated through him, and he shivered in her embrace. "A part of me still does. For the memory of the man I initially fell in love with, for the father of my son. With time and distance, and loving Aiden, who is a part of Gage, I can't hate him. He was a man with faults, with issues and weaknesses. But he was also everything you remember him to be. A great, loyal friend. A loving son. A brother who would literally lay down his life for you. You can love those parts of him and dislike the parts that made him a horrible husband. There's no guilt or betrayal in that, Darius."

He pushed off the desk, spun around and grabbed her close, closing his arms around her. Crushing her to him. As if she were his lifeline. His absolution.

She clung to him just as tightly.

"I have a confession," she whispered against his chest.

"Yes?" he asked, the word scratching his raw throat.

"I never betrayed Gage, but…" She hesitated, tilted her head back. He lifted his gaze, meeting hers. She studied him for several long moments before dipping her head in a slight nod. "I noticed you, admired you. Somehow I instinctively knew you would never mistreat a woman. You were too honorable. And you've always been beautiful to me."

The soft admission reverberated in the room like a shout. He stared into her eyes—eyes that had captured his imagination and attention from the first glance.

"Sweetheart," he growled. It was all he got out before he cupped her face and crashed his mouth to hers. He couldn't stop, couldn't rein himself in if he'd wanted to.

And he didn't want to.

The avalanche of emotion that had eddied inside him burst free in a storm of passion and need so sharp, so hungry that fighting it would've been futile.

Her fingers curled around his wrists, holding on to him. Maybe designating him as her anchor as she, too, dove into the tempest. She leaned her head back, angled it and opened wider for him. Granting him permission to conquer, to claim more. More. Always more with her.

He dragged his mouth from hers, and turning with Isobel clasped to him, swiped an arm across the surface of his desk, sending books, folders, the cell and his home phone tumbling to the floor. After grabbing her by the waist, he hiked her onto the desk, following her down. Covering her. Impatient, with a desperation he didn't want to acknowledge racing through him, he jerked her pants and underwear down her legs, baring her. Her trembling fingers already attacked his pants, undoing them while he removed his wallet and jerked a condom free. Within seconds, he sheathed himself and thrust inside her. His groan and her cry mingled, entwined together as tightly as their bodies.

And as they lost themselves in each other, as he buried himself in her over and over, he forgot about everything but the pleasure of this woman.

Of Isobel.

And for those moments, it was enough.

Thirteen

Isobel leaned closer to the vanity mirror, applying mascara to her lashes. When the doorbell rang, echoing through the house, she almost stabbed herself in the eye.

"Damn," she whispered, replacing the makeup wand.

It was Thanksgiving Day. Who could that possibly be?

She glanced at the clock on her dresser. One o'clock. A loud holiday meal with her mother, brothers and plethora of aunts, uncles and cousins was set for three o'clock at her mom's house. They were supposed to leave as soon as Darius returned from the store after a last-minute errand. For someone to show up uninvited on their doorstep on a holiday, it must be important.

Quickly rushing down the hall to Aiden's room, she leaned inside the doorway. "Ms. Jacobs, I'm going to get the door. But we should be ready to go in just a few."

The older woman smiled from where she played blocks with Aiden. "We're fine until then, Ms. Hughes."

"Isobel," she corrected, but the nanny just smiled and returned her attention to Aiden. Shaking her head and chuckling, she descended the steps. She'd been waging the war of getting Ms. Jacobs to call her Isobel, but to no avail. In the short time she'd known the woman, they had grown fond of each other. So much so, Ms. Jacobs was spending Thanksgiving with them since she didn't have children of her own.

It'd been Darius who had thought of that kindness.

Darius.

A spiral of warmth swirled through Isobel's chest, landing in her belly.

Ever since that evening a week ago, when he'd come home to find her with Ken and heard her full admission about Gage, a…connection had forged between them. One that, while tenuous, had her heart trembling with a cautious hope that what had started out as a marriage bargain between them might evolve into a real relationship. A relationship based on respect, admiration…trust.

Love.

The nervous snarls in her stomach loosened, bursting into flutters.

There'd been a time—not too long ago—when she wouldn't have believed herself capable of falling for another person. She hadn't thought she could ever take the risk of trusting someone with not just her heart, but with Aiden's.

But here, only weeks later, she stood on the crumbling precipice of a plunge into something powerful and dangerous—love.

And it was a beautiful, strong, loyal and fierce man who had her heart whispering with the need to take the fall.

She was afraid. Even as a fragile hope beat its wings inside her, she was *afraid*.

She reached the foyer and glanced out the window next to the door. Shock rocked through her.

Helena and Gabriella.

What…?

As if on autopilot, Isobel unlocked the door and opened it.

"Hello," she greeted, surprised at the calmness in her voice. "Please come in." As they passed by her and entered the house, she shut the door behind them. "Darius isn't here at the moment…"

"That's fine. We can wait," Helena said, turning to face Isobel with a coldly polite smile. "We apologize for showing up unannounced, but he told us you were having Thanksgiving dinner with your family. We wanted to catch him before you left."

Unease sidled through her veins, but she pasted a smile on her lips and waved a hand toward the living room. "He should be back shortly, if you'd like to wait for him in here."

Part of her wanted to run up the stairs and let Darius deal with his visitors when he returned, but at some point she had to become accustomed to being around them without Darius as a buffer. She could handle a few minutes.

"You and Darius seem to be getting along well," Helena commented as she moved into the room and settled on the couch.

Isobel nodded, stalling as she considered how to answer. As if a physical trap waited to be sprung at the end of her reply. "Darius is a kind man."

Gabriella strode over to the mantel and studied the array of pictures there. "Yes, he is. It's both a blessing and a curse," she said. "Have you two set a wedding date yet?"

Unease knotted Isobel's stomach, at both the cryptic comment and the switch in topic. "Not a definite date," she replied. But remembering the stipulations Darius had set in their contract, she added, "Sometime in January, I believe."

"You believe," Helena echoed, and Isobel couldn't miss the sneer in her words as her gaze flicked to Isobel's left hand. "No ring yet, I see. Doesn't that tell you something, Isobel?"

"No," Isobel murmured, sensing the shift in the other

woman's demeanor and steeling herself. "But I suppose you have an idea about that."

"He hasn't set a wedding date and hasn't even bothered buying you a ring." Helena cocked her head, her steady contemplation condescending, pitying. "What you said earlier is very true. Darius is a good man. The kind who would sacrifice his own happiness for those he loves. Yet he's obviously reluctant to shackle himself to you. A man who is looking forward to marriage publicly claims his fiancée."

"I'm afraid she's correct, Isobel," Gabriella agreed, strolling the few feet to stand next to the couch her mother perched on.

A smirk curved the younger woman's lips, and a sinking, dread-filled pit yawned wide in Isobel's chest. Was insulting her the purpose behind their visit? Or just a bonus since Darius wasn't home yet? She glanced toward the bottom of the staircase. *Please, God, let Ms. Jacobs keep Aiden upstairs.*

Briefly, she considered exiting the room. But that smacked too much of running, and she'd quit doing that when she returned to Chicago.

"You don't know anything about my relationship with Darius," she said, tone cool. "But why don't you go ahead and have your say so we can get all this out in the open? That way we no longer have to indulge in this pretense. You don't want me with Darius."

Helena's lips firmed into a flat, ugly line, anger glittering in her eyes. "I thought we were rid of you for good. But you found a way to sneak back in, didn't you? It wasn't enough that you used my son and took him away from us, but now you've latched onto my other son. And if we don't want to lose him or our grandson, we have to deal with *you*," she spat out.

"I would never come between you and Darius," Isobel objected.

"As if you could," Gabriella snapped. "We have a real relationship. We love each other. You don't know anything about that."

Dragging in a breath and struggling to contain her temper in the face of their venom, Isobel straightened her shoulders and tipped up her chin.

"As I was saying," Isobel gritted out. "I would never come between you and Darius. His relationship with you is yours. And if it's as strong as you say, then there's nothing I could do to harm it," she pointed out. Ignoring Helena's outraged gasp, Isobel continued, "But while you might revise history with Darius, don't look me in the eye and speak it to me. We both know I've never tried to keep you from your grandson. You were the ones who didn't believe he was a prestigious *Wells*." She uttered that name as if it were sour. "You decided he wasn't worthy of your time and attention. Your love. As for me, I don't need your approval or acceptance. I don't even want it. But now, for some reason, you've changed your mind, and I won't deprive Aiden of knowing his father's family. But if you believe for one second that I'll let you twist and poison him, then you're absolutely correct. You won't see him."

I won't allow you to turn him into his father.

"Twist him? Poison him?" Gabriella bit, her lips curling in a snarl. "That is rich coming from you of all people. You, a gold-digging wh—"

"What's going on here?"

All of them turned toward the living room entrance at the sound of Darius's voice. A steadily darkening frown creased his brow as he scanned Isobel's features before moving to Helena and Gabriella.

Relief coursed through her, but she locked her knees, refusing to betray any sign of weakness in front of the two women.

"Helena? Gabriella?" he pressed. "What are you doing here?"

Isobel desperately needed to retreat and regroup. Shore up her battered shields.

"They came by to see you. I'm just going to check on Aiden. I'll be right back." Forcing a smile that felt fake and brittle on her lips, she left without a backward glance at Helena and Gabriella.

"Isobel," Darius murmured, catching her arm in a gentle grasp as she passed him. "Sweetheart…"

"No, Darius," she said, slipping free of his hold. "Just give me a minute."

She left the room and prayed that when she returned, the two women he considered a surrogate mother and sister were gone. If not, she might not be responsible for her actions.

Fourteen

"What happened?" Darius demanded as soon as Isobel disappeared from sight. "And can one of you explain to me why I received a phone call from my nanny to return home as soon as possible because two women were attacking Isobel?"

Fury simmered beneath his skin. They both stared at him, their faces set in identical mutinous lines. Helena rose from the couch, turning fully to face him.

"Helena? Gabriella?" He strode farther into the room, halting across from them. "What. Happened? And don't tell me 'nothing' or 'everything is fine,' because both would be lies."

He'd glimpsed Isobel's face when he'd first entered the room. That cold, shuttered mask had relayed all he needed to know. She only wore that blank expression when hurt or angry. And from the shadows that had swirled in her eyes before she'd pulled away from him, both emotions had applied.

"I love you, Darius," Helena said, approaching him with her hands outstretched toward him. "You know I do. But how much longer is this supposed to go on? How much longer are we supposed to pretend that that...*woman* is welcome in our family?"

"Helena," he warned, his muscles tensing when she clutched his forearms.

He'd never pulled away from her touch before, but with those vicious words ringing in the room—no matter the pain they originated from—he couldn't take it. He stepped back, her arms dropping away. Hurt flashed across her face, her lips parting in surprise.

"Darius," Gabriella murmured, glancing at her mother, then back at him. A plea filled her gaze. "That's why we came here today. To tell you that we know you went through this farce of a relationship so we could have Aiden in our lives. You've sacrificed for us, but you don't have to anymore. Mother told me about the DNA test. And now that we have the results back—"

He slashed his hand through the air, dread spiking in his chest. "Did you tell Isobel about the DNA test?" he growled. Driving his fingers through his hair, he glanced away from the women. His motives—bringing closure to the family—had been pure, but Isobel would see it as a betrayal. He needed to talk to her first, to explain. "Gabriella, did you say anything to Isobel about the test?"

"No, I didn't say anything to your precious Isobel," she snapped, whipping around and pacing away from him. "But you should know that we've been talking and have come to some decisions."

The unease that had coiled inside him slowly unfurled. "What are you talking about?"

For a heartbeat, Helena and Gabriella didn't respond, just stared at him. The tension thickened until it seemed to suck all the air out of the room.

"Answer me," he grated out.

"Now that we know for certain that Aiden is Gage's son, we intend to go forward with the suit for sole custody," Helena announced. "We've already contacted our attorney."

"You. Did. Not," he snarled. Betrayal, rage and despair churned in his chest, and he fought not to hurl curses and accusations that would irrevocably damage his relationships with these people. "That wasn't my plan or my agreement with Isobel. The terms of which I expressly discussed with you."

Helena scoffed, waving a hand. "That was before we knew that Aiden was our grandson. *Ours*," she stressed, pressing a fist to her heart. "Gage would've wanted him raised with us. By *us* and not that…that deceiver, that liar. And no judge on this earth wouldn't see that we're much more fit parents than her."

"Darius, don't you see?" Gabriella implored, moving closer to him. She clutched his upper arm, and he curbed his automatic reaction to shake her off. And that reaction sent a blast of pain through him. "This is for you, too. Now you can break off this joke of an engagement. You did all this for us, and we love you for it. But now, with us suing for custody, you don't have to chain yourself to a woman you hate. We know you might not agree with this, but we believe it is for the best."

"For the best," he repeated. "Do you know all Isobel has been through with her marriage to Gage? He wasn't a loving, faithful husband. He emotionally beat her down, cheated on her. He mentally abused her. Now, after she survived that, you want to rip her child away from her."

"How dare you?" Helena hissed, anger mottling her skin. She advanced on him, eyes narrowed and glittering. "I love you like a son, Darius, but I won't allow you to speak ill of my son in this house. Who told you these lies that you're so willing to swallow? Isobel?" She spit the name, her mouth twisting into an ugly sneer. "So, you believe her over a man who you loved as a brother? Did she warp your mind? Is that it, Darius? Do you think you're in love with her?"

He parted his lips, but no words emerged. His pulse pounded in his ears, and his tongue suddenly seemed too thick for his mouth. Helena's question ricocheted off the walls of his skull.

Do you think you're in love with her? Do you think you're in love with her?

Over and over. *No*, his mind objected. *Not possible.*

He pivoted sharply on his heel and strode to the bank of windows. After Faith, he hadn't believed himself capable of having deep feelings for another woman. Just the idea of opening himself and risking that kind of pain once more... He'd vowed never to make himself vulnerable—*weak*—again. And Isobel...

She had the power to hurt him like Faith never did.

If he gave her the chance, and she betrayed him, she could wreck him.

The knowledge had fear and anger cascading through him. Could he take a chance? Could he crack himself open and lose not just his family—because the Wellses would view him as choosing her as the biggest betrayal—but also risk losing himself?

No.

Coward that he was, no, he couldn't risk it.

"Darius."

He jerked his head up, spinning around.

Isobel stood in the doorway. *How long had she been standing there? How much had she overheard?* He moved towards her, but she shifted backward.

And that one movement supplied the answers.

"Isobel, please let me explain."

She stared at him, numb. The blessed nothingness had

assailed her from the moment she'd returned to the living room and overheard his conversation with Helena and Gabriella.

Did you tell Isobel about the DNA test?

We intend to go forth with the suit for sole custody.

No judge on this earth wouldn't see that we're much more fit parents than her.

Do you think you're in love with her?

That awful, damning silence.

The two women had left soon after she'd appeared in the room, but she hadn't moved. Hadn't been able to. And now, as pain invaded her body, she prayed for the return of the numbness.

"Yes," she agreed, voice hoarse. "You're right. Which should we talk about first? The violation of running a DNA test on my son behind my back? Or how *your family* intends to take my son away from me?"

He closed his eyes, and a spasm of emotion passed over his face. But it disappeared in the next instant.

"I'm sorry for not telling you about the DNA test, Isobel," he murmured.

"You're sorry for not telling me, but not for doing it," she clarified. A sarcastic chuckle escaped her. "You promised me we would make decisions regarding Aiden *together*. Without interference from the Wellses. You betrayed my trust."

"I didn't…" He broke off his sentence, briefly glancing away. "Yes, I did break that promise. And I'm sorry," he said, returning his gaze to her. "I am, Isobel. But my motives weren't to hurt or betray you. I thought if Baron, Helena and Gabriella knew for certain that Aiden was their grandson and nephew, he could bring healing to them. To this family. I wanted to give them that. But also, knowing you told the truth about him being Gage's would start to change their view of you, as well. Not only do they need to know their grandson and nephew—they need to begin to know you."

"No, Darius. Now they just think it was luck that Gage fathered him, out of all the other men I supposedly screwed." She shook her head. "But this isn't about them. It's about how you lied to me. It's about how you put them—their feelings, their welfare—above Aiden." *Above me.* "And you handed them cause to take him away from me."

"I won't allow that to happen," he growled, moving toward her, his arms outstretched. As if to touch her.

No. No way could she allow that. Not when she was so close to crumbling. She shifted backward, steeling herself against the glint of pain in his eyes.

"Agreeing to marry you, to move in here, to put my son under your protection was supposed to stop it from occurring. But it didn't. I still find myself at their mercy. A place I vowed two years ago I would never be again. And all because I trusted you."

"Do you really believe I would throw you to the wolves? That I would abandon you to face this alone? Do you think I'm capable of that?" he demanded, stalking forward, but he drew up several feet shy of her.

"Would you want to? No," she whispered. "But would you do it all the same? Yes. If Baron, Helena and Gabriella made you choose between them and me, I have no illusions about whose side you would come down on. And I'm so tired of waging a losing battle between the past, your mistrust and Gage's family. *Your family.* Because I'll never be considered a member of that perfect unit."

"That's bullshit," he snapped, his features darkening in anger. "We've been building something here. Something good. Our own place, our own family. You can't deny that."

She shook her head once more. Desperately needing space, she backpedaled, then caught herself midstep. She was through running. Through letting others dictate her life, her truth.

"What we've 'been building' was founded on blackmail, lies and mistrust. It'll never be 'something good.'"

Raising her head, she committed every one of his features to memory. Though she might wish she could evict him from her heart, she never would.

That didn't mean she wouldn't try. She had to. For her peace. For her sanity. For her future.

"I love you, Darius," she admitted quietly.

His body stiffened, and lightning flashed in his eyes, brightening them so the gold almost eclipsed the dark brown. "Isobel," he rumbled.

"No." She slammed a hand up, though he hadn't moved toward her. "Let me finish. I didn't think I would ever be able to open my heart to another man. But you did the impossible. You made me trust again. Love again. Made me believe in second chances. And I thank you for that. And I might hate you for that," she whispered. "Because you showed me what happily-ever-after could be, then snatched it from me."

"Isobel," Darius rasped again, erasing the distance between them and cradling her cheek.

And for a moment, she cupped her hand over his, pressing his palm to her face and savoring his touch. But then she dragged his hand away from her.

"Do you love me?" she asked, staring into his eyes. Glimpsing the surprise flicker and then the shadows gather in them.

Darius stepped backward, a dark frown creasing his brow. But he said nothing. And it was all the answer she needed.

"You awakened something in me," she said softly. "Something I wish would fall back asleep, because now that it's alive, I hurt. I…hope. The Isobel from two years ago would believe she could change you, make you accept her. Fight for her, if she just loved you hard enough. That Isobel would be happy with the parts of yourself you were willing to give her. But I'm not that woman anymore. I deserve to be a man's number one and to be loved and cherished and valued and protected. I deserve a man who will love me beyond reason, and though I'm not perfect, he will love me perfectly."

"What you want, I…" he trailed off.

The raw scrape of his voice and the sorrow in his gaze should've been a balm to her battered soul, but it did nothing.

"I'm not telling you this to emotionally blackmail you, Darius. I'm admitting this for *me*, not you. So when I walk out of here, I won't have regrets."

"Walk out of here?" he repeated on a low growl. His arms lifted again, but once more he dropped them, his fingers curling into fists. "We had an agreement. A contract. You can't just break it."

"We've been breaking the contract from the beginning. Becoming lovers. The DNA test. Falling in love with you." The contract was supposed to have been a defense against that. A reminder of who she was marrying and why. But it hadn't shielded her heart, just as Darius hadn't protected her and Aiden. "Do what you feel you need to do regarding the consequences. But I won't remain in this home, in this… arrangement knowing I can't trust you. That I will continue to pay the price for Gage's lies and the Wellses' grudges. I refuse to be someone's emotional and mental punching bag again. And every time you side with Gage's memory and his family, you deliver another blow. No, Aiden and I will be leaving today. But I won't keep him from you. He loves you, and I know you feel the same. We'll set up a schedule after we're settled…"

Her arms tingled with the need to throw themselves

around him. Her throat ached with the longing to ask him to say something, to beg her not to go. To declare his love and loyalty.

But nothing came from him.

She straightened her shoulders and inhaled past the pain. Then she turned, exited the room and climbed the stairs. Once she entered her bedroom and shut the door, her back hit the wall and she slowly slid to the floor. The tears she'd been reining in fell unchecked down her cheeks. How long she sat there, quietly sobbing and hugging herself, she didn't know. But during that time, her resolve to do right by Aiden, and by herself, firmed until it resembled a thick, impenetrable wall.

She might be losing Darius, losing the future she'd so foolishly allowed herself to imagine for her and Aiden, but she was gaining more.

Her self-respect.

Her dignity.

Her.

And it was more than enough.

Fifteen

Darius stared down into the squat glass tumbler and the amber-colored bourbon filling it.

At what point would the alcohol send him tumbling into oblivion, where the memories from Thanksgiving couldn't follow? He'd been seeking the answer to this for four days now. But while he'd been fucked up, that sweet abyss of forgetfulness had eluded him. No matter how many bottles he'd gone through, he could still see Isobel's beautiful face etched with pain and fierce determination as she confessed she loved him—and then left him. Could still hear the catch in her voice as she accused him of betraying her trust. Could still hear the sound of the front door closing behind her and Aiden that afternoon.

Closing his eyes, he raised the glass to his lips and gulped a mouthful of the expensive but completely useless liquid. But he was desperate to not just escape the mental torture of his last, devastating conversation with Isobel, but the terrible, deafening silence of his house. It'd chased him into his study, where he'd shut himself away. But there was no refuge from the emptiness, from the *nothing* that pervaded his home.

I deserve a man who will love me beyond reason, and though I'm not perfect, he will love me perfectly.

If Baron, Helena and Gabriella made you choose between them and me, I have no illusions about whose side you would come down on.

You betrayed my trust.

Do you love me?

Her words haunted him, lacerated him...indicted him.

But goddamn, he'd been crystal clear that he hadn't gone into this arrangement for love. He'd been more than upfront that he'd wanted to save the Wellses and her from an ugly custody battle. To protect Baron from any future health risks that a custody suit could inflict. To provide for Aiden. To unite the boy with his father's family. And everything he'd done—the engagement, the dinner with the Wellses, the DNA test—had been to work toward those ends.

He'd never lied. Never had a secret agenda.

He'd never asked for her love. Her trust.

When you let people in, they leave. He'd learned this lesson over and over again.

Isobel had left him.

Like his parents.

Like Faith.

Like Gage.

Anguish rose, and he bent under it like a tree conceding to the winds of a storm.

She'd begun to hope. Well, so had he.

In this dark, closed-off room, he could admit that to himself. Yes, he'd begun to hope that Isobel and Aiden could be his second chance at a family. But just when he'd had it within his grasp, he'd lost it. Again. Only this time... This time didn't compare to the pain of his marriage ending.

As he'd suspected, Isobel had left a gaping, bleeding hole in his world. One that blotted out the past and only left his lonely, aching present.

A knock reverberated on his study door, and Darius jerked his head up. Before he could call out, the door opened, and Baron appeared. Surprise winged through Darius, and he frowned as the older man scanned the room, his gaze finally alighting on Darius behind his desk.

With a small nod, Baron entered, shutting the door behind him. Darius didn't rise from his seat as Baron crossed the room and lowered himself into the armchair in front of the desk.

"Darius," Baron quietly said, studying him. "We've been trying to contact you for the past few days, but you haven't answered or returned any of our calls. We've been worried, son."

The apologies and excuses tap-danced on his tongue, but after taking another sip of bourbon, "Isobel left. Her and Aiden. They left me," came out instead.

Baron grimaced, sympathy flickering in his eyes. "I'm sorry, son. I truly am."

"Really?" Darius demanded, emitting a razor-edged chuckle. "Isn't this what the plan was from the moment I announced my intentions to marry her? Trick her into complying with my proposal long enough to order a DNA test. And once the results were in, take her son and free me from her conniving clutches?" he drawled. "Well, you can tell Helena and Gabriella it worked. Congratulations."

He tipped his glass toward Baron in a mock salute before downing the remainder of the alcohol.

"I'm sorry we've hurt you, Darius. I truly am," Baron murmured. "Their actions might have been...heavy-handed, but their motives were good."

"Why are you here, Baron?" Darius asked, suddenly so weary he could barely keep his body from slumping in the chair. He didn't have the energy to defend Helena and Gabriella or listen to Baron do it.

Baron heaved a sigh that carried so much weight, Darius's attention sharpened. For the first time since the other man had entered the room, Darius took in the heavier lines that etched his handsome features, noted the tired slope of his shoulders.

Straightening in his chair, Darius battled back a surge of panic. "What's wrong? Are you feeling okay? Is it Helena? Gabrie—"

"No, no, we're fine." Baron waved off his concern with an abrupt shake of his head. "It's nothing like that. But I…" He faltered, rubbing his forehead. "Darius, I…"

"Baron," Darius pressed, leaning forward, bourbon forgotten. Though his initial alarm had receded, concern still clogged his chest. "Tell me why you're here."

"This isn't easy for me to say because I'm afraid to lose you. But…" He briefly closed his eyes, and when he opened them, a plea darkened the brown depths. "I can't keep this secret any longer. Not when the reasons for keeping it are outweighed by the hurt it's inflicting."

The patience required not to grab Baron and shake the story from him taxed his control. Darius curled his fingers around the arm of his chair and waited.

"On Thanksgiving, you told Helena and Gabriella about Gage and Isobel's marriage. That he'd been cruel, abusive and faithless. Everything you said…" He dragged in an audible breath. "It was true. All of it. Their marriage was horrible, and Gage's jealousy, insecurity and weakness were to blame."

Shock slammed into Darius with an icy fist, rendering him frozen. He stared at Baron, speechless. But his mind whirred with questions.

How do you know? Why didn't you say anything to your wife and daughter?

How could you not say anything to me?

"How?" he rasped. "How do you know?"

Another of those heavy sighs, and Baron turned away, staring out the side window. As if unable to meet Darius's gaze.

"Gage told me," Baron whispered. "The night he died, he told me the truth."

"What?" Darius clenched the arms of his chair tighter. If they snapped off under the pressure, he wouldn't have been surprised.

Baron nodded, still not looking at him. "Yes, he found me in the library that evening and broke down, confessing everything to me. Isobel had demanded a divorce, and he'd been distraught. I'd barely understood him at first. But as he faced losing Isobel and Aiden, he'd come to me, horrified and ashamed."

Baron finally returned his attention to Darius, but the agony on the older man's face was almost too much to bear.

"My son... He was spoiled. Yes, he had a big heart, but Gage was entitled, and the blame for that rests on Helena's and my shoulders. He'd defied us by marrying Isobel but hadn't been prepared for the separation and disapproval from his family. Hadn't been ready to live on his own without our financial resources. But instead of faulting himself, he blamed Isobel. Yet he loved her and didn't want to let her go. So he'd alienated her from us physically and with his lies of mistreatment and infidelity. He admitted he lied about the cheating, but at some point he'd started to believe his own lies. Became bitter, resentful, jealous and controlling. It transformed him into someone he didn't know, someone he knew I wouldn't be proud of. Who he'd become wasn't the man I'd raised him to be. And I think that's why he confessed to me. His shame and guilt tore at him, and in the end it drove him out into the night, where he crashed his car and died." Baron swallowed, his voice hoarse, and moisture dampening his eyes. "Do I think Gage killed himself that night? No. I don't think it was intentional. But I also believe he was reckless and didn't care. He just wanted the pain to stop."

Air whistled in and out of Darius's rapidly rising and falling chest. A scream scored his throat, but he didn't have enough breath to release it. He squeezed his eyes shut, battling the sting that heralded tears. Tears for Isobel's senseless suffering at her husband's and family's hands. Tears for the man he'd loved and obviously hadn't known as well as he'd thought. Tears for the agony of conscience Gage succumbed to at the end.

"I'm sorry, Darius," Baron continued. "Sorry I lied to you, to Helena and Gabriella. Gage didn't ask me to keep the truth a secret, but I did because I couldn't bear causing them more pain on top of losing him. Even if keeping the secret meant standing by while Isobel was villainized. I made a choice between protecting his memory and protecting her, and now I realize my lie by omission is hurting not just my wife, daughter and Isobel, but *you*, a man I love as a second son. I can't continue to be silent. I can't allow her to be crucified when she's been guilty of nothing but falling in love with my son. Both of my sons."

Trembling, Darius shoved to his feet, his desk chair rolling back across the hardwood floor. He pressed his fists to the desktop, wrestling against the need to lash out, to rail over the injustice and torment they'd all inflicted on Isobel.

Stalking across the room, he tunneled his fingers through his hair, gripping the strands and pulling until tiny pinpricks of pain stung his scalp.

"You're going to tell Helena and Gabriella the truth," he demanded of Baron, who'd also stood, silently watching him.

"Yes," he murmured. "I planned on doing it today, but I felt you deserved to hear it first. Darius." Baron lifted his hands and spread them out in a plea of mercy, of surrender. "I'm so sorry."

"Sorry?" Darius laughed, the sound crackling and brittle with cold fury. "Sorry doesn't give her back the years where she was abandoned, left to raise a child on her own. If you knew Aiden was Gage's, why didn't you help her?"

"Gage said he believed Aiden was his, but I didn't know for sure. And she'd refused the paternity test, which deepened my doubts. And honestly, I hated her after Gage's death. I wanted her to suffer because I no longer had my son. I didn't want any reminders of him around—and that included her and a baby that might or might not have been Gage's. It was selfish, spiteful. Yes, I know that now, and I don't know if I can forgive myself for it. Gage told me I'd raised him to be a better man. But I don't know if I did."

Darius clenched his jaw, choking on his vitriolic response.

Helena and Gabriella might not have known the truth, but their behavior toward Isobel since she'd reentered their lives had been spiteful, hurtful. So unlike the gracious, kind, affectionate women he'd known for over a decade.

And he'd excused it.

Which meant he'd condoned it, just as Baron had.

Grief and searing pain shredded him.

He'd told Isobel he would never leave her out to dry. Throw her to the wolves. But he'd done it. He'd broken more than a contract. He'd shattered her trust, his word.

His concern had been about betraying the Wellses, when he'd ended up betraying and tearing apart the family he'd created, the family he'd longed for—with Isobel and Aiden. The roar he'd been trying to dam up rolled out of him on a rough, raw growl. Every moment they'd shared since the night of the blackout bombarded him.

Laughing together in the hallway.

Sharing the stories of his parents' death and Gage in the dark.

Touching her.

Her fiery defiance in her apartment.

Her surrendering to the incredible passion between them.

Her quiet dignity as she confessed about her marriage.

Her resolute pride as she admitted she loved him, but could, and would, live without him.

Jesus.

He slammed a fist against the wall, the impact singing up his arm and reverberating in his chest. He'd marched into her apartment, self-righteous and commanding, accusing her of being deceptive and manipulative, when he'd been guilty of both to maneuver her into doing what he wanted. He'd entered their agreement acting the martyr. When in truth she'd been unjustly persecuted. It'd been he who'd entered their relationship without clean hands or a pure heart.

She was the only one—out of all of them—who could claim both.

And he loved that purity of heart. Loved that spirit and bravery that had looked at all the odds stacked against her and plowed through them one by one. Loved the passion that had stealthily, without his knowledge, thawed and then healed the heart he'd believed frozen beyond redemption.

He loved her.

The admission should've knocked him on his ass. But it didn't. Instead it slid through him, warm and strong, like a spring nourishing a barren field.

He loved her.

Maybe he'd started falling from the moment she'd coaxed him out of his panic attack with talk of movies and Ryan Reynolds. No doubt he'd fought his feelings for her, but if he were brutally honest with himself, the inevitable had occurred when she'd embraced him and assured him his love for his friend—her abusive husband—wasn't wrong.

A weight that had been pressing down on his shoulders lifted, and he could breathe. He could suck in his first lungful of air unencumbered by the past. Turning, he faced Baron. Darius loved him. But if it came down to a choice between him, Helena and Gabrielle, and Isobel and her son—*their son*—then Isobel and Aiden would win every time.

"I'm going to go find my family," Darius said.

His family. Isobel and Aiden.

From the slight flinch of Baron's broad shoulders, the emphasis hadn't been lost on him.

"I don't know what this means with you, Helena and Gabriella in the future. Maybe after you tell them the truth, they can find it in their hearts to forgive Gage and let the past go, including their hate of Isobel. But right now, that's not my issue—it's theirs and yours. If they can't, then we won't be a part of your lives. And that includes Aiden. I won't allow them to poison him, and you can inform them that if you continue in the pursuit of custody, I'll stand beside Isobel and fight you."

Darius pivoted and strode out of the study without a backward glance, steady and determined for the first time since Isobel and Aiden had left.

He had his family to win back.

If they'd have him.

Sixteen

Isobel pushed open the front entrance to her mother's apartment building, shivering as she stepped out into the cold December air. Her arms tightened around Aiden for a second before she set him on the ground.

"You're okay?" she asked, kneeling next to him and making sure his jacket was zipped to the top. "Warm?"

Aiden nodded as she tugged his hat lower. "See Darry?" he asked, his eyes wide, hopeful.

A dagger of pain slipped between her ribs at his expectant question. Just as it did every time he asked about Darius. Which was at least five times a day since they'd moved out of the house. At least. Aiden missed Darius, and to be honest, so did she. It'd been a long week. One where she forced herself not to dwell on him every minute of the day. She only succeeded a quarter of the time.

She smothered a sigh, shaking her head. "No, baby," she said, crying inside as his little face fell, the sparkle of excitement in his eyes dimming.

He didn't understand that they were no longer living with Darius, that he would no longer be a permanent part of their lives. And it crushed her to hurt and disappoint her son. Darius had called a few times, but as soon as she saw his number, she'd passed the phone to Aiden.

Hearing his voice, talking to him—she wasn't ready for it yet. Didn't believe she would still have the courage and determination to say no if he asked her to return home.

Home.

She'd constantly told Darius his house wasn't hers, but somewhere along the way, she'd started thinking of it as home. And she missed it. Missed Ms. Jacobs.

Missed him.

"See Darry," Aiden whined, tears pooling in his eyes. His bottom lip trembled.

She hugged her son tight, as if she could somehow squeeze his hurt and confusion away. "I know, baby. But right now we're going to see the lights and animals at the zoo, okay?"

She'd kept Aiden—and herself—busy with outings. They'd visited the Children's Museum at Navy Pier, the Christmas tree at Millennium Park and the model trains at Lincoln Park Conservatory. And now they were headed to Zoolights at Lincoln Park Zoo. Yet, during all the trips, she couldn't help but imagine how different they would be if Darius had been by her side. As a family.

Standing, she forced the thoughts away. Yes, she loved Darius. Maybe she always would. But he didn't return the feeling, and there was no getting past that.

They weren't a family.

"Good," she said, injecting cheer into her voice for Aiden's benefit. "Let's go—"

"Darry!" Aiden's scream burst in the air seconds before he yanked his hand out of hers and took off across the tiny courtyard.

"Aiden!" she yelled, but her footsteps faltered, then jerked to a complete stop as she took in the man stooping low to catch her son and toss him in the air before pulling him close for a hug.

And the love on that face as he cuddled Aiden... It stole what little breath her baby's mad dash away from her hadn't.

Darius.

Oh, God. Darius. *Here.*

Stunned, she watched as he kissed Aiden's cheek, grinning at whatever Aiden chattered about. Joy, sadness and anger filled her, and heat pulsed in her body at the sight of him. The wind flirted with his hair, and her fingers itched to take its place. Hair that just passed the five-o'clock shadow covered his jaw and emphasized the sensual fullness of his mouth. A long black, wool coat covered his powerful body. But she remembered in vivid and devastating detail what was beneath it. She craved the strength of it at night.

Darius shifted his attention away from Aiden and pinned her with that golden gaze. The intensity of it snapped her out of her paralysis. Still, her feet wouldn't move, and she stood, immobile, as he approached her, carrying her son in his arms.

"Isobel," he said, and she worked not to reveal the shudder that coursed through her at the velvet sound of her name.

"What are you doing here?" she whispered. Damn it. Clearing her throat, she tried again. "What are you doing here, Darius?"

Sighing, he lowered Aiden to the ground, and turning, pointed in the direction of the curb where his town car idled. "Aiden, look who came to see you."

The window lowered, and Ms. Jacobs popped her head out, waving to him. Shrieking, he ran to the car, and the older woman opened the door, scooping him up. In spite of the emotional maelstrom whirling inside her, Isobel smiled. Aiden had asked about her only slightly less than he had asked about Darius.

Rising, Darius slid his hands into his coat pockets. "I hope you don't mind. I didn't want him to overhear our conversation."

"No. He's missed her," she admitted softly. Shifting her gaze from the ecstatic pair back to him, she murmured. "You, too."

Darius nodded, studying her face as if he, too, were cataloging any changes that had taken place in the last week. "You look tired," he observed in a gentle tone.

She hardened her heart against his concern, shielding herself against the tenderness that immediately sprang to life. "What are you doing here, Darius?" she repeated her question.

"To see Aiden. And you," he said, his eyes gleaming. "I've missed you both. I just needed to lay eyes on you." Then he loosed a short bark of laughter that fell somewhere between self-deprecating and rueful. "That's not quite the truth. I came to find you and beg you to come back home. To give me—give us—a second chance."

Beg you to come back home.

The words echoed in her head and her chest, and swirled in her belly. A yearning swelled so high, so strong, that it nearly drowned out the steely resolve to not give in. She wanted to—God, she wanted to just walk into his arms and have him hold her.

But she couldn't live a life without love, acceptance, trust and loyalty.

She refused to settle anymore.

"Darius, we can't," she murmured, but he clasped her hand, and the *goodness* of his touch cut her off. But just as quickly as he'd reached for her, he released her.

"Please, sweetheart. I know I don't have the right—don't deserve the right—to ask you to hear me out. But I am." He paused, as if gathering his thoughts, then continued. "Everything you said to me was true. I betrayed your trust. I betrayed you. Our family. And I do mean *our family*, Isobel. Because that's who you and Aiden are to me. You two are who I look forward to coming home to when I leave the office. And that's who you are for me, Isobel—home. All these years I believed the memories of my time there with my parents made it that. But I forgot the reason I love the house so much is because it means family. It means love. And I didn't realize what was missing until you and Aiden came to live with me. The moment you left, it was empty, a shell. And I need you to come back, to return it to my haven, my sanctuary."

Her heart thudded against her chest, her pulse deafening in her ears. Hope—that stubborn, foolish hope—tried to grow. But she shut it down. Only more pain led down any road hope traveled.

"I can't…" She shook her head. "Darius, I know you love Aiden. And we…we…" God, she couldn't get it out.

"We burned together, Isobel," he supplied, and her breath snagged in her throat. "But that's not all that was between us. Is still between us. Before I knew who you were, I trusted you with things I hadn't spoken to another living soul in years. I didn't need to see your face to tell you were special, loving, kind and compassionate. You didn't change, Isobel. I did. I turned on you. I allowed the past with Faith and Gage to warp what my heart acknowledged all along."

He shifted closer, but still didn't reach for her. But his gaze… It roamed her face, and she shivered as if his fingertips had brushed her skin.

And inside…oh, inside she couldn't battle hope anymore. It broke through her shields and flowed into her chest, filling her.

"I love you, Isobel." He raised his arms, and after a moment's hesitation, he cupped her face between his palms. "I love you," he whispered. "Remember when I told you about my fear of the dark and falling asleep in our burning building?" She nodded, his tender clasp, his soft words rendering her speechless. "I didn't tell you everything. I believe I heard my mother and father shout my name, and that's what woke me up. I know how insane it sounds, but even from where they were, they saved me. And now I think it's not just because they loved me, but because they knew what waited for me. You and Aiden.

"I've waited for you. And I hate that I almost threw away our future, *us*. Sweetheart," he murmured, sweeping his thumb over her cheekbone. "I promise I'll never place anyone else above you and our son and any more children we have together. But if I've hurt you too badly and you can't give me your heart and trust right now, I understand. Know this—I'll still provide for you and Aiden until I can convince you to forgive me. Because, sweetheart, my heart *is* yours. And I refuse to give up on us ever again. I'll love you perfectly."

He'd gifted her with her own words. She blinked, trying to hold back the tears, but they slipped free. And he pressed his lips to her cheek, kissing them away.

"Talk to me, sweetheart. I need to hear your beautiful voice. You're the only thing keeping me sane," he whispered, his voice carrying her back to that dark hallway where they'd first connected. Where she'd started to fall for him.

Where they'd begun.

"I love you." She circled his wrists and held on to him. "I love you so much."

He crushed his mouth to hers, taking and giving. Savoring and feasting. Loving and worshipping. And she surrendered it all to him, while claiming him.

"Sweetheart," he said against her lips, scattering kisses to her mouth, her jaw, her chin. "Tell me again. Please."

"I love you." Throwing her arms around his neck, she jumped, and he caught her, his hands cradling her thighs. Laughing, she tipped her head back, happiness a bird catching the wind and soaring free. "Now take us home."

Epilogue

Six months later

Isobel groaned through a smile. "This is your fault. And you're going to deal with the fallout."

Beside her, Darius snorted, laughter gathering in his chest and rolling up his throat. "Do you want to go over there and tell him to leave the bouncy castle?"

She scoffed. "And face World War Three *and* Four? God, no." She elbowed him in the side. "I thought we had a conversation about this party, though. Low-key. Nothing too big or grand."

Darius scanned their backyard, where they were holding Aiden's third birthday party. The aforementioned bouncy castle claimed a place of honor right in the middle of the lawn, surrounded by a petting farm, a huge slide, games, face painting, clowns... Their place could double for a carnival.

He shrugged. What could he say? Having missed Aiden's previous two birthdays, he'd really wanted to handle this one. So, he might have gone a little…overboard. Still, as Aiden's high-pitched laughter reached Darius, he had zero regrets.

"Well, he is having a blast," Darius noted, watching their son slide down the "drawbridge" of the castle. "And look on the bright side. At least the party is out here, so in case of a blackout, no one can get trapped inside. With all these animals."

She laughed. "True." Smiling, she slid an arm around his waist and leaned her head against his shoulder. "He'll never forget this. All of his family here to celebrate him." Including Isobel's mother and brothers. They mingled with the children and parents with ease, laughing and talking.

Well, not with Darius's family. Since Baron had confessed the truth to Helena and Gabriella, they'd dropped the custody suit. Discovering Gage's faults hadn't been easy on them, and even now, months later, they still struggled with the magnitude of his lies. And his death. Though he knew Isobel held sympathy for them, relations between her and the Wellses had been put on hold. It would take a while to heal years' worth of pain, and Darius refused to push that reconciliation. Isobel had to move forward when she was ready, and until then Darius had her back. At least she'd allowed Aiden to see them, but only if Darius was there to supervise. And he would never betray her trust again.

It'd been six months since he'd gone to Isobel to plead for her forgiveness and love. Six months since she'd given him both, plus her trust, her heart and her body. She'd given him his family back. That had been the happiest day of his life. And the days that followed were just as wonderful, filled with laughter and joy.

She'd been accepted into the University of Illinois and was majoring in psychology to become a domestic-violence counselor. He wholeheartedly supported her. Isobel was living proof that a person could emerge from a destructive situation stronger, whole, and with the ability to find happiness and peace.

"And just think," Darius said, sliding behind her and settling his hands over the small bump under her tank top. "In another five months, we'll have another one to spoil. A girl. Just imagine the princesses and unicorns that will be prancing around here in another two years."

Isobel groaned, but it ended on a full-out laugh. The joy in it flowed over him.

"Thank you," he murmured, pressing a kiss under her ear. And when she tipped her head back, he placed another kiss on her generous, lovely mouth. "Thank you for filling my life with love and family. I love you."

Her grin softened, and she lifted an arm, cupping the back of his neck. "I love you, too. Always and forever."

"Always and forever."

* * * * *

COMING SOON!

We really hope you enjoyed reading this book. If you're looking for more romance, be sure to head to the shops when new books are available on

Thursday 13th June

To see which titles are coming soon, please visit

millsandboon.co.uk/nextmonth

LET'S TALK

Romance

For exclusive extracts, competitions
and special offers, find us online:

📘 facebook.com/millsandboon

🐦 @MillsandBoon

📷 @MillsandBoonUK

Get in touch on 01413 063232

For all the latest titles coming soon, visit

millsandboon.co.uk/nextmonth